RACING ORION

RACING ORION

ZACH FRANZ

ISBN 978-1-09837-913-1 (print)

ISBN 978-1-09837-914-8 (eBook)

ACKNOWLEDGEMENTS

One name on the cover, plenty of others propping it up.

First and foremost, my family: Anna, Mom, Pop. There are no words, except to say that without you, this wouldn't have happened.

Thanks to Mike Hoogland, who's attention, encouragement and industry expertise took this book to new heights. Also, in the same vein, to Matt Martz and Dan Weiss, for recognizing the manuscript's potential and spurring its development.

Stephanie Phillips was the first professional to edit the manuscript; her insight and kind words were the exact jumpstart it needed. And I am in deep debt to Jessica Turcios and Kevin, Kyle and Seth York. Each of you is a great writer in your own right, and an even better friend.

A special salute must also go out to authors John DeKakis and Terry Irving, who readily donated time and talent to a novice at the Killer Nashville Writer's Conference. Their selflessness will not be forgotten.

Additionally, many more were instrumental in making this book a reality: Ryan Brockschmitt, Matt Clark, Joe Consiglio, Ollie Drake, Matt Ellis, Ethan and Vic Gerson, Cindy McGrew, Robert Presnell, Andy and Mikey Riva, Patty Ann Schemenauer and Teri Wimborne. I'm grateful for every one of you.

Thanks, finally, to God, who is the source of all the preceding human generosity. This book is praise to him.

It is wonderful what you can do when you have to.

- C. S. Lewis

1

Jerry Banks couldn't believe his luck. That was the word, too. What else could you call it when two blokes appeared out of nowhere and offered you a boatload of cash?

It's not like his mates were there and he beat them to the punch. The pair of strangers seemed to come just for him, and had the briefcase with them. Once they opened it up…he'd never seen so much money in one place.

And for what? Admittedly, staying in a single room for nearly two weeks had been a bit rough. But that was the only downside. They'd drawn his blood on the first day, and would do so once more at the end.

Each morning they'd come for a few minutes, checked his heart rate and blood pressure. There was a machine with some sticky probes, for running tests. But it was all painless. If the worst thing he had to deal with was a few needles, this would be even easier than he thought.

Even the drug had no side effects. He felt better now than the day he'd started. He didn't care what they'd injected him with. It probably wasn't slated for MHRA approval, but that wasn't his problem. If his hosts wanted to make a profit off some illegal vaccine, he wasn't going to stand in their way. Especially when he could almost feel the pounds in his pockets.

Pausing the football match on his iPad, Jerry glanced for the fiftieth time at the briefcase against the far wall. They'd let him keep it. An 'act of good faith.' It was all the motivation he needed. Less than twenty-four hours to go.

Meantime, he'd had much worse surroundings. The iPad was linked to a database of entertainment, including the internet. Somehow, they'd blocked access to any site that allowed for communication with the outside world. All social media. He didn't mind. It made sense; they had a lucrative secret to protect.

He still couldn't wait to tell his pals, though. They'd ask where he'd been, but forget everything once he mentioned the briefcase. Especially Tommy Shales, whom Jerry hadn't seen in over a month. Where'd he gone? Some guessed he'd taken his younger brother Cameron up to Leeds. Their uncle had a pub; they were going to start work, escape this life.

Jerry didn't buy it. Life on the street would always be better than a dead-end job. What were three squares and a roof over your head when you had no freedom? Out here, sure, it got hard. But they'd always leaned on each other, made it through. Jerry knew his friend: Tommy didn't have what it took to handle the change.

Or are you just jealous?

Jerry quickly glanced around the rest of the room, distracting himself with its other positives. The food was good; better than he'd had in years, actually. Other than a simple bed, on which he currently sat, there was only a small table and chair to break up the concrete. Another thing he didn't mind—not when it was temporary. Soon he'd never have to worry about shelter again.

He was a bit surprised he wasn't familiar with the space. Living in and out of so many empty buildings nearby, he figured every area had been explored. Apparently this one, about the size of a kitchen, had remained a secret. Smooth, stark walls, with no windows. The door locked from the outside. Some kind of old storeroom? It was surprisingly comfortable. Never too hot or cold.

The final piece in the setup would have bothered some, but again, he understood. There were tiny surveillance cameras mounted on the wall of both his room and a small adjoining loo. Just a sink and toilet. He had to sponge off when the smell got too strong.

As for the cameras, his hosts needed to see everything. Documentation. On the whole, still a small price to pay.

Turning back to his iPad—he got to keep that too—Jerry was about to hit play when something stopped him. A thought. One of those peculiar ideas that was so obvious, it often avoided detection. He rolled it around in his head a minute, made sure he had it right.

Why the secrecy? If he was going to leave tomorrow, why did they care if he told anyone today? What about when he was gone—did they just trust him to keep his mouth shut? That seemed a little thin.

Maybe—

It was the last word Jerry Banks ever processed. Each one after was erased by shock, fear and astonishing agony. He'd once considered gradual pain a death sentence; right now he would have killed for it.

It all came at once, an explosion inside his body. Razor sharp pangs sliced through every inch of muscle. His blood pressurized like the bottom of the ocean, an invisible vice crushing his frame.

At the same time, he felt the life draining out of him. He was dying, literally and instantly. He tried to reach out, yell, anything. All he managed was to tumble off the bed, collapsing onto the concrete floor. It felt colder now.

There might have been questions. *What's happening to me? Why?* Jerry couldn't form them, couldn't reach that far up. He writhed feebly on the ground, knives still stabbing, vice still grabbing. He'd have screamed or kicked, but any kind of strength was already a memory.

The only thought, the one shred he could picture, was a gun. Just a merciful bullet to end this nightmare. But then, a second later, he didn't need it. The room went quiet.

A wall away, on the other end of the surveillance cameras, Simon Clarke nodded to himself. Their creation was performing perfectly, consistently. He glanced to his counterpart. Linus Boxler smiled behind a pair of steel-rimmed glasses. "She's ready. These homeless rats have proven useful."

"*Mice*, Linus. Your English isn't fluent until your metaphors are straight."

"Like I care." Boxler set a pair of headphones down on a nearby desk. "In a few days I'll be rich enough to say whatever I want, and pay the rest of the world to shut up."

Clarke almost nodded again. They were, indeed, close. Plenty of hard work was about to pay off. He glanced back toward the camera feed. Now they just had to dispose of one more body. He still hated that part—the weight, the mess. At least it was secure. No one seemed to miss the homeless.

Boxler sat down and began making notes on a pad. Clarke reached forward to switch off the cameras when he felt his phone vibrate. Retrieving it from his waist pocket, he eyed the name on the screen and answered. "We've just finished the final trial. Full success."

"Right now it doesn't matter." The Russian voice on the other end, usually confident, held an air of tension. "We've had a setback. A mole."

Clarke's stomach immediately soured. He could feel the shock creeping toward his chest like latent fire. "Who?"

"One of the Americans. We have him, but he's hidden a key and canister. We'll know where soon."

Boxler, reading his partner's expression, straightened in his chair. Clarke felt the weight of fear, and its accompanying anger, but masked both with cynicism. "You sound confident."

"And you're not one to talk. Our field, our fix. It will get done." A pause. "Move up your schedule. We have to finalize Orion."

"How soon?"

"Three days."

Clarke exhaled. Such speed would be difficult. But he bit his tongue. The man on the other end understood their situation. The Russian spoke with no anger, or even condescension. Just rigid efficiency. "Yes sir," he finally said.

The call ended and Clarke pocketed the phone. Boxler stood. "What's wrong?"

"A fly in the ointment."

2

The stone wall rushed forward, slamming into his body like an unforgiving freight train. *No*—he was the one moving, thrown against it from across what appeared to be a small room. Hard to tell with the drug still coursing through his veins. It was some kind of hallucinogen, blurring everything. A piercing headache threatened to split his skull.

At that same moment, a heavy boot surged into his midsection. He dropped to the floor and the wind left his lungs. A pulsing knot of agony sprouted within, freshened a second later with another kick to the same spot. This folded him onto his back before a third tenderized his right kidney. He opened his mouth to cry out but was cut off by a kick to the face, this time from a different set of shoes. A busted lip joined three cracked ribs.

Another blow to the face threatened to knock him out, but before darkness came two pairs of large hands lifted him off the ground. One held his arms back while the other delivered a volley of jabs to his torso. A final uppercut across his left eye sent him to the ground once again.

His body stubbornly clung to consciousness. Through a cloudy haze, he could see red pooling at the bottom of his vision. His skin was split open, oozing blood and exposing a damaged cheekbone. Between this and the drug, he was practically blind.

But they weren't done. He was lifted off the floor again, and now caught a glimpse of his attackers. One was tall, the other stocky, both well built. That was enough. He knew who they were.

The tall one thrust forward an open palm, but the victim summoned a final ounce of strength and blocked the attack. In the same motion, he connected with a chop to the man's neck. The tall one staggered in surprise, clutching his throat, then was knocked back by a kick to the midsection.

The shorter man froze an instant too long. The victim seized the opportunity with an elbow to his opponent's face. Bone met cartilage and a fountain of blood spurted from the stocky man's freshly broken nose. He grunted in pain and fell to one knee.

The victim still couldn't see straight, but knew the exit must be directly ahead. As he leapt forward, a wave of vertigo assaulted his surviving senses. The ground came fast. He stretched his hands out to soften the impact. It mostly worked as each palm donated strands of skin to the stone floor. But his face still found a way through, widening the cut on his lip and chipping a few teeth.

His head felt like it weighed a hundred pounds; pain was everywhere. The only remaining resolve came from his gut. *Don't quit.* Right now, it was that simple. If he could just get up, start running…

He pressed both hands to the ground and rose on shaking arms. A knee helped out, then folded into a foot that brought him to a standing position. The room swirled. He forced himself to lunge forw—

The surging mass closed from the left like an angry bull. Lowering his head, the tall man rammed the victim, lifting him off the ground and driving him into the room's far wall. His skull flew back and collided with the stone barrier. Everything went black.

3

How long had he been unconscious—four hours? Five? Not much more. His wounds were too fresh, the pain still too strong. Part of him wished he'd never woken up.

Thin, labored breaths began in his battered chest, then escaped through a mouth that could hardly handle them. The bleeding—on his face, his head—had dried, forming a jagged maroon cap over each throbbing wound. From what he could feel, small bandages held his skin together.

That was the idea. They needed him alive. At least until the information he possessed could be extracted. *By any means necessary.* He couldn't let it get that far.

There was a last resort. It was essentially impossible, but he had to try. Not yet, though. Both his physical and mental reserves were dry. Only will remained, and barely. The recent beating had taken his last shred of defiance and reduced it further.

Even worse, his head had cleared, allowing his brain unadulterated access to his present physical state. There was no haze to deaden pain within, no headache to distract from the contusions blackening his torso, like marks of a disease. The cold was the final arrow, an enveloping frozen cloud that never quite numbed the skin. A lone pair of cotton shorts was his only protection from such charitable surroundings.

Surroundings which he'd memorized the moment he awoke. The room looked to be the site of his earlier punishment. This time, though, details were clearer. It was a cell. Perfectly square, with walls and floor made of stone.

The space was small and old, but clean—no stench. No windows either. He glanced up. Just a solitary light, glowing dimly atop the low ceiling. It was plastic and in the shape of a saucer. No discernible wires or glass bulb with which to end his misery.

He sat on the floor, reclining against one of the walls. To his left lay the entrance to the cell, currently occupied by a set of floor-to-ceiling bars. Beyond ran a hallway, then another stone wall. Set into this far partition were two mini surveillance cameras, staring back at him through furtive lenses.

He slowly exhaled, crystalized breath wafting upward in curls of smoke. A sharp pain suddenly knifed his ribs, earning a grimace. He had time to kill and needed an escape—something to take his mind away from the agony that was and was to come. The first random thought to materialize won.

A desk. *His* desk, in his office. He was surprised he still recognized it. *Long time.* Nothing fancy, and no pictures of loved ones on the surface. Other stands, in different sections of Langley, held the framed smiles of family, friends, even pets. For him just a clock and computer.

At least it was clean. The janitorial staff would keep the dust off. Did they ever wonder? An empty chair, day after day—who was its invisible occupant? Was he or she saving lives in some foreign land?

If only he'd been on the other side of the Humvee. Would he be somewhere else right now? Despite his current predicament, it wasn't a regret. Just an irresistible question.

He hadn't heard the IED, only the shrapnel. Screaming past his ears, then slicing through his leg. The injury was bad enough to bring him stateside, but he'd always planned to go back. Then one day a pair of suits walked into his room at Walter Reed. *"Why don't we go someplace we can talk."* That should've been the first clue.

He could still hear the words, as clear as yesterday: *"Lieutenant, how'd you like to make an even bigger difference? Save even more lives?"*

Footsteps interrupted his thoughts. A heavy, deliberate pace—they're owner was an easy guess. Pulling his gaze back, he eyed the man emerging from the corner to his left.

Gerhardt Berger. German, late-thirties, solid as a rock. A patchwork of bandages held the broken cartilage in his nose together. Studying the prisoner through black eyes, he silently strode to the far wall at the center point of the bars.

In the next moment a second man came into view. He was familiar too: Gunnar Scharp, a six-four Swede with razor-like features. A signature cap of silvery hair belied his relative youth. The damage was harder to see, but a dark bruise just above his larynx told the story.

By this time the captive, ignoring the protesting screams of his muscles, had pushed his five-foot-eleven frame up the wall and slowly drifted to the center of the cell. He could hear one more set of footsteps, soft and relaxed. They belonged to a man in control.

Sergei Ryov. Near the top of his class at Moscow State University, then a standout in the Russian Military. Recruitment to Spetsnaz followed, before a post in the SVR as his country's most valuable foreign asset. All leading up to the day when he abruptly disappeared. Into thin air, it seemed. An untraceable speck on an infinite map.

So went, in similar fashion, the stories of his present comrades. Each a one-man army, and now a breathing ghost.

An instant later Ryov's thin figure emerged from the shadows. Barely out of his twenties, he wore his shoulder-length black hair in a ponytail and clasped both hands behind his back. He approached the bars with a stoic gaze. "Jeremy Kent." A deep voice for his size. "Thirty-two years old, unmarried. Field Operations Officer for the Central Intelligence Agency of the United States. Proficient in hand-to-hand combat, tactical weaponry and improvised critical thinking. Speaks eight languages, including the dialect of a traitor. Can fly a helicopter under pressure, control a car at high speed and betray his friends without thought."

Kent shook his head slowly. "You think you know someone."

Ryov showed no frustration. "Proof that a file is only half the story." He stopped a foot from the bars. "To think, I almost liked you once."

"Tragic loss to my pool of friends."

"Can't be that deep anymore. I might be all you've got left."

"And here I was despairing."

Locking eyes with Kent, Ryov eventually nodded. "You're brave, I'll give you that. It's fear wrapped in a stink of desperate wit, but still brave." He turned away. "I call myself your friend because I hate torture. This can all end with a simple bullet to your head. No mess, no time wasted." He spun with expectant eyes. "Just tell me where the canister is."

Kent said nothing.

Ryov stepped back to the bars. "This is a one-time offer, Jeremy. I prefer expediency, but I will not hesitate to hurt you. You and I both know every man has a breaking point."

Kent thought about feigning incredulity. Had they not been trying to hurt him earlier? Maybe he'd missed the invitation to tea. Yet, he knew exactly what Ryov meant. Pain was relative; the beating had just been a primer. Whatever they had coming down the pike would be much worse. Unbearable, in the truest sense of the word. He exhaled, hoping the dread in his gut wasn't visible on his face. "I'll take my chances."

Ryov shook his head, almost sadly. "You have none." Turning, he began heading back down the hall. Scharp and Berger quietly followed.

"The station in Linz," called out Kent. Ryov stopped. "How did you know?"

The Russian turned, slowly, his face half-obscured by the shadows of the corridor. As ruthless as he was, he followed a certain code. Kent was an adversary, but a *worthy* one. He'd earned this…professional courtesy.

Ryov let a handful of seconds fall away before responding. "Scharp happened to step off the train for a smoke. He saw you move around the far corner, not where you said you'd be. A bad feeling crept up. He climbed back on, we checked the bag." Ryov zeroed his gaze on the cell. "One canister missing. It was…"

"Pure chance," Kent realized.

Without a word the Russian spun and strode from sight. Moments later the click of a distant door returned Kent to his previous solitude. He remained standing at the bars, playing out the next few hours in his mind.

This was the end of the line. His opponents' strategy was obvious: give him a taste of violence, then promise more before stepping away. Let the fear simmer. Soon a simple bullet to the head didn't sound so bad.

It only worked if the threat was real. In this case, Kent had no doubt. He could still feel his enemy's resolve leaking from a dozen wounds. These men were lethal because they were cold, unswayed by emotion or prejudice. They didn't toy with you, they just killed you.

He cleared his mind. The last thought to pass through was the ace up his sleeve. It was bent and soiled, but still a card that counted. He needed a bit more time. More strength, before ten frantic seconds drained it all away.

4

Down the hallway, beyond what amounted to a soundproof door, Ryov sat with his legs resting on a small table. The stand was pushed to one side of a room twice as large as Kent's cell. Beside his boots, a simple array of recording equipment displayed their captive's every move.

Though wireless cameras tended to transmit images in lower resolution than their corded counterparts, the video before him was in color and high definition. Not that it mattered. He didn't need to see each individual hair on Kent's head.

Over his shoulder, Berger entered the space from a smaller anteroom with two bottles of water. Placing one in front of Ryov, the burly German strode across to the far wall and sat down in front of a second table with a laptop. Ryov took a swig of liquid and set the bottle down. He would have killed for it to be vodka, but this interrogation wasn't planned. There'd been no time for a trip to the store.

His lament was interrupted by the sound of a flushing toilet. Seconds later a door opened onto the room and an Asian man emerged. Strutting forward while still fastening his belt, Kaito Tanaka stopped beside Ryov and stared at the screen. "Counting his blessings?"

"If he has an imagination."

Tanaka smiled and glanced at another monitor on the table. This one was divided into eight sections, each displaying a live camera feed from a deserted forest. One of the sectors had been covered in gray until a moment ago. "All quiet on the western front?" he asked.

Eyes still on Kent, Ryov nodded. "On their way back."

Almost before the words were spoken, Scharp and a shorter man entered the space through a door behind Berger. Their tracks were damp and garnished with white powder. Ryov looked up. "Snow on the lens?"

Sebastian LeRiche, a French explosives expert, nodded. "Gust of wind, maybe an animal."

"We walked around, saw nothing," said Scharp. "Forest is clear."

Ryov nodded and turned back to the monitors. Checking the grounds was prudent, but hardly necessary. The facility they presently occupied was entirely subterranean. The only surface marker was a steel hatch, flush with the ground and covered, the majority of the year, by a healthy layer of snow.

They were in Russia, about 150 kilometers west of Moscow. The facility was an underground bunker, originally an ammunitions store during World War II and later used by the KGB for "persuading" its enemies. Bars had been affixed to the space's handful of supply rooms, creating an inescapable prison.

To call the bunker rustic was generous. Stone walls and cement floors dominated each room. Electricity came from a portable generator under Ryov's table. That powered the monitors, recording equipment and a couple space heaters. Flat lights, like the one in Kent's cell, provided illumination. There was also indoor plumbing, added in the 60's and still surviving. A few cots in the anteroom completed the setup.

Abandoned by the Russian government in the mid 80's, Ryov had recently learned of the space and taken hold. Most had forgotten its existence, and those that did remember had no desire to reminisce. It was an invisible relic of history. A perfect hiding place.

Tanaka had taken a seat beside Ryov. "Did you ask him about Baker?"

"Not yet. Less on his mind, more space for the coming pain."

The Asian leaned back, eying the monitor. "Then it's only a matter of time."

5

Kent slowly opened his eyes. *Almost there.* As a last step, he let the details of the entire operation role around in his head. Worth putting it in perspective before betting the house on a sliver of hope.

It all began with an accident. Nearly six years ago, a pair of virologists—Simon Clarke and Linus Boxler—were working in Brussels on a cure for liver cancer. They created hybrid strains of the disease to encourage the process. One night, after inoculating a lab mouse, they had trouble locating the infection. Extracting blood samples at twenty-four-hour intervals, they found nothing until the fourth day.

It was the seed of a virus.

Several months later and hundreds of miles away, Nicholas Kerr, longtime deputy chief of MI6, accepted a gift from a colleague. The giver was Eric Stanton, the agency's head of research and development. The gift was *War and Peace*.

For the past three years the pair had been at constant odds. But Stanton was leaving for a private company, and the novel was his token of reconciliation. In fact, he'd given every senior officer a different book. This particular title was Kerr's for obvious reasons.

But whether he read it or not was irrelevant. What mattered was that he kept it, because the book was more than just a binding with pages. It was a bug. Retribution, not reconciliation.

Within the lining of the cover, Stanton had planted a listening device. He kept the receiver at his house, occasionally eavesdropping on conversations. It wasn't much more than a practical joke. A final, random prick.

One day, though, he had a visitor: his nephew, Nathan Brooks, who also happened to be the Prime Minister's Chief of Staff. After too much to drink, Stanton showed Brooks his receiver. He flipped it on for fun. Immediately they heard a conversation. Three distinct voices, all male. One of them was Kerr. Seconds later Stanton began recording. The words were chilling. A lethal disease, massive death.

The other two men on the line were Clarke and Boxler. The latter was Swiss, but Clarke was British and had only been a year behind Kerr at Oxford. The connection, if not explicit, was undeniable. They'd stumbled upon a biological weapon and joined forces with one of the most powerful men in Europe.

Kent broke from his thoughts for a moment. He'd always wondered why Clarke and Boxler even started down this road. They could just as easily have scrapped their findings or used them to continue toward a cure. At the most basic level, what made men go bad? Or were they already that way, their vice just waiting for the best time to take control?

Profound questions, and also the least important. Moral philosophy wasn't something Kent had time for. All that mattered right now was stopping this enemy.

For what it was worth, he'd already figured Kerr out. There'd been the problem of how the scientists knew they could trust someone with such incriminating evidence. Just as Clarke and Boxler had a choice to turn away, so did Kerr; he could've brought them into custody and ended the whole thing. But then Kent had seen the deputy chief in person. His face—his *eyes*. They'd glowed with a certain darkness.

Nicholas Kerr's greatest loyalty lay with himself. He'd sacrificed thirty years and two marriages to MI6, as well as a couple bullet wounds from the field in his younger days. Yet he'd remained at the number-two post for nearly a decade. Revenge was a likely motive.

His problem had been those eyes. There was a detachment, a calculation with Kerr that some in his country's government found unnerving.

He seemed to elevate the mission—progress—above human life. The word 'sociopath' was mentioned once.

It sounded like an extreme, and obvious, issue. But these observations were merely shades, mild suspicions spread over the course of years. A time period during which Kerr was still excelling at his job. In the end, though, the reservations were strong enough to keep him from receiving a final promotion.

Kent had wondered if that were enough motivation to end millions of lives. *Depends on how you value the lives.*

From the beginning, they'd called the virus Orion. Kent originally found it trivial, naming such a deadly creation after a simple group of stars. But then he thought it through: not the constellation—its namesake. In Greek mythology, Orion was a hunter. So went the virus, stalking and killing its victims without mercy.

As for the recording, there was no doubting its authenticity. The trio of voices carried all the emotion of a board meeting. Cold, results-focused. The furthest thing from an act.

Upon hearing the conversation, Brooks commanded Stanton to silence. Beyond that, he wasn't sure what to do. He was out of his depth. Nicolas Kerr was already one of the most decorated officers in the history of the Secret Intelligence Service.

The threat was far-fetched, but too much of a risk to ignore. Yet Brooks didn't know who to trust, who Kerr had already recruited. Finally, the Chief of Staff told the one man he knew was clean: his boss.

But the prime minister was in the same position—young and overmatched. He couldn't even trust his own security detail. The only choice he had was to reach far away, outside Kerr's sphere of influence. The PM used a third-party phone and called the President of the United States. Two days later, the Secretary of Defense, headed to Berlin for a security summit, rerouted his plane to Stansted Airport for a 'maintenance check.' Brooks personally delivered the recording.

Despite their discovery, Clarke and Boxler were a long way from a tactical weapon. A period of testing and refinement would likely follow. Ultimately, it didn't matter whether they meant to use it or sell it. The only objective was to locate and stop the virus before it became operational.

Both scientists, though, had vacated their known addresses. Neither was a convicted felon, eliminating any real database knowledge. Credit card activity had been abandoned. They'd obviously been coached by Kerr and, while probably still in Europe, could technically have been anywhere in the world.

The one hope for success was through Kerr himself. While he remained with MI6, his extracurricular activities were clearly beyond his agency's purview. He would likely recruit a small, skilled team to ensure protection and intelligence for Clarke and Boxler.

This was where Kent came in. He and another agent were given posts in Europe—now that he thought about it, almost five years ago to the day. They had separate covers in separate cities. A path toward recruitment onto Kerr's team.

The goal was to involve them in as many joint intelligence ventures as possible. Kerr had always been hands-on. They would likely come in contact with him. Perform well—even advertise their willingness to subvert protocol—and he might notice.

Kerr certainly held the scientists' location among his most prized possessions. Clarke and Boxler were synonymous with victory itself; if they were found, so was the virus and all the data associated with it. The gambit would be over.

Kerr would eventually tell someone the secret, though. Perhaps a pair of his most trusted allies. If given enough time, Kent or his counterpart could become one of them. The mission had never been described as "short-term."

Was this really the easiest way? Kent had asked that at the beginning, and, during moments of acute struggle or weakness, still wondered. But the answer was always the same.

This operation required a scalpel, not a machete. Deploying a larger team to kidnap Kerr and force him to give up the scientists had been seriously considered. Ultimately, though, it held no weight. MI6's deputy chief would be prepared. Whether it be a call that wasn't made, a text that wasn't sent—something would alert Clarke and Boxler that their ally was taken, and they'd disappear forever. Kerr, to protect himself further, would likely know nothing of their destination.

There was only one opportunity to get this right. *And it's sitting in prison.* With a beaten body and odds longer than a national lottery.

6

Kent eased himself up against the stone wall. The moment had come. He took a deep breath, galvanizing each frayed nerve one last time. Then, with a quiet shudder, he turned his head right and bit into his shoulder.

He clenched his jaw to the utmost. Every tooth made its mark on the cold epidermis; a few broke the surface. Releasing his grip, a wave of intense pain subsided as the punctures oozed blood.

The sound of a door being thrown open down the hallway came just when he expected. Five seconds, maybe, until his captors invaded the cell.

He reapplied his iron grip in the same spot, though this time with the added weapon of adrenaline. Biting down once more, he squeezed harder as tears of pain began soaking his eyes. Still not there. *Four seconds.* The hall was now filled with sprinting footsteps.

Releasing for an instant with the pain screaming in his ears, Kent attacked the spot one more time. He clenched the now-mangled patch of skin with a strained jaw and jerked back, tearing a piece of flesh away. Surprised at his success, he immediately reached with his left arm into the wound and dislodged a minute plastic capsule.

Two seconds. The footsteps were closer and louder. He tore off the top of the container, filled with an orange liquid. A shot rang out and blistered a padlock off the bars. *One second.* Kent swallowed the liquid as Scharp, ahead of two companions, barreled into the cell like a rhinoceros. The big Swede righted himself just in time to see his prisoner lose consciousness.

The other two men, Ryov and Tanaka, joined Scharp as Kent's body was still crumpling to the floor. A second later they were huddled around his supine frame. Tanaka checked the neck for a pulse and the mouth for breathing. Both were faint. "We have very little time," he told Ryov, who was inspecting the shoulder wound.

The Russian nodded without looking up. "Some blood, not bad."

Scharp had been sweeping the floor for something and now held *it* in the beam of a flashlight. "Poison?' he asked to no one in particular, studying the empty cylinder. Ryov called for the vial as LeRiche, who'd stayed behind to watch the rest of Kent's actions on the monitor, approached the cell.

"Some kind of poison," announced the Frenchman. "Has to be."

The next instant Berger arrived with a first aid kit. Tanaka quickly turned to Scharp. "You checked him for hidden substances?"

"Extensively. Both ends."

Just then Ryov opened Kent's mouth and thrust the fingers of his right hand down their prisoner's throat. The body quickly convulsed and Kent, his head jerking forward, regurgitated onto his chest. Ryov took a cloth from his back pocket and wiped his hand. For a moment each man was silent, watching the limp form with mounting anxiety.

Tanaka soon exhaled. "If he just vomited up the poison, we might have a chance." He scanned the other faces, finally resting on Ryov. "If it entered through the mucosa into the bloodstream instead of going to the stomach, we're already too late."

Further seconds passed like hours. The whisperings of failure began to attack their exteriors, though panic had yet to set in. Another instant and Tanaka tried the pulse again. "Gone," he announced.

Kneeling over Kent's torso, he began alternating compressions and breaths. One minute went by. Nothing. Two. Tanaka diligently continued his regimen with his counterparts looking on, each feeling more helpless than the next. Ryov slowly rose and took a step back. He already knew it was over. Failure was something you could feel, especially when it didn't come often. Like a deadly stench emanating from Kent's limp body, the air of defeat prickled the hairs on the back of his neck.

Three minutes. Other than Tanaka's breathing, the cell was eerily quiet. The Asian gave it another thirty seconds before looking at Ryov in disgust. "Forget it," said the Russian.

More silence, before LeRiche rose from his crouch. "Did we just lose Orion?"

Tanaka stood too. "It's likely."

"He must've sent a message from the station in Linz," added Scharp. "Someone coming to pick the canister up."

"Or they already have," offered LeRiche.

"You don't know that," said Ryov, stepping forward. "You don't know any of it."

Tanaka looked down at the body. "Then why this? Why kill yourself unless you have all the pieces in place?"

Ryov followed the Asian's eyes. "Because he had no choice. He knows our ability, our methods. No hope of escape, looming agony—this was his only option." He looked up. "Kent was desperate before we caught him. His plan couldn't have been airtight. Maybe the serum was left in a place where its discovery relies on chance; spotting it would be possible, but not probable. Perhaps it was passed off to someone who didn't know what it was in hopes they'd deliver it to the proper authorities."

"I never knew you to be an optimist, Sergei," said Tanaka.

"I'm only saying this is no more likely to hurt us than to fall away." Ryov looked around. "We'll put eyes on the station, but we're not giving up Orion." The finality in his voice was clear.

The cell went quiet. Eventually, Berger reached down for the first-aid kit. "What do you want to do with the body?"

Ryov thought a moment. "Bury it outside." He eyed Kent's shoulder. "Dress the wound first. The last thing we need is an animal finding blood in the snow and digging him up."

Berger nodded as each man began to move. Tanaka joined him at the wound while Scharp and LeRiche gathered supplies to clean the cell. Ryov took a step back, his eyes glazing over with a distant look. Their prisoner had been a formidable pest, but it took something special to do the most damage as a corpse. *Bravo, Jeremy Kent.*

7

Berger wasn't apt to complain, but the weight was becoming a nuisance. It wasn't physical—he and LeRiche had just dragged Kent's 200-pound frame through a mile of three-inch snow without breaking a sweat.

Still, it was heavy. They'd been minutes from eliminating the only obstacle in their path, snipping off the final loose end. Now the threat was still active. Doubtful, but in play. And the clammy torso sliding along was a constant reminder.

Kent had been one of them. Now he was the slain enemy, failed and forgotten. *Then why does it feel like he's won?* Every boot crunch, every tug across the cold ground seemed to echo his triumph. It was as if he were laughing at them from the other side.

Yet they continued on. Ultimately, Berger knew, his thoughts were fruitless. Lamenting unchangeable occurrences, Ryov liked to say, did nothing for the mind but satisfy its taste for immaturity. No matter how things felt or seemed, the fact remained that Kent was dead and they were alive. It would all be over soon.

Approaching a small clearing in the trees, each man clutched a shovel with one hand and one of Kent's limp arms in the other. The body, flecked with dried blood and still covered by a lone pair of shorts, faced backward like a prisoner being pulled to the gallows. The bare feet cut a trail through the snow, but it would melt before any discovery occurred.

The opening soon came in sight as a chilling wind rushed through the forest. The air was below freezing, but the ground, recently thawed from back-to-back weeks of temperatures in the forties, would be penetrable. The area was isolated too. No need to go a full six feet.

Sitting in the bunker's main chamber, Tanaka methodically navigated the laptop's worn keyboard. Its 16" screen displayed a flurry of scheduled flights in and out of Sheremetyevo International. The majority of his attention, though, was focused on Ryov.

Pacing the length of the room, the Russian hung his head in thought, eyes distant. He'd been silent for the past five minutes, boots softly brushing the stone floor with each controlled step. Tanaka checked his side. The cell phone was out, but had yet to be raised above the waist.

For any other man the Asian would have understood. Reporting a critical failure to your superior—especially one as powerful as theirs—was not something to which you looked forward. Ryov, though, was different. He was capable of anger, even surprise, but, as far as Tanaka had seen, never fear. He just didn't seem to care enough.

And that was only the beginning. Most in their group had a single motivation for the risks they were taking: money. But not just any amount. Orion was a weapon the likes of which the world had never seen. Its implementation was exceedingly simple. For anyone wanting to inflict widespread fear and pain on a boundless target, it was perfect. A terrorist's Holy Grail.

Which commanded a tantalizing price. It'd seemed odd at the time, but that was the first thing Kerr had told them. *"The world will laugh at you. 'All this for money. You're nothing more than a common thief.' Leave it. Your ego is your enemy. Let them laugh when their cities are on fire with terror, and you're living the life of a king."*

For Kerr it wasn't only about the money. In person, Tanaka could practically feel the sea of envy roiling beneath the man's composed exterior. He didn't blame him. Not when an unforgivable lack of promotion made Kerr's current post—one he'd mastered a decade ago—seem like a crude gift, a perpetual slap in the face.

The last straw had come nearly seven years back. With the Chief of MI6 having announced his impending retirement, Kerr's moment was at hand. How could it not be, after a leak of information directly connected

Kerr to recently foiled terrorist attacks against the London Eye and Houses of Parliament?

Wonders never cease. You could've seen it coming, like a bad movie. The Foreign Secretary had already made his choice. Soon, a well-coiffed deputy from MI5 officially became Nicholas Kerr's new boss. Tanaka imagined the fatigue set in quickly. It had to be tiring, taking orders from a man more symbol than spy, ten years your junior and hideously underqualified.

But Kerr soldiered on. Quietly, until an old college friend dropped a golden egg in his lap. The last few years, as Orion continued to develop, Kerr's day job had become easier and easier. Every cold morning, every hollow meeting brought him closer to the day when his enemies would hit their knees, begging for mercy from a chemical killer that didn't care.

Tanaka brought his mind back to the room and stared at his pacing counterpart. *But Ryov.* Sergei was different than Kerr. Different than all of them.

Tanaka knew the Russian's file back to front: no daddy issues, nor unrequited love. Yes, the money, the comfort, were absolute incentives. But not everything. And the missing link wasn't tangible.

Ryov wanted—needed—something more. His Promised Land was cerebral, almost spiritual. Was he going to get there through this op? *As likely a place as any.* Maybe, when he was sipping his pina colada on the beach—if the alcohol didn't suffice, nor the woman on his lap, nor the waves at his feet—knowledge would. The knowledge that he'd beaten the world, won the impossible game. Each time the thought came it would bring a high more bountiful than all the money any of them could fathom.

Something like that. Tanaka refocused. Ryov still hadn't made the call. He was about to say something out of sheer curiosity when the Russian, facing away, suddenly stopped pacing. There was an eerie silence. Tanaka felt a cold shiver trace his spine. He'd have given anything to see the look on Ryov's face.

"The substance…in that capsule…" Ryov's voice was low, distant.

Tanaka sat up straight. "From Kent?" He thought a moment. "Could've been anything. Plenty of drugs stop a man's heart."

Ryov turned, eying Tanaka directly. "How many start it again?"

Tanaka stood involuntarily, but found he couldn't move beyond that. The shiver instantly became a tremor, coursing through his torso. Should they have thought of that? Why? The chances were so small… Already, it didn't matter.

Ryov, characteristically, looked as if he'd expected this. Gaze still on Tanaka, he pressed a button on the phone and brought it to his ear.

—

8

They were at the edge of the clearing when Berger's right hip began to buzz. Squeezing the shovel between his arm and side, he snatched up his cell phone. "Yes?"

"Pull out your gun and check Kent's pulse."

"What?"

"He may be—"

Neither Berger nor LeRiche heard another word. They still possessed all their faculties, but their attention was quickly diverted. It wasn't everyday a dead man came back to life.

Planting numbed heels into the snow like a stubborn zombie, Kent pushed off with shaky legs, sailing in front of his captors. He passed LeRiche's inside hip and freed a 9mm Beretta from its holster. Swinging his arm right, he pulled the trigger. The Frenchman's shocked face barely changed as a slug tore into his chest. Still airborne, Kent swept the barrel left and fired a second round.

At the mercy of a rapid decision, Berger forsook his own gun and gripped the shovel. He swung the spade head toward his chest like a pendulum. It intercepted the bullet just before impact, the deadly projectile ricocheting into the trees.

Kent saw this and squeezed the trigger again, but the gun failed to fire. The shock of his bruised body colliding with the frozen ground kept his finger from pulling back completely. Another chance never came as Berger, still in motion from blocking the bullet, violently flung the shovel toward his exposed attacker. The tool whirled forward like a helicopter blade. Kent desperately threw his legs up to block.

Arriving like a frozen hatchet, the spade hacked into Kent's improvised barrier. He'd tried to lead with his heels, which were still numb, but the shovel also made vicious contact with both shins. He grunted in agony and raised the Beretta for retribution. Berger was already too close and chopped the gun from his hand.

Ryov and Tanaka bolted for the door before the first gunshot sounded over the phone. Gaining the entryway, the Russian quickly spun and pointed at the monitors. "In case he doubles back."

Tanaka complied as his counterpart raced up a narrow stairwell and threw open the hatch. Scharp approached with his pistol out and a half-burnt cigarette dangling between his lips. "Gunshots?"

Ryov slammed the hatch down. "Kent's alive. Follow me."

Picking up the trail of footprints, both men broke into a frantic sprint.

Straddling Kent's midsection, Berger reached down and clenched a pair of bear-like hands around his opponent's throat. Kent immediately felt his vision begin to blur. He tried to pull the heavy arms off but knew it was an impossible task.

He balled his right fist and lunged for Berger's jaw, but fell short as the German swiftly cocked his head back. The mighty hands regained their leverage, and Kent felt his neck continue to constrict. Darkness began creeping past the edges of his sight. Berger's goal was simply unconsciousness—they still needed information from him. But there was no escaping a second time. Capture was the same as death.

Kent feverishly clutched the snow for some kind of weapon: a stick, a rock, anything. Instead, he found only white powder. The German leaned forward, putting the full weight of his torso onto his opponent's already-bruised larynx. Kent's entire upper body throbbed in pain as the shapes before him lost definition.

He grunted through the choke hold and pushed the cloud of unconsciousness back for one more second. Twisting his torso to the left, he brought his right hand up in a final attack. Berger maneuvered as before, but this time Kent's arm was on a straighter trajectory. At its fullest extension his fist plowed into the German's jaw. Each knuckle howled in pain, but Berger's grip loosened. The darkness began to recede.

Kent felt a flurry of hope. He sent his left arm surging into Berger's stomach. Dazed and sucking air, the German released his hold. The window widened further as Kent connected with another right cross to the face before kicking Berger off into the snow.

His gasped in some cold breaths, his vision rapidly clearing. He spotted the Beretta to his right and lunged for the handle. Instantly it was in his grip, the trigger close. He swung the gun around, but failed a second time to fire as Berger cut his shovel through the air like a sword. The spade head smashed into Kent's right hand with a dull roar and the pistol flew from his grasp.

Ignoring a pair of freshly broke fingers, he waited on Berger's follow-through and dove for the German's right hip. He snatched an exposed Glock, then somersaulted ahead and brought it around. This time he didn't even get turned halfway.

The shovel arrived like a sledgehammer. Kent toppled to his knees as the spade rammed into his bare back, just missing the spine. He tried to yell but choked on the pain. One more hit like that and it was over.

Berger obliged, bringing the steel head down once more. Kent sensed the blow and rolled to his right. The shovel bit hard into the ground inches away. Fumbling the Glock, an idea flashed in Kent's mind and he tossed it into the air.

The move surprised Berger, who instinctively relaxed his grip on the shovel and reached for the gun. In the same motion Kent pulled the spade free and swung it north. The German had just enough time to feel the Glock's handle before his left temple exploded with a concussive thud. Both eyes quickly rolled back as his thick frame toppled to the frozen ground.

Kent was already there, breathing heavily through cracked ribs. For a moment his gasps were the only sound; the forest was quiet. Feeling the cold seep into his pores, he fought the urge to shut down completely. It would have been so easy. *But you won't be the only one dying.*

Besides, they were coming. Planting his palms in the snow, Kent pushed to his feet and retrieved the Beretta. He wanted to put a bullet in Berger's forehead, but couldn't afford to give his position away. He scanned the two prostrate forms before grabbing LeRiche's shoes and forcing them on. Then came Berger's jacket, and he darted off through the trees.

Seconds later Ryov and Scharp broke into the clearing, guns up. Both were breathing heavily from the extended run. The Russian pointed to the prone bodies without taking his eyes off the forest beyond. Spotting a pair of footprints, he crept toward the tree line like a lion on the prowl.

Kent raced through the maze of evergreens in fleet desperation. He didn't know where he was headed, other than away from his enemies. He had to put as much distance as possible between himself and the clearing. Careful not to snap any fallen twigs, he nevertheless winced each time his boots crunched into a patch of wet snow.

Then it hit him.

He'd heard the pistol's report but was in full stride and unable to attempt anything evasive. Arriving with surprising force, the slug tore through his newfound jacket and dug into his left side just above the waist. He spun forward, barely sidestepping a thick tree and spiraling toward the snow. *Stay on your feet!* The time interval between the gun's firing and the bullet's impact was miniscule; they were close. If he fell he was finished.

The space between his chest and the ground rapidly diminishing, Kent at last extended his left leg and planted it in the snow. He pushed off with phantom energy just before another shot sounded. The round coursed through the wooded maze like a miniature missile. He flinched as it exploded into a patch of bark inches behind his flailing jacket. He managed to keep his balance and continued sprinting forward.

His side shuddered in pain, cold blood wetting his back. Were any organs hit? For the next two minutes, it didn't matter.

Then he saw another clearing. Less than a hundred meters away, it was larger than the one before. Much larger. In fact, it was *the* clearing—the end of the forest. Its expanse of white snow glowed like light at the end of a tunnel.

Kent pushed his exhausted frame forward. He had to increase the lead he had on his pursuers. The area ahead was his best chance of escape, but was looking more and more like an open field that offered no cover. If his hunters could shoot him through a maze of trees, they'd have no trouble doing so in the clear.

Fifty meters. No further shots, but he couldn't risk a look back. Ahead the space began to take shape. The woods in which he ran painted the edge to his right and far beyond. The left side held a house. One-story, simple wood exterior. Smoke puffed from a small chimney. Kent knew it was his best option. Despite the long stretch of untouched snow in between, if he could round the corner of the house without being hit he might have a chance.

He forced himself through the last few meters. The gunshot wound had gone numb, but continued to bleed freely. His right shoulder, through its patch, burned sharper with every new stride. The rest of his body was freezing, any sweat it generated turning to ice on his raw skin.

He finally burst into the clearing and veered left. His prints would read like tracking lights in the snow, but there was nothing he could do.

A moment later he reached the halfway mark and stole a glance back. No one. Spinning forward, he bore toward the house, gasping through each labored breath.

Five more seconds passed before he grunted in relief as his right boot crunched beyond the far corner of the shelter, fully shielding him from the woods behind.

9

Ryov gained the clearing in time to see the last vestiges of Kent's jacket disappear around the edge of the house. Maintaining his pace, he followed the footpath to the left and scanned the expanse for movement. It was unlikely Kent would attack, but nothing was certain.

His gun still out, the Russian slowed and broke off from the line toward the back of the dwelling. He reached its wooden exterior and strafed right, toward the corner. Once there he paused for half a second, then spun into the open.

Nothing. Except more tracks, which curved around the front of the house. Ryov could see the front grill of a snow-covered Yugo decades past its prime. Beyond that ran a slatted fence, most likely the companion to a lengthy driveway. He heard the quiet crunch of powder behind and turned to see Scharp, breathing evenly with pistol poised. "LeRiche is dead. Berger's unconscious, but he'll live." The Swede paused for an instant. "Did you hit him?"

Ryov nodded. "Near the left kidney."

Moving forward, the Russian led his companion to the front edge of the house and they peeked around. Kent wasn't visible. Neither were his footprints. They'd most likely melded into the indistinguishable city of slush spread across the muddy drive. The frozen metropolis had surely received most of its shape from the group of young boys in a snowball fight on the far side of the yard. To the right of the battle a large hedge of pines connected the forest to the driveway.

Both men leaned back behind the corner. "I'll ask the boys," said Ryov, "but I'm betting he's inside. You take the drive, just in case."

Scharp nodded. "If he made it to the tree line, their view is cut off."

Holding their guns discreetly, they rounded the edge. Scharp broke off to the right as Ryov continued forward. Each boy, distracted within the heat of battle, failed to notice the movement. Except one. He might've been eight or nine, with brown hair and a frightened face. He stood inside a circular snow fort, its walls as high as his chest. Upon seeing Ryov he stopped firming up a series of snowballs and froze.

One by one, whether en-route to the fort for more ammunition or after a random spin, each of the others did the same. By the time Ryov crossed the drive, he had a captive audience more silent than the wind gently slipping through the trees.

Moving carefully, he fished out a leather wallet and flipped it open. "My name is Oleg Borodin. I work for the Federal Security Service. Did any of you see a man run through this area just seconds ago?"

A few of them instinctively scanned the surrounding landscape, finding, with Scharp already obscured by the line of trees, nothing of note. The rest stared back at Ryov with blank expressions. He took a step forward. "This is very important, boys. Did you see anyone?"

A second later the one in the fort responded. "No sir." His youthful voice quivered. "We saw no one."

Ryov eyed the rest of them. "And you? Anything?"

A quintet of shaking heads was the answer. Ryov had spoken softly, hoping to ease the shock of his presence. But this was better. They were all too afraid to be lying. He turned back to the boy in the fort and motioned toward the house. "Do you live here?"

"Yes sir."

"Is anyone inside?"

"My mother and sister, sir."

The Russian extended his palm. "Stay here." Turning, he noticed a worried look on the boy's face and produced a thin smile. "They'll be fine, I promise."

It was one of the few he intended to keep. The last thing they needed was anyone here to die. Nothing left a trail like collateral damage.

Reaching a small wooden porch, Ryov climbed its pair of steps and rapped on the front door. Soon it swung open, revealing a brunette in her late thirties. Perhaps expecting to ask her son why he was knocking, she instead eyed the man before her with a mixture of surprise and caution. "Yes?"

"Sorry to disturb you, ma'am," said Ryov, flashing the ID and introducing himself once more. "I've been tracking a fugitive over the past several days and have reason to believe he may, at this moment, be inside your house."

The woman's eyes quickly widened, but there was still hesitation. Ryov caught her take a furtive glance toward his gun. "With respect, sir, my daughter and I have been inside for several hours. I'm sure no one is here."

Behind her Ryov noticed a kitchen and small living room. A girl, maybe twelve, stood in nervous interest beside a worn sofa. He motioned inward. "Was there a period in the last five minutes when neither of you were in this front area?"

The woman thought for a moment. "Yes, but just for a short time."

"That would be enough. This man is an expert in stealth and deception. It would be nothing for him to be hiding in a bedroom right now." Ryov saw his host waver in consideration. "Please," he urged, "time is critical."

"How can you be sure he's not outside somewhere? And what about my son?" Her voice took on a new shade of concern as she peered left toward the yard.

"He's fine. I already spoke with him. None of the boys saw anything." Ryov took a half step forward. "May I suggest the two of you join them directly?"

It was barely a request. After glancing into his eyes, she turned around. "Kata, outside, quickly."

Ryov stepped aside as they grabbed coats from near the door and descended into the snow. Taking one more look at their visitor, the woman led her daughter away. Ryov raised his weapon, crossed the threshold and closed the door.

Silence permeated the interior. Most of the details from the scene were burned into his memory after a single glance. Wood floors covered the entire area. The kitchen featured an old refrigerator and even older gas stove, on top of which sat a simmering pot of what smelled like borscht. Beyond was a small space with a round dining table. Down the back wall, a glowing fireplace warmed the nearby couch and pair of stuffed chairs. Further to the right, past a small bookshelf, a dim hallway beckoned.

Gripping his pistol with both hands down in front, Ryov advanced with vigilant strides. The snow caked on his boots was quickly melting, creating a liquid mirror off of which the flames of the fire danced brightly. The corridor's only illumination came from the waning day's gray light, streaming through a tiny window halfway down. Two doors stood to the left, with a third at the end. All were open, but none of the rooms beyond glowed any brighter than the hallway.

Sliding his back against the far wall, Ryov inched forward before suddenly bursting into the first room. Empty, outside of a dresser and pair of twin beds. He checked underneath each item to confirm. There was no closet.

Turning back, he stepped into the hallway and immediately dove through the next door. Before him lay a simple bathroom. Shower curtain drawn, empty. Finger still on the trigger, he swiveled toward the final space.

Another bedroom, slightly larger than the first. A dresser lay straight ahead, with a modest bed further left. Checking low, Ryov again found nothing. No closet here either. He stepped forward and turned left to trace the near wall. His last chance was a bulky armoire sitting in the corner.

Tensing for one final assault, he reached for the handle. Suddenly, though, he stopped. His body relaxed, he lowered his gun. A scowl materialized on his face as the revelation passed over: Kent wasn't here. Somehow he knew. Pulling open the cabinet's double doors confirmed his conviction.

Ryov removed his phone and dialed. After a ring the line picked up. "Scharp."

"Status."

"*Noll*. Driveway leads to a small road, more houses. Street is empty. The only definable tracks are too small to be Kent's. Probably boys walking over for the snow fight."

"Understood." Ryov started for the front door. "The house is empty. Have Tanaka pick you up. Berger and I'll bury LeRiche."

"Where could he have gone?" asked Scharp after a slight pause.

"Right now it doesn't matter." Ryov walked onto the porch and eyed the woman and children, now huddled near the Yugo. He kept his voice low. "We'll never find him in the dark, and searching this area would be too conspicuous. Kent's in no position to travel. If he doesn't freeze to death, he'll hole up somewhere. I want to be a step ahead before he moves again."

"Copy."

Ending the call, Ryov stowed his gun and descended the steps. The woman shielded the kids as he approached. "Your home is empty, ma'am. Thank you for your patience. I apologize for the intrusion."

Relief spread across her face, but not completely. "It is no problem."

Ryov continued for effect. "If you should notice anything suspicious, please call your local politsiya station. Contact instructions have been disseminated along the chain of command. Any news will soon reach us."

She gave a curt nod.

Ryov returned the gesture and spun to leave. Striding purposefully across the driveway, he rounded the corner and broke into a swift jog. There were no new tracks behind the house. Snow on the roof and car was untouched. Kent was gone. But where?

Taking his own advice, Ryov brushed the question aside. This was only the beginning.

10

Boris Poushkin didn't like to drive fast. In Russia there was always snow on the ground, especially off the beaten path. Plus, he'd only bought the Isuzu pickup months ago. It was five years old with plenty of mileage, but still new to him.

Today, though, he *was* driving fast. It'd only started seconds back. There was just something about the man. Tall, silver hair, walking along the roadside. Poushkin didn't recognize him. That wasn't necessarily alarming—theirs was a small community, but hardly immune to the occasional visitor.

No, it was the way he carried himself. The gait held a direct purpose; his arms seemed ready for action. When the truck passed by he waved, but never really showed his face. Everything about the man was unusual. Foreign.

With his family less than two kilometers away, Poushkin needed no further motivation. Attempting to keep his speed reasonable, he nevertheless spun the Isuzu's tires aggressively over the gravel road. Bits of snow and rock kicked up behind as he negotiated a few curves before arriving at his driveway.

He slowed slightly to turn, then barreled ahead. Seconds later the house came into view. He was still a distance away, but everything looked fine: interior rooms glowed yellow through the front windows; smoke wisped evenly from the chimney up top. Set above the front door, a bright floodlight washed the driveway in stark illumination.

Rolling closer to the scene, Poushkin's heart calmed significantly as he spotted his wife and son on the porch. Despite his approach, they seemed to be paying most attention to each other through what looked like a heated exchange. He cut the engine and dismounted. "Everything okay?"

Turning, his wife spoke through the rising wind. "We're fine." She placed her hand on their son's shoulder and said something. Poushkin could see his little boy nod and exhale. Alexandra was gifted in the art of combining strength and love when dealing with her children. She signaled for her son to stay and descended into the snow.

Hugging a thin blanket tight around her shoulders, she strode through the frozen muck toward her husband. Poushkin had stayed near the truck, assuming whatever she had to say was not for their children's ears.

Instead of offering an explanation, she opened her arms and embraced him. At six-six, 280 pounds, Poushkin was a big target. Despite his surprise, he managed to respond, wrapping his own arms around his wife. Coupled with the blanket, she was barely visible.

After a second he squeezed a bit tighter, rubbing her back. Alex was a strong woman. She had to be; they lived a hard life. Still, it was a two-person job. As much as he hated to see her overwhelmed, a part of Poushkin secretly reveled in moments like this, when his wife truly needed him. Yet as she released her hold and looked up, he saw no fatigue in her eyes. It was fear.

"Someone came by a few minutes ago," she said. "An officer with the FSB. He told me they were looking for a fugitive in the area and thought he might be inside the house."

Grasping his wife's shoulders, Poushkin returned her gaze. With some effort he kept his face calm. "What happened, Alex?"

She shook her head. "Nothing. I took Kata outside. Anton was with his friends and we all huddled together. The man was in and out of the house in two minutes." She paused. Her voice was controlled, but clearly under stress. "He said it was empty. He told us to contact the authorities if anything happened. Then he was gone and I brought all the kids inside. That was just ten minutes ago."

Poushkin didn't immediately respond. He looked down at his wife, the two of them warm silhouettes against the floodlight and whipping wind. She took a deep breath and continued. "It's just, the man—the officer. There was something…wrong about him. Something sinister." She looked up. "I'm sorry, I know it sounds strange. Maybe it's just been a long day."

"No," said Poushkin, thinking of the man on the road. "I believe you." He was about to ask another question when he noticed his wife's face. Whether it'd happened in the last second or he'd missed it earlier, she was exhausted. *Later.* "But I'm here now," he offered. "Nothing's going to hurt us."

He turned her toward the house and they started walking. Boris thought about calling the police. What if this stranger returned? But he had no proof of any threat. And this man—or men—really might be with the FSB. If word got out that the house they'd visited had made an inquiry, things could become awkward. Or worse.

Poushkin took a breath. No physical harm had come to his family. He would sleep on it before making a decision. He gestured up at their son, still standing on the porch. "What were you and Anton talking about?"

She sighed. "He wanted to wait outside for you. I told him no."

"Why did he want to do that?"

"He wouldn't say." She shook her head. "Maybe on a brighter day, but certainly not after what just happened."

At that moment the young boy leapt from his perch and ran out to meet them. "Papa, it's been long enough, please." He tried to move his father by tugging on his right sleeve. Two men pulling the Titanic across the Sahara would've had a better time of it.

Poushkin had been holding his wife's hand and released it to bend toward his son. "Anton," he replied calmly, "what do we say to someone who has just arrived?"

His momentum halted, the boy grunted in frustration and looked down. Swaying in the snow for a few seconds, he exhaled and returned his gaze. "Hello papa." He turned to his mother. "I'm sorry for arguing, Mama."

She gave him a kiss on the cheek. "It's okay sweetheart. Come now, let's go inside and have some soup."

"No, no," said Anton, regaining his earlier zest. "This way, or he'll freeze."

Poushkin looked in the direction his son was pointing. About fifteen meters away he could see what looked to be a snow fort. "Ah, you brought Sasha out to help in the fight," said Boris, referring to his son's teddy bear.

"No, not Sasha," said Anton. "I don't know his name. He's sitting in the fort."

Both parents exchanged glances. Their son had the imagination of any child, but never to the point of complete fabrication. Poushkin moved out in front. "Anton, are you saying there is someone in that fort?"

The boy nodded.

"Is he older, like us?" asked Alexandra.

"Uh-huh."

Poushkin stared at the fort. "What does he look like?"

Anton followed his father's gaze and furrowed his brow, as if he were taking on an important task for which he would be graded. "He has dark hair and scratches on his face" he said after a moment. "And he's bleeding. He's wearing a jacket and shorts and looks really, really tired."

Poushkin's eyes widened as he looked back at his son, then his wife. Yet, as the questions piled up in his mind, he brushed them away. Now wasn't the time. "Alex, would you please take Anton inside?"

"But Papa—"

"No buts." Poushkin crouched down. "You've done a great job, Anton, but we're a team. It's my turn now."

"But I want to go with you."

"Not this time. You go take care of your mother and sister and all your friends." Poushkin gave his son a wink. "I'll be inside in a minute." He slowly stood, already envisioning the look on his wife's face. He squeezed her hand. "I'll be fine."

She didn't let go. "Boris…"

He faced her completely. "I know. I'm sorry, but I have to."

"Let's call the police first."

He shook his head. "I can't wait. Not when it's this close to my family."

Alexandra stared at her husband for a long moment. Finally, she nodded in understanding and grasped their son's hand. "Come on, Anton."

Seeing her mouth the words 'be careful' as they walked away, Poushkin smiled back and turned toward the fort. He didn't feel as confident as the grin implied, but there was no other option. He trudged ahead, reminding himself that he was probably bigger and stronger than whoever this mystery man was.

The wind had picked up, swirling snow particles around like a winter tornado. The sky was now completely dark, its canopy of distant lights struggling to illuminate the scene before him. Reaching down, Poushkin armed himself with a heavy stick from the edge of the yard.

Almost there. He could feel his heart pounding as beads of sweat began collecting near the top of his forehead. If this man were sitting out in the open in the condition his son had described, Poushkin wanted to think he would have been more welcoming. As it was, the visitor was shrouded in secrecy and darkness. The burly Russian could take no chances.

The thump in his chest reverberated into his throat as the top edge of the white structure curved closer. Poushkin could easily see over the walls, but only had an angle for part of the interior. Raising his stick, he lunged forward to see the rest.

He barely noticed him at first. Curled up in a ball amidst the white powder, the man looked more like a forgotten statue than flesh and blood. Almost instantly, Poushkin's guard dropped as the stick hit the ground. He bent closer. Anton was right: the man was bleeding. Beneath his jacket, a thick line of red stained the left side of his bare chest. Poushkin could see the stomach moving, but both eyes were closed. He appeared to be sleeping. The beginning of hypothermia.

Reaching down to pick him up, Poushkin touched the edge of his sleeve when the man instantly sprang to life. He gripped the Russian's wrist with surprising strength and plunged his other hand into his jacket pocket. Just as quickly as it had started, though, the movement stopped. His intense gaze swiftly melted into vacant exhaustion. "Forgive me," he whispered, in Russian.

Surprising himself, Poushkin stood unfazed and proceeded to lift the man off the ground. "No police, no hospital," said the stranger. "Tell no one."

Stepping over the fort wall, Poushkin was about to respond when his charge once again slipped into unconsciousness.

11

Ryov stood in the bunker's anteroom, cell phone to his ear. The voice came on after two rings. "I'm headed to a meeting. Call back in an hour."

"Kent's gone."

There was a short silence. "I hope that means dead."

"You know what it means."

Another pause. Ryov knew why. The mind on the other end worked just like his. *How could something like this possibly happen?* And yet, instantly, that didn't matter anymore. Only the next move. A race had begun, and there was no second place.

"Do you know where he's headed?" asked the voice finally.

"Right now, not far. He's injured. Soon, though, Linz, then London."

"That cannot be allowed to happen."

"I have a proposition."

"I'm listening."

Five minutes later Ryov pocketed the phone and strode into the main chamber. Scharp leaned against the left wall, his gaze piercing the stone floor. Across, Tanaka stood bandaging Berger's temple. All three immediately looked up.

"Kent's obviously headed for Linz," said the Russian. "After that we have to assume London."

Scharp straightened. "London's not a sure thing, Sergei."

"It's too much of a probability to ignore," said Ryov. "He'd have wanted to steal the key shortly before we left for Istanbul. Earlier would have been too risky."

Tanaka stepped forward. "Which means he'd have little time to move it somewhere else."

"What about mailing it away?" asked Scharp. "Or handing it off to someone? The key could be in Canada by now."

Ryov looked at the Swede. "If you were in Kent's position, would you trust something like this to a civilian?"

About to respond, Scharp cut himself off. Tanaka turned to Ryov. "So Kent lifts the key before we leave London, then grabs the canister at the station in Linz. By the time we notice, we're trapped on the train and he's headed back." He looked around. "Not a bad plan."

"But why not just bring the key with him?" asked Scharp after a moment. "Then he steals the canister and doesn't have to return to London."

Standing from a chair, Berger shook his head. "Keeping the key separate gives him leverage in case we catch on."

"Which is exactly what happened," said Ryov.

Silence permeated the chamber. Tanaka nodded toward the anteroom. "What did Kerr say?"

"He agreed with my plan." Ryov eyed all three men. "Kent can't fly to England. A plane is too confining; he'll want to stay mobile. But we can't cover the continent on our own." He took a few steps forward. "Each of us has a network of contacts from Moscow to Dublin. It's time to use them. Border patrol, police, transportation officials—anyone who owes you pays you now. Waiters, cab drivers—I don't care if they seem irrelevant. The more eyes we have on the ground the better. Kerr will mobilize his own people."

"And Baker?" This from Scharp.

"Ordered to London," said Ryov. "And pleading innocent. Without proof to the contrary, he's too much of an asset to eliminate. But twenty-four-hour surveillance began this morning. If he doesn't toe the line, we'll know his true colors."

Thinking for a moment, the trio eventually nodded.

"Good," said Ryov. "Pack this place up. I want to be gone in ten minutes."

12

Allison Shaw gripped her coffee with both hands, but gulped in the cold air instead. It felt different today. April in Scotland was a far cry from Atlanta, and she'd been getting used to the weather. But it'd finally turned. Specifically, up above. No clouds, blue skies and—wonder of wonders—a bright sun shining down.

She'd needed the light. The country was beautiful, but for the last two weeks she'd been coming and going from work at night. Her off days had been highlighted by canopies of gray. What did they call the need for sunlight? *Seasonal affective disorder.* Or just not enough vitamin D. Either way, she was getting it now.

Another minute and she finally did bring the steaming caffeine to her lips. About twenty feet ahead stood a small gaggle of fellow nurses, each with their own hot drinks. They chatted back and forth in subdued tones. Allison knew half of them, but liked her alone-time too much to join the conversation.

The closest thing to her, actually, was the building in which they all worked. 'Building,' though, was an understatement. Really a cluster of structures, the Royal Infirmary of Edinburgh occupied over forty picturesque acres along the Scottish capital's southeastern edge. Allison's eyes traced the main complex just to the left, its white, minimalist façade extending out of view.

Holding off a sneeze from another glance at the sun, she was about to take a second sip of coffee when she heard footsteps approaching from behind. A turn of curiosity revealed her best friend at the site, Rebecca Townsend.

Allison thought her own flight had been long; Becky's started in Sydney. They'd both come to the UK with a program called Continental Travelnurse. A six-month assignment. They fit the profile perfectly: single, skilled, still in their twenties. The website said it was a chance to see the world, discover a little more about yourself. Trite, sure, but maybe still true.

Certainly for Becky, who liked to stay active and had an adventurous spirit. The setup featured free lodging and good pay. Perfect conditions for extra travel. Allison was actually more unsure about herself. Why was she here, really?

On the surface, it was simple. While not as much of a globe-trotter as her friend, she valued independence. Cultivated it, too, like a budding plant. Not because it was trendy or cool; because it was part of her makeup. Crossing an ocean for a job opportunity was a big step, but a welcome one.

This trip, though, was different, and she couldn't figure out why. Scotland's natural beauty came as-advertised. She didn't hate her job, and the hospital was clean and up-to-date. On more than one occasion she and her coworkers had gone into Edinburgh—even Dublin and London—and shopped for antiques before flirting with a few cute locals at a pub.

But something was missing. Some extra piece that'd only recently made itself known. Would she find it before going back home? Maybe it would have to find her. How, though, did you search for something you couldn't identify?

Slipping in that second drink of coffee to warm her throat, Allison smiled faintly as her friend drew closer. Pretty and athletic, Becky stood every bit of 5'10" and was difficult to miss. She usually walked with a spring in her step, but today flaunted an extra bounce.

"Good morning, Ally," she offered in a smooth Australian accent. "I've been looking everywhere. Thought you southern girls didn't like the cold."

Allison's smile widened. "Life's full of exceptions." She paused. "Looks like you've got some news. Are you going to pull me back inside?"

"Oh no, this would sound good anywhere." Becky's eyes grew bright like a teen on her first date. "I noticed we've both got the same block of time off coming up. Petr has invited me down to Linz for a few days, and…I think you should come."

'Petr' was Petr Arnold, an Austrian banker who'd spent a semester at the University of Edinburgh years back. Returning recently to see some friends, he'd met Becky and they hit it off. The two had since spent a couple weekends together, but they'd always been alone. This was the first time Allison had heard mention of anyone else being invited. She made no attempt to hide her surprise.

"I know," said Becky, reading Allison's expression, the schoolgirl look still in her eyes. "Maybe our relationship is ready for the next level. But I can't introduce Petr to an entire contacts list overnight. It needs to be a slow, easy pace. Who better to start with than my best friend?"

Allison remained surprised, this time thanks to her own interest. She enjoyed hanging out with Becky, but there'd been no hesitation; she knew instantly that she wanted to go. And she'd never been to Linz. Maybe it was just the chance to see a fresh place. *And fill this hole inside.*

"I'm in," she said.

Becky squealed in delight. She reached forward and wrapped her arms around Allison, nearly spilling the coffee. A moment later she stepped back. Her body shook, a wave of excitement blending with the morning chill. "That's great! I've got to call Petr. He'll be thrilled."

Allison's face crinkled in puzzlement. "Thrilled? He doesn't even know me."

Becky kept her smile. "He knows of you. I've painted a good picture."

"Nothing impossible to live up to, I hope."

"As if you could ever fall short."

Allison was about to deflect the compliment when her eyes flashed in remembrance. "Didn't you tell me a while ago that Petr's place is only a one bedroom?" She thought about it. "I guess I could do a fold-out, but it wouldn't be the most comfortable…"

Becky was shaking her head. "That's the best part. Petr's uncle is an airline pilot and has an apartment with a spare bedroom. It's nothing special, but right near the city center. He's going to be gone while we're there."

"And he doesn't mind me using it?"

"Not at all. He trusts Petr. They're close. Gave him an extra key for anyone who visits."

Allison was silent. It was the perfect scenario—a long weekend in a vibrant city, a place to herself at its heart. "How can I say no? Thank you, Becky. And tell Petr thanks, too."

"You can tell him yourself," she said, grinning playfully. "We'll be there before you know it." She turned to head back inside, but spun around at the door. "Aren't you cold?"

"I'll be there soon."

Seconds later Becky was out of sight. Allison felt a fresh tinge of excitement, but nothing was going to keep her from savoring the sunshine.

13

Despite plenty of competition, Ten Downing Street was perhaps the most prominent of all UK addresses. Boasting close to 100 rooms, the brick and mortar structure shared several attributes—architectural and symbolic— with its Pennsylvania Avenue cousin.

Differences, though, still existed. For one, Number 10 wasn't white. It's sparse façade, now more familiar than a union jack, was a definitive dark brown. It also wasn't a single house. At least, it didn't used to be. Formerly a trio of homes, the various residences were eventually melded into a single unit over a quarter millennium ago.

Knowing facts like these was not a prerequisite for becoming Prime Minister, but they came easily for Alan Bradley. Standing in front of a mirror from his bedroom in Number 10's private upper-floor apartment, he calmly pulled a silk tie through the twists and turns of a Windsor knot.

It was the history that drew him. Ever since he was a boy he couldn't get enough. Bradley had played sports and chased girls like the rest of his friends, but in the back of his mind there was always a book waiting to be read.

Was it that knowing the past told you something about the future? The knot he was tying received its name from Edward VII, Victoria's eldest son. Ed waited a long time to be king and evolved into quite the fashion connoisseur along the way. The Windsor was inspired by his preference for cravats with wide knots. Interesting, certainly, but it wouldn't help any policy decisions.

There were other facts, though. Like knowing that when he became Prime Minister at the age of thirty-three, Bradley was the youngest to hold the post in over two-hundred years. That single piece of information had been a constant reminder to lead with humility. Two elections and seven years later, its importance was apparent.

Recently, though, his chief reason for focusing on history had been to remind himself that heroes still existed. William II at Hastings; Nelson at Trafalgar; Chamberlain at Little Round Top. It happened then, it could happen now. *It has to.*

"Don't think too hard. Remember, you're a politician."

Bradley turned to see his wife, Sarah, wearing a gray business suit and leaning against the room's door frame with folded arms and a smile. "Have no fear, milady," he said, regaining his composure and strolling toward the middle of the chamber. "I promise it wasn't important."

She moved forward too, bringing her hands up for a final adjustment of the Windsor. "Good. Important is never much fun anyway."

They locked eyes for a moment. The irony of her words brought a pall of heaviness into the room. Bradley fought it off by gazing deeper into his wife's blue irises.

He'd met her in college and fallen in love immediately. They were the same age, but, looking at her now, he swore she was ten years younger. Perhaps it was the strain of his position, hastening the wrinkles and gray hair. Then again, she'd just taken on a much larger amount of stress.

Bradley knew it was a cardinal sin to relay such classified information, but he'd been at his breaking point. Lying in bed together, hand-in-hand, whispering back and forth; he'd felt a release. Others knew, but no one could provide the comfort his wife did. He hated to burden her with the news, but she'd taken it calmly. The exact trait he needed himself.

Reading the look in his eyes, she focused back on the tie and swallowed. "There. Now you're ready to see the Queen."

"I've got to make it through a cabinet meeting first."

"Anything fun planned?" She turned to retrieve a necklace from a nearby dresser.

Bradley reached toward the bed for his jacket and frowned. "Preparation for the Commons. It's going to be feisty this week."

"Something you said?"

"Something I'm going to say."

Sarah clasped the jewelry around her neck and walked back to the center. "Well, no one says it better. Just be yourself."

"That's what I'm afraid of."

She smiled. "Did your daughter bid you farewell for the day? She's finishing her breakfast now."

The Prime Minister donned a silver watch. "Yes, she came in a few minutes ago." His eyebrows rose. "But…"

"But what?"

"I didn't give her a kiss." He leaned in close. "Perhaps you can deliver one for me?"

Sarah barely had time to react before her husband wrapped her in his arms and dipped her into a long, soft kiss. A second later she was catching her breath. "I'll relay the message, but your teenage daughter will probably decline a physical demonstration."

"She doesn't know what she's missing."

Sarah laughed and walked toward the doorway. "I'll be back this afternoon. Love you."

"I love you too."

Half a minute later Bradley strode through the doorway himself and nearly collided with his son. "Ben, pardon me. I was just about to go find you."

"Likewise, dad." The fifteen-year old was dressed for school with a backpack slung around one shoulder. "We still on for Friday?"

The PM smiled. "I thought I'd be the one having to remind you. Yes. Fish, chips and James Bond. Our second time, so, *From Russia with Love*."

Ben made a face. "I still don't get what the big deal is with Sean Connery."

Bradley looked around furtively. "Keep your voice down. You could get shot for saying something like that."

Ben chuckled. "Seriously, dad."

Bradley put his arm around his son. "Trust me, it'll come. Sometimes greatness has to grow on you."

A few hours later Bradley was back in the apartment, staring into a bathroom mirror. He washed and dried his hands before adjusting his tie. It was still pristine, no wrinkles or stains. This time, though, his wardrobe was an afterthought.

He gripped the sink counter and forced himself to stop trembling. Closing his eyes, he took a long, deep breath and flashed an ironic smile. When you were younger, secrets made you special, set you apart. The perfect prize to lord over your friends. It was only later that the truth came.

No one wanted secrets. The world said they were great, but those who had them knew: they were much more pain than pleasure. Sometimes dark, always heavy.

Slowly gathering himself, Bradley exited the bathroom and wound his way toward Number 10's grand staircase. Its yellow walls glowed brightly from sunshine cascading through a large mounted window. He took the carpeted steps one at a time, glancing to his right, as he often did, at the line of portraits descending alongside. Every past prime minister was represented. The White House had its own version, and to him the concept was the most important in a head-of-state residence.

As much as you relied on your staff, friends and family, running a country was a lonely enterprise. The only people who really knew what you were going through were those who'd gone through it before. Passing the second portrait of Churchill—the only PM on the wall twice—Bradley managed a slight grin and nodded subconsciously. *You're right, Winston. We still have a chance.*

Gaining the ground floor, he strolled into the entrance hall. Like the rest of Number 10, it was relatively unassuming. A carpeted walkway led him toward the front door, held open by a security guard. Bradley eyed the black and white tiles on either side of the rug. Still in use since their installation in the eighteenth century. They'd always reminded him of *The Twilight Zone.*

Nodding to the doorman, he stepped out into a swath of sunlight and squinted upward. The sky was an uncharacteristic blue. No clouds. Downing Street was calm at the moment, and the Prime Minister moved to his left along the sidewalk. One of his private bodyguards, wearing a black suit and sunglasses, waited nearby. "Morning, Hugh," said Bradley. "Beautiful day, isn't it?"

The man nodded. "Yes sir."

"Makes you want to take the rest of it off, no?"

Hugh smiled as they began walking forward. "You just give the order, Mr. Bradley."

"If only I could."

They were now only steps from a black Jaguar XJ, resting along the curb like an eager racehorse. Reaching out, Hugh opened the rear passenger-side door. The Prime Minister thanked his man and climbed in. Hugh folded into the front seat and nodded to the driver. Without a word, the man shifted into gear and rolled toward the security gate off of Whitehall. A Range Rover filled with additional protection followed close behind.

The PM closed his eyes and sank back into the charcoal leather. After they passed through the steel barrier and gained the larger road, a voice from the seat beside him broke in. "So, how was it?"

Bradley kept his eyes shut. "You mean the cabinet meeting?"

"Yes."

"Better than expected. We all seem to be on the same page."

"Splendid. Although I'm detecting a 'however' in there somewhere."

Bradley straightened and opened his eyes. "However, none of us are looking forward to the next few days. Who ever thought comprehensive education reform would be so difficult?"

"Glad to hear you haven't lost your sense of humor."

"The last to go, I promise."

This earned a grin. At five-foot-nine with a slight pudge, Nathan Brooks commanded much more authority than his physical stature suggested. Despite being five years younger than Bradley, Brooks served as Downing Street's Chief of Staff and was the Prime Minister's top aide.

Bradley had been university friends with Brooks' older brother. Several holiday trips back home brought the future PM in contact with the younger sibling. Not much time, but there was a connection. When the day came to start carving out his executive personnel, Bradley thought of Brooks before anyone else. He'd just graduated with a law degree and seemed smart beyond his years. The Prime Minister, in recent moments of self-pity, questioned whether his aide was exhibiting that same intelligence by sticking with him through this storm.

His mind bounced back to the present as the Jaguar turned right off of Whitehall, its elegant frame dancing in and out of the sunlight. On the left, Westminster Abbey rose to meet the clear sky. Bradley admired the majestic structure for the thousandth time, then turned back. "Any news?"

Brooks perked up. "As a matter of fact, yes." He'd been tapping on his phone, but now stopped and turned toward his boss. "As you know, it's extremely early across the pond, but a few east coast feeds seem optimistic about the day on Wall Street."

"Really?" Bradley smiled. "Knew I should have joined the Wal-Mart rush."

"Take a look," said Brooks, handing over the device.

Instead of a spreadsheet or webpage, the Prime Minister found himself staring at a simple word document. Its sparse text leapt off the screen, knifing into his gut:

**Kent still hasn't called in. That's 48 hours.
Baker may be compromised, has been
sequestered in London. I've told McCoy.**

He fought the dread off in waves. Kent had relayed the exact date
he was planning to make a move against Orion. Phones were a risk, but,
over the course of five years, exceptions had to be made. Brooks estab-
lished a third-party landline at which Kent and Baker could leave messages
to communicate.

They had one chance at success. Kent, more than anyone, knew
the gravity of this attempt. He wouldn't have waited so long to send a
good report.

Bradley forced himself to read the note again. Over the last few days,
the resident anxiety in his stomach had intensified; now it felt like an ulcer
had burst. This news was essentially proof of failure.

Silence enveloped the cabin as the V8 smoothly propelled the sedan
down Victoria. Bradley's throat had gone dry. Their enemy was not the
kind to allow second chances. For the life of him, he could imagine no
scenario outside of Kent dead or dying.

The PM steeled himself, though. He wouldn't fold, not here and
now. There was still hope. Churchill came to mind once again. "*Never,
never, never...*"

He managed an empty smile. "Looks promising." He handed the
device back. Brooks, ever composed, accepted the phone and slipped it in
his jacket pocket.

Half a minute later Bradley stole a glance toward the front. Had his
men been listening to their conversation? Would they buy this act?

He swallowed, shifting left and staring out the tinted window. His
gut churned through a mixture of weight and worry, heavy butterflies with
no place to land. He noticed Scotland Yard sail quietly by, its iconic sign
spinning like an oblivious sentry. *If only it were that simple.*

14

The cold was a memory, replaced by glowing warmth. Kent lay still, his body enveloped by the rare touch of a soft surface. For a second he thought it was all over—the threat, the hardship. His mind wandered back to his one-bedroom closet in Arlington. It'd long since been rented out, probably more than once. But had it somehow returned to his possession? Was he there, lying in his own bed for the first time in half a decade?

No. The pain, as usual, was his answer. Aching knives stabbing into his ribs and shoulder. His left side burned from back to front; the skin felt raw and charred at the same time. Still, he could breathe and think clearly. Considering what he'd been through, the agony should've been much worse.

Kent opened his eyes fully. He found himself staring at a low ceiling. He was in a room, dim and quiet. Heat seemed to be radiating in small waves over his left shoulder.

He sat up, or tried too. It was harder than he expected. Fatigue still reigned; his entire frame felt like a shell about to break. Regrouping, he managed to right himself with a grunt and looked around.

He'd been spread on a sofa, covered with a wool blanket. Behind, a dying fire reached out with its final dose of crackling, like muffled fireworks. To his right, over the back of the couch, a humble kitchen snuggled close to a small dining room table. Straight ahead, a thin bookshelf held a load of dusty hardcovers. Wood floors covered the entire area.

Kent gingerly pulled back his cover. He was dressed in sweatpants, a thick tee shirt and socks—all about six sizes too large. But how could you complain? Slowly turning, he swung his body out and planted both feet on the hardwood.

He immediately recognized his companion, sound asleep in one of two stuffed chairs. Everything about the man was massive: forest of a beard, thighs the size of tree trunks. Before diving into the snow fort, Kent had heard the boys' Cyrillic cries during their fight. This was Russia, and the bear before him proved it. Despite a rifle leaning between the chairs, though, there was a softness in the man's bearing. He looked more teddy than grizzly.

Kent remained still for a moment, fully digesting the situation. Finally, he forced himself up on wobbly legs. Edging toward the slumbering stranger, he reached the rifle and carefully laid it across the empty chair. Then he sat back down, leaned forward and spoke in Russian. "You picked the best one." Kent kept his voice loud enough to be heard in the living room, but nowhere else.

The man began to stir, stretching his long legs and rubbing his face. Sitting up, he finally noticed his guest and froze. For a second, Kent knew, he'd forgotten where he was. Kent sat straight-faced on the sofa, studying his host's actions. The Russian didn't panic, nor make any sudden movements. After eyeing his visitor for a long moment, he glanced to the right for his gun. Spotting it a chair away, he calmly turned back. "Excuse me?"

Kent cleared his throat. "I said you picked the best one." He pointed to the leather-bound Bible folded open on the man's lap. "Romans."

The Russian looked down. "This?" He idly fingered the pages. "I haven't read it in years."

"Why pick it up now?"

The big man exhaled, slowly composing himself. This couldn't have been the way he'd envisioned the conversation starting. "I don't know. The possibility of death seems to have reasserted itself lately."

Kent held up a hand. "My fault. Your son saved my life."

The host smiled slightly. "Do we look that much alike? Poor kid."

"I thought Russians weren't allowed to have a sense of humor."

"It's an underground movement." He gestured to the rifle. "Was this your own joke? I can still reach it."

Kent shifted his weight. "Just didn't want you to pull the trigger before you were fully awake. Might disturb your family."

"And put a hole in your chest."

"If you're a good enough shot."

"Something tells me you are." The host slowly pulled out the Beretta from an inside pocket, showed it to Kent, and set it on the empty chair beside the rifle. A shade of unease pricked the still air. "My son said you told him you were in trouble and needed to stay hidden."

Kent slowly nodded, keeping his eyes on the Russian. "It was my only chance. He was walking back to the fort, I'd just jumped in."

There was a short silence. "Anton is a smart boy. He said he looked in your eyes, knew you could be trusted."

Kent glanced at the weapons, then returned his gaze. "Do you trust me?"

The Russian exhaled. "You're a stranger who arrived with a gun and is now only feet from my sleeping family. Forgive me, but I'll trust you when you're gone."

Kent gestured to his wounds. He could feel the protective layer of fresh bandages. "Then why help me?"

"Trust is not the same as decency. Who doesn't help a dying man on their doorstep?"

"You could've called the police."

The man shook his head, stiffening. "Not after the encounter my wife had with an FSB agent."

Kent gazed directly at his host. "Did you see him?"

"The agent? My wife did. Slight build, long hair. He gave her a chill."

"That wasn't an FSB agent."

Poushkin paused. "And the man with silver hair I saw walking along the road?"

"Neither of them will be back here."

"How can you guarantee that?" the Russian asked, his voice gaining an edge.

"Because they think I'm somewhere else. I will be, too. Soon. Have to keep moving." Kent exhaled, letting his face crease into sympathy. "I'm truly sorry to have brought this upon you and your family."

The Russian stared back, his frosted gaze eventually melting. He stretched his large hand across the space between them. "Boris Poushkin."

Kent accepted. "The honor is mine."

"But…no name." Poushkin didn't seem surprised.

"I'm afraid your imagination will have to suffice."

The big man nodded. "I will say, you speak the language well. But you're not Russian."

Kent knew his features weren't sharp enough to pass for Eastern European under scrutiny. It was a small truth to grant the man who'd saved his life. "Fair enough." He paused. "But you've healed me as if I were a local." He motioned to his left side. "Is the bullet out?"

Poushkin nodded. "With some difficulty, and blood. Sorry—our kitchen makes a poor operating room."

Kent waved it off. "I'm alive, Boris. Do I have your wife to thank?"

"And my sister. She's a nurse in Smolensk." Kent's eyebrows rose slightly. "Don't worry. She won't tell a soul."

"And your son's friends?"

"I said you were a secret. Kids are better at keeping them anyway."

Kent nodded, and once again silence filled the room. "You mentioned your sister works in Smolensk," he said after a minute. "How far is it from here?"

"About eighty kilometers." Poushkin took a breath. "Please don't tell me that's where you're headed. I had you pegged as someone exciting."

"Oh that that were true." Kent thought a moment. "Eighty kilometers…west?"

"Yes."

"That must put us near Safonova."

Poushkin's eyebrows rose. "Impressive. Slightly north, actually. Levkovo." He flashed a small grin. "Are you heading to Moscow or Belarus?"

"Perhaps I haven't decided."

"A man like you always knows where he's going." The Russian paused. "Nowhere tonight, I hope."

On cue, Kent winced. "How long have I been here?"

"Thirty-six hours."

Kent was about to ask if Poushkin could stand him a bit longer when a thought clicked in his mind. Something he should've remembered the instant he woke. "Can I use your phone?"

"Am I allowed to know why?"

Because a few men in Washington need to know I'm still alive. It was a risk to send something out through the ether—Kerr probably had the entire continent held under a web of cellular surveillance. Use the wrong keyword and a computer worth more than Kent's pension would sprout a red flag. That would bring Ryov back, along with his fellow "FSB" agents. But this message was more than necessary, and didn't have to be specific. *No Boris, you're not allowed to know why.*

Kent shook his head.

Poushkin nodded, understanding. "It was worth a try. Of course you can use the phone." He stood up. "But only if you eat something. I'd hate to see a man survive a gunshot wound and hypothermia only to starve to death. Besides, the pain medication my sister gave you is wearing off. She left one more set of pills. They're better on a full stomach."

"What's on the menu?"

"The best borscht you've ever had, and some stale bread."

Kent moved to stand but the Russian held out a palm. "I'll bring it to you." He took a step toward the kitchen, then turned. "I have one more question, though."

"Yes?"

"Why is Romans the best book in the Bible?"

Kent thought a moment. "Because it's all about the saving."

Poushkin's brow crinkled. "Funny. I wouldn't have pegged someone in your position as a believer."

"In my position, Boris, sometimes believing is all you've got."

15

James Baker felt like he was walking through a lost Van Gogh. London, in all its iconic beauty: overcast sky, fog, drizzle. Cool, but not enough to chill the bones. As if to complete the image, he clutched a black umbrella, ebony face slightly obscured by its round canvas.

Tracing the western edge of Hyde Park, he could see the Joy of Life Fountain a few dozen meters ahead. 350 acres of generous greenery stretched to his left. The trees still had leaves to gain, but the lawns and hedges were already lush. On the right, impatient cabs weaved past tour buses along Parke Lane. Beyond, the Dorchester Hotel rose through the cloudy air, its front-entrance parade of Bentleys and Ferraris a constant through the bustle.

Normally, the weather might've been a problem. A sunny sky meant more foot traffic in the park—an easier canvas of humanity within which to disappear. But the last few days hadn't been normal, and he didn't need to disappear. It would do him no good.

He'd left his hotel in Southwark an hour ago, taken the tube to Kensington, then doubled back. It was a perfect route: enough of a detour to make the appearance of ducking a tail, but sufficiently simple to admit the one follower he expected.

He needn't have worried; the man was good. Too good. That was the rub of it all. Baker himself was a high priority. Kerr wasn't going to trust his surveillance to an intern.

In fact, his tail was three different men—a twenty-four-hour job, split into shifts. All of them, though, were essentially the same: middle age, average build, short hair. And stooping well below their pay grade.

Baker wondered what they'd done to deserve this. Each looked more and more like a pathetic pet on an invisible leash, following a mundane mark into obscurity.

He spied his companion for this morning across Parke Lane, pretending to stare through the outer glass of a Mini dealership about a hundred meters away. It was surely a greater distance than the man would have liked, but cross the busy road and he was too close. There was no middle ground.

Essentially, though, the tactic worked. Hyde Park was one of central London's rare open spaces. Even if Baker tried to escape, he'd be easy enough to spot.

But none of that mattered. If he behaved, kept to his boring schedule, he'd give no reason for a chase. Running would only serve to incriminate him further, anyway, breaking the thin tether of trust Kerr still granted.

Baker reached the fountain and circled around the far side toward a bench. Half its length was still dry, protected from the rain by an overhanging tree. Keeping his umbrella open, he sat down and casually looked around. Vehicles continued to buzz by, now about twenty meters to his left. Most park occupants were dots on the horizon, too distant to see clearly.

The only two within view were about to walk past his right shoulder. He'd spotted them several minutes back. A pair of females, also holding umbrellas. They nodded his way as they passed, one of them exhaling smoke from a half-burnt Pall Mall.

Soon they were on the other side of the fountain. Baker donned a pair of earphones and plugged them into his cell. A moment later he selected the number and a metallic ring sounding on the other end. Kerr's voice came through crisp and smooth. "You're right on time."

"I know you've got a busy schedule. Wouldn't want to delay lunch at The Savoy."

A small chuckle. "I'm afraid you overestimate my notoriety. No one cares where the deputy chief eats."

Baker glanced around once more. "Lucky you."

"I can hear the wind, the leaves," said Kerr. "You're in a park. St. James's?"

Baker knew his choice of setting made sense for the conversation. Enough space for words to carry into nothingness. "Why ask?" He glanced at his tail, who'd moved further north along Parke Lane toward a Starbucks. "Aren't you getting constant updates?"

Kerr exhaled. "Not as often as you'd think. And leave those men alone. They're dependable. If you rough one up, his absence will be noticed. The last thing I need is raised eyebrows over such a routine assignment."

"*Routine assignment.* Who did you tell them I am?"

Kerr's voice hardened. "Damaged goods. A once-great source who fell from a wall. Whether he can be put back together again is unknown."

Baker waited to respond until a jogger gliding past was out of earshot. "So that's why I'm here, in London—as punishment? Being babysat by government suits is my penance?"

"Don't ask questions to which you already know the answer. You understand the procedure. You'd do the same."

"Is that supposed to make waiting around easier?" Baker's own words had gained a stiffness. "I was days away from becoming wealthier than the sultan of Who-Gives-A-Stan. Now I'm a suspect."

"Pull your head out of the sand, James. You came from the same agency and arrived six months before the man who's jeopardized our entire operation. If I make a choice to rely on you, it won't be today."

Baker made a conscious effort to keep his voice down. "And as I while away, watching cartoons on a rented mattress, my partners risk their lives attempting to corral a rat on the run?"

"*Partners.* That's a bit more love than I think any of us would give one another."

"Forgive me for being devoted to the cause."

A short calm hugged the line. "You already know you're useful to us. Otherwise you'd be dead by now. But don't mistake value for indispensability. This endeavor will succeed, with or without you. Consider your current assignment a probationary sentence. Serve it in silence."

Baker remained still, the umbrella heavy in his hands. *Ten days ago a chef in Rome, now an unemployed Londoner.* He was still picking out traces of an Italian accent in his English. "I was a valuable foreign asset, Nicolas. My superiors will be searching for me. Are you sure such a large city is the best place to hide?"

"Counter intuition," said Kerr. "Overt is covert. The city's a melting pot of race and culture. You won't stand out."

"Last time I checked, they're pretty talented at finding faces. I guess we're lucky the CIA doesn't have a presence here."

"Your sarcasm outshines your significance, James. Don't imagine you're at the top of their priority list." Kerr paused. "That said, you've probably guessed London is Kent's ultimate destination. I can use your eyes in the city. And as emergency protection for Clarke and Boxler."

"So they're close?"

"Close enough. A gun would be made available to you, in such an event."

"I feel special already."

Kerr waited a moment. "This should be the last time you check in. We'll soon have the virus secured."

"And Kent?"

"A human expiration date. No man can outrun us forever."

"Finally, we agree."

16

"Pete…hey Pete."

The thin voice hadn't been strong enough the first time. Now, with a deeper edge, it successfully reached across the room and broke Peter McCoy from his thoughts. The senior CIA agent focused to see his assistant, Adam, standing in the doorway of his office. "You okay?" asked the younger man.

McCoy rubbed his eyes. "Yeah, sorry." He exhaled. "What is it?"

Adam straightened, as if finally put on the spot. "It's been a long day. Looks like you're feeling it too." He paused for a half-second, waiting for an objection to this fractional impertinence. None came. "A few of us are going to grab a beer. You want to come?"

McCoy respected the gesture. He liked to think he was approachable, but inviting your boss to a bar still took a bit of gusto. He almost said yes, just to reward the kid.

Instead, he picked up a pair of reading glasses and placed them on the bridge of his nose. *The overworked veteran, too old to party with the rookies.* Technically he was only forty-five, but this job had a way of draining your years exponentially.

"Thanks," said McCoy finally, "but I've got some things to finish up."

Adam hesitated; maybe he didn't believe his boss. But there was no point in objecting. Both men knew it was an argument he'd never win. "You need anything else from me?"

McCoy waved his hand, grinning. "Get out of here."

Adam nodded and closed the door. McCoy heard his muted footfalls echoing down the carpeted hallway, growing more faint by the moment.

Soon they melded with several others. The start of the evening rush. Even the CIA's clandestine wing had to punch the clock sometime.

They were an army of dedicated employees, the best their country had to offer. From analysts to linguists to technicians, each had beaten out hundreds of competitors to reach their current post. But now they had to turn their brains off for a while. Refresh their minds for the next go-round tomorrow.

And you'll still be here. Not quite, but it was too close to the truth to elicit much of a smile. McCoy stretched back in his swivel chair and surveyed his office. He supposed there were worse places to spend fourteen-hour days. This room had been his for the past eight years. Funny that he'd never really looked at it.

It was a modest rectangle, maybe two-hundred square feet of floor space. The walls and carpet were similar colors, both shades falling safely within the government-approved range of taupe to boring. File cabinets and bookshelves hugged the edges of the room. Two plush chairs occupied its center.

Facing them lay a dark-stained mahogany desk. Much of the agency's furniture had by-now evolved with the times, taking on a more modern, minimalist design. McCoy, though, had always leaned toward the classic. To him, the style of desk said something about the person sitting behind it.

His was no monstrosity, but solidly built. It simply all came back to the history. What would Washington and Lincoln have preferred? For the life of him, he couldn't envision either one of them stationed behind a jumble of right angles from Ikea.

Reaching across the desk's polished surface, he fingered a half-filled Styrofoam cup of coffee. Still lukewarm. He drained its contents and tossed the cup in a small wastebasket. He'd get a refill soon, from the cafeteria downstairs. For now, he used the jolt of stale caffeine to spin around and stare out the large window behind his desk.

Pretty soon he'd be able to open it. Spring had almost hit Fairfax County. Today had seen nearly sixty degrees, and the sunshine made it feel like more. Below, the landscaped greenery didn't seem as artificial as it had in January. Barren trees along the horizon made the most of their premature condition, jagged branches invading the deep orange sky like an Ansel Adams photograph dipped in color.

An hour from now it would all be pitch black. McCoy turned back to the room, glancing at a quadrant of classified satellite images on his computer screen. They detailed a pair of rebel encampments in eastern Iran. Just the tip to his daily iceberg of fresh intel. All of it worth every hour he contributed. Each coup, every attack was the definition of critical.

But none was the reason he stayed late. That all fell to one chance. One man. *Who's probably dead.*

Brooks had told him of Kent's failure to check in, which could only mean a botched heist. The news came during McCoy's weekly phone call with the chief of staff. The update on Baker was nearly as grim: he'd been sent to London, suspected—if not already convicted—of betrayal.

McCoy had nothing against Brooks; for an amateur, the aide had done well. But, personally, he found it agonizing having to go through a middleman to contact his officers. For all the CIA's technical firepower, they'd been forced into an archaic form of communication. Such was the delicacy of the situation, and the nature of their enemy.

Nicolas Kerr was second-in-command of one of the world's leading intelligence agencies. Considering the political duties of his superior, though, he was essentially the operational head. Kerr controlled more expertise and resources than a thousand cave-dwelling terrorists put together. And the best-case scenario placed Jeremy Kent in the middle of this maelstrom, as a fugitive. His cover as a turned agent was completely blown.

Kerr, for his part, needn't burden his senior staff, or their officers, with the truth. Anyone outside the deputy chief's circle of trust would simply be provided a false file on Kent and Baker. Maybe the two of them were off-the-books assets who'd forgotten their loyalties, or past allies with damaging secrets to spill. Either way, there was no telling how many fresh sets of eyes were now tracking the pair.

Suddenly five long years of intricate planning held no weight. The entire operation against Orion boiled down to a desperate race. But to where? Kent would do everything he could to stay alive. *And you're powerless to help.*

More than once, McCoy had caught himself glancing at his cell phone, hoping Kent might indeed call for assistance. But with the full power of MI6 at his disposal, Kerr was capable of intercepting any type of communication.

Especially messages sent to America. Those would be scrutinized the most now that Kent had been outed. It's possible Kerr would suspect Jeremy had gone rogue and interfered for his own purposes. But the most logical play was that he was still working for the CIA.

Any calls through the air were ultimately unsecure. E-mails too. Even a landline could be tapped as it ran through a landing station—most likely in the UK—before scuttling across the Atlantic via undersea fiber optic cable.

Langley, of course, could play the surveillance game too. A directive had just been sent out to every European station chief and case officer. It included the last known photographs of Ryov, Scharp, Berger, Tanaka and LeRiche. According to Kent and Baker, that was Kerr's crew.

Up until a few days ago, tracking these men had been a supreme liability. If any one of them even suspected the CIA was on their trail, Kent and Baker's turncoat identities would be forfeit, the op finished.

Now it didn't matter; the agency could search all it wanted. But where to start? None of their targets worked from any kind of home base. With an entire continent to canvas, it was truly a needle in a haystack. Even if they did manage to locate one of the men, it was unlikely he'd lead them to Orion.

McCoy leaned forward in a daze, reaching for the cup of coffee that was no longer there. Grasping the empty air failed to free him from his train of thought. For a moment, he was back in his fatigues as a Staff Sergeant, ordering privates around Camp Pendleton. Privates that reminded him of Kent and Baker. From the beginning, the two agents had been his responsibility.

But they weren't green Marines. They were the top clandestine field officers for the most powerful country's most powerful agency. The best in the world. That's why they'd been chosen.

Would it be enough?

McCoy could feel the sun setting behind him. Night, like a phantom creature, swallowing up the day's waning light. But he reminded himself of the orange glow, and the power of the sun itself. It always seemed to go down with a fight, burning deepest just before dropping over the horizon.

17

Kent walked out onto the porch and stared at the sky. Back inside all of the clocks had yet to hit five-thirty, but the coming day glowed orange in the haze above. He rubbed his hands together through a pair of cotton gloves. Smoke escaped from his mouth. Descending a trio of steps, he crunched across the icy driveway in a pair of ankle-high hiking boots. Like the rest of his clothing, they were old but still in good shape.

"They fit better than I thought." Boris Poushkin lumbered over with a slight grin. "My brother's a bit closer to normal when it comes to the size department."

Kent fingered the thick jacket hugging his torso. "Thank you. How'd you pull them away?"

"Vassily has too much clothing as it is. We told him there was a charity that needed supplies."

"Charity." Kent smiled. "Sounds about right."

"Ah, but you'll be riding in luxury." Boris gestured to the right. Five meters ahead the Yugo sat idling, its bug-like headlights piercing the frozen dawn. A healthy layer of snow still caked its olive-green roof, but the windows were clear. The muffler coughed a steady plume of smoke.

Kent took a few steps forward. "It's perfect."

"She certainly won't stand out, and I just fixed the heater last year."

Kent turned toward Poushkin, but before he could speak the Russian pressed a wad of rubles into his hands. He looked down. "What's this?"

"Some spending money, to go with your new car."

Kent fingered the bills. "This has to be six months' savings." He glanced at the house. "Does your wife know about this?"

"It was her idea." Poushkin grinned. "Looks like we'll have to wait on that in-ground swimming pool."

Kent gave a half-smile that quickly faded. After a short silence, he reached back. "I'm sorry. I can't take this."

Instead of accepting the cash, Poushkin closed Kent's fingers around it. "I have a feeling you're going to need it more than us." His face sobered further. "More than anyone."

A long moment passed. Finally, Kent pocketed the bills and extended an empty hand. "Words aren't enough, Boris. But thank you."

Poushkin shook the offering with a nod. He held on for a minute, seeming to search for the right words. Or whether to say them at all. "I know you can't give details. But, wherever you're headed...will I know if you make it?"

Kent thought about it, looking his host in the eye. "You'll know if I don't."

A minute later he was behind the wheel. The small engine made a dull roar and the Yugo's tires started rolling forward. Soon the car passed the halfway point of the driveway and disappeared beyond the line of pines.

18

Allison nearly had the gate to herself. Edinburgh Airport was the country's busiest terminal, but she and Becky were early. The flight to Linz didn't leave for another hour.

Arms crossed, she leaned against a wall of glass separating the building's interior from a modest stretch of tarmac. The planes were smaller too, but their dance in and out of jetways, between roving legions of men and machinery, remained the same the world over.

Inside, only two other travelers occupied the area's stiff seating. One was a businesswoman typing away on a laptop. She seemed oblivious to her surroundings, dutifully fulfilling the stereotype of a self-important executive. A row over sat an older man—at least seventy, asleep—with a single bag at his feet. His quiet snoring domesticated the scene, like the purr of an oversized cat.

Becky had stepped away a minute ago, hunting down Scotland's nearest answer to Starbucks. Which left only Allison. And, perhaps, the sunshine, warming her through the glass. Days ago she'd forgotten what it looked like; now it wouldn't let her go. It was almost as if it knew she was leaving. *Does anyone else?*

She frowned reflexively. The question seemed to have come from nowhere. But she knew better. Its source was four thousand miles away, in a suburb outside Atlanta. There her younger sister Amy was down from Nashville, hubby and kids in tow, visiting their parents.

Allison hadn't called home in three weeks. There was no estrangement; she honestly just hadn't thought—or felt the need—to do so. Her folks may have welcomed a ring, but they also understood her desire for space.

Amy had always been the family girl. She'd wanted a full house from a young age. Sometimes fairy tales came true. She met Ben her junior year of high school; wedding bells rang three years later. Now they had a mortgage and twin boys.

Allison moved from the glass to a nearby seat, still deep in thought. Could she ever see herself getting married? Like most young women, she'd fantasized about the ceremony, mentally arranging details down to the color of the carnations. Ultimately, though, she was still on the fence. There was just so much to see and do.

Even now, she was only twenty-eight years old. *You've got your whole life ahead of you.* But she'd used that line before. Suddenly it didn't hold quite the same weight.

Really, though, this wasn't about marriage or family; it was about anchoring herself. And what was there to fear? She was always going to crave adventure, but that didn't mean she had to be aimless. Commitment— roots—were a good thing. They didn't even need to be romantic. Or in Georgia.

Enough introspection. She'd face it all when she had to, and that wasn't today. The only thing that mattered was the trip ahead. Nothing cleared the mind like a night out on a new town.

19

A small black bag slung over his shoulder, Ryov strode calmly through the domestic terminal of St. Petersburg's Pulkovo Airport. It was closing in on 10 p.m., but the facility's streamlined corridors still bustled with travelers. This made blending in that much easier, no matter who might be watching: CIA, Mossad, even his own government, still searching for him after all these years.

The hour-long flight from Moscow had been uneventful. So, thanks to Vladimir Petrovich, was passing through airport security. Petrovich was a diplomatic security officer who bore a striking resemblance to Ryov and, conveniently, only existed on paper. The plastic badge and passport currently tucked inside Ryov's carry-on gave him all the clearance he needed for traveling with a pistol.

Keeping pace with the surrounding crowd, Ryov passed a newsstand and located the main entrance. He spotted the man immediately: late thirties, black suit; he was leaning near the doors with his head stuffed in a newspaper. As Ryov approached, the man folded the paper and led the way out. No eye contact.

They soon gained an expansive parking lot and were immediately met with solid sheets of rain. Illuminated by the stark glow of the space's towering lights, the droplets attacked like liquid needles. Their penetrating salvo was sharpened by the night's cold air and occasional gusts of wind. The suited man pulled out an umbrella and wordlessly offered it to Ryov. He shook his head and zipped up his own jacket. Opening the temporary shelter for himself, the man steadily escorted his charge across the wet asphalt.

Twenty meters farther he reached into his right pocket and pulled out a set of keys. Clicking a button on their electronic pad earned a single blink from the lights of a nearby BMW 5-Series. With its black exterior, the sedan had been nearly invisible amidst the darkened surroundings.

They approached the automobile from opposite sides. A moment later the bag and umbrella were in the backseat, both men up front. Behind the wheel, Ryov's escort pushed a button near the instrument panel to start the car. Its 6-cylinder engine promptly roared to life before settling to a steady purr.

The German sedan slipped into the gloom beyond the lights of the airport. Flipping on the windshield wipers, the driver made a series of turns before merging onto Pulkovskoye Highway. Ryov knew the route: straight north nearly all the way. He leaned his leather seat back. The trip would take at least thirty minutes. The heat in the car, activated a moment ago, combined with the soft pitter-patter on the windshield to create a peaceful symphony. He thought about using the time to consider Kent's plan, but that'd been the entire flight. He forced the questions away and shut his eyes.

In what seemed like seconds, a soft bump in the road roused him. The wiper blades were still busy clearing streaks of water off the glass, but the lights beyond the windshield had grown brighter. Larger buildings came into view as they neared the heart of Russia's former capital.

Gripping the steering wheel with both hands, the driver zipped across a small bridge and turned right on the other side. This brought the BMW parallel with the Fontanka River, one of the Neva's several offshoots. Local temperatures had just recently broken the freezing barrier; the Fontanka's black waters were still reveling in their initial freedom from what had been a winter-long prison of ice.

Soon they turned left onto Nevsky Prospekt, the city's most famous roadway. The requisite sea of shops and restaurants made their usual show until the driver curved right onto a side street. He parked the BMW a few meters down. Their destination was just steps away; it'd been visible from a much greater distance.

The Grand Hotel Europe was the oldest hotel in St. Petersburg and, arguably, the most prestigious in all of Eastern Europe. Rising five floors above the glistening pavement, the impressive structure occupied its central position in the city like a king on his throne. Its historic marble and gilt interiors had played host to a bevy of famous guests over the years, from Tchaikovsky to Prince Charles.

Striding through the front entrance, the two men made their way up to the second floor. The sentry led his charge down an ornate hallway before stopping abruptly and taking a few soft raps on the nearest door. It was opened by another suited man who ushered the two of them inside a large room. They marched across the floor before the pair of guards cut toward an adjoining door and disappeared without a word.

Ryov stood still, surveying the space. Lavish furniture and decorative accents dressed the chamber, their presence highlighting the hotel's signature Art-Nouveau style. On the far side, a large window framed the sparkling night.

Nicolas Kerr stared through the glass, his back to the door. If ever a man seemed destined for dominance, it was him. Kerr had joined the Special Intelligence Service as nothing more than a glorified desk clerk. A tireless work ethic and sharp intellect carried him up the ladder; despite a lack of field experience, he'd learned how to handle himself. At six-three, the sixty-year-old was still an imposing specimen.

A handful of seconds passed before he turned his lean frame and stepped closer to Ryov. "An executive suite for a man who grew up sleeping on a cot. You Russians do know how to welcome a guest."

"Excess has always been our specialty."

"Have a seat," said Kerr with an outstretched arm, striding across the room to the left. "How was your flight?"

Ryov stepped toward the nearest chair and sat down. "Fine."

ZACH FRANZ

Kerr reached the far side. He grasped a decanter filled with a clear liquid and raised it toward Ryov.

"As long as it's vodka," said the Russian, setting his bag on the floor.

"When in Rome, Sergei."

Soon Kerr handed his guest a glass before sitting down with his own across a crystal coffee table. Each man took an even swallow. "Where are we?" asked the deputy chief.

Ryov set his glass down. "Tanaka and Berger are in Linz. Scharp should be near Berlin by now and I have a flight to Milan in ten hours."

"What about extended coverage?"

The Russian sighed. "We're informing our contacts. By tomorrow night a solid web should be set. If Kent crosses a border on a road or uses any type of public transit, we'll have a chance."

"How do we know he hasn't been to the station in Linz already?"

"He hasn't." Ryov said this with the confidence of a math professor doing simple addition. "Considering his condition, he may not even be out of Russia."

A moment of silence passed. Kerr seemed to be measuring this information. Ryov gestured toward the window. "What brings you to St. Petersburg?"

The senior man abruptly stood and paced a few steps to his right. "U.N. idiocy. The Security Council's five permanent members have been encouraged to look into the possibility of forming an international intelligence bureau. We share data, combine resources—all in the name of tracking threats beyond borders."

"What about Interpol?"

"This would be an addition. National governments—greater force and scope."

Ryov shook his head. "What fun you boys have at the top."

Kerr returned to the bar and poured himself another glass. "It'll be over soon. Pure rubbish, the whole thing. A political fantasy." He spun back to Ryov. "The U.S. would no sooner trust us with their secrets than they would Russia or China."

"Where's the director?"

"Bradley sent him to Canberra." Kerr flashed an empty smile. "You heard about those car bombings in Jakarta? The Australian government is concerned they'll bleed south. Their PM wanted a second opinion on the threat assessment."

"So, you finally get your seat at the main table."

"Three of the five sent subordinates. This was always a show." Kerr drained half his glass. "Never had the stomach for such artifice. Maybe it's better I didn't get promoted." He sat down again. "Which brings me to the reason I called you here." There was a long pause. Kerr looked directly at Ryov. "Why are you doing this, Sergei? These past five years with Orion—everything?"

A hint of surprise leaked onto the Russian's face. "Are you serious?"

Kerr took a breath. "I remember the first time I saw you. At the summit, in Geneva. Polakoff stepped out of that Mercedes surrounded by security. Each man six-foot-forever, except you. And the greenest of all." He took a sip. "But I knew...I knew the moment I saw your eyes. The others were tensed, waiting to react. You could already see what was coming."

"In that case, nothing."

"Irrelevant. You'd shown your colors. I had to have you lead my team."

"How did you know I'd accept?"

"That, more than anything, is my job." Both men finished their drinks and set them on the table. Kerr continued. "You operate by your own rules, Sergei. Like a powerful machine that can neither be stopped nor controlled. I've always considered my role simply to harness you."

Ryov mulled the words. He couldn't tell if he was being complimented or insulted. "All this time...why ask now?"

"Because now is the tipping point. If we don't stop Kent, Orion is essentially a lost cause." Kerr paused. "It's a simpler game for the others; money is a great motivator. I'll even put myself in that category. Though

I'd be lying if I said I didn't want to see my government crumble under the weight of its own inefficacy."

The words were said with civility, but there was a hint of something deeper. Kerr's eyes burned with dark fire, a secluded storm that pierced his staid British veneer.

Ryov simply stared back, his gaze even. Kerr recovered. "I can see you have the raw material, Sergei. But a man fears what he doesn't know." The room went quiet. "I need to hear you say it. I need to understand."

"My world is simple," said Ryov after a moment. "Black and white, kill or be killed. I was orphaned at a young age, but was dealt this...raw material. A fair enough hand.

"I just want to win. Not for the sake of revenge or greed. Because I can; because it's better than losing. What else is there to life? Pleasure and victory are all that matter. All that make sense in this world."

There was a long silence, Kerr studying Ryov's eyes. Finally, the older man nodded. "Good enough for me." A pause. "One last thing, though." He leaned forward. "Don't underestimate our enemy. Tanaka, Berger, Scharp—they're all experts. You, Sergei, are the best. But Kent is a survivor. Put him in a room of assassins—he may not do the most killing, but he'll be the only one to walk out." Kerr stood up. "Remember that fact. Use it against him."

Ryov also stood, as if in agreement. Kerr reached inside his coat and handed the Russian a key packet. "You're one floor up. Sleep fast."

Five minutes later Ryov stepped into his own room and closed the door on the world. He set his bag down and turned toward the window. It offered the same glistening view as the suite, if less expansive. Kerr's final words were still fresh in his mind, and would keep him up for another hour. Because they were true.

Kent *was* a survivor. For five years he'd toed a line of secrecy that would've driven stronger, smarter men insane. Just since his capture, he'd made it through a gauntlet of pain, fear and extreme deprivation. Half of Ryov wanted to chalk his escape up to luck; the other half knew that was a lie.

But the trap was set. Ryov kept his gaze, and thoughts, trained forward. Rain still streaked the pain, blurring anonymous points of light floating distantly amidst a sea of darkness.

That was Kent right now: isolated, exposed, wavering. Destined to be extinguished by the inevitability of morning. Ultimately, it didn't matter which of them pulled the trigger. Ryov, though, found himself hoping for the chance to shine like the sun.

20

Forget sleeping—Kent was having trouble just shutting his eyes. It wasn't the cold; compared to the cell in the bunker, his current surroundings were a veritable sauna. It wasn't the pain either. After a while that became normal.

He took a deep breath and focused on keeping still. There wasn't much room to maneuver anyway. Curled up in the Yugo's backseat, he cuddled with a heavy blanket found serendipitously in the vehicle's musty trunk.

The darkness outside was western Belarus, fifty kilometers from the Polish border. Specifically, a neglected junkyard tucked off a back road. He'd angled the compact between two antique diesel trucks. With its lights shut off the small car was as good as invisible.

Getting here had been tricky, though things would be simpler once he crossed into Poland. Most of Western Europe abided by the Schengen Agreement, a contract which allowed for passage across borders of member countries without the need for documentation. It was as close as they came to being united states.

However, neither Russia nor Belarus had joined the body, which meant Kent needed a passport. If he charged through a border crossing the guards might not see his face, but surely the description of the Yugo would be disseminated, and right now he needed a car.

On his way through Smolensk, the largest city between Moscow and the border, he found what he'd been searching for. The kid didn't look old enough to shave, but he ran an active forging business. Kent had seen better work, but it would do. A few hours later he crossed into Belarus as Miro Vakkuri, a professor from Helsinki.

Outside an icy wind howled through the pitch black night. *Tomorrow.* That's why he couldn't sleep. There was only one place Kent could be heading, and his enemies knew it. They'd be waiting for him. He was a slab of meat waltzing into a lion's den.

But there was no other choice. For the hundredth time he pictured the train station in Linz, for the thousandth time the black canister hidden within its walls. As small as a cigar. *And big enough to save the world.* Or, at least, delay its demise.

It was an antidote, to Orion. Clarke and Boxler had left themselves a back door. Inside the canister was a liquid which, when injected, completely neutralized the virus. The antidote would spread throughout the entire body, imprinting its signature onto each cell. This allowed them to recognize and destroy Orion. As new cells formed, the signature was shared. One dose guaranteed a lifetime of protection.

The antidote was made valuable by its function, but even more so by the power of its opponent. If it was the solution, the problem was death personified. A monster not even its creators could have predicted.

Orion's potency lay in stealth, not speed. There were no symptoms. The virus spread through the body of a victim, latching onto cells without destroying them. Each cell was still able to perform every necessary function, keeping the immune system from recognizing an infiltration. It was frighteningly brilliant. Even from the outside, detection was impossible. The most powerful microscope in the world wouldn't reveal a thing.

After infection, there was a dormant period of about two weeks. Once it ended, Orion attacked like a synchronized bomb. Every contaminated cell—nearly the entire body—was destroyed. Like the entire process of cancer condensed into ninety seconds. Kent cringed at the thought, even now.

Contagion came from the exchange of bodily fluids. A kiss, your friend's water bottle, a sneeze—it didn't take much. Factoring in the dormancy, containing an outbreak would be next to impossible.

Kent pictured the canister again, then considered himself: one man, hunted by a team of killers, five thousand miles from safety. He'd have been the last resort if he weren't the only one.

Over the past half-decade, and especially the past two weeks, hope had turned to desperation. Locating Clark and Boxler was the prize, but now likely unreachable. Kerr had never fully welcomed Kent or Baker into his inner sanctum of trust. Did they somehow tip him off? Had he suspected their duplicity from the beginning?

Whatever the cause, the game had changed. It was now clear that Kerr intended to sell the virus, not use it. Thus, a newfound plan B: use the antidote as leverage against the sale of Orion. No buyer, no matter how fanatical, would be willing to pay billions of dollars for a disease that'd already been cured. Once momentum stalled, the CIA could exert pressure on Kerr and his men. Maybe back them into a corner, eventually a mistake.

It was thinner than a patch of spring ice, and highly impractical. If Kerr decided to call their bluff and sell Orion for a cheaper price, they'd have to duplicate and disseminate countless gallons of the antidote. The virus would spread more quickly than a mass of patients lining up for a mystery shot. Even if major population centers were covered first, people would die. Many people.

But that didn't have to happen. Plan B could work. *Don't think about the odds.* It was a miracle any still existed. This mission was—had always been—a house of cards. They just had to get out the door before the whole thing collapsed.

That meant that Linz, even if he somehow survived, was only the beginning.

The canister was developed by MI6 in response to chemical warfare. Each one had a lock that operated on a specified frequency and would only open for a key with a sonic trigger programmed to match. The outer shell was a reinforced silicon composite. Nearly unbreakable.

Even so, a sensor lay inside. The moment the tube's structural makeup was compromised, a miniature explosive literally burned its contents away. Adding to the fun, the frequencies connecting key and canister were perfectly synchronized and changed randomly every sixty seconds. Duplicating a way in was impossible. The only chance was to find the specific key made for his canister.

The good news: he already stole it. The bad: it was even farther away, in London. Kent let his mind drift as the memory flooded back. It felt so much longer than a mere week ago.

Orion was finished, ready. Kerr had lined up a buyer—a Saudi oil magnate-turned-jihadist. The exchange was set for Istanbul. Kent had no specific plan, but he was out of time. A move had to be made.

The key came first. It was a cylinder, silver, about the size of a paper clip. Kerr had summoned a couple of his men to London ahead of Orion's sale. Kent was one of them. Beforehand he'd called Brooks on their landline connection, knowing he could get away with requesting a few details. Surveillance from Kerr wasn't as heavy now as it would be once he made a play for the key and canister.

Upon receiving Kent's call, Brooks immediately contacted Eric Stanton, who still had friends in MI6's R&D division. The day Kent arrived in London the package was waiting for him, folded tightly and taped to the backside of an Underground bench in Euston Station.

It was just two papers, but they showed and described the keys' exact dimensions and specifications. Each device had a specific identifying number engraved near its bottom edge. Kerr had explained earlier that they were using even numbers for the virus, odd for the antidote.

Soon after, Kent managed to slip into a Covent Garden craft shop and custom order a plastic replica of the key. The memory brought a smile to his face. They thought it was the missing piece to a toy. *The Millennium Falcon's right rear thruster?*

Kerr was keeping a small case of keys in his Mayfair flat. A day before leaving for Turkey, he called a meeting there to review final preparations. The space was almost as secure as Vauxhall Cross, and less obvious than packing the corner of the Red Lion. Each of his men had been instructed to wear a business suit. Kerr often worked late; his fellow tenants would take the hint. This was just another case of bringing the office home.

In the study, Kent noticed the copy of *War and Peace* still on the wall. But he was alone now. Stanton's bug had only been designed to last two years.

The opportunity for the switch came five minutes before he left. The case was out in the open. No harm, as a key, without its matching canister, was useless. And, should the upcoming exchange go bad, it was prudent for all of them to know exactly what the keys looked like.

Gliding past, Kent made the trade, pocketing a real key and planting the fake in its place. He remembered the jolt of adrenaline once he realized no one had seen. The copy was a perfect match, too. Any difference was negligible.

Thirty-six hours later, he was on a train with Kerr and the others when it left Waterloo Station. A plane would've been faster, but was too conspicuous for their cargo. Once they reached Paris, they'd switch lines. Kerr had rented two private cabins on another train. He and Scharp would be in one, with Kent, Berger and Tanaka manning the other.

LeRiche and Baker were waiting as the train pulled into the Gare du Nord. They'd come up from Marseilles and Rome, respectively. Minutes later Ryov, carrying a satchel of canisters, completed the entourage. He'd presumably arrived from wherever Clarke and Boxler were still holed up.

Kent's chest hadn't stopped pounding since he stowed the key in London a day before. There was no training that fully prepared you for stakes like this. Sometimes years of tradecraft simply gave way to moments of improvisation.

His best chance to lift the canister came when they'd stopped in Linz. It was the middle of the day, plenty of activity. Tanaka, in Kent's cabin, had the case of keys. Down the hall in the other lay the satchel. Protocol banished all contact. Two separate groups drew less attention than a united front.

But as the train stopped, with passengers flooding the corridors to switch tracks or stretch their legs, Kent made his way to the second cabin. He'd grabbed a random shoulder bag from a nearby rack. He could feel his hairline begin to perspire and hoped it didn't show as he rapped on the door. Ryov opened it a second later, a neutral look on his face.

"Excuse me," said Kent, in German. He glanced down at his bag, as if searching for a tag. "Is this berth number four? I thought it was mine."

Ryov flashed a look of curiosity, but recovered with a nod. This interruption had to mean something. "You're right," he said. "I was just leaving." He opened the door a few more inches. "Please, come in."

Kent stepped through. A pair of bunks hugged the left wall with a sofa built in to the opposite side. The satchel lay between Kerr and Scharp on the couch. Baker lounged on the top bunk.

Ryov closed the door and turned, eyes narrowed. *This better be good.*

"Tanaka's sick," said Kent, to the whole room. "The flu, something he ate…I don't know. He started vomiting twenty minutes ago. Didn't make it to the toilet the first time.

"A steward overheard the commotion, knocked, offered to bring us a new trash bag. When he returned, an off-duty doctor caught a glimpse and insisted on taking a closer look."

"You didn't push him out?" asked Scharp, looking up from a magazine.

"At a certain point resistance becomes conspicuous." Kent paused, but still had the floor. "The keys are out of sight. It should be nothing, but you can understand why I didn't call."

A few seconds passed, then Ryov reached for the door handle. "Tanaka will live. Get rid of the doctor."

Kent nodded. He half-turned, then pretended to see the satchel for the first time. His voice grew quiet, reverent. "Are those…can I hold one?"

Baker sat up. "Get out of here, Jeremy."

"Have I not bled for this?" snapped Kent. "I deserve a look as much as any of you." He exhaled. "I'm sorry. A man just wants to see what he's worked for."

More silence. The outburst was rare, but not unprecedented. Kerr knew his men: they were well-trained, but still human. Five years was a long time, even without the pressure they were under and the stress it produced.

Eventually Kerr gave a small nod to Scharp. Kent knew this time that it wasn't so much a response to emotion as a recognition of odds. They were isolated; a shade was drawn over the room's lone window. Granting his request was a small price to pay to keep things under control.

Scharp opened the satchel's top flap. Kent took a step forward and stared down into the bag. He could feel the room's eyes on him, but nearly smiled. It was just as he'd hoped: every canister stood upright in a numbered slot; there were four each of the virus and antidote. More than one tube proved to their buyer that the serum could be produced in larger quantities.

Kent reached for the container marked "5" and pulled it out. He lifted it high, examining it like a jeweler would a diamond. The canisters, like the keys, were engraved with a corresponding number along their bottom edge. "Amazing," he said. "Barely the size of my middle finger."

The cabin had been a whisper, enough for the quiet shuffling of feet outside to drift through the door. Suddenly, though, a loud bang shook the partition. Each man instinctively glanced that way. It was nothing, a clumsy passenger's suitcase. But enough time for Kent.

Seizing the instant of distraction, he'd lowered the canister toward the satchel and slipped the tube up his left sleeve. In the same movement he pretended to slide the canister back in its numbered slot and closed the flap.

His limbs began to shake. The sleight of hand appeared to have gone unnoticed, but that was small consolation. If they opened the bag he was finished. Kent remembered the line about his middle finger and tried to settle himself. "Maybe there's a metaphor there somewhere."

He stepped back and eyed Kerr. "Thank you." Ryov seemed an even greater test, but Kent kept his face calm as they exchanged a quick glance. Then the door was open and he walked out. The stuffy corridor felt like freedom.

Kent turned against the flow of passengers and dropped the bag back on the rack. He continued past his cabin, which, of course, had never known any doctor. Thirty seconds later he was on the platform, searching for a place in Linz's station to hide the canister. Escaping now wouldn't do. The train wasn't scheduled to leave for another ten minutes. He would get back on, then excuse himself one last time just before departure. His enemies needed to be trapped on the tracks for him to have a chance at a clear getaway.

He'd considered fabricating a canister, as he did for the key, but ultimately it didn't matter. The true alarm would sound when the train pulled out and he wasn't on it. The satchel would be scrutinized. Any duplicate, no matter how precise a match, would be discovered.

Unfortunately, it never got that far. The moment Kent returned to his own cabin, LeRiche began talking to him. Before the Frenchman had uttered two sentences, Kent sensed the butt of a pistol surging toward his left temple. Then everything went black. The next thing he knew, he was being pummeled in a Russian bunker.

Once Scharp saw him on the platform and they discovered the missing canister, they couldn't have known he'd come back to the train. But those in the other cabin were surely searching the station for him. Berger, Tanaka and LeRiche maintained their post as a trap. One he walked right into.

A sharp gust of wind freed Kent from his thoughts. He pulled the blanket off, almost sweating; each breath had become heavier. It all still felt so real. A memory that'd quickly morphed into a nightmare.

Oh that things had been easier. If Clarke and Boxler were on the train, there could've been dual platoons of Special Forces blocking the tracks just outside of Paris. But there was a reason the two scientists weren't there. They were likely safeguarding a portion of Orion and its antidote. Perhaps it was a backup option to deliver the virus to the buyer, or simply leverage in case something went wrong. Either way, taking the others in without Clarke and Boxler was far too much of a risk. Like cutting off ninety-percent of a tumor and expecting the cancer to disappear.

One other option had occurred to Kent once he'd escaped the bunker: call for help. McCoy may have been a world away, but he could still send those same Special Forces to retrieve the key and canister. Kent would barely have to move from this junkyard. No more running for his life, or risking someone else's.

But that was a fantasy. There was no way for it to work without sending a specific message overseas, including either his own location or those of the key and canister. That information, right now, was the entire mission. Kent couldn't bring himself to risk it, even if he wanted to. And part of him didn't. As hard as this road was, it was his. Too late in the game to put the ball in someone else's hands.

Almost. She was practically a kid, Kent knew. Still in her early twenties. But she was also a trained field officer, and the only real chance he had. It was a long shot; he didn't even know if she was still in Vienna. Anything, though, was better than walking into that station himself.

He heard the wind whistle past the Yugo's doors again. A little seemed to seep through this time. But suddenly it didn't matter; he was warm enough. He left the blanket on the seat, thinking of the Bible in Poushkin's hands. He realized, for the first time, that he wasn't alone in the car. A look up. Every other expression was too much work, so he smiled. "You sure do love a challenge."

21

Rachel Jordan didn't need to look up to know it was a strange day. She could feel it. Seventy-five degrees was something of an anomaly for Austria in April. Even the sun was making an appearance. Its neighboring clouds were powerless to protest, each a mere white brush-stroke against a vast canvas of blue.

The heat, according to the papers, had come all the way from the Mediterranean, passing through northern Italy and skirting the Alps to the east. But it was only temporary—back to the mid-fifties in two days. Evidently, none of Rachel's fellow students knew. Or, more probably, they did, and were taking advantage of the rare spring warmth by crowding Vienna's Sigmund Freud Park to within a few meters of capacity.

In truth, some were simply residents of the city, happy to have the afternoon free. She spotted a couple businessmen, their suitcoats off, ties loosened. Nothing provided escape like the unexpected.

But most of the space's inhabitants, like Rachel herself, were attendees of the University of Vienna just across the street. While the school occupied buildings throughout the capital, this was its epicenter. No doubt, spread across the park's green expanse, law and med students mixed with management majors, all discussing the merits of art and philosophy.

She pulled her eyes off of them and back toward the concrete path she'd been following. She looked down, adjusting the brown pack slung over her right shoulder. Her previous thought fluttered back to mind. *Students like me.* She couldn't help but smile. An outsider's smile.

Being different still thrilled her. Not a vague, intangible difference, but the kind of concrete distinction that set you apart. Particularly when you were aware of something most others weren't. Rachel knew it was part of the reason why she'd accepted the CIA's original invitation.

Maybe it stemmed from high school. She hadn't hit a growth spurt until senior year. Walking in that first day as a scrawny freshman—five-foot-nothing, acne-faced, glasses—she'd been branded a loser from the start. It didn't help that while her peers were slipping into cheerleading skirts and running for student council she was chairing the forensics club and scoping out nearby orienteering courses.

My how things change. Rachel still wasn't tall—five-five on a good day—but her body had filled out, her face had cleared up and she'd traded the glasses for contacts. Judging by the frequent looks she received from male students, it'd been a successful transformation. She almost wished a few of her high school classmates could see her now. It really wasn't that long ago.

She made a right turn and continued down the walkway, tracing the park's outer edge. She had a class in fifteen minutes, but it could wait till the last moment with this weather. She scanned the crowd again with practiced informality, eyes open to anything unusual. She saw nothing. Just an innocent blend of Austrian citizenry, having fu—who was that?

Fifteen meters ahead stood a man whom Rachel found curiously familiar. He was actually leaning against a tree, his face buried in a paperback. There was something about him; his eyes followed the pages, but only enough to convince everyone else that he was engrossed. A name quickly materialized in her mind: *Jeremy Kent.* She was sure, and knew why.

She maintained her pace. After a second Kent casually closed the book and stepped onto the same path, moving away. Had he seen her? She studied the back of his head, peeping from side to side to ensure no one was watching this meet cute. His presence couldn't be a coincidence; he had to be here to make contact. But they'd never met before.

Rachel had seen his face only once, nearly a year ago. An agency case officer named Jakob Krauss—at least, that was his cover name—was being transferred from Vienna to Stockholm. Langley needed his replacement to pose as a student. This thinned their options, but Rachel had turned heads at Camp Peary and was quickly elected. She'd been only twenty-one at the time and still easily passed for an underclassman today.

The night before he left, Krauss invited her over to his apartment for dinner. It was strictly business. He cooked, then shared a few points on Vienna not found in any guidebook: potential contacts, law enforcement behavior, detailed traffic patterns.

Once the table was cleared, he brought her to the living room and a shelf of framed photographs. They featured a charming combination of children and adults, all smiling. And all fake. Each was a decoy, meant to paint Krauss as someone he really wasn't.

Save one. In it, a suited Krauss stood next to another man dressed the same and holding a briefcase. It was Jeremy Kent. Displaying the face of a fellow officer, Krauss admitted, was against protocol. But the picture had only been taken two weeks ago, and up on his shelf for half that time. It served as a trophy, he'd said, and as a reminder of the man whose kind he'd never see again.

They'd been on an operation together earlier that month. An arms dealer, whom both the CIA and MI6 wanted badly, was due to attend a security convention in Munich. A neutral setting, the confusion and cover of crowds—this was deemed a prime opportunity to pounce.

But there was a tight guest list. A last-minute addition wasn't possible. However, a private defense contractor based in Omaha was sending a team of five reps. They were immediately replaced by a mix of British and American intelligence, including Krauss and Kent. The Deputy Chief of MI6, Nicholas Kerr, ran point from a remote location.

Success came after-hours one night outside the convention hotel. It was undesirably public—a standoff turned into a gunfight and car chase—but no civilians were harmed. The dealer was killed, along with most of his men.

The photo was snapped on the convention floor, just hours before the deadly encounter. Rachel recalled taking a second, closer look at the two men. They were both grinning—for show, of course—but there was that hint of unease only a skilled eye could recognize.

Despite completing the mission and escaping with his life, the element Krauss remembered most was Kent. It was one thing to play the part of an oblivious salesman, but even in the team's private moments Kent was a cut up. A joke here, smile there. You almost considered him a liability.

Then the bullets began to fly, and he was a step ahead of everyone. Focus, strength, precision—where had they come from? But then Krauss realized they'd always been there, poised beneath a veneer of genuine nonchalance. It was as if Kent could switch himself on and off, embracing the essence of each emotional state. Krauss found himself jealous of such ability, yet drawn to its uniqueness.

Rachel squinted as the sun's glare hit her directly in the eyes, breaking her reverie. She mechanically brushed a few blonde strands from her face and glanced ahead. On cue, Kent marched forward in a gait that was casual, almost aloof. She was trained to read body language and found no sign of tension from his shoulders down. Yet she knew, somehow, that he was ready to act if necessary.

That moment never came. Instead, Kent reached the edge of the park and turned right, tracing the walkway along its southern flank. Rachel followed, maintaining a distance of about ten meters. She wondered how long this game would last. The park was pretty, but after a few circuits they could become conspicuous. A sliver of doubt invaded her mind. Was the man ahead really Jeremy Kent? Had she been tricked by a vivid memory into trailing some random guy?

Just as the pool of anxiety in her stomach began to boil, the man ahead reached around and scratched his back. Rachel didn't think anything of it. Then, an instant later, she slowed, her brain reflexively guiding her to a natural stop. Fighting the urge to immediately slip her pack off her shoulder, she calmly stepped left toward a long wooden bench. There was no one else within five meters. She laid the pack down and sat beside it, allowing Kent to slip from view.

In the corner of her eye she could see a small, white sheet of paper fluttering from one of the bag's pockets. She waited another minute, then reached over and removed a notebook. The sheet was stuck inside. She flipped the spiral open and scanned the paper, casually chewing on a pen.

Stadtpark—Strauss—30 minutes

22

Rachel's destination was about a mile away. She could've taken a tram or the subway, but decided to walk. She needed some space to think.

There was little doubt in her mind she could handle whatever Kent was about to throw her way. Confidence was a prerequisite for her position. Still, a faint unrest hugged her frame, weighing down each step. She preferred to be in control, and usually was. Every plan had its genesis within her own mind. Except right now.

Twenty-five minutes later, on the other side of a typical European downtown marriage between current shops and classic architecture, she reached the Stadtpark. It was the largest green space within the city center. Against its western edge ran the Ring Road, a modern replacement for the protective walls that'd encircled Vienna's Old Town since the middle ages.

Sidestepping a tram, Rachel entered the park and veered right. As expected, it too was flooded with visitors. Both tourists and locals choked its cement paths and manicured lawns. Rachel agreed with Kent on the location—it was the perfect place to get lost.

She made her way south, toward the gilded bronze statue of Johann Strauss II. The park was filled with several similar monuments, but this was easily the most famous. Still looking spry over a century later, Strauss posed with his violin below a carved marble arch. A crescent-shaped crowd gathered around its base, as if willing the composer to break free from his golden shell and start playing the *Blue Danube Waltz*.

Rachel methodically closed on the pack, looking for Kent. No sign. She continued forward. About twenty feet from the statue, a couple moved on and she stepped into the space they'd occupied. She casually checked her watch: right on time.

"Punctuality," said a voice to her left. "The first sign of respect. I'm flattered."

She turned slightly to see Kent admiring the statue beside her, hands in his pockets. She too focused back on Strauss. "You saved me from a lecture on the history of tax legislation. Hardly a favor."

Kent cracked a smile, then wordlessly moved to his left around the crowd. Rachel followed, staying a few steps behind. Once clear from the group, Kent slowed and she caught up. "We've got plenty of cover," she said, "but I could always see someone I know."

"Perhaps you're just on a harmless afternoon stroll with a new professor. I just got to the city, you're showing me around."

"Professor? In his early thirties at a seven-hundred-year-old university in a European capital? You must be some kind of wunderkind."

"I'm good at pretending to be brilliant. Never had much luck with the real thing."

"That's not what I hear."

"Did I get a mention in the agency newsletter?"

"Jakob Krauss spoke highly of you."

"Is that how you recognized me? I was glad I didn't have to wave."

"What about you? My profile must be public knowledge at Langley."

Kent's tone sobered. "Jakob showed me. Have you seen the photo of us from Munich?"

She nodded.

"An hour before that was taken, we were at the hotel bar. He flashed me a pic on his phone of a young blonde. Said she was taking his place here so he could supplant a retiree up in Sweden." He turned toward Rachel. "I remember thinking the Farm was spitting them out young these days. But you don't walk or talk like a baby."

She nodded again, this time in thanks. "There was a tenured faculty member here who'd started making anarchist statements. He headlined a few rallies, got himself arrested at a peaceful protest. He has a few friends with past ties to the IRA. The agency wanted someone here who could keep a closer eye on him."

"And who better than a student?"

"That's the idea."

"Did he get fired after the arrest?"

"Just the opposite. Became a rock star on campus. Still is."

"But no movement?"

"Nothing significant. You know the drill—hurry up and wait. My life's been almost normal for the past three months."

"Then I'm right on cue."

They stepped across a bridge that spanned one of the Danube's modest offshoots. Kent waited to speak until a family of four had passed. "Linz is one-hundred-sixty kilometers from here. I left a package in its central train station. There are men waiting there for me. They know my face. I'd never have a shot."

Rachel was silent. Kent hadn't elaborated on the men because he didn't need to. He wouldn't be asking for help to get past rent-a-thugs. "You want me to go instead?" she asked. "To retrieve this package?"

He nodded. "I'm asking. This is as real as it gets. There's no guarantee of survival." A pause. "It has to be your decision."

She felt her stomach begin to swirl, from stress, anxiety, and a slight hint of excitement. "Go on."

"The men are foreign, government trained. They've been tracking me from Moscow. There's only a handful, and they'll want to cast a wide net. I doubt all of them will be in Linz. But I expect one or two standard officers as well."

"Standard officers," repeated Rachel. "From an agency?"

Kent paused. He'd probably decided beforehand how much to tell her, but she seemed to be challenging those boundaries. "MI6," he finally said. "Nicolas Kerr has recruited a small group of elite assets. He's their leader, and our enemy."

Each word hit like a tidal wave. The smallest, though, wasn't lost on her. "*Our* enemy?"

"And that of millions more. They just don't know it."

She paused. Something was missing. "What aren't you telling me?"

Kent shook his head. "You've got to say yes first. It's a raw deal, I know, but the less you know the safer you are."

She knew enough already; the writing on the wall was etched in large print. She was a valuable government weapon. Kent wouldn't have approached her if he wasn't desperate.

"Why me?" she said. "You must know others with the same skill set."

He nodded. "But it's a small group; Kerr has seen or worked with them all. Except you."

"How do you know he hasn't contacted me without your knowledge?"

"You've been at your post less than a year. It's a risk I have to take." He paused. "And you're close. Anyone else would be flying in from multiple countries away. I can have you back in Vienna by train in time to catch your next lecture tomorrow."

"Train? Wouldn't you rather a car? It's more flexible during a getaway."

Kent shook his head. "If it comes to a getaway, it's over. The best chance—the only one—is to get in and out undetected. Arriving by train cuts this task in half: you're already inside the station. All that's left is to find the package and leave."

Still in the park, they rounded a corner and slowed. Kent leaned against a nearby tree. Rachel sat down on an empty bench a few feet away. "Where is the package?" she asked.

"In the ceiling of the men's restroom." Her eyebrows rose. "I didn't have much time to stow it."

A short silence followed. Kent said nothing else; it was time for a decision. Rachel took a deep breath, staring at the surrounding leaves as the sunlight trickled through their maze of green. "Tell me this is important." She knew, but needed to hear it. "Tell me this package is worth my life."

"It's worth mine." He stepped across and sat on the bench's far side. "The train leaves tonight for Linz. I already bought a ticket. If you're not on it, I am."

It wasn't a guilt-trip, or arrogance; it was solidarity. They both walked the same rare path. Rachel remained quiet, thinking. *Isn't this what you originally signed up for?* She finally nodded.

Kent risked a glance right at her. "Thank you." It was sincere. True to form, his levity had fallen away as the stakes had risen.

"Thank me when I'm done," she said.

"By then you'll deserve it twice." He reached for an inner pocket and slid an envelope between them on the bench. "Everything you need is inside."

He stood and walked past her. She'd stay on the bench another ten minutes, but didn't wait to reach across, pull the same notebook from her bag and scoop up the envelope beneath it. Pretending to stretch her neck, she turned in time to see Kent disappear into the still-buzzing crowd.

23

Allison was glad she'd passed on the naan. It'd looked so good, but she'd already been close to bursting from lamb and curry sauce. *Royal Bombay Palace*. She'd have to remember that name.

And dessert. Tomorrow, maybe at a café or coffee bar—in between museum stops. Today had been all about shopping. She had no idea how she was going to fit everything into her suitcase.

The moment they'd touched down yesterday, her deep thoughts— filling the void inside, planting roots—had taken a backseat. They were still there, but felt much smaller than they had in Scotland. If she stayed busy enough, maybe they'd remain hidden. She'd take the break.

Becky's boyfriend, Petr, had picked them up from Linz's Blue Danube Airport and taken them to his uncle's apartment. Last night had been a simple meal; they were tired, he had an early call the next morning. But this evening was different. The *Palace* started things, and now they were ensconced in a booth at *Easy*, a cocktail bar near the city center.

Allison paused from her second glass of merlot and looked around for the first time. The place was packed. Dozens of conversations taking place at once, but the volume remained civil. Warm lighting softened the room's sharp lines. The bar had a distinct Mediterranean feel.

They'd spent a portion of time at the restaurant discussing Petr's situation. There was the stop in Edinburgh, but he'd completed most of his schooling at the University of Vienna. Graduated with a master's in economics and quickly received job offers in the capital city. He'd been born in Linz, though; home was home.

Allison studied Petr now, enjoying his Hefeweizen and laughing with Becky. He was up for a promotion, and looked the part: gray suit, styled hair, handsome in a traditional sort of way. He was taller than Becky. Not quite as athletic, but close enough. Together they looked like the cover of a fashion magazine.

You're not so bad yourself. A cream blouse, dark pants, sleek heels— Allison knew she looked good. Several guys tonight had given her a more-than-cursory glance. One in particular was just twenty feet away, ogling her from the bar beside his clueless buddies. She fantasized about the two of them leaving here together. It could be fun, spending a few days with a stranger she'd never see again.

She brushed a brown curl from her face and turned back to her cuddling friends. "So Allison," said Petr, "Becky tells me the boys in Scotland haven't exactly been lining up at your door with roses in hand. If you ask me, they're crazy."

She fingered her wine glass, managing a smile. "Thanks. But I probably haven't given them much chance. The job's pretty intensive."

"Tell me about it. I've got to wait half a day for Becks to return my calls." He smiled at his girlfriend. "Makes me think she has guys all over town up there."

"Not even close, I can assure you," said Allison. She finished her merlot and thought about a third. *Not yet.* They'd started drinking at dinner, and she could feel a buzz coming on. The night was still pretty young. She wanted to remember it.

Becky had no such plans. She needed a refill on her apple martini and started for the bar. Allison asked her for some water as Petr continued his probing. "I hear you grew up in 'the South.' Sounds a little vague."

Allison grinned. "Not in America. 'D.C. to Dallas, except for Florida.' That's how my uncle puts it. I was born just outside of Atlanta, in Georgia. Heard of it?"

"The state, not the country, yes." Petr took a pull on his beer. "Why not Florida?"

"Too many tourists and transplants. There aren't enough roots beneath the sand." She took a breath, surprised at the ideas flooding her head. "The South isn't just an area. It's a way of life. It's a community, and a culture, and if I keep going I'll sound too much like a history professor. Suffice to say there's no other place like it."

Petr looked around figuratively. "Yet here you are." He studied her more closely. "You seem to love where you're from, but something tells me it wasn't that hard to leave."

Becky came back with their drinks and sat down. Allison nodded at Petr. "My adventurous streak. I guess I've never really been scared to try new things."

Allison took a drink and smiled as a memory came back. "My first summer in college, at Georgia Tech, I traveled to Egypt with Samaritan's Purse. Only knew one other person on our volunteer team."

"That's pretty brave," said Petr.

"And generous," added Becky.

"Not really," said Allison. "My parents paid for half the trip. We were heading to a desert town, Kharga, in the southern half of the country. I had this romantic idea of riding a camel on sand dunes, or shopping for clothes at a bazaar. Exotic experiences I could brag to my friends about. Maybe even steal some time before our flight out of Cairo and see the pyramids at Giza."

"Hey," said Becky, "there's nothing wrong with fitting in a little fun."

"I agree." Petr raised his glass. "Besides, sometimes it's not the reason we go, it's merely the fact that we're there."

Becky elbowed him in the ribs. "Easy, Descartes. Maybe I'll call my mum and have her crochet that on a pillow."

Petr smiled and turned back to Allison. "So, how many times did you get to play Florence of Arabia?"

Allison shook her head. "Every bit of zero. We were helping build an extension onto a school, and it was one-hundred degrees every day. I was exhausted." She could see the mild disappointment on their faces.

"There was a silver lining, though. One time a few of us were playing soc-cer—sorry, football—with some local kids. A little boy took a bad spill and skinned his leg on a rock. There was a decent amount of blood. I happened to have some bandages and ointment."

She went quiet, picturing the scene. "I remember the look in his eyes when I'd finished. He glanced at his knee, said 'thank you,' and never looked at it again. A second later he was back to kicking the ball around with his friends. The wound had already been forgotten. It was as if, in the smallest possible way, he was whole again. That's when I decided I wanted to be a nurse." She paused. "I know, sounds silly."

"No," said Becky, hearing the story for the first time. "Not at all."

"But why not a doctor?" asked Petr. "Why stop at nurse?"

Allison's lips curved into a smile. "Because as a doctor I'd still be in residency, either slogging through some medical journal or stuffing my face into a patient's infected spleen." She glanced around. "Instead of being here, with you two."

Becky nodded in agreement. "And on that note, I think it's time for some dancing."

Petr leaned back, feigning a grimace. "Oh, my feet are killing me. I worked all day today."

"And you're off for the next three," said Becky. "This is just a tune-up for tomorrow." She turned to Allison. "He loves the clubs more than I do."

"Only for their clean bathrooms and friendly staff," said Petr. "There are so few guarantees in life anymore."

Allison chuckled. "How often do you guys go?"

"Every chance we get," said Becky. "But never in Linz. I hear they've got some great places." She looked at Petr, grinning like a five-year-old in a candy store.

He exhaled theatrically. "I suppose I'm familiar with the establish-ments you speak of."

Becky's eyes glowed. "What do you say, Ally?"

"Why not," said Allison. "I could use the exercise."

"Oh, you'll get it," said Petr. He tilted his now-empty glass. "But not before I have another beer."

Becky, still in kid mode, frowned. "Just get it where we're going. You know they'll have the same thing."

"But it won't be the same thing. This Hefeweizen was brewed to be savored. Hard to do with heavy base notes drubbing my ears." He shrugged, grinning. "Some drinks aren't about the end result."

Becky protested with a few seconds of silence. "Fine," she finally said, keeping her spirits. "That'll give me time to call Yvonne and ask her if she wants to join us." She started fishing through her purse for her phone.

Petr glanced at Allison, then back to his girlfriend. "And who is 'Yvonne?'"

"You remember that afternoon in Amsterdam," said Becky without looking up. "You had that business call and suggested I wait in the café nearby." Now she paused her search, eying Petr. "Yvonne was at the table next to me. We started a conversation. She happens to be a waitress, here in Linz. She was on a break and spending a couple days in Holland."

Petr shook his head, smiling. "You know more people in this city than I do."

"She comes as-advertised, doesn't she?" said Allison.

"She certainly does." He playfully wrapped his arms around his girl-friend. "A perfect angel."

"Except when I can't find my phone," said Becky, having resumed her hunt and ignoring the embrace. "I wonder if—" She stopped suddenly, looking up with wide eyes. "It's not here, and I know exactly where I left it." She turned to Petr. "In your uncle's apartment, on the dresser. When we picked Ally up." She shook her head. "How could I have been so flighty?"

"You'd think you lost a child," said Petr, preparing to edge out of the booth for his refill.

"We've got to go back," said Becky, sliding out to make room.

He exhaled. "Not an issue. The apartment's five minutes away." He held up a finger. "But not before I've had my beer. I think you can survive that long."

He was gone a second later, snaking through the crowd. Becky sat back down, an impish pout spread across her lips. Allison finished her water, eying her friend. "You sure do keep things interesting."

Becky glanced in the direction of the bar. "He's too good to me, isn't he?"

Allison smiled. "Maybe that's how it should be."

"And maybe we can find you a special dance partner tonight."

Allison glanced toward the bar; her admirer was gone. Overruled by his entourage? *His loss.* "A regular dance partner should be easy enough," she said, turning back to Becky. "I keep my standards pretty low."

"Well then, you might be primed for a surprise."

24

Kent checked his watch for the tenth time in the past hour. He would never have advised such a conspicuous routine, but this was a unique situation. When the sum of all your efforts came down to one moment, and you placed that moment in the hands of another, exceptions were in order. Besides, he'd studied every surrounding face three times over. No one was doing the same to him.

It shouldn't even have been an issue, because he shouldn't even have been in Linz. There was always the risk of being spotted. Rachel could easily retrieve the canister, hop in a bus or taxi and meet him in a smaller town miles away. Better yet, a city like Innsbruck, or back in Vienna.

But, for the same reason he'd now memorized the time, Kent had to be here. They only had one shot at this. Fail now and there was no point in continuing. What good was a key with nothing to unlock?

He consoled himself with the fact that, despite his limited options, he'd chosen Rachel for a reason. She was young, but that meant little in their profession. You weren't given a post like hers without possessing a unique skill-set, honed further by rigorous training. In fact, the odds were still heavily in their favor that she'd walk into the train station unrecognized, retrieve the canister and leave without incident.

She can handle this. Kent almost whispered the words, as if making them audible would make them true. Instead, he gulped down the last of his cabernet and laid his napkin beside an empty plate. Even the sauce had been cleaned, wiped thoroughly with several pieces of accompanying bread.

The café, *Rosso*, was Italian, and the food was good. He hadn't had much of an appetite, but nothing drew attention more than ordering pasta and leaving it untouched.

Stomach now full, he paid the check, stood and was outside a moment later. The air was cold, augmented by a stubborn, biting wind. Winter's final salvo. The surrounding night complied, its darkness muffling nearby traffic and isolating windows and headlights into lonely beacons of life.

Not an easy thing to do in this town. Linz was Austria's third-largest city. Nearly 200,000 residents graced its streets every day. It had an industrial past, but, thanks to constant construction, the future was decidedly more modern. Plenty of metal and glass.

Kent headed east, threading himself through a maze of sleeping government buildings. Linz's central station was a mere block ahead. Despite the hour—it was just past 10 p.m.—he knew the terminal would be busy. It handled over thirty-thousand passengers daily and was a key railway stop between Austria and cities in Switzerland and Germany.

Kent checked his watch one last time. Rachel's train would be arriving now. He'd played the scenario out several times in his head: she could complete her retrieval and escape in five minutes, give or take. He simply wanted a line of sight to the building. Not necessarily to witness success, but to know if something went wrong.

There was no guarantee that she'd even walk out the front. He hadn't had time to completely case the building, but had given her all the specs he possessed in the envelope. It also contained, in addition to the train ticket, descriptions and background information on their enemies, as well as a rundown on Orion. He didn't include everything about the virus, but enough; she'd know the stakes.

A structure like this station had several points of egress. Rachel would choose the quietest one. They were set to rendezvous an hour from now at Danube Park on the city's northern end.

The one thing she couldn't do was leave the way she'd come. Under different circumstances, it might've worked. But departure schedules weren't tuned to her getaway. Kent wanted her out of the building as soon as possible. And if she was seen entering a train—or worse, followed on— she was trapped.

Kent wound his way through the civic corridor. It was quiet, nearly deserted. A patch of bleak starlight found its way down, gifting the scene a handful of shadows. He thought about flipping his collar up. *Make yourself a real spy.* But no. The ballcap pulled tight over his head would be enough to shield identity.

Seconds later, rounding a final corner, Kent magically stepped into another city. Or so it appeared. Gone was the silence, the darkness; even the stars seemed to dim, overtaken by a mass of artificial illumination. Linz's central railway station hummed with activity as if it were midday. Cars pulled up to its main entrance, making way for pedestrians to course in and out. In the foreground, cabs shared Karntner Street's numerous lanes with buses, bicycles and everything in between.

Kent stopped at the near curb beside a pack of teens. They waited for the traffic to thin, then jogged across. He followed, back far enough but still one of the group. On the far side they broke toward the station. He turned left.

He'd already spotted the MI6 agent. Tracing a sidewalk, maybe fifteen meters from the front doors. Well-built, alone, dark clothing—the signs were there, but the clearest was always a practiced disinterest. The man puffed on his cigarette with a little too much nonchalance. In this game, to kid a kidder, pretending not to care wasn't enough; you almost had to really let go.

Gaining a pair of concrete steps, Kent ascended halfway and sat down. He shoved his hands into his pockets. He was encased in shadow again, too hard to see from the station. To anyone nearby, just another hobo trying to keep warm.

Kent kept both eyes peeled on the building. He'd have given anything to be inside. *It'll all be over soon.* Nevertheless, a sliver of fear began to invade his stomach.

Rachel was dealing with a much greater amount. Even as everything, thus far, had gone according to plan. Imagine if it hadn't. *No, don't.* Focus needed to be on success. Identifying threats came naturally, but they didn't have to result in her death, and she certainly didn't need to picture it.

She took a deep breath. It really wasn't all that dramatic. She'd arrived on time, found the bathroom, slipped in with a hood and her head down. Three minutes later she'd pulled the canister—stored inside a leather pouch—and strode out like any other man. If the hardest thing about this operation was avoiding the notice of a few oblivious travelers, it was a true cakewalk.

Still, as she made her way up a long flight of steps, exit doors in sight, she was nervous. Small rivulets of sweat coursed beneath her clothing. A simple defense mechanism, her body preparing for a fight. But would there be one? She glanced around. The quiet was no comfort. She could still hear her instructor at the Farm: "*In this world easy doesn't exist. Murphy's law is our religion.*"

She'd brought her rosary. The Glock tucked into her right side was a jolt of confidence, even if she never used it. A backpack slung over her left shoulder, filled with generic clothing and toiletries, was the final piece. It made her just another traveler. Part of the monotonous crowd.

A thought occurred to Rachel as she reached the landing and turned toward the exit. She was doing all of this on the word of one man. Everything in the envelope was detailed, and dire. But was it true? Were there even men in this station waiting to kill her?

Kent was clearly a legitimate field officer, but he could've gone rogue. *Are you, and your youth, just his easiest target?*

For what, though? Was he setting her up, or planning to use the canister for some nefarious purpose? Every accusation fell flat. She was green, but this was still the CIA. You either knew how to read people or got yourself killed. Beyond Krauss's endorsement, her instincts simply told her she could trust Kent. The proof was in his eyes—fierce, calm and honest, all at once.

Rachel looked through the glass on the door. Outside the still night beckoned like a finish line. She strode forward.

"Jane? Jane Winslow?"

Rachel nearly jumped at the words. They were directed toward her, and came from an unfamiliar voice behind. *Just keep moving.* But then the call might grow louder. A few heads had turned at the minor commotion. After a second's worth of internal deliberation, she spun around. A woman, about her age, stepped forward with an expectant gaze. Seeing Rachel's face, her expression quickly fizzled. "Oh, sorry," she said in a British accent. "I thought you were someone else."

Rachel forced a smile and started to swivel back. She was cut short, though, by a face beyond the stairs. A man, built like a bull, staring directly at her. Kent hadn't had photos of his adversaries, but this could only be Gerhardt Berger.

She recognized him immediately, and that, sadly, was how he recognized her. Her stomach had tightened like a vice, adrenaline beginning to course through each vein. A combination of alarm and aggression glazed her sight. This all happened in an instant, but it was enough for his trained eyes to notice the skill of a rival.

There were only ten meters between them, but also a buffer of several people. Rachel didn't wait. Slinging her backpack to the ground, she spun and burst toward the exit.

A gunshot sounded. Half a second later a glass panel in the door, inches from her head, splintered into a hundred cracks. The door kept sliding open, though, and she kept running. Outside, a car in front of her slammed on its brakes. Everyone behind screamed.

25

Kent was on his feet the instant he heard the shot, and sprinting forward once he saw Rachel. This was bad. She would never run unless it was *from* something. Angling to her right outside the station, she reached into her jacket. He crossed a patch of open pavement, closing the distance between them.

The MI6 agent had traded his cigarette for a Sig Sauer. He spotted Rachel as she flew past and bolted after her. Kent, now less than forty yards away, edged right and tore through a sea of parked bicycles. He wasn't sure if Rachel had seen her trailer, who was just raising his gun. She'd pulled out her own pistol, though, and spun to fire.

Two shots. Both came from a distance. Kent glanced toward the station, but his attention was quickly stolen as Rachel let out a cry and collapsed.

"No!" It'd been meant as a yell, but, under the present exertion, escaped Kent's lips as a guttural whisper. He continued forward, beyond the bicycles and over a stretch of grass. The MI6 agent closed from the left.

Seconds later Kent was mere feet from Rachel. She lay face down on the ground, and immediately he knew she'd never get up again. She'd been motionless since falling. Her head looked intact; the bullets must've gone through the chest. The sight was like a massive fist slamming into his gut.

But there was no time to mourn. Kent reached the body half a second before the agent, who readjusted his aim to the new threat. Before the man could pull the trigger, Kent chopped the weapon from his hands and stomped down on the inside of his left ankle. A pop sounded and the man opened his mouth to yell. Nothing came as Kent sent a heavy jab toward his face and both eyes rolled back upon impact.

Kent returned his gaze to Rachel as his adversary sank to the ground. The man would be fine, but not anytime soon. All around, screaming continued to pierce the night. From the direction Rachel fell, the gunshots had likely come from near the station entrance. Someone was still inside.

Kent began rifling through Rachel's pockets. He chose to ignore the fact that the corpse he was now searching would've still been breathing without his intervention. A dense cloud of guilt materialized in his chest. He shook it off. *She knew the risk.*

Somehow that didn't cure—*there.* He fished a black pouch from inside her jacket. In the same instant, the hair rose on the back of his neck. An internal alarm, a feeling. He turned just as Berger broke from the station, pistol up. The German's exit had no doubt been delayed by a number of rocket scientists who'd chosen to run around frantically instead of duck for cover.

Kent dove behind a nearby bank of exhaust vents just as a shower of bullets kicked up the surrounding turf. He leaned with his back to the cold metal, heart racing. A survey of the scene: directly ahead of him—across from the station entrance—lay a bus lane, then the busy Karntner Street. Plenty of cars still buzzed over its dark surface, either oblivious to the gunshots or speeding to escape them.

Kent pictured Berger approaching, cautious but still at a run. There was only one move to make. Standing his ground wouldn't work; others could be nearby. Taking a quick peek inside the pouch to ensure the canister was there, Kent stowed it and removed his Beretta. An instant later, exhaling, he spun to his left.

Berger was about sixty feet away, rounding a line of metal exhaust towers. No one else nearby. Kent quickly squeezed off several rounds while surging to his right. The bullets were only half-aimed, designed to delay more than damage.

It worked. Berger leapt back behind a silo-shaped tower as the projectile spray dented its metal. Kent took the seconds of cover and darted for the bus lane. It was separated from the main road by a chain-link fence. Seeing a break in the northbound traffic, he hurdled the barrier and sprinted over the asphalt.

A glance back: Berger had recovered, keeping pace and barking into a cell phone. He might have shot, but accuracy was tough at this speed. Kent turned forward to see two SUV's bearing down from the southbound lanes. He had to make it.

Tires screeched as he burst across the first gap. The BMW skidded behind, missing him by a foot. In the same motion he dove ahead. The Volkswagen was closer, hot air from its grill nearly burning his neck. His boot clipped a front headlight.

But the far curb came. Kent rolled to his feet, finally stealing a breath.

Then the deafening crack of a handgun pierced the air. Instantly a bullet grazed his right thigh, tearing a chunk of flesh away. Kent collapsed back to the ground, the fresh wound lighting a fire up his leg. *Move.* He had to get up, run through the pain. *Move!*

Adrenaline helped. He heaved himself up and darted left. Two more shots whistled past his head, peppering squat buildings beyond. The violence now directly in front of their windshields, every car in Berger's way skidded to a stop. Kent kept running.

26

Petr turned left, passing beneath a bridge of windows and stucco with the sign *Hotel Lokomotive* displayed across its top. Straight ahead, a small street ran quietly between two long buildings. On the right, several cars were parked toward the curb at an angle. To the left, they lay parallel to the street, facing opposite. Gazing in this direction, he spotted a gap near a silver Range Rover and edged his Audi into the space.

"You know you went the wrong way down the street," said Becky, chewing on a piece of gum from her perch in the backseat.

"I always was one for breaking the rules."

She chuckled. "Oh yeah, you're a real man of adventure."

"I'm dating you, aren't I?" With a grin, Petr popped open his door. He turned to Allison in the passenger seat. "This won't take long. Just stay in the car, I'll keep it running. We'll be back in two minutes."

She nodded, smiling too. Seconds later Becky, her protest over, hugged her boyfriend's arm as they crossed the lane toward the far building's middle entrance. He opened the door and motioned her through, but stayed outside himself. He turned toward the car, then took a glance up at the apartment's windows.

What was he doing? Allison studied him, dividing his attention between the building and the Audi. Then she realized: he was watching her—for security. *What a gentleman.*

Not that it was needed. She hadn't heard so much as a car horn all night; the streets couldn't be safer.

Kent didn't have to look back anymore. Despite the frantic traffic and screams from onlookers, he could hear Berger's footsteps. Pounding, relentless, like a bull seeing red. Kent's lead was fifteen, maybe twenty meters. Still a difficult shot on the run. Berger had surely stopped when firing back near the station. He wouldn't now. Too much of a risk in falling further behind.

Soon, though, it wouldn't matter. Kent's leg continued to burn; it was only a matter of time until it went numb, then flat. His pace would lag, Berger would close the gap, and it would all be over. Kent thought of the canister in his pocket, the breath of countless lives sealed with its serum.

He pushed on, labored breaths warming the chill air. The sidewalk began to curve, mirroring the arc of Karntner Street. Across the road to the left, a canopy of trees beckoned. *No.* Even if he made the far side, there wasn't enough cover. To the right, beyond a concrete wall hugging the path, a cylindrical building housing the city's library rose into the night. Its dimmed lights and locked doors seemed to seal his fate.

A heavy burst sounded, the cement barrier beside him exploding. Kent shielded his eyes from the flying rock as a second shot whistled past his left ear. Ahead, the pavement curved into a merciless straightaway. He was about to spin and make a final stand when a side street came in view to the right. *Last chance*

27

Allison finished applying a fresh layer of lipstick and dropped the tube in her purse. She glanced out the window toward Petr—still waiting—then leaned back and took a deep breath. Dancing sounded more and more like a great idea. She knew the freedom and release of losing yourself in a crowd. It'd be the perfect end to a perfect night.

Crack. She saw Petr stiffen, then cower reflexively against the building. He was staring down the street, behind her. Panic gripped her immediately. The sound of a gunshot, that close, was unmistakable. She fought the urge to turn around, then finally did.

In the same moment the passenger window shattered before her eyes, an invisible bullet driving into the dashboard just above her knees. Allison opened her mouth to scream, but nothing came. It was like a nightmare.

Another shot smashed the right taillight, before a third tore through the rear windshield. She felt the Audi's back end sag temporarily, hearing a bump as if someone were sliding across. Then the driver's side door flew open. A man—dark hair, Caucasian—jumped inside and slammed the door. He lunged across with his arm. "Get down!"

His palm shoved Allison's head between her knees just as another flurry of bullets ripped into the sedan, shredding the leather upholstery. The man pulled the car into drive and stomped on the gas. Immediately the vehicle surged forward, its modest engine straining under the fresh demand.

Allison struggled to breathe as more shots sounded. These, though, only sparked the pavement near the tires. The Audi roared down the short lane, gunning through the next intersection and veering left onto a larger road. Parts of her body were already covered in sweat. She gripped the passenger door and center console with white knuckles.

A stabbing pain in her left side quickly rose through the fog of shock. She groaned from its sting, looked down and saw a pool of red spreading across her blouse. The man beside her swerved past a slow-moving car, then stole a glance her way. He stretched over, feeling the wound. She yelled in pain. "Keep pressure on it!" he said, shouting above the air rushing in.

Allison had no idea who this man was. He, though, wasn't the one shooting at her, and that was enough. She had no choice but to trust him.

She forced herself to press down on the crimson patch. Anguish like she'd never known swept through her body. She began to shake, forcing out each breath. Darkness threatened edge of her vision. The man reached out again, his strong hand seizing her wrist. "Stay with me!" He looked her in the eye. "Just hold on!"

Something about his gaze. He was scared, like her, but…not of dying. His eyes held a certain determination. *We're going to survive this.* Allison looked ahead, the Audi continuing to thread itself down the wide thoroughfare. Maybe he was right.

The rear passenger window exploded with a deafening crack. She could almost feel the bullets, each one missing her neck by inches and completing the destruction of the front console. Needing no push this time, she joined her companion and ducked just as a second volley splintered the front windshield

Allison then rose, instinctively, to steal a glance outside. It was a stupid move. She had just enough time to glimpse a black sedan on their right before a succession of fresh gunshots flared behind her. These were heading the other way, sent from a pistol in her driver's hand out the shattered side window.

Ears ringing, she watched the bullets spark against the other vehicle's front hubcap. Immediately, the new car surged left. Her driver tried to veer away but wasn't fast enough. The attacking vehicle slammed into its target. They were rocked in their seats as the Audi screeched into oncoming traffic. Recovering just in time, the driver swerved around an onslaught of blaring horns and careening metal.

He reached an open spot, cut the car back right and raised his gun past Allison's face. She froze as the weapon discharged two more rounds, one striking metal, the other something softer. A look out. The black sedan faltered, its left front tire going flat against the pavement.

Her driver increased his speed. The other car rapidly turned their way. With his vehicle about to be left behind, the phantom pursuer rose from his seat and leapt out the window. She lost track of his body as it flew over her door, but heard him hit the roof. An instant later a thick blade pierced the top of the Audi.

Almost before the knife cut through, the man beside her started jerking the wheel back and forth. The German sedan roared from side to side, but, like a thousand-pound anchor, the sharp weapon held its place. Once the vehicle straightened, the knife rose and cut into the roof again further up.

Allison shrank from the serrated steel. Her attention, though, was soon apprehended as her neighbor jumped from his seat. "Drive!"

She had an instant to think it was a sick joke before cringing in horror as he slung her behind the wheel. She gripped it without thinking, her foot fortuitously landing on the gas pedal. Out of desperation, or mental exhaustion, she simply pressed down. Diving right, the man reached toward the open window just as a pistol swung over the side.

He grabbed the attacking wrist and shoved it upward. A shot tore into the cab's ceiling. Further grappling ensued but Allison didn't see. Shock had turned to terror, limiting her awareness, locking her in place. She kept her foot down, eyes forward. Any other movement was too difficult, like breaking free from titanium shackles.

The pain in her side remained. She gritted her teeth and kept the Audi speeding forward. Buildings and trees lost definition, as if slinking away from the danger. Random lights turned to yellow streaks in the darkness. She noticed movement to her right. Both men swung out onto the windshield, their bodies a tangled mass of ferocity. For the first time she noticed their attacker looked Asian.

Sweat stung her eyes. She blinked it away, not wanting to risk a hand off the wheel. That's when she spotted something curious ahead. The road curved left, then seemed to terminate at a black wall. Second by second the scene became clearer. *A tunnel.*

Out on the windshield Kent lay back against the glass, gripping each of his assailant's wrists. Atop, Tanaka still held the gun in his right hand. His left was balled into a fist, poised to strike.

The scrap wasn't graceful. They continued to fly forward at over 130 kilometers an hour. Each man gave as much attention to staying on the car as he did battling his opponent. Suddenly both of them felt a decrease in speed. Eyes still on Tanaka, Kent spotted an approaching tunnel in his peripheral vision.

Could he, somehow, use the new environment to his advantage? It came too fast for any ideas to form. Tanaka continued to edge the barrel of his gun closer to Kent's head. Fighting for leverage, Kent shifted his weight and rolled his foe to the left. Momentum, though, carried them a full revolution, ending with the Asian still on top. This time they were directly in front of the steering wheel.

The driver, her view cut off, swerved frantically. The sound of screeching tires reverberated off the tunnel walls. Both men on the windshield jostled back right, finding themselves in the same place they'd started.

Tanaka continued to attack, seething eyes fixed on his opponent. The gun muzzle was now inches from Kent's temple. Quickly abandoning his hold on the Asian's left arm, Kent brought his right over and forced the pistol back with two hands. Tanaka was about to swing his left wrist down but was thrown off balance as the Audi burst from the tunnel and spun right. The car slid through an intersection, each man desperately clutching its exterior.

Finally straightening, the sedan revved up again, surging ahead with the Danube River on its left. Kent might've marveled at the driving but was interrupted as his right kidney exploded in pain. Tanaka quickly reached toward his side, pulled out the knife he'd used to slash through the roof and thrust if forward.

Kent swung his right arm over to cut off the attack. Instead of blocking the stab, though, he only forced the blade to the outside. Tanaka, taking the open path, abandoned the torso and dug the weapon into his enemy's right arm.

Kent yelled at the tidal wave of pain but immediately reached down and pulled out his Beretta. With his gun hand locked up and his other arm still gripping the knife in Kent's shoulder, Tanaka could do nothing but gasp as his opponent squeezed off three rounds, each sinking into the Asian's chest.

The life quickly drained out of him, and Kent kicked the body off the vehicle. The Audi, still speeding forward, approached a congested intersection. To the left, a concrete bridge spanned the Danube, cutting through a line of docked river-cruise ships hugging the near shore.

Fighting off waves of shock, Kent stowed the Beretta and gingerly pulled the knife out of his arm. He tossed it toward the street. Sweat and fatigue stained every inch of his frame.

He gripped the door and swung back inside the car. The woman was still trained on the road ahead: eyes wide, frozen like a statue. Kent was about to say something when the sound of a rushing engine forced his gaze to the right. In a flash he saw Berger barreling toward them in a Range Rover. The SUV was at their side in an instant; they had no room to maneuver. Spinning left, Kent dove toward the woman and wrapped her up.

A breath later the Audi jackknifed inward as the Rover's front grill drove into its exposed metal. Careening across the width of the road, the knot of vehicles hit a short concrete barricade. The SUV screeched to a stop while the mangled sedan flipped over the wall and began tumbling down a grassy slope toward the river. Kent held his charge tight, each of them pinballing between a sea of airbags and leather.

They splashed into the strong, chilly current. The Audi quickly began sinking; inside, dark water rushed through the broken windows. Kent gripped his companion's arm and dragged her out. Like him, she was bleeding from a dozen places. None of her wounds, though, appeared fatal.

The woman's natural instincts took over and she started swimming for the surface. Kent pulled her back, shaking his head at her wide eyes. He motioned forward and began towing her along.

They couldn't surface yet. The boats were too far offshore to use as cover. Berger was too good a shot, and floating corpses were an easy frisk. The item in his pocket still mattered more than anything.

The need for oxygen, though, was unrelenting. Giving two more strong kicks, Kent felt a jerk and glanced at the woman. She stared back, then up, panic spreading across her face. She'd hit a wall. He immediately began pulling her toward the surface and broke through a half-second after she did.

No shots. They were just out of Berger's sightline, flowing under the bridge. Kent pulled his companion low in the water so only their heads protruded. She didn't say a word. Like apples bobbing in a barrel, they glided downriver, angling toward the near shore. The current offered a quick getaway, but drifting toward its center would choke away any chance of controlling their landing point.

Kent decided that needed to come soon. Despite the cold water, he was still losing blood in his leg and shoulder; she was on the edge of consciousness. Back at the crash site a crowd was no-doubt forming along the river's edge. Berger would have taken a few steps down the bank, watched for them in the water, then quickly driven off. He couldn't afford attention any more than they could.

But he wouldn't consider them dead. It's possible he'd assume they were carried under the bridge and was waiting on the other side. The crowd, though, was less than a hundred meters away; sirens would be approaching soon. Kent decided to risk landing. If he were Berger, he'd be gone.

Not that any of it mattered. They had to get out of the river. The water was turning frigid and she'd already bled too much. He had to find a place where they could both get patched up. A hospital wouldn't do, too public. *What about…*

Just beyond the bridge, Kent angled around the stern of a ship and found his footing. Berger wasn't in sight. He pulled his companion from the water. She slumped down, then stumbled. He pulled her up again. "Stay with me. Just a little longer."

He walked her up the bank. They reached an asphalt boardwalk and increased their pace, aiming for a handful of cars parked twenty meters ahead. Kent suddenly realized the Beretta was gone. *Forget it.* The gun was probably on the bottom of the river by now. Even if the police found it in the car, and somehow lifted a print, the trail would only lead to a digital ghost.

She fell again. This time Kent caught her before she hit the ground. The last ounces of adrenaline still masking the pain in his arm, he scooped her up and continued forward. *Just leave her.* He considered it. But she needed medical attention, and might not be noticed soon enough. He kept walking.

To the left the Lentos Art Museum reflected the scene, its glass façade sparkling under an array of blue lights. Almost to the vehicles, Kent glanced to his right. Traffic continued to flow across the bridge, though several cars had stopped near the crash site. Flashing lights lit up the distance, closing fast.

The nearest car was an old Honda. Leaning his charge against its meager frame, Kent rammed his right elbow into the passenger-side window. No alarm, no witnesses close enough to hear the broken glass. He stretched through and unlocked the door, then laid her on the seat. Crossing to the driver's side, he bent below the steering wheel and exposed a tangle of wires. Seconds later the engine was humming, heat blasting.

A look left. The nearest intersection was empty. Kent shifted into drive and the car sprang forward. After a U-turn across the open asphalt, he slowed slightly and cruised away from the scene.

Down the road he studied his rearview mirror and spotted the police arriving near the river. Eventually they'd start looking for a stolen Honda compact. But not now, and he didn't need the car for long. She was only going to last a few more minutes.

He glanced to his right. The woman was still unconscious, leaking blood. He gripped the wheel tighter, forcing himself to stay within the speed limit. The downtown streets were a relatively simple maze. He still knew the way.

Soon lights became scarcer. Large trees began to obscure the star-filled sky. Coming up on a final turn, Kent felt himself fading and shook the haze away.

He spotted the familiar cottage on the right and veered left. A lonely gravel drive stretched out ahead, gradually sloping upward. Kent aggressively pushed the Honda over the rocks. They passed just two homes, both shrouded in darkness.

Finally hitting the end of the road, he pulled onto an expansive cement driveway. The house it led to wasn't monstrous, but certainly comfortable. Dual floodlights bathed its tidy grounds in a wash of bright ivory. A three-car garage stretched off to the left, each of its doors closed. Kent would have loved to see a familiar vehicle and confirm the owner hadn't moved. He didn't recognize the Volkswagen sitting near the front entrance.

Pulling behind it, he put the Honda in park and cut the engine. Each breath was a challenge. He stumbled around to the passenger side and lifted the woman out. His heart began to race as he climbed a flight of steps and rang the doorbell.

Ten seconds. Nothing. Kent hit the bell again. He could feel the will draining from both their bodies. An upstairs light came on this time, followed by descending footsteps. They were slow, cautious.

The foyer lit up. Glass panels hugged each side of the door. A figure peeked through one of them. The face was blurred. Kent couldn't be sure until the partition slowly swung open. He exhaled in relief.

Standing on an expanse of gray marble was a tall, thin man, mid-thirties. His wide eyes stared out through square-rimmed glasses. He managed a whisper. "Jeremy Kent."

"Roland." Kent adjusted the limp body in his arms. "Can you help us?"

28

Scowling in frustration, Linus Boxler fought to turn the Mini Cooper's steering wheel. The rusted car was too small and too old to be anywhere close to comfortable. The only things softer than the cracked dashboard were the tires, sloppily rolling over the worn asphalt as if it were sand.

The money kept him patient. It was coming soon, and would yield more than he could ever hope to spend. He knew wealth was a predictable, even boring motivation. But who cared once you had it? By then he could own whatever car he wanted, with a chauffeur to match.

He turned left and peered through the cramped windshield at a cloudy sky. Why did he even bother? Five years ago, when he'd first arrived in this country, most days had begun with at least a cursory interest in the weather. Soon, such attention was replaced by simply identifying a shade of gray. That was England for you. And, like succumbing to a disease, he'd gotten used to it.

Boxler hugged another curve. He could see the upper half of the Stanley Dock Tobacco Warehouse in the distance. The centerpiece of one of Liverpool's many famed dock systems, the building remained one of the largest brick structures in the world. Now in disrepair, it, like several smaller neighbors, was vacant the majority of the time.

That's one of the things he'd never understood about the English. Europe had plenty of old structures, but at least in France and Italy they focused on the famous ones. Here it didn't matter—government building, corner drugstore, nondescript warehouse—they never tore anything down. It was as if the entire country prized something just because it'd been around for a while.

Making one more turn, Boxler covered the final hundred meters to his destination. The warehouse's brick facade did absolutely nothing to draw notice. Its interior had a similar effect, unless you looked a little closer. Fortunately, the outside world had yet to do so.

The padlocks on the doors helped, along with boards hammered up against each window. The only people they really needed to deter were the homeless and drug addicts. The rest of the city generally stayed away from the area. There were the usual plans for civic revitalization, but much of that was political lip-service. By the time anything actually happened, they'd be long gone.

Boxler sputtered past the front of the building and curved left around the first corner. There, beneath a makeshift carport of wood and scrap metal, sat a dusty Saab about the same age as his Mini. He continued around the back to the warehouse's opposite side and a similar shelter. Kerr had told them never to park near one another.

Sliding his vehicle into place, he shut off the engine and grabbed a leather bag from the passenger seat. He climbed out and flipped the collar of his jacket up. A sharp wind whipped around the car. It was April, but today's temperature wouldn't reach fifty degrees.

Boxler glanced around casually like he'd been taught. He saw no one, nothing out of the ordinary. Walking a few paces back to a metal door, he reached toward the handle and lifted a padlock. Four scrolls of numbers. He adjusted for the correct sequence, yanked the metal lock open and removed it from the handle.

The door was heavy. He stepped through and reapplied the lock to the inside. Turning, he was met by an expansive, nearly empty space. Other than a thick layer of dust and several cobwebs, all that remained in the once-bustling storage area were the broken remnants of its skillfully crafted livelihood. Most recently—in this case, decades back—the building had been a loading house for one of the city's largest furniture manufacturers.

Boxler passed historic piles like mundane landmarks on his morning commute. Their melancholy charm had long fallen numb to his senses.

He quickly reached the far side of the space. Directly ahead, a particularly large mound of wooden refuse sat against a corner. From the outside, the heap looked impossibly dense. But pulling back a specific clump of wood revealed a thin passage through the maze.

Closing the invisible door behind him, Boxler followed the trail and came to another barrier. This one was made of rusted metal and completely hidden through the mass of wooden limbs. It held a padlock identical to the one he'd just circumvented.

He performed the same action on this device and slipped through, again clamping the lock on the inside. A flight of descending concrete stairs came next. He gained the bottom landing and turned right.

The space before him was far smaller than the level above, but still featured the same brick-wall and concrete-floor setup. It was also just as old. Much cleaner, though; there were no cobwebs or rotting wood. In fact, most of the items it contained had no business being in a warehouse, abandoned or not.

A microscope stood on a wooden table near the center of the room. Beside it, grouped in a small cluster, lay several glass vials. Some were empty, others glistened in a dull rainbow of liquids. Nearby sat a stack of petri dishes, followed by a computer and printer.

The rest of the space was close to bare. Fluorescent lights buzzed overhead, revealing a metal storage cabinet, portable generator and a couple of cheap rugs. Half a dozen cardboard boxes were stacked near the door, sagging like a limp pyramid.

Boxler stepped into the room, removed his jacket and set it atop his bag beside the cabinet. He turned to the microscope. "What are you doing?"

Lifting his eyes from the device, Simon Clarke ignored the comment. "You catch that soot smell on your way here? I'm going to miss this place."

Boxler moved closer. "You can keep it. No wonder your country couldn't wait to colonize every third world with a view of the sun."

"So I don't need to ask how your morning went." Clarke, sitting in a leather office chair, swiveled toward the vials. "I suppose Bern was a veritable rainforest."

"Zurich. At least we had some green."

"Forgive me. They all run together."

Boxler gestured toward the table. "Must I ask again?"

After a moment Clarke straightened, face sobering. "Just a few nooks of data that needed confirming, for peace of mind. Nothing serious."

"Testing Orion a third and fourth time wasn't enough?"

"A fifth and sixth wouldn't have been enough. This drug is everything. It has to work."

"It will." Boxler nodded toward an adjacent space. He could still hear the screams of anguish, wafting from the lips of so many past test subjects. He edged around the table, glancing at the computer screen. "Besides, Kerr wants us to be out of here by tomorrow. No trace."

"Yes." Clarke punched a few numbers on the keyboard. "I hope it matters."

Boxler paused. "What was that?"

Clarke stood. He'd nearly whispered the words before; now they rang through the room like a curse. "I said I hope it matters."

Boxler gazed directly at him. "Kent?"

Clarke nodded. "I spoke with Kerr an hour ago. Kent made it to the station in Linz. There was a chase, gunshots. Tanaka's dead."

"And Kent? The canister?"

"Both gone. We have to assume he has it."

Silence. Boxler leaned over the table, staring into nothing. "Is Kent still headed for London?"

"According to Kerr, yes. Scharp is moving down to Munich, Ryov up to Geneva. Berger will stay in Linz for the next day or so. He thinks Kent may be injured, unable to travel." Clarke paused. "There is something else. It seems Kent picked up a companion during his escape. A woman."

Boxler straightened. "How do we know?"

"Berger saw them both in the same car before he rammed it through an intersection. The whole vehicle tumbled into the Danube. He couldn't pick them up again. Too many witnesses."

"Any chance they drowned?"

"Have we ever been that lucky?"

Boxler sat on the end of the table. "Do we know who she is?"

"You must not have seen a news report in the last six hours. Her name's Allison Shaw. She's American, a nurse. Single, late-twenties—here in Europe on some work-transfer program. She'd evidently been in Linz on a break with some friends. They've been talking with authorities."

A flash of worry lit Boxler's face. "Could she be working with Kent? Is she CIA?"

Clarke shook his head. "According to Ryov, Berger shot another woman, presumably an actual agent helping Kent. If this Allison Shaw was connected to them, why was she spending time with unrelated third parties?

"Also, according to Berger she was sitting in the passenger seat of a running car when Kent jumped inside. She didn't react as if she knew him. It's all a bit too thin."

Boxler took a breath, fighting to control his rising anger. "So, what... she was simply in the wrong place at the wrong time?"

"It would seem so. Kerr is in the process of turning her life inside out, but he doesn't expect to find anything."

"Then Kent will drop her, if he hasn't already."

"Unless he can use her."

Boxler's eyes narrowed. "How so?"

"He might have told her something about the canister, even given it to her. All our eyes on him, she could slip away and deliver it to safety."

"Do Kerr and Ryov think this is a possibility?"

"Absolutely. We don't have the luxury of loose ends."

29

Kent opened his eyes and, like the cabin in Russia, didn't immediately remember where he was. *You've got to stop doing this.*

He sat up slowly, exhaling. A grunt of agony followed. Now it all came back, once again led by the pain. It felt wrong to consider yourself lucky after having been beaten violently, shot twice and stabbed in the span of a few days. But he knew it could've been worse.

The latest wound was Exhibit A. His right shoulder was impossibly sore, but he still had full range of motion. Tanaka's knife must've missed the critical tendons and bone.

Kent forced his attention off the pain and onto his surroundings. He was in a fairly large space, probably a guest suite. Simply decorated, but decidedly less rustic than Poushkin's living room.

He spotted the canister lying harmlessly on a nightstand beside his bed. The details of the night before—of Rachel's death—rushed in like acrid breath. A heavy, sickening pall draped his shoulders, slipping down his torso. Kent knew he couldn't let it shake him. *You're a professional.*

But he was also human. Whether you wore a uniform or not, losing a fellow soldier was always the worst case. He eyed the canister again, Rachel's question reverberating in his mind: *is it worth my life?*

The answer was up to him. Right now, without a key, the canister was nothing more than a paperweight. But complete this mission and it became salvation. A cure worth the sacrifice of anyone—even a talented young agent at the dawn of her career.

She, though, was no longer the only woman in his life. Kent eyed the room's door, then swung both legs over the edge of the queen-size mattress.

He planted his bare feet on a thick pad of carpet and stood. Dizziness. He steadied himself against the bed.

Once the feeling passed, he gingerly made his way toward the entrance. His borrowed ensemble—a tee shirt and cotton pants—fit better this time. Drawn shades on both windows kept most of the pale sunlight from streaking through.

Reaching the door, he softly turned the knob. A short catwalk stretched ahead, leading to a hallway and set of descending stairs. The house was almost completely silent. The only sounds he heard were the tick-tock of a large, unseen clock and a pair of feet climbing the staircase.

A moment later he saw his host gain the upper landing with a stack of towels. "Afternoon," said the man. "What are you doing up?"

"Bathroom," answered Kent, his voice hoarse. "And to check on her."

The man set the towels down. "She's all over the news. Name's Allison Shaw. A nurse from Atlanta, Georgia. She was evidently up in Scotland on some foreign work program."

For a second, Kent forgot his pain. "How do they know?"

"Her friend told them. She's Australian, a fellow nurse…I can't remember her name. The two of them came down here on a break, to meet the other woman's boyfriend. The woman and her boyfriend each said they were close to the shooting when it started. Press is eating it up."

"Of course they are." A young, American female involved in a shootout and car chase through the streets of a European city—you couldn't dream up a better headline. The fact that she was still missing was even better.

The man glanced down the hall. "Are you sure you want to disturb her? I was going to change her dressing an hour ago, but she was sound asleep." He hesitated. "Her meds are about to wear off. When she wakes… from what you told me, she's going to wonder where she is. It could get awkward."

"Story of my life." Kent nodded reassuringly. "Don't worry, I'll tiptoe."

The man gestured ahead. "Second door on your left."

Kent crossed in front of his host, then remembered something. He turned. "How long have I been out?"

"About twelve hours."

Seconds later he was turning the handle to another bedroom. Larger than his, with an attached bath. He stepped through and shut the door quietly.

Same spare design, but not a speck of dust in sight. After tracing the edges, he ran his gaze up the plush covers of the bed in the center. The woman was still asleep, breathing evenly. She lay on her back, one arm stretched atop the blankets. Kent stepped closer, keeping his eyes on her face.

She was pretty—very. Smooth features, brown curls down just past her shoulders. He hadn't noticed last night. *But you do now?* He shook his head to no one in particular. Still, of all the girls in all the gin joints...

Kent continued to stare, his mind changing tracks. He thought of the live female body in front of him and couldn't help but visualize the dead one from last night. By now Rachel's corpse would've been moved to a morgue, cooling in some anonymous locker, tagged with whatever false name her ID indicated.

Naturally, Langley would be familiar with her cover identity. Once it hit the news—perhaps even before that, through law enforcement channels—they'd know she died in a firefight. The station chief in Vienna might get involved, try to pull some strings and minimize the local investigation. Either way, nothing would lead back to Washington. For any enterprising inspector, Rachel Jordan was already a dead end.

She deserved better. Kent felt his remorse inside turning to anger—at Orion, Berger, himself. Slowly, though, he brought his focus back into the room, onto the bed. Last night was last night; there'd be time for guilt tomorrow. Today, all that mattered was the woman before him.

Kent turned for the door. He was reaching for the handle when a soft rustling of the comforter broke the room's silence. He spun around, trailing his eyes up the bed again. A pair of hazel irises stared back this time. They studied him, fighting a mixture of fear and fatigue. Then came a dash of calm as recognition seemed to set in. More than anything, though, Allison's gaze reflected the bullets and pain of yesterday. They signified a situation that was clearly beyond her.

After a moment, Kent cautiously raised his arms. "It's alright. You're safe." He retrieved a chair from the far wall and pulled it close to the edge of the bed. She didn't slink back, didn't move at all. He sat down. "Do you remember me?"

A nod.

"That was last night, about twelve hours ago. We're still in Linz. I brought you to a friend's house, to get patched up."

"Who are you?"

He needed to offer something specific. Personalizing things would help her feel secure. "My name is Jeremy. I'm an American."

"Military?"

"Close enough."

She shifted up onto an elbow. "Why did you choose my car?"

She seemed to be asking herself as much as him. "It was already running. I needed a quick getaway." Kent took a breath. "I wish there were a deeper reason. If there'd been any way to let you go free before taking off, I would have."

He could sense her mental gears begin to spin. A slight shade of confidence now colored her eyes. His answer seemed to pass muster, but she was going to have more questions. She sat up further, wincing in the process. Kent took the opportunity to direct the conversation. "How are you feeling?"

"Fine." She paused. "The pain is still there, but not as bad as before."

He nodded. "Our host is going to come in soon to replace your bandages. He's a surgeon at the city's trauma hospital."

"Why aren't we there, at the hospital?"

You walked right into it. Nothing would suffice here except the truth, and he wasn't sure she was ready for it. Maybe a partial answer would be enough. "The men from last night are still out there. This house is more secure than anywhere public. No one knows we're here."

"I thought they were only after you." Her voice had gained a hint of extra anxiety.

He was out of options. But she was deep enough into this. She deserved to know. "They were. But not anymore. They want something I have, and they've seen us together. If they even suspect I've given it to you, nothing will stop them from knowing for sure."

"What happens when they find out I don't have it?"

"Same thing that'd happen if you did. People in their position…they can't afford to leave things undone."

She froze, understanding glazing her face. He was glad he didn't have to say the words. The pain and dread in her eyes, though, were punishment enough. "I'm sorry, Allison. Your life was in danger the moment I jumped behind that wheel."

She pulled away. "How do you know my name?"

Kent leaned back in his chair and put his hands up again. "Easy. You're the top news story, probably for most of the northern hemisphere."

"Me? I'm just one person."

"That's the point: you're the star. Last night played out like the climax to a James Bond movie."

She was silent for a long moment, eyes distant. "It didn't feel like a movie."

"It never does."

Kent could feel exhaustion tugging at his bones, ordering him back to the other bedroom and its soft mattress. She was fading, too. This conversation couldn't last much longer.

"The only solution," he said, "is long-term safety. No embassies, not even a military base. The best option is to get you back across the ocean, inside the U.S. border. But you're not ready to travel. You need a few more days of rest."

It wasn't her choice; the decision had already been made. But Kent kept his tone diplomatic. She needed to feel that her input was valued, that she still had some control.

More quiet. Kent could see the tug-of-war behind her eyes. Was she really safe here? What if she'd been kidnapped and was now being held for ransom.? But she wasn't wealthy or well-known. And this bed was a bit too comfortable for a prisoner. Ultimately, the man before her hadn't tried to kill her last night and wasn't hurting her today. What other choice did she have?

She nodded.

"Thank you." Kent stood. "Can I get you anything—another pillow? Some water?"

She shook her head.

He forced a small grin and lifted the chair to its original spot. He'd turned toward the door when a hollow gasp sounded. He looked back to the bed. She was halfway out, breathing in a fresh dose of agony and fear. "Becky, Petr—they were on that street."

Kent shuffled back toward the bed. "Your friends? They're fine. They're the reason the press knows who you are."

She retreated, slightly, from her emotional edge. "And my parents? They're all the way in Georgia. I can't imagine what they're thinking."

"They'll be fine," said Kent, knowing the words rang hollow. "You'll see them soon."

Tears started to pool in her eyes; her breathing became ragged. He knew it wasn't just her parents. It was the cumulative effect of the past four-teen hours. She'd seen and experienced the kind of stress most people were never trained to handle. He felt a sudden desire to embrace her, if only to squeeze some of the pain away.

She gathered herself enough to form another sentence. "Can I call them…tell them I'm okay?"

Kent didn't try to hide the grief on his face. "I'm sorry, it's not safe. The call could be tracked."

That was the end of her remaining strength. Almost immediately a heavy glaze deadened her expression; both eyes went blank. She nodded absently, her body beginning to shake. She climbed back into the bed, looking at nothing in particular, frozen in a cage of fear and helplessness.

At that moment Kent hated himself. He hated his job, hated the evil in the world that made a scene like this possible.

Then he walked out.

30

For the first time in his life, Nathan Brooks studied his pint. He looked closely, trying to read between the lines of the dark, amber liquid. Was this how they did it—the philosophers, the movie stars? Right about now the patented epiphany was set to break through, lifting the weight of some sinister dilemma.

He had nothing. The thick alcohol just stared back at him, barely asking to be drunk. So he did, idly licking the lingering flavor from his lips. He glanced at the beer again, this time in admiration. Taste was never a problem. Nothing about this place was, actually. The Flask had always been one of Highgate's bright spots. It was just a few blocks from his flat. He'd been coming here even before he knew names like Kent, Baker and Ryov.

It was different now. He tried to imagine what things had been like half a decade earlier. *How did you feel—only the weight of your job, maybe a stalled relationship?* He couldn't remember. Another drink, this time to forget. He'd have done anything for a second's peace.

Brooks forced his gaze around the pub's main seating area. Business was good. No surprise for a historic bar in an affluent borough. Dark wood and warm lighting gave the place a rustic charm. A patio lay out back— ample room to party—but you could still enjoy a quiet, solitary drink inside.

Plenty of history's finest had done so, including Byron and Shelley. Local lore had it their main objective was Coleridge's house across the street, where opium resided like a guest. Brooks felt a smile creep onto his face. Pride? Yes, the best kind. They'd needed a powerful drug to make it through; he only had hops. Sure, *Frankenstein* and *Don Juan* changed the world. But no poet had ever dreamed up a part like his.

Tilting his glass back, Brooks drained the contents and suppressed a belch. He casually checked his watch. *Right on time.* Peering up toward the bar, he locked eyes with the man behind it and scratched his nose. Harry Johns could have hired someone to tend the front, but he preferred a closer look. "If I'm going to run this place, I want to see it," he'd told Brooks.

The two men went back to the days when Brooks was at university, prone to enjoy a pint with friends on summer and Christmas holidays. Johns had tolerated his patron then—big head and a bad haircut. For the past five years, he'd been doing a much larger favor.

Standing, Brooks watched his friend casually stride through the room and pass his table. He followed, descending a few steps into the bar's cellar, now converted to additional seating. Walking the depressed corridor, he held no fear of being recognized. His face rarely saw the cameras and it was 6 p.m. in the middle of a long week. He was just another high-class reveler tiding himself over until Friday.

Nearing the space's far table—occupied by what appeared to be a pair of retired couples—Johns quickly broke into his familiar address. *"How are you all tonight?" "Yes, we're keeping busy." "Fancy another round of my expensive alcohol?"* Perhaps a bit unusual for the owner of a pub to check in on his customers, but it worked every time.

Brooks didn't catch each word. He was too busy walking past the conversation—slowly, furtively, trying to blend into the wall. The distraction didn't have to be airtight, just enough to discourage a second glance as he reached the door at the far end marked 'no exit'.

Knowing its alarm had been disabled, he pushed through. Shadows reached out and quickly enveloped him as he shut the barrier. The bar's signature noise—clanking dishes, idle chatter—immediately faded. Total darkness reigned, save a ribbon of yellow light glazing the door's base.

Brooks exhaled and pulled out his phone. He knew the layout by heart, but saw no reason to risk tripping over a fallen obstacle. He activated the device's flashlight and instantly a pale beam cut through the dim. He waved it around, confirming everything was as it had been a week earlier.

The room was small, essentially a glorified maintenance closet. Wooden shelves holding seldom-used supplies covered each wall. In the center a humble desk and chair did their best to entice an entrant into coming closer.

They always failed. Yet Brooks had no choice. Nicolas Kerr, through the power vested in him by MI6, had a long reach. While there was no proof that he was monitoring the chief of staff or the prime minister, anything was possible. For Brooks, lounging at home with his feet up, gabbing on his mobile, all seemed a little careless.

That's why the Flask's landline was so important. He could trust Harry. The man didn't know specifics, just that the calls were critical. Even so, Brooks and his counterpart on the other end always kept the conversation vague. No real names.

He sat down and took a breath. Outside of the phone's light, the room remained dark. There was an overhead lamp, but he never used it. Chief among the benefits of such gloom was the ability to spot a disruption in the door's bottom illumination. Eavesdropping would've taken an acrobat.

With a sweaty palm—*every time*—he reached for a telephone receiver and brought it to his ear. The first step was to check for messages. This line was the only way for Kent and Baker to leave updates on their progress. A month ago, Brooks had borrowed a key from Harry. In addition to these regular meetings, he'd stop by the pub multiple times a week—in the morning, when it was closed—to check the phone for news.

This time there was some. Brooks' stomach settled slightly as he heard Kent's steady voice on the line. Again, no specifics, but they'd developed their own bit of verbal shorthand over time. The message was clear enough.

Now came the main event. Still holding the receiver, Brooks cleared the line and dialed the number burned into his memory. Despite their indirection, he and Pete McCoy still needed a way to refer to their duo in the field. The Hardy Boys seemed appropriate enough; Kent was *Frank*, Baker *Joe*.

As the first ring sounded, Brooks tried to picture McCoy on the other end, three thousand miles away. Maybe the CIA man was in some recommissioned townhouse in a D.C. suburb. A cracked leather armchair, even a glass of scotch.

Maybe not. But the romanticism helped. It reminded Brooks of the stakes and, if only for a second, made him feel like a professional.

The second ring had yet to finish when McCoy's voice broke through. "Evening."

The chief of staff exhaled. "Afternoon for you."

"Sometimes they run together."

"Occupational hazard, I suppose."

"For both of us."

Brooks appreciated the comment. A small recognition of his efforts. "Perhaps I can ease the pain."

"You have something?" McCoy failed to suppress a timbre of hope.

"You're aware of last night's activity, east of here?"

"In the center of the continent. Yes."

"I just received a message from Frank. That was him. He's split the prize in half. Has one piece."

"And his companion?"

"A temporary accident. Separation will occur."

"What then?"

Brooks kept his focus on the door, both eyes now accustomed to the dark. "Heading west. Toward my area, and the second piece."

A patch of silence hugged the other end. "What else?"

"That was all."

"Anything from Joe?"

"I'm afraid not. Do we still assume he is in a holding pattern?"

"Yes."

Now it was Brooks' turn to pause. He realized, for the first time, that this entire operation was nearing its end. His experience—these calls, this room—had been surreal. The surface of a clandestine world as foreign to him as a distant planet. "Will this be our final call?" he asked.

"It appears that way. But not our final meeting. Let's make it face-to-face next time."

The aide was taken aback, then understood. "To celebrate?"

"To celebrate."

Brooks could hear the doubt in McCoy's voice and felt it in his own. Kent, miraculously, had survived, and he'd evidently formed a plan. But by no means was he out of the woods. Kerr remained at large; there were likely still highly-trained assassins on Jeremy's tail.

Brooks chewed on his last patch of stale faith. "I'll keep my fingers crossed."

"You've done a lot more than that. Godspeed."

Abruptly, the line went dead. There was nothing more to say. Brooks slowly stowed the receiver, then stood. This part was always tricky.

Harry, naturally, couldn't engage a single table for the length of the phone call. Thus, it was entirely possible for someone to glimpse Brooks as he exited the room. Even someone who'd seen him originally walk through. It'd happened before. Thankfully, never with the same patron twice. Still, he had to be quick on his feet.

Sure enough, he closed the door just as a member of the nearby retiree club was bringing two full glasses back to his table. Their eyes met. Brooks produced a sheepish grin. "Seem to have lost my way."

The man set the beers down with a laugh. "A pint or two'll do that to you."

Brooks kept the smile as he walked by, thinking that sounded right, and thinking he could still use a third.

31

Allison opened her eyes to quiet and darkness. She couldn't see much, but the bed was still soft and warm. She pulled the blankets off and sat up. A little too fast. Her whole body ached, left side the most.

She had a gnawing urge to inspect the wound, but didn't want to undo the work her host had completed. She pictured him again, hunched at her side: he was tall, with a soft voice and kind face. He'd mentioned his name, but she was still groggy from the drugs and couldn't remember. She'd drifted back to sleep the moment he left.

Twisting toward the edge of the bed, she let her legs dangle over. She wore an oversized tee-shirt and shorts pinned at the waist. She took a breath, listening for any sounds outside the room. Except for the possible distant clanking of pots and pans, there was nothing.

Through the shadows, Allison spotted a lamp a few feet to her left and pulled its cord. Yellow light instantly colored the walls and floor. She stood. Her legs began to wobble and she braced herself against the bed. A few seconds later the feeling passed. An attached bathroom lay directly ahead. She stepped forward, but never made it.

Instead, after glancing to her right, she gasped at the sight of a man sitting in a chair near the door. *Slouching* was the more accurate term. He was asleep, head resting against his left shoulder. She'd been groggy during her dressing change; had she not seen him? Had he come in later? Either way, his name she did remember.

Nature's call was growing louder. Allison looked to the bathroom, but instead padded toward his chair. Once she was within a few feet she whispered. "Jeremy." He didn't stir. She spoke a little louder. "Jeremy."

She wondered how the lethal weapon from yesterday could be so dense today. Then she realized he was probably drugged too. She took a breath, moved closer and shook his shoulder.

His right shoulder.

Immediately he grunted awake, snatched her hand and bent over in pain. Allison tried to pull away and let out a gargled scream. Kent held on, then looked up with wide eyes and quickly released his grip.

She staggered back, shaking. The fear she'd felt during their earlier conversation, momentarily forgotten, came rushing back. Kent dropped to his knees. Reflexively touching his shoulder with his left arm, he cut the motion short and reached out toward her, palm open. "I'm sorry."

All she could do was breathe. Mentally, she'd already decided earlier that the man before her wasn't a threat. She'd also come to believe his assertion that this house was, relatively speaking, safe. But emotionally and physically, terror squeezed her like a snake.

Kent slowly rose to his feet. His face no longer displayed any pain. Instead, just calm. He stared across the eight-foot gulf between them, directly into her eyes. Allison reciprocated. Were those blue irises, or grey? She couldn't quite tell at this distance.

Each held their gaze, without words, for nearly a minute. The focus helped; Allison could feel her heartbeat slowing. After another thirty seconds, she realized he wasn't going to make the first move. He didn't want to frighten her again.

She took a step forward; he followed. If nothing else, they were now at a normal speaking distance. Finally, he exhaled. "I'm sorry."

"You said that already."

"I need you to believe it."

She glanced toward the chair, then back to him. "What are you doing in here?"

"I came back a few minutes after walking out. It didn't feel right to leave you alone."

The words were delivered without excess emotion, but there was no denying the sympathy, even chivalry, they contained. Her medication wasn't *that* heavy. This, though, was still an unfamiliar man in an unfamiliar place. Beyond a simple nod, she was unable to let her guard down.

And nature was still calling. "If you don't mind," she said, "I need to use the bathroom."

"Of course." He looked at the bed. "Are you still tired?"

She shook her head. "Not so much."

"In that case, take forty-five minutes. Freshen up—whatever you want." He pointed to the bathroom. "There should be fresh clothing hanging inside. I'll come back, we'll go downstairs together."

Allison nodded again. Kent retreated to the chair, put it in place, and was gone a moment later. She took a deep breath, letting the silence return. She was happy to have the room back to herself. Its four walls were like shields from the outside world. They offered a sense of protection, no matter how thin; they defined her sphere of power. Right now, it was the only piece of life she could control.

Two minutes later she'd used the bathroom and was washing her hands at the sink. She hadn't noticed any clothing, then turned around for a towel. Hanging, behind the door and against an adjacent wall, was an entire wardrobe. Two each of sweaters, shirts, blouses, pants, even a skirt. A clear plastic bag of lace delicates completed the collection.

Focusing on the last item, Allison felt herself flush. It was as if she'd been intruded upon, her walls of protection pierced the moment they'd gone up. *Relax.* She forced a deep breath and stepped closer to the clothing. Really, it wasn't much different than her hospital patients who complained about the flimsy paper gowns.

She fingered a navy pullover. The size of each piece looked to be close enough to fit. No doubt whoever'd bought them had seen plenty of her skin while she was being patched up.

It didn't feel great, the exposure. More than anything, it highlighted her helplessness. But everything came back to a simple fact: facing what she had last night, she shouldn't be alive right now. If not for these men… she could humble herself for a day or two.

32

The hot water felt good. Allison hadn't been able to take a full shower with her dressing, but she'd wet the upper and lower thirds of her body with a sponge. Piled neatly near the sink, alongside towels and some soap, had been a hair dryer. She'd taken the invitation and was using the device now. She studied herself through the large mirror, brown hair dancing in the loud, artificial wind.

She looked refreshed, but not cured. There were cracks to her foundation, echoes of stress that required more to fix than hours of rest and minutes of steam. They'd be with her, not until they weakened, but until she gained enough strength to leave them behind.

She'd put on a cotton blouse, loose slacks and flats. The clothes were comfortable, their fit eerily snug. Even underneath. Allison rubbed her cheek, feeling the naked skin. She'd always considered makeup the final piece to her daily ensemble. When was the last time she'd gone without it? Earlier she caught herself checking near the soap for a container of blush or concealer, knowing it didn't matter now, feeling silly for looking.

The distinct sound of a human voice pierced the dryer's din. She flipped the 'off' switch, listening. A second later, "hello?"

Allison set the device down. "Hello." It was Jeremy.

"May I come in?" His voice came from around the corner.

"Yes." Allison brushed a few stray locks from her eyes and turned. Her heavy jacket of fear was gone, but she still felt a swirl of anxiety as he stepped into view.

There was a patch of silence. For the first time, she really looked at him. He was in his early thirties, by her best guess; trimmed brown hair, maybe an inch or two under six feet; no bulging muscles, but certainly in shape. A hint of handsome lit what was otherwise a very typical face. He wasn't going to stand out in a crowd. *Probably the idea.*

He was dressed in dark pants and a gray fleece, sleeves pulled up to his forearms. He studied her. "How's the fit?"

Allison looked down at the clothing. "Good." She shook her head. "Too good."

"Compliments of our host. He has some experience shopping for women's clothing. I'm afraid you're not his first female guest."

"That's…reassuring?" She crinkled her lower lip, the seed of a smile.

Jeremy went a little farther with his grin. "He's harmless, you'll see." He gestured toward the bedroom door. "Ready?"

Yes. Her hair was dry enough, her clothing comfortable. But leaving this chamber was harder than a simple step forward. Her nervousness thickened. Downstairs was unknown, a world away. Yet she couldn't stay in here forever. And she'd already met her host; he'd taken care of her. If this was still some elaborate kidnapping scheme, her captors had aided her to an unreasonable degree. One way or another, it was time to know the truth.

She nodded. He led her out onto a carpeted hallway, then down a flight of stairs. The house was impressive—marble floors, crown molding. They turned left and strode toward a sizeable kitchen, its granite counter-top sharing space with stainless steel appliances.

A tall man stood near the stove, his back to them. Spinning at the sound of footsteps, he set down a spatula and slowly moved forward. Allison took him in, their bedside encounter during her dressing change becoming a clearer memory.

He wore glasses and a crown of black hair, thick and manicured. He might've been a few years older than Jeremy, but possessed a smoother, almost pretty, face. She could see why women found it easy to accept an invitation back to this house.

The man glanced at Jeremy, who'd stopped by her side, then turned to Allison. "Ms. Shaw." His English was clean, only traces of an accent. "I hope you're feeling comfortable, under the circumstances."

He'd offered the last qualifier as if he were ashamed. It was the jolt of guilt she needed to find the right words. "Yes, thank you. For everything." There was an awkward silence. "Forgive me," she added. "I forgot your name."

He smiled. "Prescription-strength pain relievers will do that to you." He reached out his hand. "Roland Wirth, at your service."

She hesitated, then accepted. Human touch was still a barrier to be crossed. He didn't seem to mind. Releasing, he waved a hand toward a crystal dinette table. "Please, have a seat." They did so, and he curved back toward the counter. A moment later he delivered two large glasses of clear liquid. Allison first thought it was a lot of vodka. "Sorry," he said, "but neither of you have had much to drink since last night. You should start with water."

He reentered the kitchen, fingered a bottle of cabernet and flashed a smile. "I'll have to pick up the slack."

Jeremy took a drink. "Max?"

"Yes, he can help." Roland checked his watch." Should be here by now. Can't have spaghetti without bruschetta."

Allison took a drink herself, studying her host. He'd started off this encounter cautious and reserved—perhaps for her benefit. Now he seemed to be warming up. She tilted the glass again, and kept it there until it was empty. She realized she hadn't had much to drink since the make-shift surgery.

Almost immediately, Roland walked over with the wine and traded the bottle for her glass. "A second round already." He nodded toward Allison. "Good for you."

She was just thinking how awful vodka would've been when she realized she'd missed something. Her brain switched to the new name that was mentioned and she turned to Kent. He beat her to the punch. "Max is Roland's brother. He's living here, temporarily. Helped us last night."

"Is he in the medical field too?" she asked.

"By the grace of God, no," said Roland. "He's an artist. That's usually German for 'unemployed,' but Max's done alright. Mostly painting. He's opening a small gallery downtown with a few colleagues. Once the flat above it is finished, he'll be gone." His eyes glazed absently. "I suppose it's a good thing that hasn't happened yet. Would've been tough to patch you both up on my own."

Roland brought Allison's refill and sat down. She took another drink. The anxiety within her had dulled to a more tolerable degree. It was clear now: danger still existed, but it was beyond these walls; the men before her were not part of it. She would expend no more energy bracing for them to turn on her.

Instead, she turned to Kent. "Were you awake, then—last night?"

"Only for a few moments. I passed out once we had you on the table."

She glanced down, a little surprised. "This table?"

"A larger one." Roland pointed down a nearby corridor. "In the dining room."

Allison nodded, then focused back on Kent. She'd wondered about him. His wounds from the night before were apparent. In a strange way, it was comforting to know he'd also needed medical attention. After his surreal dance atop the windshield of the car, injury humanized him. It also made her feel less alone; she wasn't the only patient here, the only victim of violence.

Still, her companions had obviously met before. She looked at each of them. "How do you know one another?"

Jeremy gave her a protective stare. "Maybe another time."

Roland was sipping his red. "Aw, c'mon Jeremy, there's no harm in a story." He smiled. "It happens to be a good one."

Allison met Jeremy's gaze. She assumed he had a reason to hesitate, but found herself nodding, curiosity outweighing caution.

Jeremy paused. The decision was ultimately his. Finally, he cleared his throat. "A few years ago, here in Linz, the Russian mafia tried to eliminate a witness at a hospital. I was there to stop them. A firefight broke out, Roland got caught in the middle. He was shot twice."

"The first was minor," said their host, rolling up his sleeve to show a scar on his right forearm. "But the second hit my brachial artery. I would've died in seconds if Jeremy hadn't turned his belt into a tourniquet. I told him I'd be there to return the favor if he ever needed it."

Immediately Allison understood Jeremy's reluctance. She could still feel the bandages at her side, and, despite a fresh dose of medication, the searing pain underneath. Such a graphic scenario was capable of dredging last night's visuals back to the surface, paralyzing her into a fresh cocoon of fear.

But this one didn't. Maybe it would have hours ago. If anything, now, it made her current world a little less frightening, the men before her a little less mysterious. A blank edge had been filled in. The bloodshed was real, but at least it had concrete limits; her imagination couldn't make it worse.

"I guess," Jeremy said to Roland, "you didn't expect to be taken so literally."

Roland waved the comment off. "I got a lovely dinner guest out of it." He turned to Allison. "I have a weakness for Italian food. Slap me if we have spaghetti again this week."

She shook her head in confusion. "Week? I'm sorry, but I'll only be here for another day or two."

His expression cracked. Just for a second, but she noticed. A small note of worry flared within her. She glanced at Jeremy, expecting—hoping for—a refutation. He returned her gaze for what seemed like an hour. Finally, "You can't leave, Allison. Not for at least a week. Maybe longer."

Her face went blank, as if she hadn't heard the words. "I don't understand."

"I said you'd be safe back in the states. That was a lie. Your only sanctuary is this house." Jeremy minced no words, but each one was tinged with empathy. "You've seen the expertise of my enemies. They have the means and ability to reach you anywhere. Hiding isn't an option, either. You can't travel back home without the press, or other authorities, finding out." He paused. "Forgive me. I would've told you sooner, but you needed more time to rest. I wanted you to spend a few minutes with Roland, down here, before hearing the truth."

Deep down, in some small, distant place, Allison understood this. It made sense. But such knowledge was powerless to stem the feeling that the floor had opened up beneath her.

The reality of the proposition, lost on her at the moment, wasn't so much of a sacrifice. She'd already made the choice to trust Roland. This house was no dirty shack; two weeks wasn't eternity. The difficult part would be the lack of communication with friends and family. She chose not to picture the grief her parents were already feeling, wondering where she was, thinking her dead.

Beyond all of this, though, was the emotional shock. It was as if she'd miraculously scaled last night's brick wall only to be pulverized by a fresh wrecking ball. Her psyche was crying out for some semblance of familiarity, of home. Instead, she was met with more isolation. Any sense of safety she'd regained was quickly stolen back.

Jeremy looked at Roland, then to Allison. She didn't know what the rest of her face was doing, but could feel moisture pooling in both eyes. "You're strong, Allison," he said. "Neither you nor I would still be alive if you weren't. You can do this."

She found herself nodding. Not because she agreed, but because there was no other choice. She was exhausted, afraid, and upset at the man before her. But she would do this. *If only you hadn't been in that car.*

"When will we know it's safe for her to leave here?" This from Roland, still at the table, trying to help.

Jeremy swung his gaze between the two of them, ending on Allison. "I'll get word to you. Somehow."

Allison had barely spoken, but found her throat dry again. She took a few more gulps from her new glass. A second later the familiar sound of a key turning in a lock echoed through the kitchen. "That'll be Max," said Roland, standing.

Soon a younger man, golden hair draped past his ears, strode into the room. He was carrying a loaf of bread wrapped in a thin paper bag. "Evening." He glanced to his left and slowed, setting the bag down on the counter. "Ah, to all of you."

Roland gestured to his sibling. "Allison Shaw, my brother, Maximillian."

"How are you feeling?" he asked, eyeing Jeremy too.

The question was clearly in reference to physical injuries. Five minutes ago, that might've been the only pain to speak of. As it was, Jeremy and Allison both remained silent. Roland stepped forward. "Ms. Shaw has just agreed to stay with us a bit longer."

Max's expression sobered. "I see." He exhaled. "Lucky are we to have such a brave guest."

The words hung in the room, their dichotomy of praise and peril spiking its still air. After a moment Jeremy, eying Roland, quietly nodded at the counter. The host's eyebrows rose. "Of course." He moved toward the paper bag, perking up slightly. "Dinner is almost ready." He glanced at his brother. "Just have to prepare the bread."

"Forgive me," said Max, laying his jacket across a nearby chair. "Rain's slowing traffic down." He walked to the table and reached for the bottle of cabernet. "I also had a chat with the owner of the house at the end of the lane." This was directed at Jeremy.

"Seems," continued Max, "that he couldn't sleep last night. Happened to see a car pull onto the road from his window. Caught the plates in the glare of the street light. He said he remembers the numbers because they were almost identical to his daughter's birthday."

"Go on," said Kent, an edge coloring his voice.

"He called the police. Only, just now. He'd forgotten until a repeat story on the news flashed the plates."

Jeremy immediately stood and checked his watch. He seemed about to move but then stopped, closing his eyes. "What?" asked Roland.

"The police know we've driven down this street."

Roland stepped forward. "We left the Honda in a ditch, just as you instructed. No prints, no trace of it here. If the police come with questions, we'll cover. Wouldn't be the first time I've lied for a friend."

"The police aren't the problem." Jeremy looked at Allison. "The men pursuing me have contacts throughout Europe. Many are in law enforcement."

Her mind had accelerated. It almost felt good—cathartic—processing information instead of emotional pain. "What are you saying?" she managed to ask.

"I'm saying they know we're here."

"You can't be sure of that," said Roland.

"I have to assume."

"But that's the worst-case scenario."

"My entire world is a worst-case scenario."

"How would they know which house to check?" asked Max, thinking.

"There are only three. It's worth their time to search each one."

Roland's eyes went distant. "The other two are empty anyway." He refocused, turning to Jeremy. "One belongs to a CEO and his wife. Month-long holiday in St. Barts. A cleaning service comes once a week. No housekeeper, but there is advanced electronic security."

"And the second?"

"Vacant. A bit unusual for this area, but it won't last long. The couple moving in hit a snag with financing. Should have it straightened out in another ten days or so."

"My," said Allison, "you don't miss a thing."

"I ran into the seller's real estate agent as he was pulling up the sign. It's easier to keep up with your neighbors when you've only got two." He paused. "At least neither home will be occupied until this storm blows over. No more innocent lives in danger."

Max frowned. "Except ours."

"We'll be gone before the sun comes up," said Jeremy. Everyone went quiet. He eyed the brothers. "All of us."

Both Roland and Max hesitated. This was all happening incredibly fast. But their faces displayed no shock; they had to know what the situation meant. Allison did too. This house had become a deathtrap, its walls already seeming to close in. She thought of the assailant last night. He fought atop the car like a cold machine, each movement a brutal mix of precision and ferocity. The others could be just like him, and on their way here.

Max's words brought her back into the room. "Together?" he was asking. "All of us in the same car?"

"For a short time," answered Kent.

Roland was studying Jeremy and Allison, a step closer to incredulous than his brother. "You're injured."

"We can move," said Jeremy. "Right now, that's enough."

"Where are we going?" asked Allison. The three men turned her way. The question had come out of nowhere, but felt natural. She sat up, a hair more confident. Her heart was beating faster, glued to this new threat, galvanized by adrenaline.

"Southwest," said Jeremy. "For about twenty miles." He turned to Roland. "There's a transit station in Wels. From there, you and Max will each buy a ticket for the next train south to Graz."

"Why Graz?" asked Roland.

"The larger the city, the easier it is to hide. Staying in Austria simplifies this. But Linz isn't an option, and Vienna has too much of the spotlight."

"Wouldn't flying there be faster?" asked Max.

"Yes, but it's too risky. Even if you could find a red eye, your names would be on the passenger manifest."

Both brothers blinked in understanding. Roland was quickest to continue. "What do we do when we get to Graz?"

"Walk to separate hotels. Rent rooms for two weeks and lay low. Pay for everything—rail, hotel, food—with cash. Don't use your cell phones while there, don't call anyone you know." He paused. "Before we leave, each of you will e-mail a coworker and say you've come down with the flu. You're not sure when you'll be back."

Taking it all in, Max slowly nodded. Roland was unsure. "My patients...I've got major surgery scheduled in forty-eight hours. If I leave I won't operate for a month."

"If you don't leave, you never will."

Roland went quiet. It was hard to argue with life and death. He nodded.

"What about Allison?" said Max. "Is she coming with us?"

Jeremy paused. Allison instantly stood as the realization came. She'd been so focused on the details of the scenario, she completely forgot about herself. Now there was no escaping. Despair gripped her skin, chilling the blood within.

"I can't. My face is all over the news, remember? I won't blend in anywhere." Max seemed about to protest when she cut him off. "And whoever I'm with will be in danger too. If these men think Jeremy gave me something, I could've passed it along to a companion myself."

Roland shook his head. "I refuse to believe that. We can make this work."

"No." Allison was resolute, and all the worse for it. Paths of escape flew through her mind, but every one crashed upon entry. Tears began blurring her vision. "One mistake," she said, "and all of us would be dead. I'm a poison to whomever I'm with."

Max leaned forward against the table, desperation clouding his face. "Allison, you can't do this. It would eliminate all your options, everyone who could help you."

"Not everyone." Jeremy had spoken the words. Everything within earshot—simmering pasta, rain outside—seemed to go silent. He turned toward Allison. "You could come with me."

At first, she thought she hadn't heard him right. Based on last night, wherever he was headed would be the most dangerous road of all. And yet, he was capable. She again pictured the battle on the Audi's windshield. No ordinary person could've survived that.

She looked at the brothers, but soon turned back to Jeremy. This decision was hers to make. She wiped her eyes dry, then took a long, deep breath. "Alright."

Kent slowly nodded. "Alright." He turned toward Max, shifting into a new gear. "Go and buy some blonde hair coloring. Come right back." Then to Roland: "Do you own a straightener?"

The older brother tilted his head. "Actually, yes."

"Of course you do. Good." Kent swiveled back to Allison. "Those clothes are fine."

For leaving. She froze, realizing that's what they were preparing to do. The walls of her room, this house, would no longer protect her. That all fell to the man by her side. A skilled operative, but still a perfect stranger.

Three minutes later Kent stood in the living room, Roland's cell to his ear. Two rings passed before a male voice sounded. "Good evening, J. J. Fox cigars."

"Charlie, please."

"May I ask who's calling?"

"Jeremy."

The man on the other end hesitated slightly. Then, "one moment."

Soon the line picked up. "Jeremy?"

"Charlie."

"Always good to hear the voice of my favorite customer."

"You should've been a politician."

"I'm in sales; what's the difference?" He took a breath. "Calling for an order, I suppose. What'll it be this time—Churchills? Torpedoes?"

"Give me a box of Gran Coronas."

"Always an excellent choice. It will be done."

"I'll leave the brand to your good taste. You do have my card on file?"

"Of course." A pause. "Anything else?"

"Just take care of yourself."

The phase carried an air of finality. Charlie seemed to understand. "Same to you."

33

The moon, nearly full, glowed brightly amidst a sea of twinkling stars. Closer to the surface, surrounding hills reflected its pale brilliance. Gliding over a stretch of deserted asphalt, Kent gripped the steering wheel of Max's Volkswagen with steady hands.

Roland owned three cars, but they were all tied to his name. Which meant they were also tied to anyone hiding out with him. Max was a different story; no documentation put him, or his vehicle, at the house.

Kent and Allison had parted with the brothers over an hour ago. Wels Station—smaller than Linz's, and sparser at such a late hour—was cold and bleak. A perfect match for Roland and Max, who'd peered back toward the car with a kind of hollow fortitude. This was hard for them. But they'd survive. Their chief enemies would be boredom and isolation. Hardly life-threatening.

Allison was a different story. It began with her appearance. Kent himself was still mystery enough, but her brown curls were now blonde and straight, freshly cut just below the ears. Kent had also asked Max to buy a pair of eyeglasses with false frames. As long as Allison wore them in public, she'd have a realistic chance of avoiding detection.

He was still getting used to her new look, despite barely having known the old one. A glance toward the passenger seat: she sat curled against the far window, sleeping, her shoulders rising and falling with each breath.

Kent brought his eyes back to the road. Each moment they'd spent together had been colored—dominated—by violence and fatigue. As unpleasant as these factors were, they had the effect of compressing time, lengthening every moment; he felt like he'd known the woman across from him for months. *Does she feel the same?* Did it even matter?

They hit a small bump. She rustled awake, slowly uncurling her frame. She rubbed the haze from her eyes and glanced out the window. Then turned to Kent.

"Sorry," he said. "Road crew must've missed a spot."

Allison looked back outside. "Are we still in Austria?"

"Barely. Those are the foothills of the Alps."

She was quiet for a moment. "I've wanted to see them since I was a little girl. We had a decent view flying over, but…they're not the same from a plane."

Kent glanced her way as the Volkswagen entered a tunnel. "What brought you to Europe?"

She turned back to him with a weary face. "You don't have to do this."

"Who says it's for you? We've got a long drive. I bore easily."

She pursed her lips, not quite ready to smile. More silence came, enhanced by the steady hum of tires rolling over asphalt. Finally, she took a breath. "I was a delivery nurse at St. Joseph's, outside Atlanta." Now she did smile, a bit amazed. "*Was*—I suppose I still am. Right now it feels pretty far away."

She looked directly at Kent, a speck of wonder still lighting her eyes. It was as if she was realizing something for the first time. "I remember, about nine months ago, standing at a window on my break at work. Had a beautiful view of the parking lot. I was eating a candy bar, feeling guilty about it.

"Then the thought came: 'do you still want to be doing this forty years from now? Working in the maternity wing of a suburban hospital, twenty miles from where you grew up? Fretting over earthshaking issues like a lack of scenery and keeping your figure?'

"It wasn't for lack of a challenge. I could've applied for promotion, even gone back to school." She paused, her gaze clearing. "I came to Europe because I wanted to know my vocation—my life—didn't begin and end with me. It needed to have wider implications."

"You wanted to be part of something bigger than yourself," said Kent.

She frowned. "That's a bit too dramatic. I think I just needed to know that what I did mattered."

Kent didn't immediately respond, and her attention was diverted out the window. They were skirting Salzburg to the north, its lights an island of white amidst the surrounding black. "Is that how you feel?" he asked, pulling her gaze back. "That your job and your life are synonymous?"

She thought a moment. "It sounds bad, I know. But other than travel, there's nothing more fulfilling to me. My first day in Scotland, I had a fresh perspective. Medicine really did make a difference."

Kent nodded. "What about someone to share it with? Any little Allisons going to be running around in the future?"

She looked at him sharply. It was a personal question, but he needed to know. The more information he had about this woman, the better he could protect her. And, by consequence, the greater the mission's chance of success.

After some hesitation, she relaxed. "Not yet. There *was* someone in college. I thought it might work; he checked a lot of boxes. But we had no spark." She swallowed. "Finding a match…it feels like such a needle in a haystack. I'm not sure I have the energy anymore."

Kent thought about another question, but bit his tongue. She'd already revealed a lot, and he felt a pang of empathy at her latest words. It was easy to forget that about twenty-four hours ago her life had been normal, safe. Now she was having to rely on fragments of strength and courage buried deep within, like unused muscles. For most people they never even materialized.

"What about you?" The words jarred him slightly. Was she just curious, or did she want to reverse the flow of inquisition? She clarified her question. "Is your work your life?"

Absolutely. He wanted to smile, but instead simply nodded. "Recently, I haven't had much of a choice."

Kent navigated an interchange along the German border. Silence reigned, and he knew why. Within the space between them lay the knowledge—metastasizing like a tumor—that he was still a stranger. What did she know about him, and what would it hurt if he told her? Once she'd entered this car, she crossed the threshold. She couldn't be in any more danger now than she already was.

"My last name is Kent. I'm a clandestine field officer for the CIA."

She turned his way, eyes alight, as if seeing him anew. A moment passed. "Who are you?"

It sounded silly, like requesting the same information he'd just provided. But in truth, it was the most logical question to ask. "You guessed military originally. Not that far off. I joined the Army just after college. Two tours overseas, a promotion. Then I was offered the chance to trade in the fatigues for..." He looked down at his clothes. "Well, I guess the uniform depends on the day."

"Why join the CIA?"

Kent took a breath. He was a little shocked to realize he'd never actually asked himself this question. It'd always seemed so basic as to be understood. And yet...did he really know?

"It's impossible to fully understand what you're getting into. There's information, things you'll never see or hear until you commit to the agency. Even then, data arrives in crumbs, trickling secrets. Your whole life becomes 'need to know.'"

Kent paused, aware he was beating around the bush, circling the truth like a confused guide. "I joined the CIA because there's nothing more precious than human life. The agency isn't perfect, but it's better than its reputation. Overall, not much different from most other groups of talented people, working together, trying to do the right thing."

"Those men last night were trained killers," said Allison. "And we survived. You're not like most others."

It came out as a compliment. Which was, Kent knew, how she meant it. He shrugged. "Sometimes luck gets lazy enough to land on me."

She paused. "How do you do that?"

"Do what?"

"Sarcasm, self-deprecation. I wouldn't think there was room for comedy in your field."

Kent returned her gaze. His weary eyes held a shade of mirth. "You take trips, I tell jokes. We all have a way to keep from going crazy."

The hills outside dominated the landscape, each approaching peak slightly higher than the last. Allison studied the darkness for a few moments, then turned back to Kent. "Why are *you* here, in Europe?"

He shook his head. "Not your problem."

But it was her problem. As soon as she'd entered this car, she'd committed to becoming a target. He looked across; she hadn't responded, but, eyes still on him, didn't appear satisfied with his short answer. A few second's deliberation and he decided to give her a longer one.

Kent cleared his throat, gripping the wheel a little tighter. "It all began with an accident..."

34

Five hours later the stars had given way to a blue-gray sky, its pallid sheen pierced by the glow of a waking sun. The surrounding hills were now full-scale mountains; their snow-capped summits glistened like white crowns.

Slowing the Volkswagen, Kent made a right turn off the main motorway, then a quick left. The new road, like the last, was hugged on either side by rows of tall evergreens. The neighboring peaks slowly became harder to see as the asphalt sloped upward.

He stared through the windshield as the sun continued to split the clouds. In his peripheral he could see Allison, knees folded to her chest, taking in the landscape. *With a new perspective.*

Her old one was obsolete; every aspect of life changed once you knew the massive attack it was under. She'd listened, with surprising calm, as he'd described Orion and the key and canister. Linz's violence had prepared her for this. The information was horrific, but—at the moment—still just information.

Once he'd finished, the cabin went silent, each of them thinking. Minutes later she fell asleep again. She'd just woken up half an hour ago.

Now the Volkswagen was leveling out; soon it broke through the trees. Ahead, a small village came into view on the mountainside. Pulling forward, Kent entered a parking lot to the right and shut off the engine. He motioned for her to exit, and they met at the back of the car. "Welcome to Soglio," he said.

Allison stood still, gazing through her fake glasses at the town. He'd told her where they were headed, but words didn't quite do it justice. They were just inside the Swiss border. The scene ahead could've been the centerpiece of an alpine postcard.

Narrow, cobbled lanes wove through a quaint maze of buildings. Most of them were modest in size, their slanted roofs blanketed with wooden shingles. To the right, a steeple rose toward the sky. "The Church of St. Lorenzo," he offered, following her eyes.

"It's beautiful," she said, quietly. Talking any louder felt like a sin against the setting. There was only one other car in the lot; no other people were visible. Other than the rush of a morning wind whipping down the mountain, they were surrounded by silence. She slowly turned his way. "How did you find this place?"

Kent gestured ahead. They started walking up a small road toward the church. "A couple years ago," he said, "I flew to Milan to track down a lead on a smuggling ring. Ran into trouble with a local arms dealer. His men trailed me through the mountains. This was my refuge."

"Did you know it was here?"

"Once I got close. Too many signs and tourists to miss."

"We passed other buildings, other towns. What made this different?"

He eyed her with a slight grin. "I'll show you."

Reaching the church, they turned left toward the center of the village. Both wore jackets donated by Roland, which were now zipped to the hilt. Soglio sat at 1100 meters; despite the sun's increased presence, the temperature hadn't reached 40 degrees.

Minutes later they were still walking in silence. Allison continued to take in the town's architecture; Kent was more concerned with its inhabitants. So far, they'd only passed a few locals, receiving nothing beyond a cursory glance. The day's tour buses had yet to arrive, but early-morning hikers were a common sight.

Still, they needed a story. "Can you speak with an accent?" Kent asked.

Allison turned to him. "Why?"

"Even folks in Soglio get the news."

She thought a moment, nodding. Another pause. "I played an Irish maid in high school drama class."

"That'll work." Kent arranged the details in his mind. "You'll be Sophie, I'm Colin. We met in Dublin a year ago and are celebrating the anniversary with a trip through the Alps."

"My lilt may be a little rusty."

"You'll be fine. Neither of us will have to say much anyway."

On cue, an old man walking toward them waved in greeting. "Bonjourno."

"Bonjourno," returned Kent, doing his best to mimic an Irishman's timid Italian. "Bonjourno?" asked Allison, once they'd passed.

"The border with Italy's just two kilometers west. Most of the residents speak Italian."

They walked along quietly, gaining an intersection and turning right. Gradually, across the new street, a weathered sign came into view: *Orologi di Calatini*. Kent gestured to it. "Our destination."

Crossing, they neared the front entrance of what looked to be a simple house. Large windows—cut into a façade of stone and wood—swallowed the incoming natural light. "'Orologi,'" continued Kent, "is Italian for 'clocks.'" They climbed a short set of steps to a humble porch. "This shop's proprietor, Enzo Calatini, hid me that first day." He reached the front door and took a few soft raps.

"Would he be open this early?" asked Allison.

"No, but he's up."

Seconds later an old man, at least eighty, walked around a corner and peered ahead through a pair of glasses. When he saw Kent, a slight smile crept onto his face. He unlocked the door and pulled it open. "Yes sir?" he asked in quizzical Italian.

"The street's empty, Enzo. We weren't followed."

The smile quickly widened as he waved them through in thickly-accented English. "Please, please, step inside."

They filed into a modest rectangular room. Hardwood floors and a purchase counter shared space with several clocks, displayed on various tables and all four walls. Sunlight filled the space, illuminating dust particles as they wafted through the bright, thin air.

Locking the door, Enzo gripped Kent's shoulders and studied him. "You look good, Jeremy." He glanced up. "But your eyes…they're older."

"Occupational hazard. You, on the other hand, haven't aged a day."

"And you're still a good liar. Another occupational hazard, I suppose." Enzo rubbed his face. "I'll take it. Blame the wife's cooking. New recipes—taste like mud, but less wrinkles."

Kent smiled and gestured to his left. "My companion, Allison."

Enzo held out his hand. "Lovely to meet you, my dear."

"The same," she said, accepting.

They moved further into the room. "Any other visitors?" asked Kent.

"Not yet."

"It may not happen anyway."

"I'll be ready, just in case."

They continued around the corner from which Enzo had emerged. Kent looked to the right at a door marked *Bagno*. "I'm afraid we don't have time for chit-chat."

The old man gripped his friend's hands. "Less is more, Jeremy." He smiled. "You know where to find me."

A nod as Enzo turned and strode through another door. Kent pulled Allison toward the partition he'd been eyeing and opened it. She stared inside. "The bathroom?"

He flipped on a light and gestured through. "Please."

A second later they were both inside, the door closed. The space was small: toilet left, sink right; wood walls and ceiling. "One moment," Kent said. Bending down, he removed a loose plank from the floor. Below it was a metal lever. He reached inside and pulled it toward himself. A muffled 'click' sounded through the wall. Replacing the plank, he stepped onto the toilet and removed a similar board from the ceiling. Another pull from an identical handle yielded the same result.

Re-covering the gap above and dismounting, he pushed on the far wall. Almost magically a seam formed, eventually widening as the panel slid inward. Allison, entranced, found herself obeying as Kent signaled forward. All that lay ahead was darkness, its dim mystery impervious to the bathroom's meager glow.

They crossed the threshold onto solid ground. He reached toward what she assumed was a wall and flipped two switches. Immediately the bathroom light shut off and a nearby bulb blinked on. He then shifted the partition closed. Beside the door, matching levers protruded from a concrete wall. Kent pushed them back in place and familiar clicks sounded.

Ahead lay a cement stairway, illuminated by the single bulb and descending toward a heavy wooden door. He nodded for her to follow and led the way down. She began hesitantly, then increased her pace as the steps proved dry and level.

Once at the bottom, Kent bent down to the left. He ran his hand along a dark section of wall, beyond the light's dim glow. Reaching inside a small crevice, he fingered an object and pulled it out. A metal key. Allison couldn't help but feel a pang of excitement, like they were hunting for treasure or traversing the bowels of a haunted mansion.

Kent slid it into the door's tarnished handle and turned clockwise. Pushing forward, he flipped on another light inside and ushered Allison through. Before locking the door behind, he pulled a switch down at the bottom of the stairwell to douse the bulb. The lights that led their way now left no trace of their location.

The square room ahead, though, was hardly a chest full of gold. Like the stairway, it was small and spare. A concrete floor and walls gave way to weak lighting hung from a low ceiling. Temperature wasn't much warmer than outside.

The entry door filtered in from the left side of the chamber. Directly ahead, three plastic chairs and a card table sat caked in dust. To the right, a crate filled with canned food straddled the far wall beside a pair of cots. Kent glanced at Allison. "Perhaps you'd like some details."

"That would be wonderful."

He nodded toward the ceiling. "Enzo moved here from Italy as a child during World War Two. His father had heard about Hitler's concentration camps and was afraid Mussolini would follow."

Kent walked across and switched on a small lamp near the cots. "They moved in to the house above shortly after arriving in Soglio. This room was a storage area." He strode back to her side. "Enzo's father quickly had it sealed with a new bathroom, though he kept a secret passage."

She looked around the room with fresh eyes. "A hiding place."

Kent nodded. "After the war they maintained it, entrance and all. Enzo said his father thought they'd need it again. He was less sure himself, but did the same after dad died. Just in case."

Allison stepped toward the chairs. "You continue to use it?"

"Only when I have to. Soglio is a convenient spot, near the center of the continent. Most people in town don't know about this room." He brought her to a corner and flipped open a metal box resting in the shadows. Inside were several bundles of cash and a black pistol. "Turns out it's still a pretty good secret."

Allison's looked confused and gestured up. "He won't take it?"

Kent shook his head. "Doesn't' even come down here anymore."

"How do you know? How can you trust that?"

"Because he trusts me. Enzo doesn't need the money, doesn't want the trouble." Kent glanced at the cots. "Why don't you get some sleep. I'll wake you if he comes."

"Who?"

"A friend."

"My, you've got them everywhere."

"Not like this."

35

Allison woke at the sound of a distant click. She sat up and saw Kent at the door. He was holding the gun. She pulled a small blanket off. "Someone coming?"

He put a finger to his lips and motioned for her to stay still. Just outside, soft footsteps could be heard on the stairs. Soon they stopped and a series of knocks sounded near the bottom of the door. Two raps, a short break, then another two.

Kent immediately stowed his gun, unlocked the door and swung it open. In stepped a man around the same age as Kent, perhaps a shade taller. Once he cleared the door, it was sealed shut again. The man eyed Allison for a moment, then turned to Kent with the slightest hint of a smile. "You're crazy."

"No choice," said Kent. "We'd gone to Roland's, the police might have known."

The man swung back to Allison. "Allow me to apologize for my partner. He hasn't had a date in years. Evidently roping in hapless females for jaunts across the Continent is plan B."

She stared at the entrant. "Partner?"

Kent faced her and gestured to the man. "Allison Shaw, James Baker. Same employer. He cheated on the test, though."

"I was copying off of you."

"First mistake."

"Of many." Baker reached his hand toward Allison. "A pleasure, Ms. Shaw."

She accepted. "So you've been after Orion for five years too? Undercover from the beginning?"

He raised an eyebrow. "I see Jeremy's subjected you to all of our secrets. Yes, I started at ground zero. Give or take six months, to allay suspicion." He flashed a distant look. "Surprised we've made it this far, actually."

Kent brought the chairs closer. "James's cover as a turned agent is still intact."

"Barely," said Baker. "I've been sequestered in London. Consider this visit a violation of parole."

"We're honored." Kent gestured toward the seats. "And interested. Any news?"

Baker folded into the nearest chair. "You mean I wasn't invited for my charming personality?"

"Is that what they're calling it these days?" Baker grinned as Kent shuffled toward the crate of food. He returned with a few bottles of water and handed them out. "Are you still being kept in the loop?"

"Yes, probably as a precaution. Kerr can't have me deaf and blind if they suddenly need another hound on the hunt. It may not be every detail, but it's enough."

"What's the story on Tanaka?"

Baker's face stiffened. "Scharp has a contact with the Linz police. Tanaka's body hasn't been ID'd yet. License and passport were deemed fakes. They're moving on to DNA."

"That won't get them anywhere."

"Neither will the Beretta that washed upon the shore of the Danube. Audi's clean too—no prints. You're still a ghost, in the flesh and on the computer."

"Are they on the move?"

Baker nodded. "West. Kerr and Ryov have figured on London for some time."

"Only logical."

"They're also saying you have the antidote."

Kent reached into his jacket and pulled out the canister. "I touched my pocket a few times during the chase in Linz, just to make sure. Berger must have seen."

Baker was quiet, almost reverent. "And the key?"

"Buckingham Palace."

Allison straightened. Baker nearly choked on his water, then allowed himself a smile. "Why not?" He sobered. "But how did you…"

"The rescheduled tours."

"Ah."

"I'm sorry?" asked Allison, trying to keep up. She'd taken her own seat long ago, but still felt like an outsider.

Kent turned her way. "The interior of the palace is usually only open to view during August and September, when the Queen is on holiday at Balmoral. Last fall, though, she got sick and came back to London early, cutting off the tours.

"This month, she returned to Scotland for a couple weeks. Tours resumed in her absence. I caught the last day, hid the key inside."

"Actually, that's a perfect spot," said Baker. "Secure, low foot traffic. Accidental brilliance, I'm sure."

"How do you plan on retrieving it?" asked Allison.

"The Queen's birthday celebration. Two days from now."

Silence enveloped the room. Baker eyed Kent. He seemed on the verge of a quip, then decided against it. "Okay. If you're sure, you're sure."

Kent sighed. "It's the only way."

"What about getting there?" asked Baker. "You obviously have a car."

"I haven't decided on the Channel, but we'll go through Paris. Need a passport."

"Marcel?"

"Yes. I'd like to avoid the city, but…"

"He's the best."

Another pause. "How will you get into the palace?" asked Allison. "There's got to be heavy security for something like that."

Kent simply grinned. "I know a guy."

Thirty minutes later Kent lay asleep on one of the cots. Allison, sitting across from Baker, ate her way through a can of pineapple chunks. Halfway finished, she dropped the plastic fork in the container and set it on the floor. "How long have you two been meeting here?"

Baker looked up from cleaning the gun Kent had been holding, a .40-caliber Heckler & Koch. "A few years," he said. "It's a bit theatrical, I know. But expedient." He looked around. "No bugs in these walls."

"Was it hard to slip away from England?"

"Yes." Baker paused from the gun, looking up at Allison. "I joined the fray in Europe and was recruited by Kerr shortly after Jeremy. Too short, as it turns out. These last few days...my head's been inches from a silver platter. Like I said, I only have a chance because of my specific knowledge and skill set. I *might* still be needed.

"I've been under twenty-four-hour surveillance from the moment I stepped onto British soil. Once I got Jeremy's message to meet, I turned my collar up and started coughing. Then some cold medicine from Tesco, make sure my admirer across the street sees the purple bottle. I took it straight back to my hotel, the Bedford.

"I've seen the staff for a few days now. I'd bet my life—I suppose I have—that none of them are undercover MI6. But Kerr might have access to indoor security footage. I couldn't just use the nearest hallway and walk out the back door.

"So, when I returned to my room I stayed there, until after midnight. Then I edged out the window. I was on the third floor. I used the sills below to climb down the rear façade. There were mostly trees in the quad behind the hotel. It was dark; easy enough to disappear."

Allison's eyebrows had risen a moment ago and stayed there. *Easy*— that's not the word she'd have chosen. And the hotel was just the first step. "You still had to fly."

Baker nodded. "Out of Gatwick, at dawn. I bought a passport years ago for private use. Not too many flags raised for a cellist from Prague."

He reached into his hip pocket, pulling out a cell phone. "The real issue is this. I have to assume it's bugged, and tracked. A while back I managed to slip it to an agency programmer stationed outside Rome." He glanced at the screen. "Now I just key a cover location. Today, any device reading this signal thinks I'm still in London."

"What about the meeting time?" asked Allison. "How do you know when?"

"There's a man named Charlie, manages a cigar shop in London. I'll spare you the details, except to say he's on our side. When one of us needs to meet here, we call him and place an order. He leaves a message for the other, saying it's on the way. The combination of cigar type and number determine the date and time of the rendezvous."

"So much work," Allison said after a moment. "Is it really necessary to meet like this?"

"Afraid so. Our opponent isn't just a man, or men. It's an entire intelligence network. Most of Europe is tangled within a web of electronic surveillance. Face-to-face is about the only option left."

"What about having a programmer doctor your phone again?"

"Apples and oranges. It's one thing to reroute a signal, quite another to mask whole conversations." Baker paused. ""As for the content, it's paramount that Jeremy and I share information. We've got to be on the same page. This operation, by necessity, only carried the bones of a plan. Most of it has been two agents reacting and improvising, and bailed out by luck on more than one occasion."

"*Luck*." She glanced at Kent. "I'd say both of you are modest to a fault."

"If only that were our chief vice."

Allison thought about resuming her pineapple, but wasn't finished. "How long have you known each other?"

Baker casually resumed cleaning the gun. "Just the length of this mission." He smiled. "So, a lifetime. Our situation...we were the only ones on this continent who really knew what the other was going through. We may not have been close by the map, but in every other way it didn't take long." He took a breath. "Has Jeremy told you his background?"

"He joined the Army after college."

"That's right. Stood out quickly, too. He had a rare combination of intelligence, strength and drive. Special Forces material. But the CIA snatched him up first."

"And you?"

"Born and raised just outside Philly. Graduated from the police academy near the top of my class. Early on I felt they were grooming me for leadership, or something more tactical. Personally, I had my sights on the FBI. Things just went a bit more international."

Allison glanced down at the gun. "I assume you and Jeremy had similar training." She hesitated. "Do you ever wish..."

"That we could switch places." It was a statement, not a question. "Every single day. It's killing me to sit on the side, watch him—now the two of you—go through this."

She paused. "How did you decide who would steal the antidote?"

"Jeremy was stationed in Amsterdam. About six months ago he got rear-ended. Pair of guys, too much to drink. Once insurance was mentioned, they started throwing fists. He let them get a few hits in, for show, but eventually had to put both on the ground. He kept his movements simple, no technique. Just a clumsy street brawl.

"There were a few witnesses, a police report. It all went away quietly, but Kerr got nervous. After that, it seemed he had a hair's more confidence in me than Jeremy. That was enough to make one of us expendable, and keep the other an inside man."

"What about grabbing the key yourself, now?"

Baker shook his head. "Jeremy'd never agree, and frankly neither do I. We may need whatever leverage I still have with Kerr. If I'm even suspected of making a play for the key—and there's really no simple way to get inside the palace—it's game over.

Baker had finished cleaning the gun and putting it back together. Now he laid the weapon aside. "I'm just a glorified cheerleader. I hate it, but it's all I've got left. This continent is like a chessboard; we're running out of moves."

Allison sat back, her gaze soon resting on Kent again. Baker leaned forward. "How'd you end up with him? This is not a club anybody wants to join."

She was quiet for a moment. "I guess it never would've happened if I hadn't come over here. I flew to Europe on an overseas project. An *opportunity*." She paused once more, trying to find the right words. Finally, a smile forced its way onto her lips. "I wanted to be part of something bigger than myself."

Baker gestured around the small, cold room. "Well, Ms. Shaw, mission accomplished."

36

People-watching, Ryov had decided, was a lost art. Everyone seemed far too interested in themselves to care or even notice what others were doing around them. This, of course, was exactly what he wanted and one of the reasons he'd chosen this particular bar. But the trend still nagged him. And it wasn't just Brussels; the entire world had suddenly become starved for attention.

A thought for another time. Right now, sitting near the end of a long string of wooden tables, the Russian did his best to look like a tourist enjoying the liveliness of Belgium's capital. The bar itself, *A La Morte Subite*, was nearly a landmark. Its tall ceiling, supported by square columns jutting up from the center, looked down on a vibrant collection of the city's eclectic population. Nicotine-stained walls glowed a deep yellow in the thick lighting that bounced off numerous mirrors

11 p.m. had just rolled around, and the place was still packed. And loud. Another reason it'd been chosen. Ryov sat back and sipped his Chimay Blonde; it had a strong hop flavor. Trappist beers weren't his first choice, but he'd drunk worse, and the bar was known for them.

Gazing casually at the crowd, he soon spotted Scharp coursing through. The burly Swede had traded his purposeful gait for long, relaxed strides. Ryov stood as they shook hands. "So glad you could make it," he shouted over the surrounding din.

"Wouldn't have missed this for the world."

They sat down and continued the small talk. A waitress appeared from the direction of the room's long, wooden bar. Scharp pointed to Ryov's beer and she returned shortly with the same for the Swede. They sat quietly, drinking and picking at a plate of cheese and sausage Ryov had ordered. Both sprinkled in frequent comments on everything from football to the weather.

About to finish off his beer, Ryov spied their final member and smiled widely. Seconds later, after greetings were exchanged, Berger folded into the seat between them. They flagged the waitress down to take his order and refresh the table.

Soon after the trio sat with full glasses, nothing more to the surrounding crowd than friends having a harmless drink. Ryov kept the smile but lowered his voice. "Anything?"

Scharp shook his head. "But the bulk of my contacts are west of Berlin."

The Russian eyed Berger. "Are you sure you hit him?"

A nod. "Right leg, at least a graze." He paused. "Maybe her too. The Honda they dumped had blood on the passenger seat. Doubtful they'd have been able to continue without getting patched up."

Ryov sat back. "Which means there's no way they've made England yet."

"Can we even assume they're still together?" asked Scharp, leaning in. "She's an anchor; if it were any of us she'd be gone."

"Not necessarily." Ryov took a sip of his beer. "Kent knows her identity's public, which means we could go after her. She's not safe."

"But what if he didn't tell her anything? He jeopardizes his entire mission to save a single life?"

Ryov continued to smile, though part of it was now real. "You have to remember, Kent plays by a different set of rules. You may think them stupid, but don't ever mistake his behavior for weakness."

A short silence followed. "So what's their next move?" asked Berger.

"The Channel is the key," said Ryov. "Planes and trains are too obvious, but there are only so many routes across the water. Kent's options will narrow considerably."

"I'd take the shortest distance," said Scharp. "The less time I'm stuck on a boat, the better."

Ryov nodded. "I'm heading to Calais tomorrow." He turned to Berger. "I want you further south, in Normandy. It's still a launching point for ferries and close enough to Kent's optimum path."

Scharp took a drink. "And me?"

"Paris. You have the most contacts there. It's unlikely Kent would risk such a public area, but if he needs certain supplies—a gun, or a passport—it's the easiest place to find them."

Scharp nodded in assent as Berger finished off the last sausage from the tray. Ryov took another drink of his Chimay. It was beginning to taste better.

37

Brushing the curtains aside, Kent gazed into the night. Lake Geneva's northern waters lay five kilometers ahead; beyond his sight, but surely sparkling under the silver moon. Closer in, the town of Lausanne radiated a soft glow.

They'd departed Soglio in the afternoon, an hour after Baker. Kent had steered the Volkswagen on a southern route through Switzerland, arriving near the French border at dusk. Some take-out pizza from a nearby restaurant capped the day's journey.

He pulled the fabric shut and turned around. The room was a healthy size, especially for Europe. This Novotel was a little busier than he'd have liked, but plain enough. A double bed highlighted the space's modern décor, surrounded by a desk, TV and stuffed chair.

He was about to sit down and rub the stress from his eyes when Allison appeared from the bathroom. She wore a purple two-piece pajama set. A small remnant of steam followed her out as she flipped off the antechamber's light.

Kent caught himself staring a little too long, and looked away. Whether she noticed the movement or not, Allison was hesitant, fighting the awkwardness of the moment.

They couldn't sleep in their clothes; the wrinkles would start to build up, and they'd stand out. Allison's outfit covered most of her body, but pajamas were still nightwear. Being exposed at Roland's was simply trauma and recovery. This felt different.

"What's the verdict?" asked Kent, hoping to deflect some of the tension.

She managed to eye the clothing. "Comfortable...though I might've chosen a different color."

"Call it lavender. Maybe Roland has a thing for flowers."

She started to smile, then stopped as she noticed the single bed.

"I'm sleeping on the floor," he said.

"I guess I didn't think about it. Are you sure?"

"Absolutely." He walked forward and grabbed one of the pillows. Stepping between the mattress and the door, he dropped the cushion on the ground and removed his jacket.

Allison pulled the top blanket off the bed. "At least take this."

Kent held out a palm. "You'll need it."

"And you'll just have that."

She was nodding to his own ensemble, the same tee shirt and pants he'd woken up in at Roland's. "They're warmer than they look."

He strode into the bathroom, splashing a few handfuls of water on his face. She was sitting up in bed when he emerged. "We're going to Paris tomorrow?"

He stepped forward. "Yes, but not for long. Have to keep moving."

"Who's Marcel?"

"Marcel Molyneux, French black market. If you need something special in Paris, there's no faster way."

"And I need a passport?"

He nodded. "For England. Not part of the Schengen Area."

"What about you?"

He walked to a duffel bag, filled mostly with clothing from the brothers and cash from Soglio. Fingering a side zipper, he retrieved a small maroon booklet and handed it to Allison. "Miro Vakkuri. I'm a Finnish professor. The pouch of my jacket protected it from the Danube."

She studied the document, then looked up. "What do you teach?"

He thought for a moment. "Haven't decided."

"Well let me know when you do. I might need to enroll."

It was just an innocent joke. *Or was it?* Silence arrived as she handed the passport back, their eyes locking. Kent forced his gaze away. "Get some sleep. It's been a long day."

"Wait." He'd turned toward the door, but now spun back. "One question," she said. "I'd just like to know the hands my life is resting in."

Kent was about to brush her words off as overly dire, then realized they were about right. "Okay."

She took a breath. "Where were you born?"

He raised an eyebrow. "That's your tell-all question?"

"My mom likes to say you haven't met anyone until you know where they're from."

He moved back to the bed and sat down on the edge. "Winfield, Kansas."

"I don't suppose you'll take it personally if I've never heard of it?"

"I'd be worried if you had. Though last I checked we did put in a second stoplight."

"Center of the state?"

"Bottom edge, about forty miles south of Wichita."

"Still, the heart of the heartland."

Kent nodded. "Geographically, I'm about as American as they come."

"Are your parents still there?"

"You said one question."

"I lied. Now we're even."

He paused, the whisper of a smile on his lips. "Yes, they're both still there. Dad in a house at the edge of town, mom at the cemetery down the road."

A shadow passed over Allison's face. "I'm sorry."

Kent waved it away. "Cancer, ten years ago. She's in a better place."

"What about your father?"

"A strong man with a soft heart. Part of it'll always be broken, but he's mended the pieces enough to get out of bed each morning."

"And you?"

Kent looked into Allison's eyes. He could see in them genuine interest, but also the fear that she'd overstepped her bounds. He put worry to rest with a disarming tone. "Forgive the cliché: my mom was the best in the world. Full of comfort, security, love—everything a growing boy needs." He paused. "I enlisted a month after she passed. Think I wanted her death to mean something."

"Did it?"

"Yes and no." He patted his chest. "She's always close. But we live in an imperfect world. Sometimes bad things just happen."

Silence. After a moment Allison changed tack. "What does your father think you do? You've been over here all this time."

"I graduated from college with a BS in civil engineering. My dad thinks I'm in the middle of a long-term construction project on an Army base in Germany. I call or e-mail when I can."

"In your situation? Is that safe?"

"Par for the course for a clandestine officer. Kerr understands the game better than anyone. Part of our play was hiding as little as possible from him, to strengthen our credibility."

"Doesn't this put your father in danger?"

Kent shook his head. "He's over four thousand miles away. Even if Ryov or the others took the detour and threatened me with his life, they'd still have to find me to deliver the message. Simpler just to put a bullet between my eyes."

Allison paused. "You haven't made that very easy."

It's early. He swallowed. "What about your parents?"

She shifted on the bed. "Dad's a lawyer, mom's a teacher. They're both smart, healthy, strong enough for…"

"For this," finished Kent, looking around the room. "For not knowing whether their daughter is alive. I'm sorry you couldn't call, even to tell them you're okay."

She nodded. "I understand."

Suddenly there was nothing left to say. He stood. "Goodnight."

"One more thing," said Allison. She focused directly on him. "Thank you for saving my life. I never told you, back in Linz."

"You never had to."

"Because it's your job?"

Kent shook his head. "My job is not to involve you in the first place." He shrugged. "Which of us is perfect?"

He turned the room's lights off a second later. Complete darkness was held at bay by random strands of moonlight. Allison laid down; Kent did the same. He felt his heart beating a little heavier than usual, its steady drum receding within like an elusive memory.

A moment later the rhythm was interrupted. "Thank you," said Allison, her soft words cutting through the silence. "For the bed."

"Of course," he managed.

"Are all spies such gentlemen?"

"You should see us in our tuxedos."

38

They approached the City of Light under an overcast sky. Looking across, Kent noticed Allison gazing through the windshield at the skyline ahead. He thought about asking if she'd been here before, but it really didn't matter. Paris was Paris, on your first visit or hundredth.

Right now, though, he cared about the city's population more than its architecture. More people meant more eyes, a greater chance of being detected. Their stay here needed to be brief.

The Volkswagen wove through heavy afternoon traffic that'd be even worse in a few hours. Soon Kent pulled off the E05 Motorway and into the heart of the city. He scanned each street as they passed, steering the car toward Montparnasse in the city's 14th arrondissement. After a turn down a narrow lane, he stopped along the curb and shut off the engine. "Ready?"

Allison nodded. They both exited the car. Walking over to her side, Kent grasped her hand and led her down the sidewalk. Sophie and Colin were still their best disguise.

Thirty meters up he guided her across the street toward a five-story concrete building. Its first floor appeared to be a café. No outdoor seating, but busy inside. Reaching for the door, Kent followed Allison through. The atmosphere within was much closer to a New York deli. A line of customers snaked toward a front counter, where several young men moved quickly back and forth, slicing meat and preparing sandwiches.

The pair stepped in line and soon reached the front. Directly ahead lay a glass case displaying several types of meat and cheese. The attendant behind wiped both hands on an apron and looked up with an expectant face.

Inspecting the spread, Kent leaned forward and replied in French. "Two roast beef and brie." He waited a moment as the man put his head down and went to work. "And I'd like to see Marcel."

"No one here by that name," said the man without looking up.

Discreetly laying fifty Euros on the counter, Kent kept his voice low. "Tell him it's Jeremy."

The man stopped. He eyed the money, then Kent, for several seconds. Finally, he muttered something to one of his partners, collected the cash and disappeared around a corner. The sandwiches were quickly finished; Kent paid for them and stepped aside with Allison.

A moment later the man returned and walked over. "Outside, around the corner. There's a door ten meters down. Knock three times."

Kent nodded. "Merci."

They strode out and began tracing the sidewalk. "Food in front, document forging in back?" asked Allison

Kent calmly eyed the street's other occupants. "Café's a cover for money laundering. Marcel's cousin runs it. A perfect setup, though I doubt he wants it that busy."

"The police don't know?"

"Some do, but Marcel's white-collar. Doesn't hurt anyone, and he's been smart enough to avoid helping wanted criminals. Always bigger fish to fry."

Soon a steel door came into view. Taking one more look around, Kent rapped on the barrier. A moment later it opened slightly, revealing a massive man in a black leather jacket. He examined the pair with a trained scowl, eventually settling on Kent. "She stays outside."

"No," Kent said flatly. "She stays with me."

Pausing for another moment, the man offered a disgruntled wave forward and they were through. He locked the door behind, then turned and motioned for them to raise their arms. Kent nodded to Allison. They each complied.

The guard found nothing on her. He moved to Kent and gripped the Heckler & Koch a second later. Meeting Kent's eyes, he pulled the pistol free and stowed it in his own jacket. The search continued, but produced nothing further. The guard then motioned forward and led them down a dark, concrete corridor.

Things soon opened, and brightened, onto a large room. Two overhead lamps bathed the space's worn hardwood floors in yellow light. Muted walls backed a row of thin chairs set in the corner. Across, a stone counter jutted out from the near wall.

Against this last partition leaned two men, both smaller than the first but owners of the same hard look. They straightened upon the trio's arrival. Neither appeared surprised.

Once he reached the center, the big guard flashed a palm at Kent and Allison and strode past his colleagues toward another door at the back of the room. A second later he was gone and the space filled with silence, its four occupants wordlessly measuring one another.

The standoff didn't last long. The tall sentry soon emerged, followed by two more men. The first had the same look and air as the guards near the counter. The second, slightly shorter, wore softer features. Gliding past the other men, he extended his hand. "Jeremy."

Kent accepted the offering. "Marcel."

Their host glanced around the room. "Forgive the cold reception. My men don't know you like I do."

"Does that mean I can have my gun back?"

"Not before you leave. Standard procedure." Marcel smiled. "You could probably kill us all anyway, but at least we'll have a fighting chance."

"You always did know how to flatter a guest." Keeping the grin, Marcel turned to Allison. "My companion," said Kent, gesturing with an open hand.

The Frenchman bowed slightly. "Mademoiselle." Staying on her for a moment, he eventually brought his eyes back to Kent. "I assume you're not here for a marriage license."

"We need a passport."

"Just one?"

Kent nodded. "For her. Finnish if possible."

Marcel looked back and forth between them again. "Don't ask, can't tell?"

"You wouldn't care anyway."

"I wish I were that self-absorbed. Life would be simpler." Marcel checked a silver watch around his wrist. "How soon do you need it?"

"Very."

A moment of thought. "I can have it ready in an hour. Discount for a familiar face. Two thousand Euros."

"I'll give you five if you make it thirty minutes."

The Frenchman exhaled slowly. "Done."

Twenty-five minutes later Kent and Allison sat in two of the chairs against the back wall, each fingering a can of soda. She had managed a few sips, but the anxiety of the moment kept the sandwich on her lap unopened. She saw Kent's was identical and wondered if it was for the same reason.

Just one of the guards was with them until the big man stepped through the far door. Leaning against the counter, he muttered something to his partner in French. A few more lines of dialogue and Kent suddenly straightened. Both men turned as he spoke to them in the same tongue. The smaller guard responded and Kent stood, offering what sounded like an order. Glancing at his oversized counterpart, the sentry abruptly turned and strode out the back.

Sixty seconds later Marcel entered with the three other guards. Approaching Kent, he handed over the finished document. "Something we said?"

Kent flipped the passport open, scanned the pages, and tucked it in his pocket. "Forgive me. Something's come up." Motioning for Allison to stand, he reached in his jacket and gave Marcel a stack of Euros. "Six, for the rush."

The Frenchman passed the notes to one of his underlings, then gestured to another, who returned the pistol. "*Bon chance.*"

Kent simply nodded and began pulling Allison toward the exit. Beating them to the door, the big guard slid it open and they stepped into the gray light. The pair crossed the street amidst a sea of fellow pedestrians; Kent's gait was a step short of frantic.

The far curb came and they continued toward the car. Allison wanted to ask what was going on. It was obviously serious. She decided to wait, hoping Kent would explain when he was ready.

"They were talking about another guard," he said abruptly. "The man had just eaten a large lunch, but went out for something more."

She rolled the information over in her mind. They reached the Volkswagen and climbed in. "You think he told someone about us?"

Kent gunned the engine. "We can't afford to assume otherwise."

The car jolted forward. He pushed it as fast as possible without drawing undue attention. Soon they were at the Boulevard Peripherique, then back on the E05. Increasing his speed, Kent merged into the westward traffic tracing the city's southern edge.

Several miles later downtown Paris was just a speck on the horizon. Allison glanced behind, then to Kent. He appeared calm, but she couldn't help wondering what defensive machinations his brain was cycling through.

"This could be nothing," he said. "I *hope* it is. But chance is never a friend. Not where we're headed."

"I understand," she said, turning her gaze toward the front windshield and the asphalt beyond. "Still Le Havre?"

He nodded. "It's a full ninety miles from the English coast. Not the most obvious place to cross the Channel."

39

Twenty minutes on things were still quiet, though hardly ideal. The road seemed to be collecting new cars by the minute. Kent fought to maintain a steady pace. Above, the plain sky had grown angrier, its gathering clouds beginning to pelt the concrete with an arsenal of fresh droplets.

The Volkswagen accelerated past a semi. Kent gripped the wheel firmly and divided his gaze between the soaked windshield and rear and side mirrors. He'd yet to spot anything suspicious, but it was impossible to monitor all of the roadway's moving parts.

Across the cabin, Allison sat focused. Neither of them had spoken much since Paris. It was agonizing—watching, waiting for a phantom threat that might never come. Kent had learned to wear the discomfort; Allison's wardrobe was brand new. In deciding to come along, she'd subjected herself to the relentless broadsides of a clandestine life. Even if it only lasted a week.

Considering all of this, she was acquitting herself admirably. Other than ten white knuckles gripping her vinyl seat, she displayed no outward signs of panic. Still, Kent felt the urge to say something. "Distance is an ally. The more road we put between ourselves and Paris, the less chance something will hap—"

Two gunshots. Kent heard neither, but their impact was impossible to miss. One busted the Volkswagen's right taillight, its counterpart shattering the back windshield and driving into the center of the dashboard. A cloud of nightmarish déjà vu instantly filled the cabin.

Allison instinctively recoiled against the passenger door. Kent shot a glance toward his drivers-side mirror. He barely had time to look as a second pair of rounds sounded. The reflector was blown off its mount just before the front passenger-side window burst into a dozen pieces.

Allison gasped, cold wind and rain rushing inside. Kent frantically swerved away from where he thought the shots had come. He scanned for a threat—nothing. Half the surrounding vehicles seemed not to notice, maintaining their speed and position.

Removing his gun, Kent glanced at Allison. A few cuts from the glass, but she was alright. "Stay down!" he yelled. He floored the gas, speeding past a freight truck. The sedan cleared the lorry's front grill and he peered left. Just in time.

Surging out from the far side of the truck, a man on a motorcycle—his identity hidden behind a dark-lensed helmet—veered across and fired three shots toward the Volkswagen. Kent jerked the wheel right. Two of the bullets dented the left hubcap; the third demolished his drivers-side window before thudding into the upper half of Allison's door.

They were now desperately skidding across the pavement. Kent sent two shots the other way before cutting behind another large truck. Both bullets, more defensive than deadly, blistered the bike's undercarriage for minimal damage.

Shielded for an instant, Kent saw Allison ducking low and holding on. He thought about trying to outrace their attacker, but knew the Volkswagen's four-cylinder wasn't up to the task. *It ends here.* One way or another.

Despite the continued gunshots, several vehicles—especially the bigger trucks—remained oblivious. Others sped up or slowed down, but there was hardly space to move. Glancing around, Kent found an open seam and threaded the sedan toward the center. He didn't see the bike until it was nearly on top of them.

He lifted the HK and let loose two quick rounds. Both made contact, sparking off the bike's back end. In the next instant time seemed to stop. Kent had his adversary painted, his finger poised on the trigger. Then the car in front of them slammed on its brakes. Suddenly, there was only time to react. To choose.

He dropped his aim and swerved, just scraping around the oncoming vehicle. The Volkswagen shook from the contact and he lost his grip on the pistol. It fluttered to the floorboard near his feet. At the same time, their assailant quickly sent a burst low and hit his target. Kent felt the sickening dip of a tire deflating.

Too many bad things had happened too quickly; it was hard to keep the misery straight. The motorcycle—having backed off momentarily—now sped in for the kill.

Kent's mind raced. The HK was somewhere at his heels. *If I can reach it...or maybe Allison could...*

There was no time for either. They were already slowing, the punctured rubber struggling over its asphalt track. He heard the bike's approaching whine a mere ten feet outside his window. Surrounding traffic continued to move, but they were in an open pocket. No cover, no weapons.

Kent stiffened. *One weapon.* Immediately he jammed the pedal down. "Hold on!"

With the motorcycle gaining on his side, Kent slammed the brakes and jerked the steering wheel severely left. The Volkswagen, its modest horsepower taxed to the limit, screeched over the wet pavement. As it turned, its back end swung forward and around like a battering ram. The motorcycle was moving at over 100 kilometers per hour; its rider had no time to react.

The side of the sedan's trunk smashed into the bike and sent its occupant flying forward. In the same motion, Kent pounded back down on the accelerator. The Volkswagen jolted forward with new life, its injured tire now a bald rim sparking against the concrete road.

Meters ahead, the rider tumbled over the asphalt but popped up quickly. His helmet had been knocked off, and Kent immediately recognized Gunnar Scharp. The Swede, staring back, raised his gun as the Volkswagen sped by.

No shots came. Instead, every ounce of Scharp's attention was arrested by the roar of an oncoming tractor-trailer. It was heading directly toward him, and much too close to stop in time.

In a flash, he dove to the right just as the truck's large wheels rolled past. Any celebration was cut short, though, by an SUV keeping pace on the far side of the truck. Man and machine saw each other too late, and the result was a predictable explosion of flesh against surging metal. Scharp's body disappeared beneath the car, but it was clear life had already left him.

Kent caught the entire scene through his rearview mirror. He turned toward Allison, who'd been looking back. She now swiveled forward with a trembling hand over her mouth. Death was ugly, no matter the victim.

Wind and rain continued to swirl through the interior. Kent stole a final look back: between the errant motorcycle and dead body, screeching brakes and headlights dominated the highway. Police would arrive soon. Had anyone seen his plates? Nothing he could do either way.

But the car, with its jagged windows and missing tire, was a virtual spotlight. He angled toward the next exit and guided the Volkswagen onto a side road. Checking around for a break in traffic, Kent steered the sedan into some grass behind a line of trees.

By now Allison had gained control of her breathing. Her eyes, however, were still wide with shock. She slowly wiped a sheen of rain from her face and turned to Kent. "You'd think I'd be used to this."

"Forgive the pun, but it takes a bit more than a crash course." He flipped up his collar and opened his door.

"Are you changing the tire?"

He nodded. "And clearing out the broken glass." He scanned the cabin. "There are no bullet holes on the outside. Taillight and body damage are common enough. It won't be pretty, but we'll survive."

He pulled the trunk release lever and climbed out into what was now a complete downpour. Stepping toward the back, he was about to reach in for the spare when he saw her approach. He grabbed a musty blanket and held it over her head. "Stay inside. No reason for you to get soaked too."

She looked into his eyes. "I already am."

Kent stared back for a long moment. Finally, he nodded. Five minutes later the spare was on. He lifted the punctured original into the trunk while Allison used a tire iron to clear out the windows and wipe away the loose glass.

The rain continued as they re-entered the vehicle. A handful of cars had passed during the repair process, but none noticed them through the foliage. Flipping his headlights on, Kent carefully steered through the wet grass and back onto the E05.

40

They'd driven for more than an hour when the lights of Le Havre began to creep over the darkening horizon. It was still mid-afternoon and the rain had slowed to a drizzle, but the sky remained near-black. Guiding the car over the wet pavement, Kent kept the radio on. Word of the crash had come through minutes before: twelve vehicles, one fatality. So far, no mention of a battered Volkswagen.

But that was now a secondary concern. Over the past eighty kilometers, Kent had forced the car through more than one toll barrier. Each time they'd used an un-manned booth, but cameras still caught the plates. Would the right people put the correct pieces together in time? He took a deep breath. *Probably not.* The odds were still good that he and Allison would be over open water by the time anyone even found the Volkswagen.

A quarter hour later they'd officially entered Le Havre. Kent wound his way onto Boulevard Jules Durand, paralleling the city's extensive port system to the north. A handful of turns later they were tracing Avenue Lucien Corbeaux. When the ferry came up on their left, it was hard not to stare. Surrounding gray swells lapped innocently against its massive hull; the blue and white vessel was more cruise ship than transport boat.

It was also no longer an option. Scharp might've reported his position, and theirs, back on the E05. Le Havre was a likely destination for many on that roadway. If Kerr or Ryov even suspected they'd taken the ferry, an ambush could be waiting across the water in England. Or even here, in France.

Kent's mind searched for other options as they crossed through a roundabout and headed west. The first task was dumping the car, away from the ferry. After passing over a short bridge that spanned an inland basin, he turned right and followed the body of water north. Soon a lot appeared on the right. He quietly pulled into a space.

It was a busy part of town, but the weather kept the sidewalks nearly empty. The drizzle had thinned to a heavy mist as more black clouds hung low. Pulling the key from the ignition, Kent reached toward the back seat and grabbed a shirt from the duffel bag. He ripped it in half and handed a piece to Allison. "We'll wipe down the interior, then outside."

"For fingerprints?"

A nod.

She started on the dashboard. Kent climbed outside and pretended to stretch, scanning the landscape. There was a fair amount of traffic, but few pedestrians and nothing suspicious. He ducked back inside and helped her finish the front console. They moved toward the rear next.

Two minutes later they completed the exterior at the trunk. Stuffing the shirt scraps into the duffel, Kent slung the bag over his shoulder. No windows meant no reason to lock the doors. He led Allison away, taking one final glance at the trusty sedan.

Then he froze. "No." It was a whisper, as if his breath had been choked away.

"What?" she asked, alarm and confusion sharpening her voice.

Remaining silent, Kent forced himself through the stiffness of shock and strode back toward the car. Each grueling step matched a prayer that he was wrong, that what he saw wasn't what he thought it was.

No such luck. On the underside of the trunk, its solitary red light flashing off the wet pavement, a quarter-sized disc protruded from the car's metal frame. Immediately Kent stole another glance around. Still nothing. Grasping Allison's arm, he again led her away from the Volkswagen, more briskly this time.

"What?" she asked once more, obvious fear now shaping the word. She craned her head back toward the trunk. "What is that thing?"

Kent maintained his pace. At the same time, he released her arm and reached into the duffel bag. Pulling out a small stack of Euros, he stuffed them in her jacket pocket before she could react. "If anything happens," he said, looking around again, "hail a cab and have it take you to the U.S. Embassy in Paris. Contact your family from there."

Rising tension colored this command, but Allison simply shook her head. "I don't understand. Wha—"

"Promise me," said Kent, stopping and eyeing her directly. "Promise me you'll do this."

Staring back for a long second, she finally nodded. "I promise."

They continued moving. "That disc," said Kent, "was a tracking sensor. Scharp must have fired it between gunshots. I never heard it."

They traced a line of shops on the right as Allison began to look around herself. "Does that mean they know where we are—our exact location?"

"The car's exact location. If the signal went to anyone other than Scharp."

"Do you think it did?"

He was about to mutter something about probabilities, but quickly relented. "Yes."

Kent had to suppress a desire to pull out his HK. They were still, for the moment, the same old Irish couple strolling through Europe. This could just blow over; he might not even need the gun.

He steered Allison toward Rue de Drapiers. Beyond lay further streets and heavier traffic. The more people the better. They also needed to put distance between themselves and the Volkswagen.

The meters stretched like miles. Ahead, the commotion seemed impossibly far away, but Kent knew they were close. Glancing to the left, he quickly swung back as a flash in front caught his eye. It was a reflection, faint, from a ground-level window straight ahead. He spun behind to find its source, but saw nothing through the mist.

His heart was pumping, thick beads of sweat sliding down his spine. Still, nothing had actually happened. The reflection could've been anything.

For the briefest of moments, he doubted himself, doubted his ability to feel a threat before it surfaced. Such a skill had been driven into the marrow of his bones the moment he'd joined the—

Kent heard the steps before he saw them. They were light, quick— almost like a child. In the next instant Berger burst through the curtain of mist, sprinting forward with his pistol out.

Kent jerked Allison ahead as two shots cut the wet air. He felt each bullet tear through the edges of his jacket and rapidly pulled out his own weapon. A third shot sounded just before he emptied a chunk of his clip toward the German. The duffel bag plowed into Kent but was thick enough to stop the deadly projectile; his own barrage pelted the walls and pavement around Berger. The desperate spread delayed their opponent enough for them to swing around the next street corner.

Scattered screams pierced the empty void. The few pedestrians nearby either ducked or ran for cover. Out of the attack line for a moment, Kent pulled Allison past a salon before cutting left around the edge of a café. He wanted to tell her to run but couldn't let Berger intercept. He dropped the duffel and spun with his gun up. Inching toward the corner's fringe, he peeked out.

Nothing. Same for the next ten seconds. Other than an occasional muffled scream, the area swiftly attained a chilling silence. After his third check of the street, Kent glanced behind Allison to make sure Berger hadn't doubled back. Swinging his gaze forward again, he was about to lead her away when his body tensed. This time he didn't hear a thing.

Like a lion Berger surged around a low-lying apartment building on the left. Just ten meters away, he had his gun trained and fired two rounds.

Kent's first instinct was to push Allison away. The only other thing he had time for was a frantic tilt of the head, which was just enough. Both slugs cracked into the wall beside his right ear. Seeing his shots miss, Berger aimed again but was thwarted by a frantic volley from Kent. Despite his forced hesitation, the German barely broke stride as the bullets sparked the pavement near his feet.

Now almost on top of his prey, Berger dove forward instead of shooting. Kent shouted for Allison to run just as his attacker rammed him into the concrete wall. They hit with a violent thud, each man losing the grip on his weapon. Both guns clattered to the ground.

Berger recovered fast and swung his left arm at Kent's midsection. Kent blocked the attack just in time to see his adversary send his right fist upward. A quick duck. The German grunted in pain as his knuckles collided with the wall.

Kent took the open window, knifing his hand into Berger's throat and driving his boot into the German's midsection. The burly attacker staggered back and was rapidly cut down by a sweep of Kent's leg. By now Allison was still sprinting to the left down the alley. Kent saw his gun lying several feet in that direction, but his opponent's, on the right, was closer. He dove for it.

His fingertips were nearly wrapped around the handle, but he came no closer; a brutal kick from Berger loosed the grip and cut his legs out from underneath. The gun was still in reach. Kent waited to see Allison round the far corner, then lunged again for the handle. The delay proved costly—Berger launched another kick, this time toward Kent's face.

The impact jarred him to his back as the German, completely ignoring the pistol, jumped onto his opponent's midsection. Kent's nose was busted and bleeding. He looked up through blurry eyes; the scenario was painfully familiar. Berger, though, wouldn't bother with strangulation this time.

Balling a fist once more, the German swung his arm toward his victim's right side. Kent hardly saw the move and thrust both hands out to block. As if expecting this, Berger instantly shifted left and connected with two blows to the kidney. Kent grimaced, but had no breath to yell. A final chop to the face marred his vision further.

He looked up through splotches of light and darkness. Berger quickly pulled a knife from his ankle and wasted no time in cutting it in a savage arc toward his victim's jugular. Kent was powerless to stop the attack. He watched the blade slice down in a blur, faster than a guillotine.

But still slower than a bullet. Before the jagged steel could cover the final inches to his neck, the back of Berger's head exploded. Bits of blood and brain matter splattered across Kent's face. He noticed the German's eyes go empty, their leaden host slumping onto the pavement like a rock. In his place, several feet down the alley, stood Allison.

A dose of adrenaline cleared Kent's vision. He sat up and stared. She was motionless, breathing rapidly, pointing his pistol forward like a terrified statue. Kent forced himself up. Staggering to the duffel bag, he took another look at Berger to confirm death. It didn't take long. He darted toward Allison.

She was trembling, eyes glazed. Kent wondered if she'd even seen him approach. Gently he pushed the gun down and removed it from her hands. The daze lifted. She caught her breath as he stowed the weapon. Without looking back, he wrapped an arm around her and led her away through the mist.

41

Luc Bouchard exited the café clutching the sandwiches like a bag of gold. They were that good. Easily worth the time to stop. *Like you're on a schedule.*

In a way, though, he was. Vacations should never be about hurrying, but how could you not when your destination was the Cote d'Azur?

Weather was incentive enough—both the paradise he was headed toward and the overcast dungeon he currently found himself in. Heavy rain had morphed into a fine mist over the last two hours, but fresh clouds above seemed anxious to start a second wave. He sidestepped a puddle between claps of thunder and prepared to cross the street ahead.

Before the chance came, a police car abruptly sloshed by. Its lights were flashing, the telltale siren piercing the dense air with its signature melodic wail. Bouchard followed the vehicle with his eyes, then glanced back toward the café. Had those been gunshots?

He'd heard a handful of distant cracks while waiting in line for the sandwiches. His first thought was a small car accident or dockworker dropping a crate. There'd been no reason to assume anything worse. Now he wasn't so sure.

But what can you do? Bouchard let the issue go, resuming his trip across the pavement. He was curious, but not enough to further endure such a dreary port. Whatever the trouble, the police surely had it under control. There was nothing left for him to do but leave. He angled toward the harbor.

Two minutes later the water came into view. Its dark swells were plentiful, but not nearly as rough as they could've been. And nothing his sweetheart couldn't handle. He caught her in the distance and smiled:

twenty-five meters from bow to stern, nearly brand new. *LadyMine.* People often asked him about the name: "Which lady do you mean?" His answer: "All of them."

Closing in on the portable gangway, Bouchard spotted his captain, Serge Duval, sneaking a cigarette near the bridge. "You're clouding your pallet," he said, holding up the sandwiches. "These things deserve a blank slate."

"I think you're confusing me with someone who cares," muttered the seaman, without removing his smoke. "Maybe one of your chef friends at *Le Cinq.*"

Bouchard kept his grin. Duval was the kind of seasoned officer— mid-fifties, salt-and-pepper hair—who only seemed at home on the water. Nothing got the man too excited, but he cleaned up enough for their ritzier stops and knew how to handle a boat.

Bouchard gained the *LadyMine*'s deck. "I'll win you over." He turned toward the interior. "Are we ready?"

"Five minutes. The boys are prepping her."

Bouchard nodded. *The boys.* A first mate and cook, the latter doubling as an engineer. He knew he could've gotten by with even less—two crewmen, maybe just Duval. But there were plenty of berths, and no plans for guests other than the occasional—hopefully frequent—female border. This trip was about doing the least amount of work as possible. The extra help was worth it.

Bouchard snaked through the lavishly appointed living room and state-of-the-art galley, laying the sandwiches on a marble island and continuing on. He wanted to switch his damp jacket for a dry sweater.

Descending a short flight of carpeted steps, he turned to the door of his master suite. Closed. *Didn't I leave you open?* He reached for the handle and pushed through.

The last thing he expected was still a welcome sight. A young, attractive woman lay in the center of his bed. Her black skirt rode high up a smooth thigh, while the teasing corner of her blouse had slipped over the edge of a bare shoulder. Bouchard prided himself on a polished approach with women, but the surprise in front of him stole every word. It never occurred to ask how, or why, she was aboard.

"I hope I'm not interrupting," she said. *In English.* American? Right now, he didn't care.

Bouchard took an involuntary step forward. "Of course not. Welcome to—"

The door closed behind him, it's lock clicking in place. *Something's wrong.* He spun to see a man with a beaten face leaning against the wall, cutting off his exit. The dream faded. As if seeking confirmation, he turned back to the bed. The woman was already covered up and sitting on the edge, a million miles from the sultry specter of a second ago.

There was no time for anxiety; fear cut directly into Bouchard's stomach. He spun back. The man broke the silence. "Relax, Luc. If we wanted to hurt you we'd have done it by now." He spoke French. Clean, but accented. *Also American?*

A dozen more questions flooded the Frenchman's mind. For a second, curiosity trumped caution. "How do you know my name?"

The stranger gestured to a desk in the corner. It held a framed certificate, as well as a pen and neatly stacked paper. "Not too many attorneys with their own stationary. And a yacht already...you're barely pushing forty." He straightened. "A bit odd to bring your law degree on board. Is that how you get the ladies to stay the night?"

Bouchard found himself confused. Who were these two? Thieves? He looked into the man's eyes. *No.* Thieves were gutless, rash. The stranger before him exuded a control several rungs above the common burglar. Bouchard's unease slowly gave way to interest. "How did you get on this boat?"

The answer was in the man's eyes. *It's what I do.* Suddenly the fear was back, melding with defiance. And yet...his legal mind couldn't bear the loose thread. He glanced at the woman. Her eyes had grown distant, as if in a trance. Back to the man. "How did you know she'd be a distraction to me?"

The man made a show of scanning the room. "Every picture in here frames your face, alone. A single lawyer from Paris with his own yacht—the odds were worth the risk."

Quiet. Bouchard glared at the man, soon backing away. "No," he said, shaking his head. "Whatever you're asking for, my answer is no." He turned toward a phone at the far end of the room. "This is my boat and you're not welcome."

The unmistakable sound of a pistol being cocked stopped him cold. He slowly spun around. The man took a step forward, calm still covering his face. The gun must have been tucked behind his back. "There's no reason for this to get ugly, Luc. But we're not asking. You're going to help us, conscious or not."

A tense silence followed, each man staring at the other. "Fine," Bouchard said finally. "What do you want?"

"Your boat, temporarily." He glanced at the woman, who'd stood and was inching his way. "We need to get to Newhaven."

Bouchard thought for a moment. "England?"

A nod.

"And where am I to go in that time?"

"Nowhere. Give an excuse for staying in your cabin, and the detour. No one else can know we're aboard."

Bouchard thought about asking why they were doing this, but already knew it was out of the question. "How can I trust you?" he asked.

Without hesitation, the man softly laid the pistol on a nearby dresser. A second later, the craft's diesel engines thundered to life. Bouchard stared back for a long moment, then turned to the phone and picked up the receiver.

"Speaker," said the man.

Bouchard pressed a button and the other end of the line filled the room. "Yes?"

"Serge, forgive me...this is going to sound strange. I'd like to detour north. Set a course for Newhaven."

There was a lengthy pause, uncertainty clouding the gap. "Whatever you say, Luc. It's your boat." Bouchard nodded reflexively, but didn't speak. "Anything I should be aware of?" pursued Duval.

The Frenchman leaned forward quickly. "No, just something to check off the list. And Serge, I've just been hit with a wave of fatigue. Going to stay in my cabin for...perhaps the entire trip."

Another pause. "Understood. Give us a few minutes to reroute and check the weather before putting her out."

"Of course. Patch me down to Pascal, will you?"

There was a short click, then another, higher voice came on. "Monsieur Bouchard?"

"Pascal, I'll be staying in my room for the next few hours. Please bring the sandwiches I purchased down, along with some fruit and tea."

"Very good, Monsieur."

Bouchard hung up. "Thank you," said the mystery man.

The Frenchman turned and nodded.

"Is Serge going to be a problem?"

"No. He's smart, but obedient. Cares more about his paycheck than anything."

A short silence passed before Bouchard gestured to both the man and woman. "What do I call you?" He mustered a weak smile. "This long of a trip, it could get awkward without names."

The stranger pointed at himself, then his companion. "I'm John, this is Jane."

Bouchard nodded wryly. A pair of Does. *Why am I the one being hunted?*

42

The rain had returned. Dodging heavy droplets, Ryov pulled his phone out and dialed. Kerr answered after one ring. "Yes?"

"I'm in Le Havre. Berger's dead."

A slight pause. "Kent?" The word was laced with controlled anger.

"Has to be. I walked past the body a minute ago. There's a crater in the back of his skull."

"How fresh?"

"Police just roped off the scene."

"Any sign of Kent or Shaw?"

"No, but they have to be close. The most obvious point is the ferry that just left for Portsmouth, though I doubt they're on it."

"Me too. I'll send a pair of men anyway." Another pause. "What about Scharp? There're reports of a pileup on the E05. Gunfire."

"No word." The Russian paused as he passed a few people within earshot. "He shot a tracking sensor onto Kent's Volkswagen. I found it here: bullet holes, spare tire, windows gone."

"But Kent was obviously healthy enough to get the car to Le Havre."

"No blood on the seats," added Ryov.

Silence cut through the line. "Call it like it is, Sergei. Kent's won a few battles." Kerr took a breath. "This is a war, though. He still, ultimately, has nothing."

"I agree." Ryov picked a break in traffic and crossed the street. "The finish line is the most dangerous. He has no choice but to race into the fire."

"How soon will you be here?"

"My plane lands at Heathrow in five hours."

"Good. There's something we need to discuss."

"Oh?"

"I think it's time to remove the chains."

43

Kent watched the last ounce of daylight slip over the horizon. Bouchard's cabin had a large portside window, offering a fading view of the channel's inky chop. The only illumination now came from the *LadyMine* herself, though the faint glow of England lit the distance.

It was just before 8 p.m. They'd made good time. He guessed the yacht had been cruising well above twenty knots since clearing Le Havre. It was as if the crew couldn't wait for this trip to be over. *How did they know?*

In truth, tension still hugged the air in the stateroom, but they'd settled into a relative truce. The food helped, and Bouchard had managed to procure a first aid kit without raising suspicion. *"I think I turned my ankle on the docks."* Kent's split face was now cleaned and bandaged.

Bouchard sat on the bed, idly flipping through a magazine. The Frenchman hadn't lost his irritation, but was also accommodating and made no attempt at escape. At this point he was a minor concern. Kent glanced across the room, at Allison.

She lay curled on a large chair, eyes still peering into empty space. The initial shock had worn off, and now her entire frame seemed hostage to a numbing weight. Kent knew the feeling. It all went back to pulling that trigger. She might've fired a gun before—with that aim, probably—but never killed anyone. That was something you didn't forget.

That was the greater benefit of training and experience, he realized. Not the ability to kill when necessary, but to let it go once you did.

Kent found it difficult to pull his eyes off of her. She'd made the choice to come along, yes, but she was his responsibility. *And you've failed her.* If not physically, then mentally; there was no first-aid kit with which to reach inside and heal her mind.

He stood frozen. Allison lay less than ten feet away, but the gulf between them suddenly seemed much greater. Everything he'd learned at the Farm and in the field was telling him to keep it that way.

The phone rang. Bouchard looked at Kent, then rose and walked to a small table. He picked up the receiver. *"Oui?"* A moment of listening. *"Merci."* He set it down and turned to Kent. "We're ten minutes out."

A nod. Kent wanted to reach London by the end of the night, and they were still on schedule. Ahead, really. Bouchard sidled over to the window, pausing at the blackened sea. Eventually he stole a glance toward Allison and lowered his voice. "What did she do?"

Kent almost smiled. *The meek captive grows bold.* It was a smooth attempt to slide in between himself and Allison, probably for no darker reason than simple curiosity. "Story's not for sale," he said. "We'll have to go with yours."

Bouchard countered with a shrug. "Afraid it's not too exciting. Well, most of it. Computer screens and courtrooms."

Kent raised a charitable eyebrow. "Most?"

The Frenchman took a breath. "I work eighty hours a week for eleven months so I can spend the twelfth sailing from Calais to the French Riviera. Have you ever seen Monaco in May?"

As a matter of fact... "I'll have to take your word for it."

Bouchard looked up and down Kent's frame. "It's a good fit."

Their host had volunteered fresh clothing. The two men were around the same size, and Bouchard had a few items left by a past female guest. Kent eyed Allison once more. "Yes, thank you again. We seem to be lucky in that department."

Moments later they entered the Ouse River. Newhaven harbor lay a short distance ahead. The town itself wasn't especially large, but its central waterway attracted plenty of shipping activity. Tonight, though, was quiet.

Above, the clouds began to split, allowing handfuls of bright stars to dot the water like Christmas lights.

The *LadyMine* floated smoothly up the channel, its diesels churning at a much slower rate than before. Angling to the right past the port authority office, the yacht soon kissed the east quay near the town's border checkpoint. Bouchard turned to Kent. "They may come aboard."

"We're leaving." Kent strode to the far side of the room and lifted the duffel bag. He spun to the bed, unzipped the sack and pulled out a stack of Euros. "Ten thousand. I know you don't need it, but it's all we have to give."

Bouchard studied the money, then turned his head to the door. Faint voices echoed from the dock, growing louder. "More eyes than when you got on. How do you plan on exiting?"

"Keep your crew together, near the front of the boat." Kent noticed Allison stand. His first thought was of a hypnotized pet—obedient, but only slightly aware of the situation. Then he saw her face. A measure of focus had entered her eyes, seeds of recovery piercing the prevailing haze. It was like a fever breaking. He took a breath, relief invading his chest. "Do you have a blanket?"

The question was directed at Bouchard. Puzzlement colored the Frenchman's face before he conceded, shuffling to a nearby closet and retrieving a navy cover. Kent directed him to hand it to Allison. "Thank you," she said, rolling it under her arm. The words were clearly for more than bedding.

Bouchard swiveled to Kent. "I could still yell, or run. Now you trust me?"

"Now we're on land. More options for escape." He grabbed the gun off the dresser. "But you passed the test. Next time I might even leave this loaded."

Bouchard couldn't help but grin. "Anything else I can do for you?"

Kent slung the duffel over his shoulder. "Just remember your ankle's injured. Limp a little."

44

Five minutes later they were free, slinking away from the lights of the dock amidst the shadows. Allison marveled at what a little misdirection could accomplish. They didn't even have to run.

She clutched the blanket in her right arm; Kent held her left hand and led her forward. She hadn't shied away when he'd reached for her. The act was a reflex by now. Or maybe more.

No. Allison shook the thought from her mind. She glanced to the left, across the water. The west quay showed plenty of recent development. Large apartment buildings towered over Newhaven marina, the latter's countless berths occupied by all manner of watercraft. On the opposite bank, it felt like they were walking through an industrial graveyard. The east quay was functional, simple; she could see it looking much the same fifty years before.

Still, it had its charm. A row of quaint, modest dwellings lined the right side of the lane they traced. Ahead, where the path met a larger road, more housing was visible. Windows glowed yellow; a pair of neighbors chatted between their front doors; cars buzzed along the quiet streets.

Kent scanned their surroundings—casually, relentlessly. Everything was a potential threat: the dark, open lot to their left, the man walking his terrier on the right. Allison found herself strangely calm. She wasn't afraid. Not with such a man beside her.

The tremors, though, remained. Intermittent, rumbling deep within her. Scharp had been one thing—violent, but distant. Not so with Berger. She couldn't get the image of his head out of hers: the bullet making contact, the skull rupturing into a mass of red and white.

All because of her. Because of something *she* did. But there'd been no other choice. *Why doesn't that make this easier?*

She stowed the weight, realizing they'd reached a quiet area. Homes still hugged the road to the right, but no people were visible. Suddenly Kent released her hand. "Stay here." He dropped the duffel at her feet and jogged to the left.

His destination seemed to be some kind of bus depot surrounded by a chain-link fence. No lights shone within. Several of the large vehicles sat idly. The business was obviously closed.

Reaching the fence, Kent scaled it and dropped silently to the other side. Allison looked up and down the road: no traffic. She didn't dare leave her post, but peered in closer through the fence. Amidst the buses she caught a slit of his jacket and what looked to be a car. An anxious moment passed. She spun around, knowing a sea of front doors were just feet away. *How would I explain myself?*

No need to wonder as Kent returned and climbed back to the street side. He hustled over, clutching a pair of license plates beneath his jacket. One was white, the other yellow. He stuffed the plates inside the duffel and motioned forward.

Twenty feet ahead, a lone Peugeot sat parked near a cable shop. They began angling toward it. Instantly a pair of headlights cracked the darkness ahead of them, approaching steadily. Kent linked his arm in Allison's and walked her past their target. "Smile," he said, turning her way. "That's what couples do on evening strolls."

She obeyed. The car passed without incident, steering left and disappearing behind the houses. Immediately Kent turned her around. "Not much time." They hurried back to the Peugeot and he motioned her toward the passenger side. Again she complied, listening to him work the door in the darkness.

Allison considered the fact that they were stealing a car. *Commandeering*—that sounded better. Though the owner was still going to wake up empty-handed. The act didn't bother her so much as her indifference to it. *Desperation is the mother of delinquency.*

Pop. Kent had the door open a second later and unlocked the rest. Allison jumped inside, throwing the blanket in back with the duffel bag. She'd forgotten about the cover, in a way. Why did they need it?

She buckled up just as the French sedan pulled into the street and headed north. She allowed herself a sigh of relief, and thought she heard Kent do the same. *We're just part of traffic now.* The escape was complete.

Soon they reached a large intersection and Kent cut through to the A26. He increased his speed, the space around the road opening up. Little by little homes and businesses gave way to fields and trees. Five minutes later Newhaven was a memory, traded for the mystery of a looming black night.

The first thing it held was a stop. Near a bend in the road, Allison noticed a few structures to the left; Kent doused the headlights and turned right, slowing onto a gravel drive. It was quiet, deserted. One hundred feet ahead he pulled to the side, leaving the car running. "Three minutes," he said, stretching in back and removing the license plates from the duffel bag.

She peered forward. They were surrounded by flat, open land. A soft glow warmed the distance, maybe a house or barn. Still plenty far away. She turned to her side mirror, catching a glimpse of Kent just as he kneeled at the bumper with the yellow plate. Sixty seconds of gentle tinkering and he made his way toward the front with the white marker. Same time, same result.

He was walking back to the door when she glanced at the car's clock, its invisible seconds ticking by behind a digital readout. The number changed. *Three minutes.* She wondered what it was like to achieve precision so casually. Then she realized there was nothing casual about it.

Kent climbed inside, stowing the Peugeot's original plates in the duffel. "That should buy us enough time, even if the car's reported tonight." He backed up toward the road, waited to turn on the headlights until they were off the gravel, then headed north again.

They drove in silence. Above, the sky had completely cleared, its moon washing the landscape in bright shafts of silver. Allison stared into the Peugeot's headlight beams, hypnotized by the car's steady hum along the road. How were they still alive? Surviving today alone felt like summiting Everest. Yet, somehow, she sensed the gauntlet was only now thinning, preparing to offer its greatest obstacle.

The clock had hit 9:30 p.m. when they slowed at the outskirts of a village. "Where are we?" she asked.

"South Godstone," said Kent, quickly veering left off the road. "Still about twenty miles from London."

She looked around. They were tracing a small drive, lined by foliage and wooden fencing. Ahead looked to be a small parking strip, beyond it some kind of structure. She remembered a sign she'd noticed at the turn. "The train station?"

"Just borrowing the lot," said Kent, backing into a space. There were only two other cars present, both empty. "For a couple hours." He took a breath. "Right now, neither of us looks the part of a refined tourist. Entering central London…I want the lobby of any hotel we enter to be as empty as possible."

He put the car in park, then shut off the engine and pocketed the keys. For a second they sat still, each soaking up the glorious inactivity. He turned her way. "We should get some sleep." Allison doubted she'd be able to, but nodded and reclined her seat. "No," he said, opening his door. "In back."

She followed him outside, slowly. "What?"

After a quick look around, Kent opened his rear door and put the duffel bag on the floor. "We can't be seen by anyone passing by. It could draw attention, even if they haven't watched Linz or Le Havre on the news." He climbed inside and unraveled the blanket. "Come on."

Allison hesitated before opening her own rear door. She studied the backseat. The Peugeot was a decent size, but no Lincoln. "Not much room in there."

"No choice, princess."

She glanced around herself before stepping in. There was only one way to do this. Kent lay on his back, his jacket balled into a pillow behind his head. Ignoring the awkwardness of the moment, Allison lowered herself into his lap, resting her head on his chest. As if to seal the arrangement, Kent folded the blanket over the top of them, covering every appendage. Without much movement, they could easily pass for birthday presents, or a pile of junk.

Allison was more comfortable than she expected. It wasn't just physical: once again, she felt safe. Would Kent allow himself any sleep? How did he know when to wake up?

Quickly, she realized she wouldn't be conscious long enough to find out. Fatigue, and a thousand future thoughts, slid from the forefront of her mind. The last to go were the tremors themselves, powerless against the onslaught of such welcome, if temporary, peace.

45

Kent steered the Peugeot across Westminster Bridge just before midnight. Paris and London on the same day. *Not even a souvenir.* Unless you counted a battered body and face. He touched his cheek reflexively. The bandages had been removed half an hour ago. He still felt conspicuous.

A glance at Big Ben. Its lofty tower glowed orange, crowned by a rim of pale green light. To the right, stately offices looked out over the Thames like immortal diplomats. The river itself sparkled under a clear sky, its patented murk made clean by the darkness.

There was little traffic to disrupt the scenery. For a city its size, London turned in early. Areas with pubs and clubs still held life, but the government district ahead was quiet. They'd be even better off once they distanced themselves from the main roads.

He began the process by turning right onto Victoria Embankment. Sitting on his left, Allison straightened. She was drained beyond description, but remained focused. They'd gone over the routine. Just one more test.

Despite their recent nap, the red brake lights ahead seemed to blur in his own vision. He shook off the haze in time to see Hungerford Bridge growing near in the gloom. Just before reaching it, Northumberland Avenue came up on the left and he turned.

More government behemoths presented themselves, this time squeezing the road from both sides. Kent checked the stone facades from his periphery. His eyes may have lapsed, but every other sense was heightened. Kerr and Ryov had to know they were coming. Needles in a haystack, perhaps, but nevertheless they'd entered the lion's den.

Soon the Nigerian High Commission came into view; he made another left onto Great Scotland Yard. The small road curved through to Whitehall, but the Peugeot stopped shortly after entering and nestled against the right-hand curb. The street was empty, just as he'd hoped. Cutting the engine, Kent took a breath and looked at Allison. She nodded.

They exited without a word. He began wiping down the car's exterior, she the inside. An occasional vehicle passed along Northumberland, its headlights projecting into the lane, compelling the surrounding shadows to dance. But no one came closer, and they quickly finished. Kent slung the duffel over his shoulder and grasped Allison's hand, walking her down the street without a look back.

Halfway through, they cut left along Scotland Place, then again onto Whitehall Place. Their surroundings were palatial, a living museum. Remove the modern cars and you could turn the clock back a century without blinking. It was impressive, and Kent found himself wishing for time to care.

Seventy-five meters up they hit another intersection and turned right. Their destination loomed ahead. Its unassuming entrance blended well with the neighboring architecture, but it was difficult to ignore a façade that dated to the reign of Queen Victoria. *The Royal Horseguards* was one of the most impressive luxury hotels in a city full of them.

By this hour, all the fanfare had moved on. They approached the front doors as a slight breeze rustled dual black flags anchored above. Allison spoke softly without turning. "Why here? Awfully high-profile."

Kent held the door for her. "Who in their right mind would choose such a place to hide?"

They pushed through the vestibule, entering the lobby in a hush. It wasn't cavernous, but still large. Elaborate crystal chandeliers dipped handsomely from the curved ceiling; plush red velvet furniture mingled with spotless tile floors. You could almost feel the five stars.

No other guests were present. *Thank you.* They turned left, toward the front desk. In the center an attendant—mid-thirties, probably the night manager—looked up with practiced timing. "Good evening." They even got a smile. No wide eyes at their clothing, though he did linger on Kent's battered face. "How may I help you?"

Kent placed his passport on the counter and summoned his best Finnish accent. "Miro Vakkuri. I have a reservation for three nights."

Taking the booklet, the man lowered his gaze and began typing on a computer. A moment later he looked up, lips forming a slight frown. "I'm sorry, sir. I show no reservation under Vakkuri."

Kent wrinkled his face in confusion. "Are you sure?"

A nod. "I checked twice."

Kent glanced at Allison; she obliged by meeting his eyes in mock frustration. He turned back to the desk, leaning in toward the computer. "Perhaps there was a misspelling?" He smiled sheepishly. "My secretary made the reservation. Details are not her strong point."

The man grinned, but stiffened behind the counter. He remained silent, clearly searching for the right mix of courtesy and caution. Kent beat him to the punch. "If I may offer some advice?" he said, gesturing to his face. "Don't go mountain-biking twenty-four hours before an international education conference. I'll have some fun making up stories for my colleagues."

It was a little thin, but it worked. The man's demeanor softened and he studied the passport again. "Allow me a closer look, Mr. Vakkuri."

"Thank you."

He punched a few keys once more, their plastic chatter echoing throughout the quiet chamber. Eventually he looked up, shaking his head. "I'm sorry sir. I find no variant spelling. There is also nothing made under your first name, nor for an alternate date of arrival."

Pausing for a second, Kent nodded. "Thank you for checking. I'm afraid, nonetheless, we still need a room. Do you have anything available?"

This was the greatest risk of all. A hotel like the *Horseguards* was no one's last resort, especially on a Friday night. The manager spoke after consulting his computer a third time. "I do have one room free, double bed. A late cancellation."

"Lovely." Kent offered a relieved smile that he barely had to force.

"Very good, sir." The man turned to Allison. "I simply need your companion's passport and a form of payment."

She handed over her documentation as Kent reached in his pocket. "I would prefer to pay cash."

A hint of surprise flashed on the manager's face, but he recovered quickly. "Of course." He searched the computer screen. "For three nights the total comes to…£680."

Kent was already sifting through a stack of notes. He laid £1000 on the counter. "The rest for expenses."

The man accepted the money. "Thank you, Mr. Vakkuri." He stowed the bills and collected the passports. "One moment while I make copies." Spinning, he disappeared through a door beyond the counter. An instant passed, which might've been laced with anxiety had their entire day not already strained the odds of survival.

Soon the manager returned and placed the passports on the counter, along with a registration form and pen. "Please fill in the marked portions." Kent did so and the man smiled. "Excellent, sir. Will you be needing anything else tonight?" He paused. "Perhaps the porter could bring up your additional luggage?"

It was the other elephant in the room. "No, thank you," Kent said, grimacing. "Our bags were lost on the flight from Helsinki. We've given the airline this hotel as a forwarding address."

The manager frowned, offering what appeared to be genuine concern. "I'm sorry to hear that, Mr. Vakkuri. We will certainly keep an eye out for your bags. If there's any further assistance the hotel can provide, I trust you won't hesitate to ask."

An assured smile graced Kent's lips. "Yes, thank you."

Satisfied, the man handed across a room key and mapped them toward the elevator. "It's the third floor."

Kent nodded and, with Allison, turned in the prescribed direction. A few minutes later they'd reached their destination. Unlocking the door, he ushered her inside and followed. She flipped on a light, revealing a comfortable, well-appointed space highlighted by the bed in its center. The bathroom rested left, while further up wooden furniture sat atop thick, red-patterned carpeting. Windows covered the far wall, their heavy curtains drawn. Kent walked forward and lowered the duffel bag to the floor as Allison sat down on the edge of the mattress.

He stood still for a moment, letting his body and mind relax. *Finally.* It felt like the end, like this should be victory. In reality, they'd just started. Fail now and every previous triumph was in vain.

Before it began, sleep. A heavenly word. First, though, he had one more task to complete. Why did it feel harder than all the others?

Moving carefully, he swiveled toward the bed and knelt before Allison. He let a deep breath go. "Thank you for saving my life. I never got to say it, earlier."

She let out an exhausted chuckle. "I hope we're not keeping score. Something tells me you've still got the upper hand."

He remained sober, staring directly into her eyes. "Why did you come back? In Le Havre...why did you turn that corner?"

The room fell silent. After a moment, she turned her head away. He could see from an angle her lips begin to tremble, eyes glistening. She gathered herself enough to speak, slowly, quietly. "Before I rounded the edge, I looked back. You were on the ground, getting hit. I forced myself forward, trying to run." She turned back to him, tears now coursing down both cheeks. "But every step I took became harder and harder, like weights on my shoes. I realized you still had the canister. If you died, so did everyone else."

Like the hotel in Lausanne yesterday, and the backseat of the Peugeot two hours ago, Kent's heart began beating a little stronger. He hesitated for a second, then slowly stood. Allison had stopped crying, but refused to wipe her eyes. He reached forward and gave her shoulder a light squeeze. It was all he could do.

He turned away, leaving her alone at the bed. And hoping, against every rule and reason, that one of her tears was just for him.

46

Walking through a stark corridor, Pete McCoy tugged down on his tie. It was early morning, but the patterned silk already felt tight around his throat. *Apparel imitating life?* Cute. He forced his mind away. *To where?* There was no escape from your entire world.

He'd tried, several times. A rare vacation, to Cozumel; frequent trips to the local bar; even volunteering at a homeless shelter. All diverting, but none distracting enough to take his mind off of Kent and Baker. And now, with the finish line so close, there was little room for anything else between his ears.

That's what he knew this meeting was about. It had to be connected, in some way, to the race against Orion. Why else would the agency director call just before midnight and ask to get together six hours later? Could some piece of news on the antidote's location have come available and somehow slipped his purview? Unlikely, but he was intrigued nonetheless.

McCoy reached a door at the end of the hallway and braced himself. In the next instant, he stepped outside into a grassy courtyard bridging the CIA's original and new headquarters buildings. The space was normally a pocket of peace, but today had fallen subject to a wintery invasion of spring. The forty-five-degree temperature nipped at the skin and was further chilled by a steady wind.

Fighting off a random gust, McCoy squinted through the dawn's gray light and strode toward a wooden bench in the center. On it sat CIA Director Thomas Vanning. His slight frame wrapped tightly within a wool overcoat, Vanning seemed unaffected by the cold. These morning sojourns were a constant for him, even when the ground was white.

Throughout the Orion operation, McCoy had reported directly to Vanning. But he still approached cautiously, not wanting to interrupt the patented focus which his boss had made a habit of channeling into tactical brilliance. Vanning got more mental work done in minutes of sitting alone than hours in a boardroom surrounded by advisors.

The director surely noticed McCoy, but didn't move, maintaining a rigid posture and staring into the distance. Thirty paces away, one of Vanning's bodyguards shivered near the semi-shelter of the far building. *They must have drawn straws.*

McCoy angled around a sculpture of large rocks jutting from the ground. He looked down as he passed. Were they bursting forth, or sinking back? He'd always wondered. Across the courtyard, Kryptos, the decades-old monument bearing a code that remained partially unsolved, seemed to wink in his direction. The whole area felt...uncertain. *Welcome to the CIA.*

Finally sitting down on the bench's left side, McCoy stuffed his hands in his pockets. Vanning still didn't move. McCoy glanced to his right. If, metaphorically, Vanning was the most powerful person in the agency, he was nearly the opposite physically.

When standing, he touched five-foot-eight—barely—with a thin mustache and short-trimmed dark hair. He wasn't particularly handsome and looked as though the weight of the ivy cap on his head might be too much for such a thin neck.

But who cared when you were the smartest man in the room? *Speak softly and carry a big brain.* McCoy had originally found it curious that Vanning would occupy such a high-profile position. Generally speaking, his particular talents and appearance seemed more suited to the assistant who provides brilliant insight but rarely shows his face at a press-conference.

As it turned out, Vanning's interpersonal skills reached well beyond the stereotype. He still hadn't graced the covers of *Time* or *Newsweek*, but no one at the agency challenged his authority. The man had a presence.

For a moment both of them were silent, the wind's hollow whistling their only soundtrack. Fifteen feet away a dogged squirrel descended a tree, determined to make a day of it. Finally Vanning spoke. "I suppose this is where I say something clever about the weather."

The corners of McCoy's lips curved upward. "You never were one for small talk, sir."

Vanning turned his way. "Thanks for coming, Pete."

"Of course. Though I'd be lying if I said I wouldn't have preferred it be three hours later in a warm office."

The director swung back, gazing forward. "There's always been something about this place that heightens the senses. Helps me think clearly."

"Is that what this meeting is about—thinking clearly?"

"In a way." Vanning paused, then finally cleared his throat. "What odds would you give Kent?"

"Of success or survival?"

"Is there a difference?"

McCoy gave it some thought. "I'd say one in a miracle."

Vanning slowly nodded. "So would I." This was not a flippant admission. The director's loyalty to and confidence in his field officers was acute. "Which is why I need you to start planning for him to fail."

McCoy flinched inwardly at the last word, despite already having considered it a thousand times himself. "I suppose we all do." *This can't be why he called me here.* "If Kerr manages to sell Orion, the United States is likely the buyer's prime target. We'll be facing an untraceable, unstoppable weapon."

McCoy said the words with a healthy dose of detachment. You had to. It was the only way to contemplate such a horrific scenario. In truth, though, they still didn't know the virus's full potency. Those secrets were locked away with Clarke and Boxler. Orion could easily be a more ruthless killer than even the gravest estimates predicted.

Which made the other half of the issue all the more vexing. To combat a threat of this magnitude, they needed a dream come true: every defense and intelligence agency, including the military, cooperating with unprecedented efficiency. But to this point, beyond McCoy, Vanning and a handful of suits on Pennsylvania Avenue, no one in America had even heard of Kent and Baker's operation.

That was how it had to stay, too. There were only so many people you could tell before the secret got out. A senator has one-too-many drinks at a cocktail party and lets the wrong word slip; a four-star general's misplaced document is left in sight of his aide, who's girlfriend is a reporter for the Post. It'd happened before. From the moment the public heard the word 'Orion,' the fuse from curiosity to mass panic would light faster than a firework.

McCoy had run through these thoughts in the blink of an eye, because he'd thought them all before. He still couldn't see the point of this meet. Vanning knew everything he did, probably more. "Sir, forgive me, but—"

"I didn't mean physical."

McCoy grunted to a stop. "What?"

The director turned back to him. "Your brain, Peter. If this goes south, it's all hands on deck." He glanced at the buildings figuratively. "You're one of my best officers. I need to know you can pivot mentally from the current operation to whatever future threats may form."

A long moment passed, McCoy's eyes slowly narrowing. "You think I'm too close to this—to *them*."

"Not *too* close, not yet. That's why we're having this conversation now."

Vanning possessed the rare ability to lace criticism with palpable empathy; every blunt word held a smooth edge. Still, McCoy felt a measure of defensiveness creep into his voice. "You've never questioned my objectivity on other missions."

"This isn't like other missions." The director kept his voice calm. "Two agents, isolated and undercover for half a decade. Hell, Aldrich Ames would've grown attached to these guys."

A long pause arrived, its discomfort stiffened by the stubborn breeze. "I'm not telling you to let them go," continued Vanning. "I'm just asking you to be able to."

McCoy spied the squirrel once more. It was emptyhanded, but still searching. "Fine," he said. "But I can't abandon all hope."

A glint of mirth lit the director's eyes. "Why do you think you're on this op in the first place?"

47

The sun was shining as Nathan Brooks stepped out onto Number 10's secluded front drive. Turning left, he gulped in a deep breath of fresh air. The isolation was intoxicating. No security detail, no motorcade; this was a situation his superior could only dream about.

Such was the benefit of working within the halls of executive power without actually having any yourself. Even amidst a throng of the public, Brooks knew only the most die-hard political junkies would recognize him. And even then, he was likely to receive nothing more than a superficial inspection. It was near-anonymity, and it felt like freedom.

He'd take it. The last four hours had been spent with Bradley and his team prepping—cramming—for the vote on education reform in the Commons next week. Brooks didn't mind working on a Saturday; that came with the territory. Less than eight hours before the Queen's birthday celebration, though, seemed to be pushing it. At least the PM had the presence of mind to break for lunch. Brooks needed to stretch his legs and clear his mind.

Reaching Downing's iron security gate, he passed through with a nod to the guards and turned right onto Whitehall. It was like merging onto a congested freeway. He was instantly enveloped in the crowd of pedestrians coursing up and down the thoroughfare. Some wore suits like him, others various uniforms. Most, though, were dressed casually, a good portion of them tourists.

Brooks continued forward as Whitehall changed to Parliament Street. He studied the people around him. They didn't have a clue. Some were happy, others straight-faced, but all remained oblivious to the cloud of death closing in.

Would you rather be one of them? A thought he'd had countless times. There'd be no foreknowledge of danger breathing down his neck, no taste of life's fast-approaching expiration.

In some ways, it wouldn't matter. Orion was a peculiar plague. Whether one was informed or not, there would be no buildup. The quiet now seemed slight, almost fanciful. But things would change, and instantly. Like a volcano moving from extinct to eruption in the blink of an eye.

Five thousand people could die in LA one morning, twice that in Seattle days later. Then the virus would ford oceans, mountains, all because some executive made a business trip to Hong Kong; a daughter visited family in Buenos Aires; a family planned their holiday in London. Orion wasn't human. It had no feelings. Death—abundant, absolute—would spread at a rate that was, more than anything, terrifyingly random.

The decision, Brooks realized, was easy. Of course he wouldn't want to know in advance. They might still have a slim chance at stopping it, but as each day passed he felt more and more unqualified for the job. Let someone else save the world. *Yet here you are.* If God existed, he certainly had a sense of humor.

Finally gaining Bridge Street, Brooks swung left and approached his destination. Like most everything in London, St. Stephen's Tavern had been around for over a century. Sitting in the shadow of Big Ben, the bar enjoyed a prime location and was frequently forced to denounce accusations of its illegitimacy as an authentic British pub. Not necessarily helping the cause was a gaggle of tourists peeking through the restaurant's front windows.

Brooks politely shouldered past the group and slipped through the entrance. Inside, he immediately stopped—partly to admire the décor, partly because there wasn't an empty seat in sight.

Expected, but still disappointing. He'd have loved to take a load off. Resigning the next several minutes to a standing stint at the bar, he began walking forward when he noticed, in the corner of his eye, a couple rising from a small table. Brooks almost tripped as he changed direction. Scrambling across the rich carpet, he quickly threw his jacket over one of the stand's open chairs. He glanced around to make sure the childish spurt hadn't jilted any other desperate patrons. All clear. He sat down with a sigh.

The table was strewn with empty plates and glasses, but a waitress soon came and started clearing them off. "Something to drink?"

Brooks leaned back in his leather seat. "Tanglefoot, please, and your fish and chips."

She gathered the rest of the dishes with a nod and strode away. He exhaled again and took in the surrounding activity. St. Stephen's was owned by Hall and Woodhouse, a local brewery that'd put some of its famous Badger ales on the menu. Tanglefoot was his favorite. Rich, but light enough, with a sweet finish. Imbibing during work hours wasn't common practice, but Bradley didn't care. Brooks had a tin of Altoids to clean his breath.

A moment later his waitress returned with the beer. She hadn't moved away three steps when he took a quick, appreciative study of the amber drink and tilted the glass back.

"What's a guy got to do to get some service around here?"

The voice came from his right. Brooks was immediately gripped by the fear that he'd have to carry on a labored conversation with a total stranger. Turning completely, he instead nearly choked on the liquid in his mouth as Kent calmly stared back from an adjacent table.

A thousand basic spycraft procedures flashed through Brooks' mind, none of which he was able to implement. Finally swallowing the measure of alcohol in his throat, he forced the look of shock off his face and formed what he prayed was a relaxed expression. "I wouldn't worry about that. They're rather good here, should be to you soon."

Kent looked away with a small grin. A second later Brooks spotted his waitress approaching with a plate of food. She set the fish and chips down in front of him. "Thank you," he managed to say.

She smiled, then shifted to the table beside and removed its lingering dishes. "Drink for you?" she asked Kent.

He thought about it, glancing toward the bar before returning his gaze. "Just a Guinness, please."

She nodded and stepped away. Once they had their privacy back, Kent again eyed Brooks. "Good to see you, Nathan."

The aide glanced around the tavern surreptitiously before focusing back on his neighbor. "I'd say the same to you, but there's no way this is safe. I might've been followed."

"Only by me."

Brooks was about to protest, then realized it'd be like a secondary school football team lecturing Manchester United on the fundamentals of scoring.

The waitress soon came back with Kent's black stout. After separate assurances from each man that he needed nothing else, she turned away a final time. Kent took a sip, then swiveled sideways. "You look surprised to see me. Did you get my message?"

"That you met with Baker, yes." He shrugged. "I suppose it just slipped my mind for a moment."

"C'mon Nathan, you're a better liar than that."

Brooks looked down from Kent, toward his food. How could an appetite flee so quickly? He slowly turned back. "We were dealt a rotten hand, Jeremy. From the beginning." A pause. "Forgive me—I never thought you'd make it this far."

Kent's face sobered. "Neither did I."

"Doesn't mean I'm not happy." Brooks took a breath. "Le Havre... was that you?"

Kent nodded. "Berger is gone, Scharp too."

"And Tanaka and LeRiche from earlier?"

"Yes," said Kent, taking a larger pull on the Guinness. "That leaves only Ryov, though I'm sure Kerr has a few suits up his sleeve."

"I agree. They'll be nothing of your caliber, but still capable." Brooks managed a sip of the Tanglefoot. "In your message you also mentioned that you still have your companion."

Kent nodded. "An unavoidable circumstance."

Brooks lowered his voice. "Where is she now?"

"At the movies."

The aide paused for a second, stunted by such an unorthodox answer. Upon further reflection, though, the cinema made perfect sense. A dark room with a defined, extended period of seclusion from the outside world. "What kind of film is it?" He had no idea why he'd asked the question.

"An adventure, nearly three hours long." Kent pointed toward Brooks' plate. "Your food's getting cold."

Brooks grasped the hint, reaching for a bottle of vinegar the waitress had placed on the table. He'd regained enough of an appetite to put a dent in the dish. At least the cod was fresh.

Five minutes later, a portion of his fish now gone, Brooks washed the mouthfuls down with a long drink of beer. He turned slightly back to Kent. "You said the movie was an adventure. Tell me it has a happy ending."

"I'm not sure. Haven't seen it all." Kent paused. "But I'd never say 'no.' The supporting cast is excellent."

Brooks stared across knowingly. "How do they support?"

"I need a favor."

"Something quick and easy?"

"Two invitations to the Queen's birthday celebration tonight."

Brooks was silent, his mouth slowly dropping open like a drawbridge. It crossed his mind to laugh heartily, but such an action required vocal chords that weren't frozen in shock. Whatever lines of dread stretched his face, they communicated far more effectively than words.

"I understand it's a tall task," said Kent. "You know I wouldn't ask if it wasn't absolutely necessary."

A short silence followed, the surrounding air instantly simmering to a boil. "Tall task?" Brooks felt an uncontrollable rise in his emotions, flush through his chest to the edges of his throat. "It's impossible! If I had a month to secure the spots it'd be doubtful. You can't seriously expect me to—"

"*Nathan.*" Kent's voice came through at just the right volume. Firm enough to wake Brooks from his frenzy, but still an anonymous slice of the surrounding din. The handful of heads that'd turned soon swiveled back.

Brooks calmed himself with a long exhale. "I'm sorry." He loosened his collar. "This stress…it's cumulative, you know? The threat of death doesn't disappear after each day."

Kent's face creased in sympathy. "I wish I could take it for you."

"Something tells me you've got plenty of your own." Brooks turned back to his food, forcing a few pieces into his mouth.

"I need the tickets to get the key," said Kent.

Brooks immediately perked up, glancing at Kent's jacket. "Do you have the antidote on you?"

Kent nodded.

Brooks exhaled, feeling the gravity of how close they now were. "I assume the other ticket is for Ms. Shaw?"

"Yes."

"Why bring her at all? I admit, I'm a novice at this, but wouldn't she be a liability?"

"Not as much of one as my attending solo. I'd stand out like a neon tuxedo. Kerr won't be there, but he may still have eyes watching."

"How do you know he won't be there? The Deputy Chief of MI6—certainly on the guest list."

Kent took another drink of his Guinness. "Kerr knows I'm in London, or at least close. He also suspects the key to be here. The last thing he wants is to be bottled up, especially someplace so visible."

Brooks was quiet, the details rolling around in his mind. "I don't like it," he said finally.

"Well good for you, 007. I don't think we have a choice."

"What about me?"

Kent shot back a curious glance. "What about you?"

"I could retrieve the key." Kent began a chuckle that soon grew into a laugh, testing the limits of discretion. Perhaps it was the breaking of a dam of stress—a week's worth of tension finally allowed to escape. Brooks understood, but still felt a pang of frustration. "I'm glad you can still see the lighter side."

Kent soon recovered. "I'm sorry, Nathan. I meant no offense. You're beyond essential to this operation. But you've already labeled yourself an amateur."

Brooks was prepared for the rebuttal. "This would be different. I could go inside with Bradley during his visit with the queen. What's more mundane than a weekday afternoon? It'd be low pressure, no scrutiny."

Kent exhaled, trying not to sound like a kindergarten teacher addressing one of his students. "It's your sovereign's residence, Nathan. There will always be scrutiny." He looked into his glass, casually swirling around the last quarter of black liquid. "Besides, your involvement is still a question mark for Kerr. That's valuable uncertainty. If you're caught—even suspected of—retrieving the key, the advantage is lost."

Brooks stared back, dismayed by the sense Kent was making. "Fine," he said. "Where can I reach you, if by some miracle I find two openings?"

"We're at the Royal Horseguards, under the name Vakkuri."

"*Horseguards*. Nothing like a low profile."

"It's a long story"

"Too bad you can't cover it in your memoirs. Surefire bestseller."

Kent smiled, finishing off his drink. "Who'd ever believe it?"

Brooks was about to respond when the sound of a clanging glass interrupted him. He instinctively spun toward the noise. An empty pint lay horizontal on a nearby table, its former contents flowing over the wooden stand's edge and onto the carpet.

A waitress reacted quickly with a towel as the drink's owner berated his own clumsiness. Brooks turned back with an empathetic grin. "That's too ba—"

He stopped short; the seat before him was now empty, a £5 note lying quietly beside the empty glass of Guinness.

48

Kent gazed through their hotel room's window, his hands stuffed in the pockets of a fresh tuxedo. Outside, over the past several minutes, the blue-gray sky had begun admitting shadows. One by one the surrounding buildings started lighting the landscape. The Thames loomed dark in the center, its current dissecting the glow like a black cobra.

He was nervous, afraid even. The twilight postcard before him had adopted an ominous tinge. Every rounded corner looked a little sharper, each point of light a shade or two darker.

Such anxiety felt warranted. Brooks had come through with the tickets, which meant they were less than an hour from champagne, dancing and the highest stakes Kent had ever known. By midnight the fate of millions of innocent lives would be determined. It was an obvious reason for pause.

But not the only one, which scared him even more.

He hadn't been able to get Allison off of his mind. Even during the meeting with Brooks, discussing crucial details, she'd been near the forefront. It went beyond mere concern for a charge under his protection. Beyond anything he'd felt in a long while.

He'd seen the attraction coming, but still wasn't prepared. Every time he forced it away, it only dug in deeper. Letting his guard down, though, wasn't an option. And Allison had given no sign of similar feelings.

Kent exhaled, willing his muscles to relax. Along with the invitations—delivered to their door by a courier Brooks trusted—the aide included a typed note detailing a meeting point before entering the palace.

They had a thin time window, but were still on schedule. Kent checked his watch anyway.

Then he heard the bathroom door swing open and turned around. Allison walked out. Her eyes found him and she took a few more steps forward. "What do you think? Will this do?" The words were delivered in subdued monotone, like a coworker asking for a professional opinion about a uniform.

It didn't matter. Kent immediately froze, his final defenses melting away.

It was the dress. Pale blue, form-fitting. They would've been too conspicuous shopping for it together. She'd given him a size, he'd chosen the design. Elegant, he thought, without any frills to draw attention. But that was on a rack. On Allison, every inch of the satin hugging her curves, the dress seemed to eclipse its original potential. Kent couldn't take his eyes off her.

It went beyond outward attraction. He was captive to the entire picture. The outfit was just the final straw, unlocking the beauty—the essence— of the woman underneath. He started closing the distance between them, moving as if in a trance. He knew, though, exactly what he was doing.

Kent could feel the surrender in his eyes. At first Allison looked confused, but she quickly understood; there was no mistaking what was happening. The room fell silent, every sound beyond—traffic on the street below, footsteps in the hallway—as distant as Mars.

He stopped an arm's length away. They stood there, gazes locked, for several seconds. Kent still wasn't sure if she wanted this, but her breathing had matched his, making both shoulders rise and fall in heavy waves. He had to try.

"Can I kiss you?"

The words had come out quickly, seeming to speak themselves. He felt a bit silly, but she answered with a smile. "Yes."

Kent wasted no time. Pulling her in gently, he pressed his lips to hers. For two seconds, three, he forgot everything else. It was a moment's peace—ecstasy—within the mission's maelstrom.

Then, finally, they released. The present circumstances instantly came flooding back, and Kent scolded himself for acting on such reckless desire. It only sucked Allison down further into his toxic world.

"I'm sorry," he said. "It's unfair of me—"

She put a finger to his lips. "I'm not sorry."

Kent could have kept this position for hours. Like a nagging wound, though, duty refused to let go. By now the watch was burning a hole in his wrist. He risked a discreet glance at it.

"I'm almost ready," said Allison, noticing the movement.

Kent exhaled. "You're fine." He nodded toward the bathroom. "Go ahead and finish up."

She slowly turned, striding across the carpet. Kent stuffed both hands back into his pockets, then stopped. "Wait."

Allison turned. He walked forward, fingering a diamond ring in his right hand. "I almost forgot." He held it up, the room's warm light firing each karat.

Her eyebrows rose. "My, you sure do spring it on a girl."

He smiled. "Just for tonight. Brooks didn't have much choice—we're taking the place of a married couple."

She nodded and held out a cupped hand. Instead, Kent turned her palm over and slid the ring on the appropriate finger. He paused for the slightest moment. "Comfortable?"

Allison looked at him, then down at the jewelry. "Not bad. How did you know the size?"

"Lucky guess." He gestured toward the bathroom again. "Go on."

A moment later she was gone. Kent wandered back to the window, its view having not so much darkened as sharpened, featuring a more severe contrast between points of shadow and light. He thought about Allison, donning the last of her makeup, and remembered his own. She'd done a good job applying the foundation. The cuts on his face were nearly invisible now, even upon close inspection.

But they were still there. Like the HK sitting on the bed, a stubborn reminder of death's proximity. Kent reached for the pistol, feeling its weight, the cold of its grip.

He took a breath, his heartbeat nearing the end of its long road back to normal. For all its joy, the last five minutes hadn't erased the tightrope ahead. And now he had even more to lose.

49

The black cab pulled up along the curb and Allison read its dashboard clock: 8 p.m. Right on time. Kent paid the driver, got out and stretched back an open hand. She accepted, and soon they were both on the sidewalk. The taxi quickly joined the stream of traffic flowing northward along Buckingham Gate, its headlights searching like hungry eyes for a fresh fare.

A slight wind rushed across the pavement. Allison tugged a navy wrap tight around her shoulders. Linking his arm in hers, Kent led her away from the street toward several large stone columns. She squeezed back, trying to look past the anxiety pooling in her stomach.

The columns belonged to the Queen's Gallery, a public museum attached to Buckingham's west side featuring a rotating collection of royal artwork. To the right, further up the palace's façade, a short drive hosted a parade of luxury vehicles: The Ambassador's Court, where most of the guests would make their entrance. Around the corner was the building's iconic front, more ceremonious than functional.

They continued forward. Soon Allison spotted a figure step out from the shadows and quickly recognized Nathan Brooks. Kent's description had been spot-on: shorter, with a slight pudge and a smooth, round face. He looked sharp tonight—hair combed neatly, tux a perfect fit.

During their approach Brooks glanced casually up and down the street, never making eye contact. Once they were within five meters he turned back into the darkness, still without acknowledging them. Kent didn't hesitate, guiding her onward. Soon the street was a memory.

Brooks appeared again a few steps later. This time he nodded before leading the way inside and closely steering them through a series of empty corridors. After a minute, he abruptly began describing their surroundings like a tour guide. The next moment they came within sight of two men guarding an entryway. They were also dressed in suits and appeared to be security personnel. Moving up to the pair, Brooks flashed some credentials and spoke a few quiet words. The men laughed and casually waved the trio through. This happened a few more times as the aide continued his faux narration.

Soon a final door brought them back outside. They began tracing a concrete walkway, the rear of the palace on their right. To the left lay a massive, park-like garden. Allison glanced into the expanse and noticed what looked like a pair of soldiers in black fatigues marching over a patch of fresh-cut grass.

"Her Majesty's Foot Guards," said Brooks, following her gaze. "Normally a single company is split between here and St. James Palace, but, as I'm sure you can understand, additional soldiers have been stationed around the grounds this evening."

"What of their uniforms?" asked Kent, playing along. "I thought they were red and black."

"Normally, yes. But tonight is more about function than fanfare, if you follow."

Kent nodded accordingly as they now came within feet of another pair of security guards, this one manning an entrance to the palace itself. One of the sentries, about a decade older than his freshman partner, stepped forward with a deferential nod. "Evening, Mr. Brooks. Odd night for a stroll."

The aide had already begun to smile as he covered the final paces between the groups. "Sam. I'm a bit surprised to see you out here too." He nodded up the wall of the palace. "Didn't want to rub elbows with the PM?"

The sentry lifted his gaze as well, then brought it back down. "It's a pleasant evening. Thought I'd get some fresh air, let the others cover the champagne and dancing."

Brooks continued grinning. "Why do I get the feeling you're the smart one?"

Sam did his best to hide a smile and turned to Kent and Allison. Brooks, stepping back, held out a hand in presentation. "Gordon Bishop, a new research analyst with the Foreign and Commonwealth Office, and his lovely wife Caroline."

Both guards eyed the pair politely, but maintained a customary wariness. Allison forced herself to breathe evenly; her face was still plastered on screens near the top of every newscast. Inside, during the party, there would be enough distraction to cloak her presence. But right now, these two men had an isolated view. She hoped her haircut and glasses would be enough of a disguise.

A wave of release finally came as the security men relaxed their gaze. "Gordon and I were at Oxford together," continued Brooks, traces of relief in his own voice. "It's his and Caroline's first time at the palace. I thought I'd show them around a bit." He turned back to the pair. "Ready for the inner half?"

They each nodded and Brooks gestured forward. Sam, though, stepped out before Kent or Allison could reach the door. "Sorry, sir, but we'll still have to check them."

Pausing in his tracks, Brooks sprouted a face of surprise that quickly turned diplomatic. "Of course. Forgive me, must be the excitement of the night." He eyed his companions. Kent made the first move, stepping back and slightly spreading his arms and legs. Sam's partner quietly came over with a wand and began brushing each limb.

After five seconds and no beeps, it was Allison's turn. The guard repeated the process, moving the wand a bit more delicately. Nothing came up. Sam then directed them inside with a bid for each to enjoy the evening.

Several paces later, with the outer door closed and no one else in sight, Brooks took a surreptitious glance around and pulled the HK from behind his back. He clutched it by the barrel and carefully handed it over to Kent, along with the canister. Allison watched Kent stow the items, realizing he must have given them to Brooks inside one of the darkened corridors. She'd obviously missed the switch.

Resuming their trek inward, they didn't get far before a pack of subdued voices wafted through from somewhere ahead. Brooks jumped back into his monotone chronicle of the building just as a handful of other guests peeked their heads around a nearby corner. "And now we find ourselves in the Bow Room," said the aide, glancing about with practiced formality. "Traditionally, the space ushers numerous visitors from the palace interior to the grounds in back for Her Majesty's garden parties every summer."

Following Kent's lead, Allison swung her gaze around the area, pretending to look interested. It wasn't that hard. They were walking over rich, red carpet, its deep sheen matching the gilded accents of the ceiling above. Rows of round, commanding columns occupied the space in between, making the room appear far less empty than it really was.

Five more seconds and the faces were gone. Their owners had evidently been searching for an unexplored nook and found nothing of interest. The trio pushed forward, the plush ground swallowing the sound of their steps. Soon they'd moved beyond the room and into an expansive marble hallway. More well-dressed sentries became visible, as well as the group of inquisitives they'd just seen.

Kent and Allison continued to follow their guide, maintaining polite smiles but avoiding any direct conversations with the other visitors. Half a minute later they approached a sprawling collection of steps that Brooks appropriately labeled the Grand Staircase. From the side a steady flow of guests coursed through and made its way up the incline.

Brooks stopped fifty feet from the crowd and spun, speaking softly. "This is where I leave you. Most of these guests are filtering in from the Ambassador's Court." He turned to Kent. "It's as I feared, assuming the key's not in the ballroom. Everyone seems to be getting their sightseeing of the upper rooms in before the Queen makes her entrance. Can you two play politico for a while?"

Kent nodded. "This *is* a party."

Brooks paused for a moment, exhaling as he removed a handkerchief from an inside pocket. Despite his act of composure, small beads of perspiration had begun dotting his forehead. He wiped them free, putting the cloth back. "I need a holiday."

He pointed at the staircase. "You're essentially following the crowd. Move up to the middle landing, then continue straight. The next set of doors will take you into the East Gallery. The ballroom entrance is on its far end."

Kent stuck out his hand as Brooks spun back. "You've done well, Nathan. See you on the other side."

Brooks accepted the offering with a frown. "How sure are you that we'll get there?"

"Say a prayer."

"Has that ever worked?"

"It's never hurt."

Brooks managed something close to a smile, nodded to them both and disappeared back the way they'd come. Kent glanced at Allison, then led her forward. They melted easily into the flow of guests, reaching the doors at the edge of the landing a moment later.

The East Gallery was immense. Allison looked around as they began their long trek down its length. Simple, high walls seemed to go on forever; they eventually led to a glass ceiling, its vaulted slats revealing the black night above. Along the floor, isolated parties glided forward in their own form of rapt admiration.

They were halfway through the space when Allison set her eyes on the double doors at its far end. Each partition was held open by a well-groomed attendant, his uniform resembling that of a royal butler. Beside them stood what appeared to be further security, each guard surveying the approaching groups with a familiar mix of courtesy and suspicion. Beyond the opening, Allison caught glimpses of a crowd mingling, its soft cacophony spilling into the gallery's expanse.

She felt her palms begin to sweat and discreetly brushed them against her dress. Her heartbeat, pounding outside the building, had slowly calmed to a flutter. Somehow, though, it felt just as violent. She tried to psyche herself up. *It's only a dinner party, Ally.* She needed to think of each face in the coming crowd as her equal. A few extra titles didn't change anything. People were people. *You've done this before.*

Except she hadn't; no one had. It wasn't the star power that scared her, it was a constellation—*a hunter.* Filling the room ahead with her closest friends and relatives wouldn't change the stakes.

Finally, they crossed the threshold and entered the ballroom. For the first time since stepping inside the palace, Allison was no longer surprised. Ostentation had become the norm. Along every surface of the chamber lush reds and golds mixed with brilliant whites. A series of chandeliers, each several hundred pounds of crystal, hung from the lofty ceiling like past monarchs peeking into the present.

The room itself had to be sixty feet wide and twice as long. Still, it was packed. Filling the space in between numerous round, linen-covered tables was a sea of chattering guests, many of them holding some kind of cocktail. Every male wore a black tuxedo; his female counterpart was afforded more freedom. None of the dresses present were exactly the same, but most adhered to conventional rules of solid color and tasteful cut.

Across the way, at what Allison assumed to be the front of the room, crimson carpet yielded to a hardwood floor. Half the wall was graced by a long table, its chairs currently empty. Out in the open a few couples danced to subtle chords emanating from a miniature orchestra playing Vivaldi.

Allison's focus was recaptured as they arrived at a brass stand. Behind it, an impeccably dressed man stared back with a polite, unemotional smile which the British seemed to have perfected. "Good evening. Your names, please?"

Kent gave them. The man, offering a quick nod, scanned a booklet in front of him before looking up once more. "Very good, Mr. Bishop." He scribbled something on a small card and handed it to another man on his left. "Thomas will show you to your seats. Have a wonderful evening." They both thanked him and turned to their escort, who glanced at the card before leading them deeper into the room.

Back at the hotel, Kent had relayed the contents of Brooks' note. Gordon Bishop really was a research analyst with the Foreign and Commonwealth Office; he really did have a wife named Caroline. Fortunately, he'd spent most of his young career at a security firm up in Birmingham and had only joined the government staff two weeks earlier. Anyone in town that might recognize him, including his direct superiors, lacked an invitation to tonight's event.

The Bishops themselves had benefited from a special program recently instituted by Alan Bradley's administration. Designed to increase morale and productivity, a lottery had been held amongst everyday government staffers, the winners granted admittance to some of the year's most exclusive events. The party tonight was arguably at the top of the list, and Bishop, despite his brief tenure, had been one of the lucky few to receive an invite.

Once he discovered this, Brooks had gone to Bradley for help. The PM, through a terse but desperate phone call, had convinced the analyst to stay home tonight and tell anyone curious that he'd come down with the flu. Bishop, understandably, was upset; his wife was furious. Especially when all they'd been given by way of explanation was a generic notion about safeguarding national security. Still, the analyst was a low-level employee and the man on the other line was his de facto head of state. Bishop relented, and Bradley threw in a final plea for confidentiality. It probably wouldn't last, but they only needed a few days. By then, one way or another, this hidden war would be over.

After several twists, turns and "pardon's", they made it to a table in the back. All eight seats were unoccupied, though Allison saw a few layered with jackets, scarves and clutches. Theft wasn't something you worried about in a room like this.

Thomas pulled a chair out for her, but Kent politely waved him off. The attendant stepped away and for a moment they were, relatively speaking, alone. Allison draped the wrap over the chair and laid her own clutch on the table. Kent reached out his hand and gestured toward the throng. She accepted, and they entered the fray.

Like any attempt at mingling, it was slightly awkward at first, then became easier. Thirty minutes passed quickly; they spent much of it together, though drifted apart as conversations dictated. Allison constantly reminded herself to act natural—at least, Caroline Bishop's natural. She wasn't as smooth with the British accent, but Kent had assured her it would be good enough.

The champagne helped. Kent had grabbed them each a flute at the beginning. Hers, currently, was still only half empty. She could have gone through five, pounded the nerves down. But this wasn't the night to get tipsy.

Brooks had supplied a few notes on Gordon and Caroline's background. She and Kent spent a large portion of the afternoon memorizing the information and fabricating additional details. Things were still going smoothly when Allison, excusing herself from a pack of MP's wives, backed into another person and turned to apologize. The words didn't come, however, as she stared up at the President of the United States.

He still cut an imposing figure: mid-sixties, broad-shouldered; she remembered he'd played football in college at the naval academy. Pausing for the slightest moment upon seeing her, his face quickly spread into a relaxed grin. "Finally. I was wondering when I'd run into the second-most beautiful woman in the room."

Making a conscious effort to close her mouth, Allison swallowed through a dry throat. "Forgive me, Mr. President." She forced a smile to match his. "And thank you. I consider coming in behind the queen an honor."

"The queen?" His face twisted cleverly. "She can have the bronze."

On cue, the First Lady strode up beside her husband. Allison glanced toward the woman and remembered she really was pretty, even more so in person. Her emerald gown and fair skin complemented a well-coiffed, fiery auburn crown. She was around the same age as the President, but had managed to avoid, or at least conceal, the facial lines that the passage of time and stress of such a position often invited.

"Making new friends, Matthew?" she said to her husband, glancing at Allison warmly.

"All the time," he answered, conducting the younger woman's eyes back to his wife. "My better half, Audrey."

"Caroline Bishop," said Allison, surprised her accent hadn't lapsed. She extended a hand forward. "A true pleasure."

The First Lady gently grasped the offered palm. As she did, her eyes narrowed. "My dear, have we not met before?"

Allison's heartbeat jumped to another level and she worked to keep her voice even. "Not that I recall, Mrs. Billings."

There was a second of silence before the President tilted his head. "Yes, I think we'd have remembered a face like this." He straightened toward Allison, eyes widening. "You're not here by yourself, I hope."

"No," she said, happy to change the subject. She waved her arm casually. "My husband—"

"—is terribly late," said Kent, appearing almost magically beside her. "The German Chancellor tells some wickedly long jokes."

Laughter followed, and Kent quickly introduced himself. "I see you've met my lovely wife."

"An absolute treasure," said the First Lady. She was about to add something else when the band abruptly changed its tune. All heads turned toward the dance floor, and rounds of applause began as the royal family entered and made its way to the head table. The cheering reached a crescendo when the queen came in sight and didn't die down until she sat. Her son remained standing. Given a microphone, he thanked everyone for their support and announced the start of dinner. Parting from the

President and First Lady, Kent and Allison migrated with the rest of the crowd back to their table.

The next hour featured slightly less conversation as most everyone had their mouths full of roasted pheasant and boiled potatoes. Once she'd finished, Allison slid her plate away and sat back in her chair. Minutes later it was taken by a waiter and she began sipping from a glass of water.

At the same time, a couple across the table rose and began making their way to the dance floor. Allison followed them with her gaze, swiveling from left to right until her view was abruptly cut off by Kent. He was standing beside her, arm outstretched. "Care to join them?"

Taking a breath, she stood, grasping his hand and following him out to the hardwood. They arrived and shuffled to a pocket of open space, which was starting to become a premium. The music seemed lusher now, the lights a bit lower. He matched his left palm to her right and wrapped his free arm tightly around her waist, pulling her close. "Two songs," he whispered in her ear.

"Alright."

Seconds in, though, she was wishing for a much higher number. One by one the neighboring couples seemed to disappear. She told herself to stay focused; the longer the music went, though, the more she slipped into a dreamlike haze. She began to feel a faint warmth within, the beginning of safety.

And then it was over. The orchestra hit its finale and Kent abruptly led her off the floor. She snapped back to reality. "What about the second song?"

"Change of plans," he said, steadily weaving back to their table.

She quickly understood. The dance floor remained congested, while several guests resumed the mingling game and a third portion had started something of a receiving line up front to pay their respects to Her Majesty. The room was full. Which meant the halls outside were empty, or close to it.

249

Reaching their table, Kent didn't have to direct Allison. She immediately reached for her effects as he gave the remaining couple there an excuse about using the bathroom. They sifted past the scattered crowd and quietly strode through the entrance. The music began to fade as they coursed down the East Gallery. The large space seemed even longer now with them as its only occupants. Allison forced herself to walk calmly, feeling the security guards' eyes on her back.

An eternity later, they reached the far end. Soon after the Grand Staircase's middle landing came into view. Instead of heading down the way they'd come, though, Kent guided her up the other side. Allison could have heard a pin drop; it felt like they were sneaking through a museum after-hours.

Then came a typically lavish hallway. Kent marched her through an entrance on its far side. "The White Drawing Room," he said, chiefly for the benefit of an older couple admiring a large portrait of Queen Alexandra set above a fireplace. Allison nodded as they moved further within and acknowledged the space's lone occupants. Kent looked up at the painting; she followed, pretending to appreciate its ancient brush strokes and gilded frame.

A handful of seconds had passed when the other couple turned and slowly walked out. The moment they were beyond earshot, Kent swiftly strode toward the chamber's back corner and a veneered oak roll-top desk. He took a last glance around. Seeing no one, he bent down and reached for the back underside of the stand. Allison kept her eyes on him, transfixed. Despite her paltry part, she felt a stirring sense of accomplishment.

"Hands up, no words." The room's neutral silence broke at the unmistakable sound of a gun being cocked. Kent immediately froze, Allison with him. "Turn around," ordered a Russian voice.

A second later, gingerly, Kent started to back out. She moved to give him space, and was the first to lay eyes on their visitor. Near one of the room's other entryways, a man with long hair was training a pistol at them. Kent had given her a brief description of their pursuers. This had to be

Sergei Ryov. He was young, but only in the physical sense; his dark eyes were smart, almost wise. He stood with confidence, a chilling nonchalance.

Allison felt the hair spike on the back of her neck. She worked to keep from shaking and spotted Kent slowly spin his head left. Following his gaze, she saw two suited men enter from the hallway, each holding a handgun. Directly after came a third, slightly taller and older, his charcoal overcoat flapping against a rigid frame. Behind him a final figure slipped inside and closed both doors leading to the hallway.

The newcomers, along with Ryov, closed in strategically, pinning Kent and Allison into the corner. She looked to Kent, trying to imagine his thoughts. *Escape?* Too much of a fantasy to realistically consider. How, then, had they been caught? Could Brooks have given them up? Bradley? *No.* Not after they'd worked so long and hard to get this close.

Suddenly she caught a movement beyond Ryov; an additional door swung open, then closed. The edges of a figure swayed in an out of view as someone approached. Allison trained her gaze on the spot where it would emerge, knowing Kent was doing the same. A moment later James Baker stepped past Ryov and into the center of the group.

Allison wasn't surprised by what she immediately felt inside—shock, anger, fear; but that was based on a handful of hours with Baker. What about half a decade, during which the man had been your only true ally within five thousand miles? She glanced toward Kent, almost dreading what she'd find.

His empty eyes matched her pain and surprise, but reflected something more: sorrow. His face had quickly turned pale. For the first time since she'd met him, he looked small. *Beaten.* Only one question mattered now. He didn't even have to ask.

"Get over yourself, Jeremy," said Baker. "I did it for the money, that simple. Only room for one of us on Kerr's team—had to beat you to it." He stepped closer. "We were never going to win this. Even if, by some miracle...I've spent too much time and effort in these trenches for a simple pat on the back from Washington."

Silence permeated the room. The other men kept their guns trained on Kent and Allison. Kent took a long, weakened breath, as if the wind had been knocked out of him. "Why didn't you just take the canister in Soglio?"

"Believe it or not, I was still on the fence." Baker almost smiled. "Your idea about Buckingham was the tipping point." He gestured around the room. "This plan—this entire mission—was always a dream."

Kent turned to his left, a slight shade of vindictive color creeping back onto his face. "How can you trust a man who sells me out on a whim?"

The question was directed at the older man, whom Allison took to be Nicolas Kerr. "Mr. Baker has no power, no money yet," he said. "He has a trial, in two parts. The first was to lead us to you."

"The second is to kill you," said Baker. He began screwing a silencer onto the barrel of a pistol. "Hand over the canister cleanly and you'll both be ensured a quick death."

The final word hit with cold finality. He was telling the truth. Baker's face—indeed, the countenance of every man present—betrayed no emotion. This was business, and they were about to complete a routine transaction. Allison's entire body flared in fear, its innate survival instinct raising one last objection.

She was too afraid to cry, and instead turned toward Kent. He was staring right back at her. The hurt was still there in his eyes. Fatigue too. But despair had been replaced by a kind of resigned peace. For once, she was able to read his mind: *at least we'll go together.*

Slowly spinning back to the middle, he reached toward his breast pocket. Baker raised his gun and shook his head. "Take the jacket off. Hand it to me."

Kent hesitated, then began removing the garment. He eyed Kerr again. "I don't suppose I'm lucky enough to have a security camera catching all this?"

"Friendly eyes on the other end," said the deputy chief. "Seems my title is still good for someth—"

The rest of his words were strangled by surprise as Kent rapidly tossed the jacket toward Baker. In the same motion he lunged inside the sleeve and pulled out the HK. Baker instinctively reached for the flailing suitcoat and, distracted, was met with a kick to his torso.

Pushing off his enemy's stomach, Kent bounded desperately for a nearby window. He fired an errant spray toward Ryov, counting on Baker and the jacket to impede the others' view. The Russian danced around the bullets as Kent swung his gun at the window and squeezed off an extended burst. The thick glass cracked in the middle but remained intact.

Kent closed the last few meters in furious strides and leapt, feet-first, toward the makeshift exit. His shoes collided with the glass in a muffled crunch and broke through. The resulting hole was just large enough for his body to follow as a hail of rounds splintered the rest of the pane."

50

Kent shielded his eyes from the glass and torpedoed into the night air. Scraping onto a stone balcony, he clamored for its thick railing and threw himself over. Several meters below his feet pounded into a concrete portico that ran along the back edge of the palace. The guards and soldiers surely heard the shots and would be closing.

He turned right, toward the northern end of the stage, and broke into a sprint. Immediately a streak of pain knifed into his left ankle. No bullet wound—must've been from the fall. He ignored it, surging forward and hurdling the portico's railing to soft ground below.

Shouts sounded behind as flashlight beams danced frantically in the garden to his left. Kent doubted security would shoot, but had no desire to give them a chance. Ahead, a thick hedge of trees beckoned like a forest sanctuary.

Crack. His ears registered the sound just as the pavement at his feet sparked with an orange flash. He spun, almost annoyed. *Ryov.* Whipping his legs over the balcony, the Russian hit the extended porch with a roll and popped up sprinting.

Kent hadn't stopped running, but found another gear. His ankle was beginning to throb. Could he win this race? *Don't think that far ahead.* The trees before him continued to close in. Beyond lay an open field, then another patch of foliage. He had to reach the latter before Ryov had a clear shot.

Kent wanted to check his pocket but knew the key and canister were there, rubbing securely against his right thigh. It killed him to leave Allison, but escape had been the only way to keep her alive. She was now their best bargaining chip.

He crossed the hedge without another bullet fired. Ryov was still too far back to shoot from a full sprint. Kent tore through the clearing, each moonlit blade of grass a progress marker. He wanted to dive low or jump to the side, but there was nowhere to hide. Distant shouts still pierced the night. He heard little beyond his own breathing.

With a final, desperate stride he hit the second line of foliage. At the same instant came the euphoria of cover and the horror of a pistol's report. Kent braced for impact as his face whipped into leaves and twigs. Despite the noise, he still heard twin projectiles slice the air past each of his ears, cutting into the branches beyond.

Don't stop. The ankle was burning now, but numbness would come soon; he could ride it out.

Kent broke through the other side of the hedge a second later. He saw a narrow path, then more foliage. He continued, diving across and crashing through the web of trees. He'd lost his precise sense of direction but knew the garden had to end soon.

A step later it did. He hesitated for the briefest second, staring at a twelve-foot high stone wall crowned with barbed wire. There was literally, though, no time to lament the obstacle. In a single motion, Kent stowed his gun and leapt forward, the rubber sole of his left shoe catching rock and propelling him upward.

He reached for the top of the wall and pulled himself up, stopping short of the jagged wire that jutted toward an open space beyond. He was about to jump over when he felt his weight begin to slip backward. Ryov was nearly through the trees; if he fell he was dead.

Desperately clawing at the wire, Kent caught a last-second grip and pulled himself across. He sliced both palms before sailing down the other side. The ground came fast and he hit it in a roll, popping up just short of a sedan skidding over a stretch of asphalt. The driver instinctively laid on her horn, missing him by inches and swerving away. Kent stole a frantic look up and down the busy street. He recognized it as Constitution Hill.

Pulling his gun back out, he darted into the road. Blaring, metallic shrills pierced the night as he angled between speeding hulks of metal. Two strides from the far side, he dove over the remaining pavement just ahead of an oblivious compact.

He rolled to his feet through a stretch of dirt and pushed left. A glance back: Ryov had emerged from the trees and was scaling the wall. Kent continued his sprint, more tires screeching in the background. On his right, a narrow footpath separated his thin patch of earth from a larger expanse beyond. *Green Park.* Plenty of space, but its sparse trees gave no cover.

Two seconds later a pair of cracks cut through the surrounding tumult. The cars that hadn't witnessed the chase were now awakened by the sound of gunfire as the scene became even more chaotic. Each bullet had eyes, zooming past the maze of vehicles. The first bit into a tree to Kent's right; the second ripped through his shirt below the left armpit.

He kept running, wanting to shake his head. His opponent was pulling the trigger while racing at top speed through the night amidst a sea of panicked motorists. These were his bad shots.

Kent suddenly spotted activity up ahead. It was an intersection, thirty meters away. Had to be Duke of Wellington Place; not just a cross street, but a roundabout. Which meant more traffic for cover, and more exits.

All at once, though, the security clock in his brain ticked down to zero. Kent spun, steadied his hands and fired two rounds a second after Ryov broke onto his side of the street.

The Russian had his gun up but saw he'd been beaten to the trigger. He dove for a nearby tree. One of the bullets puffed up a cloud of dirt below his flailing body, but the second caught his right hand. Kent heard a muted grunt as Ryov dropped his gun, a spray of red issuing from his palm.

Kent was already racing toward the intersection. The roadway beside him remained volatile, its frenetic sea of oncoming headlights blinding in the dark. He risked a look back. Ryov had recovered quickly, sprinting forward under a fresh scowl. He switched the gun to his left hand and raised the barrel for a shot. Kent braced himself to dive low when one of the cars, trying to avoid a collision, swerved directly into Ryov's path. The Russian slid across its hood, but not before Kent had dashed behind a line of vehicles near the front edge of the roundabout.

Kent kept his head low, sucking in frantic breaths and scanning the intersection. Should he go straight through its center garden or left toward Grosvenor Place? Just as he made his choice, a third option literally rushed by.

Knowing Ryov was still closing, Kent cut between two cars and burst toward the back end of a double-decker bus. It seemed to be speeding up. He desperately lengthened his strides, each exhausted muscle having stopped its fruitless screaming long ago. The vehicle began arcing right around the circle when Kent lunged forward, his free hand gripping the cold steel of the rear step handle as if it were gold.

He barely had time to pull himself up when a nearby window exploded. A collection of shrieks instantly pierced the interior of the bus. Kent hit the deck but caught a glimpse of Ryov racing beside a Land Rover ten meters behind. He popped back up and rapidly fired two shots. Catching the move just in time, the Russian strafed behind the SUV and the twin killers sparked harmlessly off the dark pavement.

At the sight of the shots, the Rover skidded to a halt. Kent waited for Ryov to step out. One second... two...nothing. Then his stomach began to sour as he noticed his own transportation slowing. He couldn't stay at his post; escape was paramount. He bolted through the bus's lower level.

Nearly every seat was occupied, the few open spots recently vacated by panicked riders. Seeing Kent, though, they collapsed back into their chairs. He sprinted toward the front of the cabin, gun trained at its floor. "Secret Service!" he yelled. "Stay down! Stay down!" They were all too frightened to care about an ID.

Kent nearly slammed into the plastic console up front and looked directly at the terrified driver. The man's eyes were wide and locked on the

HK. Kent kept it low, but made sure it remained visible. "Secret Service." he repeated. "Do not slow this bus down."

Almost reflexively, the driver managed a frantic nod, his knuckles around the steering wheel growing an extra shade of white. Kent was gone a beat later, racing toward the rear through a now-hushed aisle of horrified humanity. Blood continued to leak from his palms, coating the pistol's handle in a sticky glaze before dripping to the floor.

The bus's diesel engine revved back up and powered them down Piccadilly. Reaching his former perch, Kent peered out. Several vehicles, evidently oblivious to the gunshots, still followed closely behind. Kent searched for Ryov but saw nothing. Had he given up? Stopped to steal a car?

Abruptly Kent spotted movement behind a Saab trailing to the right. He craned his neck, but didn't have an angle. He needed a higher view. In the next moment he was halfway up the rear stairs.

By now a couple tenants from the bus's second floor had gathered at the top landing. Without a line of sight, they'd stayed relatively quiet, but upon seeing Kent—and his gun—they opened their mouths in terror. "Secret Service!" he cut in, reaching the top. "Sit down, now!"

They complied immediately, joining the few other riders who'd chosen the upper level. Kent counted half a dozen. They all looked at him as he turned to the back window. The view was better, but still no Ryov. The driver continued to rush forward, swerving the red monstrosity around slower moving traffic.

Kent took a few steps back and started to contemplate his next move when the lower level of the bus erupted in a rumble of screams. Half a second later each voice was choked into silence, and he knew Ryov was aboard.

A glance around the cabin: he had the higher ground, but also two entrances to cover. In the middle, the riders, prompted by the commotion below, began to mumble worriedly. He silenced them with a rapid finger to his mouth and began to inch back toward the rear staircase.

For a second everything went eerily quiet. Beyond his own pounding heart, the only thing Kent could hear was the occasional horn or screeching tire. Were they speeding up? It didn't matter anymore. They could be stopped now and it wouldn't cha—

Steps, on the front staircase. Slow and deliberate. Kent lifted his gun toward the noise; each set of eyes beside him followed the barrel. Somehow, they still noticed him lay a palm to the ground, and everyone crouched low in their seats.

The next few seconds might as well have been a week. Eventually, ten fingertips crested the staircase railing, followed by two trembling palms raised above a head of moppy brown hair. It was a man—barely. A student. Early twenties, with a face that'd already turned pale.

Kent kept his gun raised, not sure what was behind the stranger. The kid stared back, his entire body beginning to shake. He swallowed a half-breath and parted a set of quivering lips to speak. But Kent already knew.

He spun toward the rear staircase. Ryov was at the top of the incline, his gun muzzle swinging toward Kent's chest. Still in motion, Kent arched back and cut his right leg across the space between them. His foot collided with the Russian's gun half a second before the trigger was pulled. Momentum carried the barrel to a new aim, and it spit the bullet out toward one of the side windows.

The pane shattered with typical intensity. Shards of glass joined the cold air that instantly rushed through the bus. Screams resumed and the passengers instinctively flooded the far end of the aisle. Kent, continuing his pirouette, swept his left leg across the ground toward Ryov's ankles. Muscle met bone and the Russian was upended, his thin frame seeming to float in the air before crashing to the floor.

The second his shoulder blades made contact, though, he arced his legs back up. The energy created from the quick reversal pulsed through his torso until his entire body flipped off the ground. He landed on his feet.

Kent, still on his knees, hadn't been expecting the move and lunged forward in desperation. Instead of aiming for a shot, he had to shift his balance and bind the Russian's weapon-hand with his own free one. Before

Kent could then recover with his pistol, his opponent reciprocated the grip and both men locked into a power struggle.

Pressing back with all his force, Kent matched the grimace on Ryov's face and slowly inched to his feet. The Russian's hand was still bleeding from Kent's gunshot, and both men traded red liquid from palm to palm.

Their contest continued almost silently as the bus rumbled east over Hungerford Bridge. It'd only been seconds, but seemed frozen in time. Finally, Kent shifted his weight and rammed his gun-hand across, slamming it into Ryov's own pistol. Polymer hit polymer and both weapons clattered to the floor. Kent's skidded to the middle of the aisle; Ryov's disappeared under a line of benches.

The Russian's eyes flashed wide and followed the sliding guns. Seizing the opportunity, Kent thrust his right elbow toward his opponent's throat. By some trick of physics, Ryov sidestepped the blow, slung a grip around Kent's extended arm and slammed him to the floor.

Kent felt the air rush from his chest. Ryov immediately abandoned him for the nearest pistol. Kent, though, managed to throw a leg out and trip his enemy. As Ryov was falling Kent braced his feet against a nearby seat and pushed. Spinning like a turtle on its shell, he flipped to his stomach and clenched both arms around the Russian's left leg.

Another power struggle. Ryov was less than a meter from Kent's gun, but could make no progress. His opponent had a desperate foot hooked around the edge of a seat. At the far end the passengers had bounded downstairs, save two, mesmerized by the fight before them.

The Russian flexed his right leg back and kicked Kent in the face. The agent's grip loosened as several of his facial cuts split back open. Still, he didn't let go. Ryov slithered forward until Kent's HK was inches from his reach. He cocked his leg for another blow when one of the passengers—the same twentysomething who'd been forced up the stairs earlier—scampered forward and swiped the pistol.

For an instant, everyone froze. The young man gripped the gun's barrel with a kind of confused fear, as if he'd worked up the courage to snatch the weapon but hadn't thought beyond that. Ryov made a jerk forward and the boy snapped back to coherence, spinning and running to the stairs. Three seconds later he and the other onlooker were gone.

Before they'd descended from sight, Ryov brought his leg back swiftly for another blow. This one caught Kent in the side of the face. He lost his grip as a black haze stormed across his left eye. Ryov scampered toward his own gun without looking back.

Kent's mind went from a thousand scenarios to one. Rapidly pushing himself off the ground, he took a single step and dove through the broken window. In the same instant the sound of Ryov's gun reverberated through the cabin. Its lone discharge tore a chunk of rubber from the sole of Kent's shoe.

Outside, Kent still didn't know his landing point. He squinted through the blood in his eyes and tucked his body as a sedan raced underneath. Colliding with its metal roof, he bounced off and unraveled into a web of flailing limbs. The scrape of pavement greeted him a second later, his body rolling until a cement wall stopped its momentum.

Fatigue and pain melted into a suit of numbing agony. But there was still no time. He swiftly rose to his knees and recognized his location: London Bridge, one of the least-ornamented spans in the city. Big, though. Three lanes in either direction, with concrete walkways hugging each flank. He was on the bridge's east side, his entrance startling a group of nearby pedestrians.

It began to grow larger, approaching onlookers drawn to the commotion; Kent only saw collateral damage. He grunted to his feet. Ryov would be coming any second. Kent looked to his left, then right. He was in the center of the bridge—despite the human and vehicular congestion, still a hundred meters from any significant cover.

Forty meters down the bus had slowed to a roll and he saw Ryov leap off. Yelling for the group to get down, Kent spun away and dove over the bridge wall just as a pair of slugs ricocheted off the barrier. He joined his palms in front and freefell toward the rippling blackness.

The surface of the Thames swallowed his body in a cold rush. He sank several feet deep, then was quickly pulled east by the strong current. He doubted Ryov would follow, but the Russian was surely angling for a shot.

Kent faced west and opened his eyes. Dark gray, with a faint pinkness poking through the distance. Red tracking lights under the bridge. They were fading fast, but he was still too close to come up for air. Seconds passed. He kept waiting for bullets to pierce the water, but none came.

His heart skipped a beat in relief as he reached down and felt the key and canister, both miraculously still clinging to his right-side pocket. A look up: the surface had dimmed significantly. He guessed he was at least sixty meters in the clear by now. Lungs burning, he steadily kicked upward and broke the surface with a small splash.

London Bridge's surface lights blended closely with its red underbelly; the traffic and pedestrians in between were nothing more than miniatures. Kent swung back around and continued to kick through the water. Finally, escape.

But not freedom.

51

"To recap, for those of you just joining us: several eyewitnesses have reported gunshots throughout central London tonight. The first sightings occurred just over forty minutes ago and appear to involve two individuals in a foot chase originating near Buckingham Palace. These same two people, both male, may also be connected to a bus speeding through the city.

"The vehicle, according to further reports, eventually stopped midway across London Bridge. Numerous minor injuries and motor accidents have been reported, though nothing serious as of yet.

"Neither man has been found. Both are being described as Caucasian with average builds and dark hair. One may have shoulder-length hair; the other is said to be dressed in evening wear.

"Both men are considered armed and dangerous. If you have any information concerning their whereabouts you are asked to immediately contact the Metropolitan Police at the number on the screen. We will of course keep you apprised of any new developments as they become available..."

The hotel manager hit the remote's mute button and set the device down on the counter. He'd seen the story for the first time ten minutes earlier. A little exotic for London, but why not? He could use the entertainment.

Shifting his stocky frame to the other side of the front desk, he plopped down in a swivel chair and exhaled. Twelve years ago, he'd walked through the main entrance for an interview. Why did he keep coming back? He hadn't had a raise since Blair was in office, and calling the lobby before him "dingy" was an obscene compliment.

Yet here he was. Maybe one day he'd earn the last few credits for that engineering degree. For now, the bell above the door chimed, announcing his latest victim. He checked the digital watch around his wrist: 11 p.m. Just in time for the evening rush.

But as the patron stepped inside and closed the door, the manager suddenly felt in no condition to see anyone. It took him all of one second to see that something wasn't right, less than another to recognize the entrant as a suspect from the news story. He didn't know how he knew, but he knew. Developing a nose for trouble was a prerequisite in a building like this.

His stomach swirled and both hands clammed up as the stranger approached, dragging a slight limp. The man was wearing dress shoes and slacks, a white tee-shirt and a black leather jacket. Strips of white cloth were wrapped around each of his hands. Other than the jacket, every piece of clothing, as well as his tousled hair, was damp. Hadn't a different station said witnesses on the bridge saw one of the men jump into the Thames? Either way, the man's battered face was enough to confirm his identity.

For his part, the stranger made no attempt to mask his appearance. The manager looked around the small lobby, realizing for the first time that he was alone. He steadied himself against the counter with both hands and swallowed. "How can I help you?"

"I need a room," said the stranger in a quiet voice. His face was straight, emotionless.

"How many hours?" asked the manager reflexively.

The man made a strange face, as if he wanted to smile but was too tired. "A full night."

A nod. The manager began clicking at a computer to the side. He was programmed to maximize profit, but with this guest the idea never crossed his mind. "The rate is…fifty pounds."

The stranger was already removing his wallet. The manager thought he saw liquid dripping from the folds in the leather. Seconds later four bills were placed on the counter. One hundred pounds each. They were soaking wet, but would be worth the same when dry.

The man behind the desk stared down at the money and had trouble pulling his eyes away. His attention was fully apprehended, though, when the stranger leaned in slightly and looked directly at him. "I'd like a quiet room. Someplace where I won't be disturbed."

Or else. "Of course," said the manager, needing no further encouragement. Suddenly his mouth felt parched. Who was this man? The way he carried himself, how he looked—certainly no small-time crook. He'd just survived an extended gunfight with an apparently worthy foe.

Slowly moving back to his computer, the manager produced a key packet and slid it across the counter. "Second floor, last door on the left." He nodded toward a nearby flight of stairs. "Quietest room in the house."

The man accepted the key with his eyes still trained across the desk, as if he were sizing up the offer. A few interminable seconds passed before he carefully piled up the bills and pushed them forward. "Thank you," he said, turning away.

Soon the stranger was out of sight, the lobby quiet again. The manager, almost unable to gather the money—*almost*—struggled to control his breathing. He gingerly stepped back to his chair and sat down.

How many more credits for that engineering degree?

Kent locked the door and strode into the musty chamber. It held a single bed and small bathroom; paint had chipped from the dust-covered walls. Circling around to the far side of the mattress, he removed the leather jacket he'd swiped from an oblivious café patron. He set the key and canister down beside it, staring at them. It was finally over. All he'd worked for— the world's salvation—literally at his fingertips. *And you don't even care.*

He found himself praying for the message to be on the machine. They'd know to call. There was no other way.

And no use waiting. Sitting down on the bed himself, he reached toward a simple nightstand and picked up the phone. Dialing the number for his flat in Amsterdam, a few rings sounded, then the automated greeting. He typed a password in for his voicemail. Two messages.

The first, left several days ago, was a notice for his dry cleaning to be picked up. Had to maintain appearances. The second call had come just fifteen minutes back. Kerr's voice came through clear and cold.

"Impressive stall, Jeremy. But that's all it was. 6 a.m., corner of Provost and Murray Grove. Come alone, with your cargo." A pause. "It's impossible for this to be anything but a simple choice. Satisfy these conditions and Ms. Shaw will live. Don't, and she'll be dead by 6:05."

The line went quiet and Kent hung up the phone. More or less what he'd expected. His mind had been searching for options, but there were none. Tampering with the canister wouldn't work. The device had been designed with a seal, which, if broken, could never be repaired. His enemies would know if another liquid had been substituted. The same went for somehow retrieving a brand new, empty cylinder from MI6 and filling it with a benign fluid. There were tools for verifying the contents' authenticity, and Kerr would surely possess them.

None of this mattered if they were going to kill Allison anyway, but Kent knew that wouldn't happen. It made more sense to keep her alive, even let her go. But only if he showed up.

He glanced up at a cheap watercolor print of George VI mounted above the bed. Even through the dingy glass, the fatigue in the man's eyes was clear. Kent wouldn't have wished the stress of a monarch on his worst enemy. And yet, he felt it now.

Kerr was right—it came down to a decision: save a single life, or millions of others. The queen or the kingdom?

52

Allison shivered as a biting wind cut through the nylon jacket draped around her shoulders. She still wore her dress underneath, its smooth fabric just as powerless to protect her lower half. The temperature wasn't any lower than the night before, but felt like it. The sun had just awoken, its timid rays still obscured by a canopy of thick, gray clouds.

She was on the roof of a building, loosely surrounded by five men. Kerr stood directly across, hands in his pockets as the wind whipped his coat like a cape. Ryov and Baker were stationed a few meters to either side, pistols out. The other two men she vaguely recognized, probably from the palace last night. One was stationed between her and the nearest ledge; the other stood beside her, holding her arm tightly.

They'd reached the surface ten minutes ago. No one had moved or said a word since. The climb up the stairs had been about ten stories, she guessed. The structure looked to be some kind of abandoned apartment complex, falling apart but not yet collapsed.

Beyond entering the building, she couldn't remember much since the drawing room last night. Her current view was free of landmarks; she assumed they were still in London. After Kent dove out the window, she'd felt a sudden, heavy pain on the back of her skull. Everything quickly went black.

A while later she woke to find herself bound and gagged in the trunk of a car. It wasn't moving. She knew they might punish her for making noise, but decided it was worth the risk and began kicking and screaming. Ten seconds later the car's engine rumbled to life and the vehicle shot forward. She winced in fear, but continued until her throat was hoarse and both legs felt like lead. The bonds, though, held.

A minute or so after that the car stopped and the trunk was opened. Ryov and Baker stood above her. It was dark and quiet beyond them. The Russian bent down and, brandishing his gun, threatened her with a bullet to the kneecap if she made a sound. She never doubted his ultimatum and remained silent as Baker untied the cord around her limbs.

She was then given the jacket and a pair of cheap shoes—more functional than her dressy heels. A moment later she'd slipped on the items and was being escorted by both men to some kind of deserted public restroom. She had to go and used it without hesitation. Once finished, Baker offered her a bottle of water. Allison wondered at the men's kindness, but soon realized they were simply managing a hostage. After her third swig—the water had tasted a bit off—she quickly became drowsy and lost consciousness. The next thing she knew she was being hauled out of the trunk again, this time in the dawn light, and taken to the building on which she now stood.

Upon entering, she thought about yelling but knew the kneecapping threat—or worse—still held. Besides, the surrounding streets looked empty. And Kent may have gotten away. She hadn't had time to hope for it before. Any disruption from her could cause a wrinkle in his plan.

Standing atop the roof now, though, she understood. The facts could easily be inferred from the situation. Kent had escaped, but there was no getting away. Kerr checked his watch for the second time since their arrival. This was a trading post. The key and canister for, presumably, her life.

Softly, Allison began to weep. She knew Kent would come, because she knew she'd do the same if their roles were reversed. She was ashamed to admit it, and even more ashamed at how little time it took to decide. What justification was there for elevating one life above so many more?

It wasn't that simple, of course. Real life never quite fit into an equation. A million distant heartbeats were no match for the flesh and blood beside you.

If he came, though, Kent wasn't just forfeiting the key and canister—he was handing over his own life as well. The excruciating part was that she had no control. All she could do was hope: that he wouldn't come, that it would be her breath instead of his.

Whatever she'd been drugged with was starting to wear off, and for the first time her heart began pounding. Like a black fog, the situation's oppressive finality began to sink in.

Suddenly Ryov reached for his phone and brought it to his ear. "Da." A second later he hung up and nodded to Kerr.

Each man slowly turned toward the roof's entrance. The sentry beside Allison continued to dig his fingers into her arm, but she was oblivious. Following her captors' gaze, she finally saw a figure emerge. It was Kent. Immediately she began to cry more freely. His eyes found her before scanning the rest of the group.

He'd changed clothes, but somewhere along the line seemed to have taken an additional beating. He moved as if the weight of the world were on his shoulders, and the bevy of cuts upon his face now welcomed a pair of large bruises.

For a fleeting second escape flashed across her mind. She saw Kent running forward, grabbing her and heading...*where?* A quick look around highlighted the futility of such a notion. This meeting location had been chosen with care. The roof was like an open-air fortress—secluded and impenetrable.

Another guard followed Kent up the stairs. Probably posted at the foot of the building; the one who'd called Ryov. "He's clean," the new sentry said to Kerr.

The Deputy Chief simply kept his eyes on Kent, who, Allison noticed for the first time, was clutching something in his right palm. Continuing to Kerr, he gently handed over two items. Kerr kept his eyes on Kent while handing the key and canister to Ryov.

The Russian inspected the canister's seal, then used the key to open it. He removed some kind of metal cylinder from his jacket. Pressing a button on its end, a needle extended out and he lowered it into the container. A measure of liquid was extracted and Ryov pressed another button on the syringe. Five seconds later a small beep sounded and he nodded to Kerr.

"Seems you're playing by the rules," said the Englishman to Kent. "She'll live."

That was the extent of conversation as Baker began screwing a silencer onto the end of his pistol. "Ten seconds," said Kent abruptly. "Call it professional courtesy."

Baker paused as Kerr exchanged a glance with Ryov. Slowly, he returned his gaze to Kent. "Ten seconds."

Kent strode directly toward Allison. Finally releasing his hold, her captor stepped back as Kent met her near the front edge of the roof. With her arm pinned down, she'd lacked the leverage to clear her eyes. Now she did, and as she stared at the face before her, every trivial detail melted away.

Gone were the cuts and bruises, replaced by the soft glow of blue irises. Below, Kent's mouth curved into a bittersweet smile. Allison forced back another wave of tears. She managed to whisper the only question worth asking, even if she already knew the answer. "Why?"

"I was ready for everything," he said after a second. "Except you."

She wanted to say something, anything. But nothing came. He gently reached out and grasped her hand. "Someday you'll understand all this."

She understood now. *Don't you know?*

The next moment broke her thoughts into a horrific memory. Baker quickly approached, pushed her aside and raised his gun to Kent's chest. An instant later a tight, muted pinch pierced the air with appalling familiarity. Kent's eyes glossed over; he staggered limply. Lifting a leg, Baker unceremoniously kicked his victim in the stomach.

Kent's body fell back at the jolt and toppled over the ledge. Baker looked down to watch its descent. Seconds later a sickening thud sounded. Frozen in place, Allison had trouble breathing, her eyes drying up in shock. The whole thing happened so fast.

Her first instinct was to jump herself, rid her body of its instant misery. Before she could think to move, though, Baker grabbed her arm and handed her off to the guard who'd been holding her before. They wasted no time in filing off the platform and reached the street a moment later. The group's composure was almost surreal; it was as if everything had gone according to some prearranged, mundane plan.

Ryov gripped Allison's arm as the three suited men broke off to the right. Leading her to the left, he followed Kerr and Baker around the corner of the building. In both directions, a line of paved asphalt stretched the cluttered horizon. Numerous parked cars garnished the street, but the closest occupied one was two blocks away. It disappeared around a bend as they came in sight of Kent's body.

He'd landed on his back; legs were tangled, a pool of blood still spreading behind his head. Allison looked up to the roof, nearly one hundred feet above. Had he lost consciousness before hitting the ground? She hoped so.

Ryov threw her to the pavement as Baker strode toward the corpse and pulled out his pistol. She had just enough time to see him put two bullets in Kent's forehead before her attention was apprehended by Kerr, crouching low in front of her. Behind him, Ryov scanned the landscape. Dawn on a Sunday, barely a sound.

"We're going to leave you now," said Kerr. "You will not follow us; you will not tell anyone of us. We no longer have reason to kill you, but if your future actions provide one, there is nothing—no one—who can protect you." He stood. "Do we understand each other?"

Her heart was pounding. Allison noticed Baker rejoin his comrades before returning her eyes to Kerr. She nodded slowly.

The Deputy Chief offered a hollow smile. "Good day."

Spinning away, he immediately followed his subordinates back the way they'd come. They disappeared around the corner a second later. Allison remained still, quickly enveloped in the silence of the scene. She lay for a long moment, yearning to look at the body, fearing what she knew she'd see. An unnerving pallor laced the end of the block, as if each surrounding building could sense the presence of death.

Finally, she crawled to her knees, then feet. She had to see him, one last time.

Glancing up and down the still-empty road, she covered the short distance between them and slowly bent down. She'd prepared herself, but not well enough. Every bone in Kent's body appeared broken, his jellied limbs splayed halfway between sidewalk and street. The face was battered from the fall, but, unfortunately, still recognizable. Below, a rim of red lined the hole in his chest while Baker's two additional shots left a fresher mark.

The eyes, though, were still blue. Blank now, but they seemed to glow a brighter shade when she looked into them. Allison found herself searching for the small handful of Sunday School memories she still possessed. She'd sworn off her parents' faith long ago, but, seeing the mangled body before her, had to believe it was no longer the man she knew. Just a shell. The real Jeremy Kent was in a much better place, away from the pain and sorrow she was now shouldering alone.

At that moment her left side began to shake. It had to be the gunshot wound from Linz, making a final entrance. Her first memory with Jeremy, now coupled with her last. Poetic, as—*there it is again*. Same sensation, same length of time. A second later came a third vibration. Allison stood and reached into her jacket pocket, feeling something that hadn't been there before. She cautiously pulled out a cell phone; it shook again as she checked the screen. A number she didn't recognize. The device buzzed a fifth time, and curiosity grew. What did she possibly have to lose?

Pressing the button to talk, she brought the phone to her ear but didn't say anything. A familiar voice came across. "Allison?"

"Nathan?" she said, surprised.

"Yes." Brooks' words were clear, but coated with anxiety. "Where are you, exactly?"

She was hit with too many questions too quickly, but still answered. "Standing over Jeremy's dead body..." She lost focus, fighting the urge to look down again.

Brooks' voice came through like a tonic, waking her. "Concentrate, Allison. It's almost over. What buildings are you near?"

She glanced up. "An old apartment tower, I think."

"The front?"

"I'm not sure." She peered across the road, voice quivering. "There are a bunch of stores and shops on the opposite block."

A short pause. "Okay. If you're facing the building, start walking to your right immediately."

The line went dead before she could wonder further. Something inside compelled her to stand, and, letting out a final breath, she forced herself away from the corpse.

She pocketed the cell phone and crossed her arms as the wind picked up. The rumble of waking traffic began to color the distance, but nearby remained quiet; the loudest sound Allison heard was the soft pad of her own bare feet on the pavement. She didn't know how far to go and kept walking, hoping the phone would ring again. Instead, a silver Volkswagen spurted around a corner fifty feet ahead. She was close enough to look inside and recognize Brooks.

A few feet later he alighted like a frazzled valet and circled around to open the passenger-side door. She had to cross the street to accept the invitation. As she climbed in, he offered a brief moment of eye contact before scanning the area with a sober face.

A second later they were rolling. "I'm sorry to be so abrupt," he said, "but you couldn't stay near the body."

She turned toward him, realization cutting through a fresh wave of fatigue. "You knew. About Jeremy, about today."

Brooks kept his gaze on the road. "Not now. We're ten minutes from central London. I have a room at the St. Giles Hotel. It's safer there. I'll explain everything."

53

Brooks was true to his word. Less than fifteen minutes had passed when they pulled into an underground car park off New Oxford Street. Allison wiped her eyes reflexively, but they were dry. Tears replaced by the now-familiar state of shock.

Somewhere within the last eight hours she'd lost her glasses; Brooks supplied a ballcap as substitute, which she pulled tight over her head. They traversed the lobby without incident and were soon riding an elevator to the tenth floor. Its doors opened onto a plush hallway. Brooks led her to a room halfway down. Keying the lock, he ushered her inside and latched the door behind.

"Please, sit," he said, gesturing to the nearest of two twin beds. They occupied the center of a room that was like the corridor—simple but well-appointed. Allison complied, sinking onto the edge of the mattress as Brooks stepped toward the bathroom.

He quickly reappeared with a cold glass of water and steaming towelette. She gulped down the drink, then rubbed the cloth over her eyes and behind her neck. It seemed to renew her, if only a fraction.

Brooks pulled up a chair and sat down across. His face adopted a shade of sympathy. She'd still been applying the towel, but now stopped. "I'm sorry, Allison. Jeremy was a friend of mine, but..." He paused. "I can't imagine how you're feeling."

Her heartbeat, having settled, threatened to ramp up again. "Was it that obvious?"

"I saw you dancing together. There's pretending to be a couple, and then there's the truth." He exhaled. "Jeremy called me. Last night, after he'd survived a chase with Ryov. He told me about the meet and asked me to be near the apartment building this morning. To pick you up."

Allison's eyes went distant. "He'd already decided."

"For what it's worth, I'd have done the same in his position."

She lowered her head after a moment. "Why didn't they kill me?"

Brooks shifted, his tone evening. "Last night, they probably would have. Exiting the palace without you would've been much simpler. But this morning, in a setting of their choosing, things were different."

"I don't understand."

"A tourist was shooting video with an iPhone on London Bridge last night and caught Jeremy's face in the firefight. Police and MI5 matched the image to a security feed at Buckingham earlier in the evening. You're on his arm. It didn't take much to confirm you as the missing Allison Shaw, despite the haircut and spectacles."

He gestured beside her to the hat she'd worn in the lobby. "Which means you're back as the top story on every newscast from Moscow to Los Angeles. For Kerr and Ryov, leaving you alive is the straightest route to the least attention.

"As it stands, the focus will be intense, but fleeting." He offered the slightest hint of an exasperated smile. "As long as you pass on the inevitable book and movie deals, this should blow over in a month or so. If, however, you were found dead—or not found at all—the mystery of these events would never really go away."

Allison's gears were now spinning. "They kicked Jeremy off the roof after shooting him. Is that why…so his body would be found?"

Brooks' eyebrows rose. "I didn't realize you'd been on the roof, but yes, that follows. His body would be discovered either way. This just expedites the process, helps the storm blow over more quickly."

He glanced at his watch. "While you were walking to my car, I called the Prime Minister. As we speak, a small team of well-compensated policemen are retrieving and disposing of Jeremy's body. There may be a few rumors from pedestrian sightings, but I doubt anything will stick."

A silence passed. "What about Kerr and Ryov?" she asked.

"We'll probably never see them, or their companions, again."

"Does that mean Orion is lost?"

Brooks leaned back in his chair. "Not necessarily. Kerr still has to sell the virus, and he'll have less resources away from MI6." He paused. "I'd be lying if I said Kent wasn't our best chance at stopping this thing, but you never know."

Allison nodded, understanding, condemning herself. *If it wasn't for me...* She stowed the guilt for later. "What about this?" She fished the cell from her pocket.

Brooks stared at the device. "I don't know. Jeremy said he'd get it to you."

Her mind went back to the roof. When Baker stepped in—the confusion. It seemed to make sense. She brought what was now a lukewarm cloth up to her forehead, which had begun to throb. "What next?"

Brooks straightened. "Extraction. It's impossible to avoid all questions; eventually you'll have to brave the lights and microphones. And not just from the press. Homeland Security, Justice Department—a number of agencies will want interviews. No matter how many are granted, the best place to face them is within your own country, closer to friends and family. Your personal effects will be shipped from Scotland."

She nodded slowly. "However," he continued, "we can't simply put you on a commercial flight across the Atlantic. The American Embassy is less than two kilometers away. I'm close with the Defense Attaché, a Brigadier General. He's arranged to meet us there this afternoon.

"The building is closed on weekends. No public access, and staff will be minimal. The general will get us past security. At that point, we will part." Brooks took a breath. "There's a Gulfstream on its way to Stansted Airport as we speak. The general has strict orders, from much higher up the line, to put you directly on it. A CIA Officer named Peter McCoy will be waiting when the plane lands in Maryland.

Allison was silent for a long moment. "The questions," she said, worry clouding her mind. "I was just threatened by Kerr never to speak of him or his men."

Brooks surprised her, abruptly reaching forward and grasping her hand. "Jeremy said that would happen. But don't worry—you'll simply tell the truth." He released his grip. "Just not all of it."

Brooks stood up and slowly began to pace. "To start, everything happened as it really did. Kent rescued you in Linz and a car chase followed. You were involved in a shootout in Le Havre and attended the Queen's birthday celebration last night.

"However, you never got a clean look at your enemies, and never knew the name of your companion. You thought he was some sort of government agent, but were too afraid to ask. Escape was never an option, and he didn't let you go for fear that you'd be killed.

"Kent will go down, like his enemies, as an unbreakable code. We're two of the few who knew his real name. His personnel files are buried behind a mountain of passwords and firewalls."

Allison remained quiet, slowly thinking the scenario through. "What about me? Like you said, it won't just be reporters asking questions. I don't know if I can hold up under a government interrogation."

Brooks stopped mid-stride, nodding gravely. "The short answer is we have no choice. It would be far too suspicious to shield you from all questioning." His gaze cleared slightly. "But if you don't quite believe in yourself, know that I do. So did Jeremy. The fact that you're alive today is proof enough. This past week was no game."

She looked down, resenting the complement despite its truth—*because* of its truth. "One last thing," he added. "My involvement, as well as that of the Prime Minister, can never be mentioned."

"So this is goodbye?"

"Not for a few more hours." He sat down beside her on the bed. "And who knows…I've never been to Georgia. Perhaps one day you could show me around."

She took a deep breath, but couldn't finish it before turning to embrace him. Whether or not he meant the words, they were like gold to her heart. She found herself grateful just for someone to hold.

After a moment, Brooks gently pulled back and gestured toward the bathroom. "Why don't you take a shower. Relax." He pointed to a small suitcase in the corner. "Fresh clothes. I'll order up some room-service. After that, I'm sure you'd welcome a nap."

She shook her head, looking down again. "I don't deserve this, Nathan. I shouldn't be the one alive."

"You act like that's the easy part."

54

"Repeating our top story, authorities continue to investigate details surrounding what can only be described as a high-speed foot chase and gun battle through the streets of central London last night. According to eyewitnesses, the pursuit involved two male individuals and may have originated on or near Buckingham Palace grounds.

"It is unclear whether these events are connected to similar occurrences having taken place across the continent in the past week. What is certain is that the confrontation left an indelible mark on those who glimpsed it. Last night, our Stephen Haynes caught up with a few such onlookers near London Bridge, where the chase reportedly concluded. Here's what they had to say..."

Alan Bradley stopped the video and set his phone down. He didn't need to see the interviews: poised microphone, breathless mix of confusion and excitement. Twice was enough. He took another swallow of the amber liquid before him.

He'd have found it funny if it weren't so distressing. Each person glared toward the camera with wide eyes, like they were in the cinema. They'd seen the action—the violence—from afar. Once it'd passed them by, they could gush about it like the latest blockbuster.

But you don't know what you're seeing. What if you can't walk out of this theatre? What if it won't let you go?

Even now, nearly twenty-four hours later, the incident maintained its pull. St. Stephen's was bustling, and many of the faces within were fixed on their own mobiles, some assuredly still glued to the well-coiffed anchor's every word. He doubted they even knew he was here, or that there was a football match today. A first time for everything.

The Prime Minister raised his beer for another healthy gulp when a hand gripped his left shoulder. The lack of movement from his accompanying security gave away the visitor's identity.

Brooks slid into the booth a moment later, gesturing at the guard standing behind. "He slaves to protect you all hours of the day and you don't even offer a drink?"

Bradley smiled weakly. "He likes it that way. Seems to think being inebriated isn't the best plan for protection. It's the reason I never became a security specialist."

"I can think of a few others." Brooks flagged down a waitress and ordered a pint for himself.

Once she was out of earshot, Bradley exhaled. "Everything go smoothly?"

"Yes. I dropped her at the embassy a few hours ago. Attaché said they'd leave ASAP, should land at Andrews by midnight our time."

"Thank you, Nathan."

"Don't thank me yet."

The PM brushed off the comment. "It matters. Only one life, I know. But she's one less casualty of this…invisible war."

"*Casualty.*" Brooks spoke the word distantly, letting it hang in the air as the waitress delivered his drink. She walked away and he refocused. "The woman—Allison Shaw…in a way, she has been damaged. Emotionally, mentally."

"You said she was strong."

The Chief of Staff nodded, taking a drink from his beer. "She'll need all her muscle to recover from this. Plenty of time, too."

"The one thing she has."

"And us?"

Bradley glanced at his phone, then the crowd. "I hope so." He paused, then found there was nothing left to say. He emptied his glass, reminding himself you only had to hit a jackpot once.

55

Allison lay on the sofa, its faux leather baking in the warm sun. Golden rays streaked through a nearby floor-to-ceiling window. Springtime in the south—today's high was eighty-five degrees. No matter. She could live with the heat, and welcomed the sunlight. Milo, her parents' Jack Russell Terrier, lay quietly at the foot of the couch, his steady breathing in sync with the room's muffled air conditioning.

It'd been three weeks since she crossed the Atlantic. She'd found an apartment in downtown Atlanta, but there was still some paperwork to complete. She doubted her mom and dad would let her leave yet anyway. They thought they'd lost their oldest daughter; she could still see the tears in their eyes when they were reunited.

So, for now she remained tied to a brick ranch in the Atlanta suburb of Druid Hills. In reality, she didn't mind. She owed her folks that much.

Her sister Amy had come down from Nashville with Luke and Jacob. They were four years old; all they knew was that Aunt Allison had finally come back from a long trip and everyone was very happy. Allison herself was glad to soak up their innocent energy. She found herself wishing for the simplicity of a child's mind, and memory.

Becky had called several times. She probably would have visited if she weren't back in Sydney, nine-thousand miles away. She still, though, sounded shaken over the phone. Merely hearing the gunshots in Linz had thrown her off her typically adventurous axis. There was no shame in this, of course, but Allison found it curious that she herself hadn't had a single nightmare involving bullets or brawling. The tables, at least temporarily, had been turned. Is that how it worked—the more times your life was threatened, the less you felt it?"

Whatever the case, she did feel the fatigue. Like a car with a broken fuel gauge, Allison hadn't known she'd been on empty until she pulled off the proverbial road. There'd been signs, of course, but her complete exhaustion—mental, physical, emotional—had hit like a freight train once her plane touched down at Hartsfield-Jackson. Europe was the obvious reason; D.C. made a close second.

Just as Brooks said, they'd slipped past security at the American Embassy on the heels of a stern-looking general. Then Brooks bid a subdued, but genuine, farewell, and the general personally drove her thirty miles northeast to Stansted Airport.

Another handoff followed as the general walked her to the base of a set of steps anchored to a waiting private jet. She climbed up and found three people: a flight attendant and two men in suits. The latter pair flashed CIA badges; they could just as easily have been fakes, but she had no reason to doubt them. In fact, despite the unusual surroundings, Allison found herself edging back from the pit of anxiety. If nothing else, she was being treated with the care and delicacy of a priority package.

They touched down at Andrews Air Force Base just after sunset. A pink hue lingered over the horizon as she stepped onto the tarmac. Fifty feet away, a lone figure stood beside a black Chevy Tahoe. She approached and soon shook hands with a man who introduced himself as Pete McCoy. He also offered ID, but by now she needed no convincing.

McCoy, though haggard, carried an authoritative presence. And while she was relieved to be back on American soil, there would be no melting into another man's arms. Allison had had plenty of time to think on the flight. She was untrained for what lay ahead, but nevertheless comprised the centerpiece of proceedings. She had a responsibility, to everyone involved, to remain composed and see this through. *Even if part of you is already dead.*

McCoy took her to some kind of safe house outside downtown Washington. He let her sleep—protected by 24-hour armed security—but came back the next morning to begin his own questioning. More of a debriefing, really. He said he was the handler for Kent and Baker, and he clearly knew as much as Brooks. She was really just filling in blanks.

Not so later in the day. McCoy offered the best preparation possible, then delivered her to FBI Headquarters. Here she spent the next day-and-a-half, fielding queries from what seemed like a dozen different agencies. Her story, though, held up. Despite creeping exhaustion, she felt a commensurate rise in confidence as the hours wore on. It helped that she wasn't so much remembering lies as forgetting the whole truth.

At the end of the second day she was released, with the knowledge that she could be summoned if anything more was needed. McCoy drove her back to Andrews, a trip during which she called her parents for the first time. The same Gulfstream then flew her down to Hartsfield-Jackson International Airport, where the local FBI office quietly ferreted her out to the suburbs. That marked the end of the stress.

And the beginning of the nightmare.

Someone—perhaps a security guard at the embassy, it didn't matter—leaked her flight out of Europe to the press. Maybe they got a free pint, or tickets to Wimbledon. Allison wasn't so lucky. She didn't have a permanent address, and her parents' was the next logical step.

One by one they converged, like flames tracking oxygen. Antenna-capped vans, cameras and microphones crowded the manicured streets of Druid Hills. *The New York Times, People Magazine, 60 minutes*—everyone wanted a piece. Investigators from Scotland Yard and Interpol showed up for good measure.

The actual interviews were easier than Washington. Allison had been counseled by those in the Hoover Building to further trim what they thought was the entire story. But she hardly needed the truth; most news outlets lapped up her clipped facts with baited breath. She could practically see the dollar signs in their eyes, like tragic cartoons.

Then, like a swift breeze that blew through town, it all ended. Brooks was right: as quickly as they'd arrived, the vehicles packed up, the lights shut down. Thank the world for its short attention span. Stories didn't get any sexier than this, but the next wave of information—chiefly involving a trail of dead bodies across Europe—was well above most reporters' security access. On the air, or on the page, there were only so many ways you could describe a dead end.

Which brought her, finally, to laying on this sofa today. Allison adjusted her body as the sun continued to splash the window. Quiet had returned, but peace would have to wait. It had nothing to do with Jeremy Kent, and everything to do with the one thing she hadn't been asked about: a virus.

She was one of the chosen few to see death coming. Or rather, wait for its sharp, remorseless ambush. The thought was enough to chill her bones through the heat. But then, what was the alternative? She could still hear the defeat in Brooks' voice. They'd already taken their best shot.

56

Ryov hadn't removed his gun, and he was starting to think he wouldn't need to. This wasn't amateur night. Every man present seemed to understand that the trade was simply a means to an end, not an opportunity to burn off some sense of pointless machismo.

They were scattered about the ground floor of the warehouse in a rough circle. The Russian might've preferred a different venue than the site where Clarke and Boxler had taken up residence, but it made sense. They needed to minimize their footprint, which meant no new buildings. But the only people who'd purposefully stumble near them were still society's outcasts. Even then, a pair of guards stood on the roof, scanning below for anything approaching through the industrialized haze.

One of the men was part of their team, one of Kerr's suits. Two more sentries currently stood beside Ryov, along with Kerr himself, Baker and both scientists. The other man on the roof belonged to the tall figure positioned directly across from the now-former MI6 Deputy Chief.

Abdul al-Asani. The Saudi national, a few years younger than Kerr, had made a fortune in oil. Evidently that wasn't enough as he later added real estate, getting in on the ground floor in places like Dubai and Baku. The $5 billion he was paying them for Orion would be nothing more than a drop in the bucket.

The entire reason he was here, though, was his brother. Al-Asani's older sibling, a self-professed "true believer," had been trying to convert his secular-minded brother for years. Somehow, recently, he'd succeeded; Orion was to be their instrument of spiritual vindication. Personally, Ryov thought the whole thing idiotic. He had no problem with seventy virgins, but he'd prefer to experience them in this life, where he could do the picking and choosing.

Al-Asani, though, was his path to such an existence, and thus he had to respect the man. Truthfully, it wasn't hard. The Arab had proven himself professional in every facet, most notably discretion.

It started with not bringing an army. Al-Asani's team was the same size as Kerr's and included a lab-man of his own to verify Orion's authenticity. They'd flown in from Athens under papers identifying each as British citizens. The group had even developed accents to match and, committing a severe sacrifice, shaved off their facial hair.

Beyond all of this, though, Ryov, Kerr and everyone else was indebted to Al-Asani's perseverance. He'd been the buyer waiting in Istanbul when Kent stole the antidote. Fortunately, Orion was a big enough draw to bring the mogul back. His one condition had been the presence of Clarke and Boxler at the meet, as a sign of trust. Kerr could hardly refuse.

Up ahead, al-Asani's scientist was running a final test on Orion. Half a minute later he turned to his boss and nodded. The Arab then summoned another one of his men, who walked forward with a laptop and set it on a makeshift wooden table. He punched a few keys and swiveled the screen toward Kerr and Ryov.

"The correct amounts in your desired accounts," said al-Asani in clean English.

Both men leaned in. It was all there, every zero in place. The Arab then gripped a metal briefcase from the same man and opened it on the table beside the computer. Rows of crisp bills sat neatly within. "Your down payment. Five million Euros."

Eying the cash with satisfaction, Kerr nodded and al-Asani closed the case. The Deputy Chief reached out a hand. His counterpart accepted, then passed the money across. Ryov glanced at the scientist packing up Orion. They'd smuggle it back to Riyadh by train over the next few days. Beyond that, he didn't care. The antidote had been pumping through his veins for the last several weeks.

And resting in his pocket for good measure. He imagined the world-wide hysteria once Orion was let loose. Millions dying, mass panic, governments helpless to stem the tide of terror. But the wealthy and powerful would survive. They always did. And he'd be among them.

One day, the antidote would be anonymously introduced into society. The chaos, like waves from a departing storm, would eventually level out. This, of course, wasn't al-Asani's aim; he wanted global destruction. But he was insane. Who would be left for the fortunate few to stand upon? Every yacht needed a captain, every gilded survivor a staff to serve him.

Then, in an instant, none of it mattered.

There was more than one bang, but, synchronized perfectly, they all sounded together. Each entry door immediately blew off its hinges and a line of black-clad soldiers poured through. Within seconds they'd flooded the area in a semi-circle and flanked the men in the center.

Ryov checked his companions on both sides. Each had managed to remove a weapon but was frozen beyond that. The Russian tightened the grip on his own pistol and studied their invaders. The group was perhaps thirty men strong, each training a C8 carbine assault rifle toward the middle. SAS.

The entire breach lasted less than ten seconds. Before Kerr, al-Asani or any of their men made another move, one of the soldiers stepped forward near the middle of his comrades. The man was clearly the leader and his ultimatum required no utterance.

Ryov felt a cold sweat running down his back. He glanced at Baker, then Kerr. Their expressions mirrored his: initial shock, followed by anger and now confusion. How could this happen?

But then, who cared anymore? All that counted was the current. Their profession was a game—you either won or lost. Some days defeat was obvious; others it sliced quicker than a guillotine.

As the SAS leader stepped back behind the firing line, Kerr locked eyes with al-Asani. Ryov knew their thoughts: escape was impossible. Upon surrender, none of them would see the inside of a courtroom; most wouldn't make it to a prison cell. Sometimes life simply became a choice of when to die.

No words were said between the trading parties, but the verdict was clear. A second later their sentence was carried out. Moving in unison, each leader raised his gun toward the soldiers and his men quickly followed. None made it to squeezing the trigger.

In a fraction of a second every aimed carbine opened up in a mechanized thunderstorm. Countless 45mm rounds slashed through the air with merciless efficiency. The entire group of victims was down in seconds, each man floating in a pool of his own blood.

Except one. Ryov had no idea why, but at the last instant, instead of raising his gun, he'd dropped it. His body followed just as the carbines erupted. Hitting the deck unscathed, he'd frozen as the cacophony of killing screamed by overhead.

As the figurative smoke cleared, he remained still and heard several pairs of boots begin to crunch forward. Seconds later a few men yelled "clear," while another set of shoes soon strode up beside him. "One live." The next moment, a knee between his shoulder blades. Then his arms were pulled behind his back, both wrists were secured together and he was lifted to his feet.

Almost as if they'd planned to find someone breathing, a small group of soldiers began escorting him past the carnage toward one of the entry doors. The movement felt eerily routine. No rough pushing or overblown emotions. Professionals didn't do that.

Ryov's mind was nearly blank. Five minutes ago, he was on the cusp of hundreds of millions; now all he had was in front of him. But he felt no fear. *Why, then, did you duck?* It was the only question left worth answering.

The soldiers ushered him through the warehouse door. He hadn't been inside for long, but the interior was dim. It took his eyes a few seconds to adjust to the bright gray above as their small band turned right along the building's exterior. At the same moment a line of unmarked Range Rovers pulled up beside them.

Reaching the first vehicle, one of the soldiers opened a rear door and forced Ryov through. Just before his view was cut off the Russian stole a glance at the sky above. It might be the last time he'd see it.

Ryov was pushed to the middle of the seat as his enforcer followed him inside and another soldier slid in to his right. He was effectively surrounded when a third man joined the driver up front. They started rolling. Outside, pockets of soldiers streamed in and out of the warehouse. All moved with a purpose. Whatever the SAS's responsibility here, it'd be complete soon. For the same reason, Ryov never considered escape. One of these men would be handful enough; four was certain failure.

Inside the cabin, as the Rover pulled away, silence. Ryov could think of half a dozen places they might be taking him, but they were all essentially the same. The only choice he had was—*wait.* Something wasn't right. He thought back to his glance toward the sky.

The roof. Why hadn't the men up there radioed a warning? He didn't care how good the SAS was, you couldn't hide thirty men. Then again, a few well-placed snipers could drop the lookouts with suppressed rifles before the larger force moved in. But how did they know which building to hit? How did they know which *city?* One more question worth asking. The answer, though, came instantly.

Kent. Somehow, some way, Jeremy Kent was responsible. You stayed alive long enough, you developed a sense for these things. They'd been too careful. Al-Asani as well. The info on their meeting spot had to be taken, not given.

Ryov had no idea what Kent did, but there was no doubt. He stared forward, eyes glazed through the front windshield as the Rover swiftly navigated Liverpool's vast dock system. He thought Kent had reached out from the grave back in Russia; now it'd really happened. The only thing left to do…was smile. *Bravo Jeremy Kent.*

A prick brought him back to the present. It felt soft, though the syringe the soldier lifted from his right thigh was large. He had little time to contemplate the move further as his vision quickly began to blur. Seconds later the fuzziness became dark and, a few breaths after that, faded to black.

57

Allison paid the driver and stepped out of the cab. Fifth Avenue was buzz-ing. *Why does that feel redundant?* Closing the door, she watched as the yellow Toyota merged back into the southbound traffic. Soon it was barely visible, a common speck on the thoroughfare's moving, metallic rainbow.

She turned around and immediately found her gaze drawn upward. Looming near the top of her vision, several oak trees basked in the after-noon sun. Their fresh leaves seemed to breathe in the spring air. Beyond, she could just make out the top of the Metropolitan Museum of Art, its stone façade gently grazing the cloudless blue sky.

Her driver had offered to swing onto 79th Street, deeper into Central Park. It would've only meant another buck or so, but she'd declined. He, like the flight attendants and hotel staff, was just a means to an end. This trip was about solitude.

That's why she'd chosen New York. Her image had just recently fallen out of the news cycle; many would remember. Where better to disappear than in a city of eight million strangers? So far so good. A few double-takes, but either no one fully recognized her—hair back to its normal brown curls by now—or they'd decided to give her peace. Or they just didn't care any-more. *Even better.*

Traveling was hard on her family and friends. It'd only been a month since Europe; the pain of thinking they'd lost her was still raw. At the same time, she needed the change of scenery, a fresh perspective. The two issues that brought her up here were blocking every other direction in life.

In the irony of ironies, the first had already been resolved. She'd been walking through JFK and spotted the scene on a TV in the concourse. As if hypnotized, she moved toward the monitor. It showed a large brick building, surrounded by police and blue caution tape. Pictures and video looped through the feed every few seconds. She was still too far back to hear, but the images and scrawl across the bottom told the story.

Orion was dead. More than a dozen bodies had been found in a warehouse in Liverpool, thanks to an anonymous tip. All were male, all fatally shot with what appeared to be military-grade weaponry. Not every corpse had been identified, but two were hard to miss: Nicolas Kerr, the recently missing Deputy Chief of MI6, and Abdul al-Asani, a Saudi billionaire with rumored ties to Islamic fundamentalism.

Something clicked inside. Allison didn't know how, but she was certain: this was the meeting to sell the virus, and by some stroke of magic it'd been foiled. Not everyone may have been there—Ryov or Baker, Clarke and Boxler—but that seemed thin. The men aligned against this were too invested to make a move unless it solved everything.

This realization flowed over her in seconds and hit with the force of a tsunami. She stood frozen in the terminal, paralyzed by elation. How many hours had been stolen from her, wrapped up in worry over innocent lives? Orion was like an atomic bomb, one whose launch date and trajectory were unknown. Frankly, she didn't know what coming to New York would've solved. You couldn't start a new life when you knew so many others—your own among them—were in danger of ending.

But that was all over now. Allison remembered staring at the people swirling around her, each of them forever oblivious to the fear and violence they'd just been spared. The scene drifted into slow-motion, a moving snapshot. She imagined the handful of men and women who knew as much as she did having similar reactions, their celebration tempered only by exhaustion.

She'd started into the park on an asphalt walkway, but still had her sunglasses tucked away. The canopy of foliage was shade enough, thinning any rays of sun that managed to spill through. A soft breeze rustled her cotton skirt; the temperature couldn't have been more pleasant; bright blues and greens popped ahead and above, filling her vision.

The weather was mocking her. It was a simple conclusion to arrive at when what you felt inside wasn't nearly so clear and colorful. Her relief over Orion had to share space with the second issue she faced. This not about millions of other lives, but one.

Despite efforts to the contrary, she often drifted back to those moments on Buckingham's dance floor; her heart had been on fire. Now it was a numbed shell. No less full, but cooled and crusted by the ravages of loss.

Kent wouldn't let her go. That's how it felt, anyway—out of her hands. She'd come here to set him aside, regain some degree of normalcy. She knew, though, that she'd never completely be free of him. She didn't much want to be. Haunting memories were better than nothing at all.

She continued through the park, smiling weakly at the few other strollers who made eye contact. The trees gave way to a grassy expanse. Frisbees flew, dogs barked. She felt apart from the scenery, deadened to its diversions.

A snack vendor came in view on the left. She slid into his short line for a bottle of water. She'd decided to pay with her card, but changed her mind to cash once it was her turn to order. She apologized to the vendor as she buried her face in her purse, fumbling for the right amount of change.

"Just tell him you're good for it."

Allison immediately straightened, a jolt from her heart interrupting the synapses firing within her brain. She knew that voice. But it no longer existed. It couldn't.

The words had come from behind. She held on to her purse, but lost all feeling for it. Her chest began pounding; the hair on both arms stood up as goosebumps covered her skin. She took a deep breath and silently commanded her frozen body to turn. A second later she found what she expected, and began to cry.

Jeremy Kent stood ten feet away, living and breathing. For a moment he remained still. Everything else around—the vendor, tourists, trees—faded from Allison's consciousness. Kent slowly stepped forward, his eyes never wavering from her own.

In an instant they were face to face. "I'm sorry," he said, wiping one of several tears streaming down her cheeks. "I deserve every one of these."

Allison's breath caught in her throat. *So many questions.* At the moment, though, they all took a back seat to instinct. She reached forward and pulled him close. Kent reciprocated, wrapping his arms around her until his own cheeks tasted her tears.

They stood locked in place for a long moment. Passersby turned their heads, but no one stopped to gawk. Releasing slightly, they leaned in and kissed. Allison kept waiting for the scene to dissolve into a dream.

But when they parted and she opened her eyes, Kent was still there. She looked down his body, then back up to the familiar pair of blue irises. Only one word came to mind. "How?"

"I told you you'd understand everything." He grasped her hand and nodded to a nearby bench.

They both sat down and turned toward one another. People continued to stream past. Allison realized she probably wasn't looking her best anymore: tousled hair, wet eyes and cheeks. She didn't care.

She did, though, feel a chill slice through her chest as a familiar image came to mind. Kent opened his mouth to speak, but she beat him to it. "I saw your body on the ground." Each word was an effort. "They shot you."

He paused, searching for the best response. "You saw *a* body, already dead. They shot a corpse." He shifted on the bench. "It was a John Doe, fresh from one of London's morgues. Hit and run. He'd died from internal bleeding earlier that night." She stared back, unblinking. "Roughly my height and weight. Contacts, some hasty plastic surgery completed the picture. It wasn't perfect, but the violence of the fall gave us some leeway."

She was initially silent. Kent had spoken softly, uttering each word with care. But the news was still jarring. Allison found herself shaking her head. "I saw you fall, heard you hit the concrete."

"SAS soldiers were camped in two rooms, one above the other; each had a window facing the side of the building where I fell. On my way down, I caught a rope from the top room and swung past the men in the bottom just as they were heaving out the corpse." He shook his head, thinking back. "Not quite magic, but certainly a trick."

Allison wasn't convinced. "What about the roof? You were shot there too. Baker saw you fa—"

And then she knew. *Baker was the only one who saw you fall.* She closed her eyes, then opened them after a long moment. "The gunshot—it was a blank."

Kent's gaze narrowed. "I always knew you were a smart girl."

"How long ago did you plan this?"

"Not long enough to make it easy." Kent stole a glance at the pack of pedestrians, still strolling by. "But the antidote could only prevent so much. This was always about locating the source of Orion. We had to find Clarke and Boxler.

"Baker was our best chance to do this, but it became clear he needed complete acceptance into Kerr's circle of trust. I'd made waves trying to steal the antidote. Kerr got suspicious of Jim. Giving me—us—up at Buckingham was the only way to save the mission."

By now Alison's breathing had normalized, her brain taking some of the burden from her heart. "I thought you and Baker had to meet face-to-face to communicate safely. How did you coordinate the betrayal?"

"Jim took the initiative; I didn't know until it happened. Once I heard Ryov's voice, I put the pieces together. The rest was improvisation."

She thought back to the White Drawing Room. Baker's little speech, the pain in Kent's eyes. She shook her head. "I don't believe that."

"I don't blame you, but it's still the truth. Survival doesn't mean preparing for every contingency. It means adapting when something inevitably goes wrong."

"What about the roof? You couldn't possibly anticipate needing blank cartridges, or knowing what side of the building to fall off."

"You're right. But by then, Kerr wasn't going back to MI6. Which meant he lacked access to their surveillance capabilities. I was able to text James directly. SAS planted a blank mag near the staircase in the building, along with a phone for you. Kerr had no reason to suspect anything. Why would you betray your ally only to save him eight hours later?"

Allison thought a moment. "Baker led you to the warehouse in Liverpool."

Kent nodded. "Even brought his own fake blood. He's lucky the SAS is just as good at aiming to miss a target as they are at hitting one."

She exhaled, trying to reconcile this new information with the traitor she thought Baker had been. "Where is he now?

"On a well-earned vacation." Kent paused, looking her in the eye. "He and I both know the part you had to see him play, Allison. No one's asking your thoughts of him to come up rosy."

"It just might take some time."

"A commodity in healthy supply, now that CNN no longer wants your life story."

She was silent for a moment, dredging up the one question about which she cared the most. "Is that why you didn't tell me you were alive— the press?"

Kent took a deep breath. She knew he'd heard the pain in her voice. "Yesterday afternoon, while your 737 was leaving the runway at Hartsfield-Jackson and your parents were at work, a pair of FBI agents let themselves into your house in Druid Hills."

Her eyes widened slightly, but he continued. "Their field office had received instructions to search the home for hidden surveillance equipment. They were there one hour and found six devices. All were miniature wireless cameras planted within fixtures on ceilings and walls throughout the house. They each recorded video and audio."

The pavement dropped out from beneath Allison's feet. She had little control over the look of shock spread across her face. Kent marched on. "These cameras weren't merely storage tools. They transmitted data to an unknown receiver. Probably Kerr's phone."

Kent went quiet, allowing Allison to digest the information. "They were…spying on me?" she finally asked.

He nodded. "Baker's last test. Before they told him the virus's location, they had to believe he'd really killed me. You were the key to his credibility." Kent paused. "Kerr and Ryov saw enough of our relationship on the roof. If I was still alive, and you knew it, no amount of discipline would mask the relief you held inside."

"And they'd know Baker was a fraud."

Another nod.

Allison shuddered. The invasion of privacy felt miniscule beside the reminder of the past month's torment. Sickness, sleepless nights, emotional exhaustion—the knowledge that they comprised such a vital contribution took some of the edge off. Still, wounds to be mended.

Kent seemed to read her thoughts. "Forgive me. If there was any other way—"

She found herself, once again, pressing her fingers to his lips. Fresh tears stung both her eyes. "I'm not sorry."

He straightened, face claiming a mix of surprise and admiration. A moment passed. "How did they plant the bugs?" she asked, still curious.

Kent refocused. "Ryov. We only spotted him yesterday, from archived airport surveillance. He'd altered his appearance and used a fresh passport.

"He flew into Charlotte and rented a car, probably while you were still being questioned in Washington. The drive to Atlanta would've taken about four hours. Slip into the house, slip out, and drive back.

"Based on the time of his flight's arrival and departure, he aimed to install the devices in the middle of the day, when both your parents were gone. They were never in any harm. The last thing he'd have wanted was detection."

She tilted her head in confusion. "If you just learned about this, how could you have possibly known it beforehand?"

"We didn't. But it's what we would've done in their position."

"*We?*"

"We happy few. McCoy, the president, a handful of others in between."

"What about Brooks? Did he know you were alive?"

"Yes."

She thought back to the St. Giles in London. "He's quite the actor."

"He's got nothing on you, Sophie."

Allison mustered a smile for the first time. "What's the next line?"

Kent was on his feet a second later, arm extended toward her. "I could stand to stretch my legs. Care for a walk?"

She accepted, placing her hand in his and rising. The sun's army of rays had begun to infiltrate the canopy. He glanced around at the collage of greens and yellows. "Which way?"

"Doesn't matter to me." She tightened her grip. "Just tell me you won't let me go."

He squeezed back. "I'll show you."

ABOUT THE AUTHOR

Zach Franz studied journalism at Webster University before moving on to pen over seventy-five monthly film reviews for two St. Louis area outlets. These days, he's always on the lookout for the next great story. When he's not writing one, he's likely reading, watching a movie, or cheering on his favorite ice hockey team, The Blues. Zach lives with his family in St. Louis, Missouri. "Racing Orion" is his first novel, and he would welcome your feedback at zachfranzauthor@gmail.com.